## LORD OF THE ISLES.

DAUGHTER, SHE SAID, THOSE SEAS BEHOLD,
ROUND TWICE AN HUNDRED ISLANDS ROLL'D.

Canto 1. Stan. 8.

THE

# LORD OF THE ISLES.

By SIR WALTER SCOTT.

WITH

NOTES AND APPENDIX.

**Fredonia Books**
**Amsterdam, The Netherlands**

The Lord of the Isles

by
Sir Walter Scott

ISBN: 1-58963-739-9

Reprinted from the 1871 edition

Fredonia Books
Amsterdam, the Netherlands
http://www.fredoniabooks.com

In order to make original editions of historical works available to scholars at an economical price, this facsimile of the original edition of 1871 is reproduced from the best available copy and has been digitally enhanced to improve legibility, but the text remains unaltered to retain historical authenticity.

# CONTENTS

---

# NOTICE.

[The composition of "The Lord of the Isles," as we now have it in the Author's MS., seems to have been begun at Abbotsford, in the Autumn of 1814, and it ended at Edinburgh, the 16th of December. Some part of Canto 1. had probably been committed to writing in a rougher form earlier in the year. The original Quarto appeared on the 2d of January, 1815.

It may be mentioned, that those parts of this poem which were written at Abbotsford, were composed almost all in the presence of Sir Walter Scott's family, and many in that of casual visitors also; the original cottage which he then occupied not affording him any means of retirement. Neither conversation nor music seemed to disturb him.]

1 *

# INTRODUCTION

## TO

# THE LORD OF THE ISLES

# INTRODUCTION

## TO

# THE LORD OF THE ISLES.

I COULD hardly have chosen a subject more popular in Scotland, than any thing connected with the Bruce's history, unless I had attempted that of Wallace. But I am decidedly of opinion, that a popular, or what is called a *taking* title, though well qualified to ensure the publishers against loss, and clear their shelves of the original impression, is rather apt to be hazardous than otherwise to the reputation of the author. He who attempts a subject of distinguished popularity, has not the privilege of awakening the enthusiasm of his audience; on the contrary, it is already awakened, and glows, it may be, more ardently than that of the author himself. In this case, the warmth of the author is inferior to that of the party whom he addresses, who has, therefore, little chance of being, in Bayes's phrase, "elevated and surprised" by what he has thought o with more enthusiasm than the author. The sense of this risk, joined to the consciousness of striving against wind and tide, made the task of composing the pro posed Poem somewhat heavy and hopeless; but, like the prize-fighter in "As You Like It," I was to wrestle for my reputation, and not neglect any advantage. In

a most agreeable pleasure-voyage, which I have tried
to commemorate in the Introduction to the new edition
of the " Pirate," I visited, in social and friendly company,[1] the coasts and islands of Scotland, and made
myself acquainted with the localities of which I meant
to treat. But this voyage, which was in every other
effect so delightful, was in its conclusion saddened by
one of those strokes of fate which so often mingle
themselves with our pleasures. The accomplished and
excellent person who had recommended to me the
subject for " The Lay of the Last Minstrel," and to
whom I proposed to inscribe what I already suspected
might be the close of my poetical labours, was unex-
pectedly removed from the world, which she seemed
only to have visited for purposes of kindness and be-
nevolence. It is needless to say how the author's
feelings, or the composition of his trifling work, were
affected by a circumstance which occasioned so many
tears and so much sorrow.[2] True it is, that " The
Lord of the Isles" was concluded, unwillingly and in
haste, under the painful feeling of one who has a task
which must be finished, rather than with the ardour
of one who endeavours to perform that task well. Although the Poem cannot be said to have made a favourable impression on the public, the sale of fifteen

---

[1] [See a note to the lines superscribed " Pharos loquitur,"
included in volume 1st; and see also " Fragments of a Tour in
the Hebrides," &c., printed in the Edinburgh Annual Register
for 1812.]

[2] [Harriet, Duchess of Buccleuch, died 24th August, 1814. Sir
Walter Scott received the mournful intelligence while visiting
the Giant's Causeway, and immediately returned home.]

thousand copies enabled the author to retreat from the field with the honours of war.

In the meantime, what was necessarily to be considered as a failure, was much reconciled to my feelings by the success attending my attempt in another species of composition. " Waverley" had, under strict incognito, taken its flight from the press, just before I set out upon the voyage already mentioned: it had now made its way to popularity, and the success of that work and the volumes which followed, was sufficient to have satisfied a greater appetite for applause than I have at any time possessed.[1]

I may as well add in this place, that, being much urged by my intimate friend, now unhappily no more, William Erskine, (a Scottish judge, by the title of Lord Kinedder,) I agreed to write the little romantic tale called the "Bridal of Triermain;" but it was on the condition, that he should make no serious effort to disown the composition, if report should lay it at his door. As he was more than suspected of a taste for poetry, and as I took care, in several places, to mix something which might resemble (as far as was in my power) my friend's feeling and manner, the train easily caught, and two large editions were sold. A third being called for, Lord Kinedder became unwilling to aid any longer a deception which was going rather farther than he expected or desired, and the real author's name was given. Upon another occasion, I sent up another of these trifles, which, like schoolboy's kites, served to show how the wind of popular taste was setting. The manner was supposed to be that of a rude minstrel, or Scald, in

---

[1] [The first edition of Waverley appeared in July, 1814.]

opposition to the "Bridal of Triermain," which was designed to belong rather to the Italian school. This new fugitive piece was called "Harold the Dauntless;"[1] and I am still astonished at my having committed the gross error of selecting the very name which Lord Byron had made so famous. It encountered rather an odd fate. My ingenious friend, Mr. James Hogg, had published, about the same time, a work called the "Poetic Mirror," containing imitations of the principal living poets.[2] There was in it a very good imitation of my own style, which bore such a resemblance to "Harold the Dauntless," that there was no discovering the original from the imitation; and I believe that many who took the trouble of thinking upon the subject, were rather of opinion that my ingenious friend was the true and not the fictitious Simon Pure. Since this period, which was in the year 1816, the Author has not been an intruder on the public by any poetical work of importance.

W. S.

Abbotsford, April, 1830.

---

[1] [" Harold the Dauntless" was first published in a small 12mo volume, December, 1816.]

[2] [Mr. Hogg's "Poetic Mirror" appeared in October, 1816.]

THE

# LORD OF THE ISLES

A POEM.

IN SIX CANTOS

## ADVERTISEMENT.

THE scene of this poem lies, at first, in the castle of Artornish, on the coast of Argyleshire; and, afterwards, in the Islands of Skye and Arran, and upon the coast of Ayrshire. Finally, it is laid near Stirling. The story opens in the spring of the year 1307, when Bruce, who had been driven out of Scotland by the English and the Barons who adhered to that foreign interest, returned from the Island of Rachrin on the coast of Ireland, again to assert his claims to the Scottish crown. Many of the personages and incidents introduced are of historical celebrity. The authorities used are chiefly those of the venerable Lord Hailes, as well entitled to be called the restorer of Scottish history, as Bruce the restorer of Scottish monarchy; and of Archdeacon Barbour, a correct edition of whose Metrical History of Robert Bruce[1] will soon, I trust, appear, under the care of my learned friend, the Rev Dr. Jamieson.

ABBOTSFORD, 10*th December*, 1814.

---

[1] [The work alluded to appeared in 1820, under the title of "The Bruce and Wallace." 2 vols. 4to.]

THE

# LORD OF THE ISLES

## CANTO FIRST.

2*

## THE

# LORD OF THE ISLES.

### CANTO FIRST.

AUTUMN departs—but still his mantle's fold
Rests on the groves of noble Somerville,[1]
Beneath a shroud of russet dropp'd with gold
Tweed and his tributaries mingle still;
Hoarser the wind, and deeper sounds the rill,
Yet lingering notes of sylvan music swell,
The deep-toned cushat, and the redbreast shrill,
And yet some tints of summer splendour tell
When the broad sun sinks down on Ettricks western
    fell.

Autumn departs—from Gala's fields[2] no more
Come rural sounds our kindred banks to cheer;
Blent with the stream, and gale that wafts it o'er
No more the distant reaper's mirth we hear.

---

[1] [John, fifteenth Lord Somerville, illustrious for his patriotic
devotion to the science of agriculture, resided frequently in his
beautiful villa called the Pavilion, situated on the Tweed over
against Melrose, and was an intimate friend and almost daily
companion of the poet, from whose windows at Abbotsford his
lordship's plantations formed a prominent object. Lord S. died
in 1819.]

[2] [The river Gala, famous in song, flows into the Tweed a few
hundred yards below Abbotsford; but probably the word *Gala*
here stands for the poet's neighbour and kinsman, and much
attached friend, John Scott, Esq. of Gala.]

The last blithe shout hath died upon our ear,
And harvest-home hath hush'd the clanging wain,
On the waste hill no forms of life appear,
Save where, sad laggard of the autumnal train,
Some age-struck wanderer gleans few ears of scatter'd
    grain.

Deem'st thou these sadden'd scenes have pleasure
    still,
Lovest thou through Autumn's fading realms to stray,
To see the heath-flower wither'd on the hill,
To listen to the wood's expiring lay,
To note the red leaf shivering on the spray,
To mark the last bright tints the mountain stain,
On the waste fields to trace the gleaner's way,
And moralize on mortal joy and pain?—
O! if such scenes thou lovest, scorn not the minstrel
    strain.

No! do not scorn, although its hoarser note
Scarce with the cushat's homely song can vie,
Though faint its beauties as the tints remote
That gleam through mist in autumn's evening sky,
And few as leaves that tremble, sear and dry,
When wild November hath his bugle wound;
Nor mock my toil—a lonely gleaner I,
Through fields time-wasted, on sad inquest bound,
Where happier bards of yore have richer harvest
    found.

So shalt thou list, and haply not unmoved,
To a wild tale of Albyn's warrior day;
In distant lands, by the rough West reproved,
Still live some relics of the ancient lay.

For, when on Coolin's hills the lights decay,
With such the Seer of Skye the eve beguiles;
'Tis known amid the pathless wastes of Reay,
In Harries known, and in Iona's piles,
Where rest from mortal coil the Mighty of the Isles

---

## I.

"WAKE, Maid of Lorn!" the Minstrels sung.
Thy rugged halls, Artornish! rung,[1]
And the dark seas, thy towers that lave,
Heaved on the beach a softer wave,
As 'mid the tuneful choir to keep
The diapason of the Deep.
Lull'd were the winds on Inninmore,
And green Loch-Alline's woodland shore,
As if wild woods and waves had pleasure
In listing to the lovely measure.
And ne'er to symphony more sweet
Gave mountain echoes answer meet,
Since, met from mainland and from isle,
Ross, Arran, Ilay, and Argyle,
Each minstrel's tributary lay
Paid homage to the festal day.
Dull and dishonour'd were the bard,
Worthless of guerdon and regard,
Deaf to the hope of minstrel fame,
Or lady's smiles, his noblest aim,
Who on that morn's resistless call
Were silent in Artornish hall.

---

[1] [See Appendix, Note A.]

## II.

"Wake, Maid of Lorn!" 'twas thus they sung,
And yet more proud the descant rung,
"Wake, Maid of Lorn! high right is ours,
To charm dull sleep from Beauty's bowers;
Earth, Ocean, Air, have nought so shy
But owns the power of minstrelsy
In Lettermore the timid deer
Will pause, the harp's wild chime to hear:
Rude Heiskar's seal through surges dark
Will long pursue the minstrel's bark;[1]
To list his notes, the eagle proud
Will poise him on Ben-Cailliach's cloud:
Then let not Maiden's ear disdain
The summons of the minstrel train,
But, while our harps wild music make,
Edith of Lorn, awake, awake!

## III.

"O wake, while Dawn, with dewy shine,
Wakes Nature's charms to vie with thine!
She bids the mottled thrush rejoice
To mate thy melody of voice;
The dew that on the violet lies
Mocks the dark lustre of thine eyes;
But, Edith, wake, and all we see
Of sweet and fair shall yield to thee!"—

---

[1] The seal displays a taste for music, which could scarcely be expected from his habits and local predilections. They will long follow a boat in which any musical instrument is played, and even a tune simply whistled has attractions for them. The Dean of the Isles says of Heiskar, a small uninhabited rock, about twelve (Scottish) miles from the isle of Uist, that an infinite slaughter of seals takes place there.

" She comes not yet," grey Ferrand cried :
" Brethren, let softer spell be tried,
Those notes prolong'd, that soothing theme,
Which best may mix with Beauty's dream,
And whisper, with their silvery tone,
The hope she loves, yet fears to own."
He spoke, and on the harp-strings died
The strains of flattery and of pride ;
More soft, more low, more tender fell
The lay of love he bade them tell.

### IV.

" Wake, Maid of Lorn ! the moments fly,
 Which yet that maiden-name allow ;
Wake, Maiden, wake ! the hour is nigh,
 When Love shall claim a plighted vow.
By Fear, thy bosom's fluttering guest,
 By Hope, that soon shall fears remove,
We bid thee break the bonds of rest,
 And wake thee at the call of Love !

" Wake, Edith, wake ! in yonder bay
 Lies many a galley gaily mann'd,
We hear the merry pibrochs play,
 We see the streamers' silken band.
What Chieftain's praise these pibrochs swell,
 What crest is on these banners wove,
The harp, the minstrel, dare not tell—
 The riddle must be read by Love."

### V.

Retired her maiden train among,
Edith of Lorn received the song,

But tamed the minstrel's pride had been
That had her cold demeanour seen;
For not upon her cheek awoke
The glow of pride when Flattery spoke,
Nor could their tenderest numbers bring
One sigh responsive to the string.
As vainly had her maidens vied
In skill to deck the princely bride.
Her locks, in dark-brown length array'd,
Cathleen of Ulne, 't was thine to braid;
Young Eva with meet reverence drew
On the light foot the silken shoe,
While on the ankle's slender round
Those strings of pearl fair Bertha wound,
That, bleach'd Lochryan's depths within
Seem'd dusky still on Edith's skin.
But Einion, of experience old,
Had weightiest task—the mantle's fold
In many an artful plait she tied,
To show the form it seem'd to hide,
Till on the floor descending roll'd
Its waves of crimson blent with gold.

## VI.

O! lives there now so cold a maid,
Who thus in beauty's pomp array'd,
In beauty's proudest pitch of power,
And conquest won—the bridal hour—
With every charm that wins the heart,
By Nature given, enhanced by Art,
Could yet the fair reflection view,
In the bright mirror pictured true,
And not one dimple on her cheek
A tell-tale consciousness bespeak?—

Lives still such maid?—Fair damsels, say,
For further vouches not my lay,
Save that such lived in Britain's isle,
When Lorn's bright Edith scorn'd to smile.

### VII.

But Morag, to whose fostering care
Proud Lorn had given his daughter fair,
Morag, who saw a mother's aid
By all a daughter's love repaid,
(Strict was that bond—most kind of all—
Inviolate in Highland hall—)
Grey Morag sate a space apart,
In Edith's eyes to read her heart.
In vain the attendants' fond appeal
To Morag's skill, to Morag's zeal;
She mark'd her child receive their care,
Cold as the image sculptured fair,
(Form of some sainted patroness,)
Which cloister'd maids combine to dress;
She mark'd—and knew her nursling's heart
In the vain pomp took little part.
Wistful a while she gazed—then press'd
The maiden to her anxious breast
In finish'd loveliness—and led
To where a turret's airy head,
Slender and steep, and battled round,
O'erlook'd, dark Mull! thy mighty Sound,[1]

---

[1] The Sound of Mull, which divides that island from the continent of Scotland, is one of the most striking scenes which the Hebrides afford to the traveller. Sailing from Oban to Aros, or Tobermory, through a narrow channel, yet deep enough to bear

Where thwarting tides, with mingled roar,
Part thy swarth hills from Morven's shore.

### VIII.

"Daughter," she said, " these seas behold,
Round twice a hundred islands roll'd,
From Hirt, that hears their northern roar,
To the green Ilay's fertile shore;[1]

---

vessels of the largest burden, he has on his left the bold and mountainous shores of Mull; on the right those of that district of Argyleshire, called Morven, or Morvern, successively indented by deep salt-water lochs, running up many miles inland. To the south-eastward arise a prodigious range of mountains, among which Cruachan Ben is pre-eminent. And to the north-east is the no less huge and picturesque range of the Ardnamurchan hills. Many ruinous castles, situated generally upon cliffs overhanging the ocean, add interest to the scene. Those of Donolly and Dunstaffnage are first passed, then that of Duart, formerly belonging to the chief of the warlike and powerful sept of Macleans, and the scene of Miss Baillie's beautiful tragedy, entitled the Family Legend. Still passing on to the northward, Artornish and Aros become visible upon the opposite shores; and, lastly, Mingarry, and other ruins of less distinguished note. In fine weather, a grander and more impressive scene, both from its natural beauties, and associations with ancient history and tradition, can hardly be imagined. When the weather is rough, the passage is both difficult and dangerous, from the narrowness of the channel, and in part from the number of inland lakes, out of which sally forth a number of conflicting and thwarting tides, making the navigation perilous to open boats. The sudden flaws and gusts of wind which issue without a moment's warning from the mountain glens, are equally formidable. So that in unsettled weather, a stranger, if not much accustomed to the sea, may sometimes add to the other sublime sensations excited by the scene, that feeling of dignity which arises from a sense of danger.

[1] The number of the western isles of Scotland exceeds two hundred, of which St. Kilda is the most northerly, anciently

Or mainland turn, where many a tower
Owns thy bold brother's feudal power,
Each on its own dark cape reclined,
And listening to its own wild wind,
From where Mingarry, sternly placed,
O'erawes the woodland and the waste,[1]

---

called Hirth, or Hirt, probably from "earth," being in fact the whole globe to its inhabitants. Ilay, which now belongs almost entirely to Walter Campbell, Esq. of Shawfield, is by far the most fertile of the Hebrides, and has been greatly improved under the spirited and sagacious management of the present proprietor. This was in ancient times the principal abode of the Lords of the Isles, being, if not the largest, the most important island of their archipelago. In Martin's time, some relics of their grandeur were yet extant. "Loch-Finlagan, about three miles in circumference, affords salmon, trouts, and eels: this lake lies in the centre of the isle. The isle Finlagan, from which this lake hath its name, is in it. It's famous for being once the court in which the great Mac-Donald, King of the Isles, had his residence; his houses, chapel, &c. are now ruinous. His guards de corps, called Luchttach, kept guard on the lake-side nearest to the isle; the walls of their houses are still to be seen there. The high court of judicature, consisting of fourteen, sat always here; and there was an appeal to them from all the courts in the isles: the eleventh share of the sum in debate was due to the principal judge. There was a big stone of seven foot square, in which there was a deep impression made to receive the feet of Mac-Donald; for he was crowned King of the Isles standing in this stone, and swore that he would continue his vassals in the possession of their lands, and do exact justice to all his subjects: and then his father's sword was put into his hand. The Bishop of Argyle and seven priests anointed him king, in presence of all the heads of the tribes in the isles and continent, and were his vassals; at which time the orator rehearsed a catalogue of his ancestors," &c. — MARTIN's *Account of the Western Isles,* 8vo, London, 1716, p. 240, 1.

[1] [See Appendix, Note B.]

To where Dunstaffnage hears the raging
Of Connal with his rocks engaging.
Think'st thou, amid this ample round,
A single brow but thine has frown'd,
To sadden this auspicious morn,
That bids the daughter of high Lorn
Impledge her spousal faith to wed
The heir of mighty Somerled?[1]
Ronald, from many a hero sprung
The fair, the valiant, and the young,
LORD OF THE ISLES, whose lofty name[2]
A thousand bards have given to fame,

---

[1] Somerled was thane of Argyle and Lord of the Isles, about the middle of the twelfth century. He seems to have exercised his authority in both capacities, independent of the crown of Scotland, against which he often stood in hostility. He made various incursions upon the western lowlands during the reign of Malcolm IV., and seems to have made peace with him upon the terms of an independent prince, about the year 1157. In 1164, he resumed the war against Malcolm, and invaded Scotland with a large, but probably a tumultuary army, collected in the isles, in the mainland of Argyleshire, and in the neighbouring provinces of Ireland. He was defeated and slain in an engagement with a very inferior force, near Renfrew. His son Gillicolane fell in the same battle. This mighty chieftain married a daughter of Olaus, King of Man. From him our genealogists deduce two dynasties, distinguished in the stormy history of the middle ages; the Lords of the Isles descended from his elder son Ronald,—and the Lords of Lorn, who took their sirname of M'Dougal, as descended of his second son Dougal. That Somerled's territories upon the mainland, and upon the islands, should have been thus divided between his two sons, instead of passing to the elder exclusively, may illustrate the uncertainty of descent among the great Highland families, which we shall presently notice.

[2] [See Appendix, Note C.]

The mate of monarchs, and allied
On equal terms with England's pride.—
From chieftain's tower to bondsman's cot,
Who hears the tale, and triumphs not?
The damsel dons her best attire,
The shepherd lights his beltane fire,
Joy, joy! each warder's horn hath sung,
Joy, joy! each matin bell hath rung;
The holy priest says grateful mass,
Loud shouts each hardy galla-glass,
No mountain den holds outcast boor,
Of heart so dull, of soul so poor,
But he hath flung his task aside,
And claim'd this morn for holy-tide;
Yet, empress of this joyful day,
Edith is sad while all are gay."—

### IX.

Proud Edith's soul came to her eye,
Resentment check'd the struggling sigh,
Her hurrying hand indignant dried
The burning tears of injured pride—
"Morag, forbear! or lend thy praise
To swell yon hireling harpers' lays;
Make to yon maids thy boast of power,
That they may waste a wondering hour,
Telling of banners proudly borne,
Of pealing bell and bugle-horn,
Or theme more dear, of robes of price,
Crownlets and gauds of rare device.
But thou, experienced as thou art,
Think'st thou with these to cheat the heart,

3 *

That, bound in strong affection's chain,
Looks for return and looks in vain?
No! sum thine Edith's wretched lot
In these brief words—He loves her not!

### X.

"Debate it not—too long I strove
To call his cold observance love,
All blinded by the league that styled
Edith of Lorn,—while yet a child,
She tripp'd the heath by Morag's side,—
The brave Lord Ronald's destined bride.
Ere yet I saw him, while afar
His broadsword blazed in Scotland's war,
Train'd to believe our fates the same,
My bosom throbb'd when Ronald's name
Came gracing Fame's heroic tale,
Like perfume on the summer gale.
What pilgrim sought our halls, nor told
Of Ronald's deeds in battle bold;
Who touch'd the harp to heroes' praise,
But his achievements swell'd the lays?
Even Morag—not a tale of fame
Was hers but closed with Ronald's name.
He came! and all that had been told
Of his high worth seem'd poor and cold,
Tame, lifeless, void of energy,
Unjust to Ronald and to me!

### XI.

"Since then, what thought had Edith's heart
And gave not plighted love its part!—
And what requital? cold delay—
Excuse that shunn'd the spousal day.—

It dawns, and Ronald is not here!—
Hunts he Bentalla's nimble deer,
Or loiters he in secret dell
To bid some lighter love farewell,
And swear, that though he may not scorn
A daughter of the House of Lorn,[1]
Yet, when these formal rites are o'er,
Again they meet, to part no more?"

### XII.

—" Hush, daughter, hush! thy doubts remove,
More nobly think of Ronald's love.
Look, where beneath the castle grey
His fleet unmoor from Aros bay!
See'st not each galley's topmast bend,
As on the yards the sails ascend?
Hiding the dark-blue land they rise,
Like the white clouds on April skies;
The shouting vassals man the oars,
Behind them sink Mull's mountain shores,
Onward their merry course they keep,
Through whistling breeze and foaming deep.
And mark the headmost, seaward cast,
Stoop to the freshening gale her mast.
As if she vail'd its banner'd pride,
To greet afar her prince's bride!
Thy Ronald comes, and while in speed
His galley mates the flying steed,
He chides her sloth!"—Fair Edith sigh'd,
Blush'd, sadly smiled, and thus replied:—

---

[1] [See Appendix, Note D.]

## XIII.

"Sweet thought, but vain!—No, Morag! mark,
Type of his course, yon lonely bark,
That oft hath shifted helm and sail,
To win its way against the gale.
Since peep of morn, my vacant eyes
Have view'd by fits the course she tries;
Now, though the darkening scud comes on,
And dawn's fair promises be gone,
And though the weary crew may see
Our sheltering haven on their lee,
Still closer to the rising wind
They strive their shivering sail to bind,
Still nearer to the shelves' dread verge
At every tack her course they urge,
As if they fear'd Artornish more
Than adverse winds and breakers' roar."

## XIV.

Sooth spoke the Maid.—Amid the tide
 The skiff she mark'd lay tossing sore,
And shifted oft her stooping side,
 In weary tack from shore to shore.
 Yet on her destined course no more
  She gain'd, of forward way,
 Than what a minstrel may compare
 To the poor meed which peasants share
  Who toil the livelong day;
 And such the risk her pilot braves,
  That oft, before she wore,
 Her boltsprit kiss'd the broken waves,
 Where in white foam the ocean raves
  Upon the shelving shore.

Yet, to their destined purpose true,
Undaunted toil'd her hardy crew,
   Nor look'd where shelter lay,
Nor for Artornish Castle drew,
   Nor steer'd for Aros bay.

## XV.

Thus while they strove with wind and seas,
Borne onward by the willing breeze,
   Lord Ronald's fleet swept by,
Streamer'd with silk, and trick'd with gold,
Mann'd with the noble and the bold
   Of Island chivalry.
Around their prows the ocean roars,
And chafes beneath their thousand oars,
   Yet bears them on their way:
So chafes the war-horse in his might,
That fieldward bears some valiant knight,
Champs, till both bit and boss are white,
   But, foaming, must obey.
On each gay deck they might behold
Lances of steel and crests of gold,
And hauberks with their burnish'd fold,
   That shimmer'd fair and free;
And each proud galley, as she pass'd,
To the wild cadence of the blast
   Gave wilder minstrelsy.
Full many a shrill triumphant note
Saline and Scallastle bade float
   Their misty shores around;
And Morven's echoes answer'd well,
And Duart heard the distant swell
   Come down the darksome Sound.

## XVI.

So bore they on with mirth and pride,
And if that labouring bark they spied,
    'Twas with such idle eye
As nobles cast on lowly boor,
When, toiling in his task obscure,
    They pass him careless by.
Let them sweep on with heedless eyes!
But, had they known what mighty prize
    In that frail vessel lay,
The famish'd wolf, that prowls the wold,
Had scatheless pass'd the unguarded fold.
Ere, drifting by these galleys bold,
    Unchallenged were her way!
And thou, Lord Ronald, sweep thou on,
With mirth, and pride, and minstrel tone!
But had'st thou known who sail'd so nigh,
Far other glance were in thine eye!
Far other flush were on thy brow,
That, shaded by the bonnet, now
Assumes but ill the blithesome cheer
Of bridegroom when the bride is near!

## XVII.

Yes, sweep they on!—We will not leave,
For them that triumph, those who grieve.
    With that armada gay
Be laughter loud and jocund shout,
And bards to cheer the wassail rout,
    With tale, romance, and lay;
And of wild mirth each clamorous art,
Which, if it cannot cheer the heart,
May stupify and stun its smart,
    For one loud busy day.

Yes, sweep they on!—But with that skiff
   Abides the minstrel tale,
Where there was dread of surge and cliff,
Labour that strain'd each sinew stiff,
   And one sad Maiden's wail.

### XVIII.

All day with fruitless strife they toil'd,
With eve the ebbing currents boil'd
   More fierce from strait and lake;
And midway through the channel met
Conflicting tides that foam and fret,
And high their mingled billows jet,
As spears, that, in the battle set,
   Spring upward as they break.
Then, too, the lights of eve were past,
And louder sung the western blast
   On rocks of Inninmore;
Rent was the sail, and strain'd the mast,
And many a leak was gaping fast,
And the pale steersman stood aghast
   And gave the conflict o'er.

### XIX.

'T was then that One, whose lofty look
Nor labour dull'd nor terror shook,
   Thus to the Leader spoke:—
" Brother, how hopest thou to abide
The fury of this wilder'd tide,
Or how avoid the rock's rude side,
   Until the day has broke?
Didst thou not mark the vessel reel
With quivering planks, and groaning keel,
   At the last billow's shock?

t

Yet how of better counsel tell,
Though here thou see'st poor Isabel
    Ialf dead with want and fear;
For look on sea, or look on land,
Or yon dark sky, on every hand
    Despair and death are near.
For her alone I grieve—on me
Danger sits light by land and sea,
    I follow where thou wilt,
Either to bide the tempest's lour,
Or wend to yon unfriendly tower,
Or rush amid their naval power,
With war-cry wake their wassail-hour,
    And die with hand on hilt."—

### XX.

That elder Leader's calm reply
    In steady voice was given,
"In man's most dark extremity
    Oft succour dawns from Heaven.
Edward, trim thou the shatter'd sail,
The helm be mine, and down the gale
    Let our free course be driven;
So shall we 'scape the western bay,
The hostile fleet, the unequal fray,
So safely hold our vessel's way
    Beneath the Castle wall;
For if a hope of safety rest,
'T is on the sacred name of guest,
Who seeks for shelter, storm-distress'd
    Within a chieftain's hall.
If not—it best beseems our worth,
Our name, our right, our lofty birth,
    By noble hands to fall."

### XXI.

The helm, to his strong arm consign'd,
Gave the reef'd sail to meet the wind,
    And on her alter'd way,
Fierce bounding, forward sprung the ship,
Like greyhound starting from the slip
    To seize his flying prey.
Awaked before the rushing prow,
The mimic fires of ocean glow,
    Those lightnings of the wave;[1]
Wild sparkles crest the broken tides,
And, flashing round, the vessel's sides
    With elvish lustre lave,
While, far behind, their livid light
To the dark billows of the night
    A gloomy splendour gave,

---

[1] The phenomenon called by sailors Sea-fire, is one of the most beautiful and interesting which is witnessed in the Hebrides. At times the ocean appears entirely illuminated around the vessel, and a long train of lambent coruscations are perpetually bursting upon the sides of the vessel, or pursuing her wake through the darkness. These phosphoric appearances, concerning the origin of which naturalists are not agreed in opinion, seem to be called into action by the rapid motion of the ship through the water, and are probably owing to the water being saturated with fish-spawn, or other animal substances. They remind one strongly of the description of the sea-snakes in Mr. Coleridge's wild, but highly poetical ballad of the Ancient Mariner:—

> " Beyond the shadow of the ship
>   I watch'd the water-snakes,
> They moved in tracks of shining white,
> And when they rear'd, the elvish light
>   Fell off in hoary flakes."

It seems as if old Ocean shakes
From his dark brow the lucid flakes
   In envious pageantry,
To match the meteor light that streaks
   Grim Hecla's midnight sky.

### XXII.

Nor lack'd they steadier light to keep
Their course upon the darken'd deep;—
Artornish, on her frowning steep
   'Twixt cloud and ocean hung,
Glanced with a thousand lights of glee,
And landward far, and far to sea,
   Her festal radiance flung.
By that blithe beacon-light they steer'd,
   Whose lustre mingled well
With the pale beam that now appear'd,
As the cold moon her head uprear'd
   Above the eastern fell.

### XXIII.

Thus guided, on their course they bore,
Until they near'd the mainland shore,
When frequent on the hollow blast
Wild shouts of merriment were cast,
And wind and wave and sea-birds' cry
With wassail sounds in concert vie,
Like funeral shrieks with revelry,
   Or like the battle-shout
By peasants heard from cliffs on high,
When Triumph, Rage, and Agony,
   Madden the fight and rout.

Now nearer yet, through mist and storm
Dimly arose the Castle's form,
 And deepen'd shadow made,
Far lengthen'd on the main below,
Where, dancing in reflected glow,
 A hundred torches play'd,
Spangling the wave with lights as vain
As pleasures in this vale of pain,
 That dazzle as they fade.

### XXIV.

Beneath the Castle's sheltering lee,
They staid their course in quiet sea.
Hewn in the rock, a passage there
Sought the dark fortress by a stair,
 So strait, so high, so steep,
With peasant's staff one valiant hand
Might well the dizzy pass have mann'd,
 Gainst hundreds arm'd with spear and brand,
  And plunged them in the deep.[1]

---

The fortress of a Hebridean chief was almost always on the sea-shore, for the facility of communication which the ocean afforded. Nothing can be more wild than the situations which they chose, and the devices by which the architects endeavoured to defend them. Narrow stairs and arched vaults were the usual mode of access; and the drawbridge appears at Dunstaffnage, and elsewhere, to have fallen from the gate of the building to the top of such a staircase; so that any one advancing with hostile purpose, found himself in a state of exposed and precarious elevation, with a gulf between him and the object of his attack.

These fortresses were guarded with equal care. The duty of the watch devolved chiefly upon an officer called the Cockman, who had the charge of challenging all who approached the castle. The very ancient family of Mac-Niel of Barra kept this attendant

His bugle then the helmsman wound;
Loud answer'd every echo round,
    From turret, rock, and bay,
The postern's hinges crash and groan,
And soon the warder's cresset shone
On those rude steps of slippery stone,
    To light the upward way.
" Thrice welcome, holy Sire!" he said;
" Full long the spousal train have staid,
    And, vex'd at thy delay,
Fear'd lest, amidst these wildering seas,
The darksome night and freshening breeze
    Had driven thy bark astray."—

---

at their castle about a hundred years ago. Martin gives the following account of the difficulty which attended his procuring
entrance there:—"The little island Kismul lies about a quarter
of a mile from the south of this isle (Barra); it is the seat of Mackneil of Barra; there is a stone wall round it two stories high,
reaching the sea; and within the wall there is an old tower and
an hall, with other houses about it. There is a little magazine
in the tower, to which no stranger has access. I saw the officer
called the Cockman, and an old cock he is; when I bid him ferry
me over the water to the island, he told me that he was but an
inferior officer, his business being to attend in the tower; but if
(says he) the constable, who then stood on the wall, will give
you access, I'll ferry you over. I desired him to procure me the
constable's permission, and I would reward him; but having
waited some hours for the constable's answer, and not receiving
any, I was obliged to return without seeing this famous fort.
Mackneil and his lady being absent, was the cause of this diffi
culty, and of my not seeing the place. I was told some weeks
after, that the constable was very apprehensive of some design I
might have in viewing the fort, and thereby to expose it to the
conquest of a foreign power; of which I supposed there was no
great cause of fear."

### XXV.

"Warder," the younger stranger said,
"Thine erring guess some mirth had made
In mirthful hour; but nights like these,
When the rough winds wake western seas,
Brook not of glee.  We crave some aid
And needful shelter for this maid
    Until the break of day;
For, to ourselves, the deck's rude plank
Is easy as the mossy bank
    That's breathed upon by May;
And for our storm-toss'd skiff we seek
Short shelter in this leeward creek,
Prompt when the dawn the east shall streak
    Again to bear away."—
Answered the Warder, "In what name
Assert ye hospitable claim?
    Whence come, or whither bound?
Hath Erin seen your parting sails?
Or come ye on Norweyan gales?
And seek ye England's fertile vales,
    Or Scotland's mountain ground?"—

### XXVI.

"Warriors—for other title none
For some brief space we list to own,
Bound by a vow—warriors are we;
In strife by land, and storm by sea,
    We have been known to fame;
And these brief words have import dear,
When sounded in a noble ear,
To harbour safe, and friendly cheer,
    That gives us rightful claim.
    4 *

Grant us the trivial boon we seek,
And we in other realms will speak
      Fair of your courtesy;
Deny—and be your niggard Hold
Scorn'd by the noble and the bold,
Shunn'd by the pilgrim on the wold,
      And wanderer on the lea!"—

### XXVII.

" Bold stranger, no—'gainst claim like thine,
No bolt revolves by hand of mine,
Though urged in tone that more express'd
A monarch than a suppliant guest.
Be what ye will, Artornish Hall
On this glad eve is free to all.
Though ye had drawn a hostile sword
'Gainst our ally, great England's Lord,
Or mail upon your shoulders borne,
To battle with the Lord of Lorn,
Or, outlaw'd, dwelt by greenwood tree
With the fierce Knight of Ellerslie,[1]
Or aided even the murderous strife,
When Comyn fell beneath the knife
Of that fell homicide The Bruce,[2]
This night had been a term of truce.—
Ho, vassals! give these guests your care,
And show the narrow postern stair."

### XXVIII.

To land these two bold brethren leapt,
(The weary crew their vessel kept,)

---

[1] [Sir William Wallace.]        [2] [See Appendix, Note G.]

And, lighted by the torches' flare,
That seaward flung their smoky glare,
The younger knight that maiden bare
    Half lifeless up the rock ;
On his strong shoulder lean'd her head,
And down her long dark tresses shed,
As the wild vine in tendrils spread,
    Droops from the mountain oak.
Him follow'd close that elder Lord,
And in his hand a sheathed sword,
    Such as few arms could wield ;
But when he boun'd him to such task,
Well could it cleave the strongest casque,
    And rend the surest shield.

## XXIX.

The raised portcullis' arch they pass,
The wicket with its bars of brass,
    The entrance long and low,
Flank'd at each turn by loop-holes strait,
Where bowmen might in ambush wait,
(If force or fraud should burst the gate,)
    To gall an entering foe.
But every jealous post of ward
Was now defenceless and unbarr'd,
    And all the passage free
To one low-brow'd and vaulted room,
Where squire and yeoman, page and groom,
    Plied their loud revelry.

## XXX.

And " Rest ye here," the Warder bade,
" Till to our Lord your suit is said.—

And, comrades, gaze not on the maid,
And on these men who ask our aid,
  As if ye ne'er had seen
A damsel tired of midnight bark,
Or wanderers of a moulding stark,
  And bearing martial mien."
But not for Eachin's reproof
Would page or vassal stand aloof,
  But crowded on to stare,
As men of courtesy untaught,
Till fiery Edward roughly caught,
  From one the foremost there,
His chequer'd plaid, and in its shroud,
To hide her from the vulgar crowd,
  Involved his sister fair.
His brother, as the clansman bent
His sullen brow in discontent,
  Made brief and stern excuse;—
" Vassal, were thine the cloak of pall
That decks thy Lord in bridal hall,
  'Twere honour'd by her use."

## XXXI.

Proud was his tone, but calm; his eye
Had that compelling dignity
His mien that bearing haught and high,
  Which common spirits fear;[1]

---

[1] [" Still sways their souls with that commanding art
That dazzles, leads, yet chills the vulgar heart.
What is that spell, that thus his lawless train
Confess and envy, yet oppose in vain?
What should it be, that thus their faith can bind?
The power of Thought — the magic of the Mind!
Link'd with success, assumed and kept with skill.
That moulds another's weakness to its will:

Needed nor word nor signal more,
Nod, wink, and laughter, all were o'er;
Upon each other back they bore,
    And gazed like startled deer.
But now appear'd the Seneschal,
Commission'd by his lord to call
The strangers to the Baron's hall,
    Where feasted fair and free
That Island Prince in nuptial tide,
With Edith there his lovely bride,
And her bold brother by her side,
And many a chief, the flower and pride
    Of Western land and sea.

Here pause we, gentles, for a space;
And, if our tale hath won your grace
Grant us brief patience, and again
We will renew the minstrel strain.

---

Wields with their hands, but, still to these unknown
Makes even their mightiest deeds appear his own.
Such hath it been — shall be — beneath the sun
The many still must labour for the one!
'Tis Nature's doom.''— BYRON's *Corsair.*]

THE

# LORD OF THE ISLES

CANTO SECOND.

THE

# LORD OF THE ISLES.

## CANTO SECOND.

Fill the bright goblet, spread the festive board!
Summon the gay, the noble, and the fair;
Through the loud hall in joyous concert pour'd,
Let mirth and music sound the dirge of Care!
But ask thou not if Happiness be there,
If the loud laugh disguise convulsive throe,
Or if the brow the heart's true livery wear;
Lift not the festal mask!—enough to know,
No scene of mortal life but teems with mortal woe.

## II.

With beakers' clang, with harpers' lay,
With all that olden time deem'd gay,
The Island Chieftain feasted high;
But there was in his troubled eye
A gloomy fire, and on his brow
Now sudden flush'd, and faded now,
Emotions such as draw their birth
From deeper source than festal mirth.
By fits he paused, and harper's strain
And jester's tale went round in vain,

---

[1] ["Even in laughter the heart is sorrowful; and the end of
that mirth is heaviness."—*Proverbs*, xiv. 13.]

Or fell but on his idle car
Like distant sounds which dreamers hear.
Then would he rouse him, and employ
Each art to aid the clamorous joy,
  And call for pledge and lay,
And, for brief space, of all the crowd,
As he was loudest of the loud,
  Seem gayest of the gay.

### III.

Yet nought amiss the bridal throng
Mark'd in brief mirth, or musing long;
The vacant brow, the unlistening ear,
They gave to thoughts of raptures near,
And his fierce starts of sudden glee
Seem'd bursts of bridegroom's ecstasy.
Nor thus alone misjudged the crowd,
Since lofty Lorn, suspicious, proud,
And jealous of his honour'd line,
And that keen knight, De Argentine,
(From England sent on errand high,
The western league more firm to tie,)[1]

---

[1] Sir Egidius, or Giles de Argentine, was one of the most
accomplished knights of the period. He had served in the wars
of Henry of Luxemburg with such high reputation, that he was,
in popular estimation, the third worthy of the age. Those to
whom fame assigned precedence over him were, Henry of Luxemburg himself, and Robert Bruce. Argentine had warred in
Palestine, encountered thrice with the Saracens, and had slain
two antagonists in each engagement:—an easy matter, he said,
for one Christian knight to slay two Pagan dogs. His death cor-
responded with his high character. With Aymer de Valence,
Earl of Pembroke, he was appointed to attend immediately upon
the person of Edward II. at Bannockburn. When the day was

Both deem'd in Ronald's mood to find
A lover's transport-troubled mind.
But one sad heart, one tearful eye,
Pierced deeper through the mystery,
And watch'd, with agony and fear,
Her wayward bridegroom's varied cheer.

## IV.

She watch'd—yet fear'd to meet his glance,
And he shunn'd hers;—till when by chance
They met, the point of foeman's lance
    Had given a milder pang!
Beneath the intolerable smart
He writhed;—then sternly mann'd his heart
To play his hard but destined part,
    And from the table sprang.

---

utterly lost they forced the king from the field. De Argentine
saw the king safe from immediate danger, and then took his leave
of him; "God be with you, sir," he said, "it is not my wont to
fly." So saying, he turned his horse, cried his war-cry, plunged
into the midst of the combatants, and was slain. Baston, a
rhyming monk who had been brought by Edward to celebrate his
expected triumph, and who was compelled by the victors to com-
pose a poem on his defeat, mentions with some feeling the death
of Sir Giles de Argentine:

> *Nobilis Argenten, pugil inclyte, dulcis Egidi,*
> *Vix scieram mentem cum te succumbere vidi.*

"The first line mentions the three chief requisites of a true
knight, noble birth, valour, and courteousness. Few Leonine
couplets can be produced that have so much sentiment. I wish
that I could have collected more ample memorials concerning a
character altogether different from modern manners. Sir Giles
l'Argentine was a hero of romance in real life." So observes
the excellent Lord Hailes.

"Fill me the mighty cup!" he said,
"Erst own'd by royal Somerled:[1]
Fill it, till on the studded brim
In burning gold the bubbles swim,
And every gem of varied shine
Glow doubly bright in rosy wine!
   To you, brave lord, and brother mine,
      Of Lorn, this pledge I drink—
   The union of Our House with thine,
      By this fair bridal-link!"—

### V.

"Let it pass round!" quoth He of Lorn,
"And in good time—that winded horn
   Must of the Abbot tell;
The laggard monk is come at last."
Lord Ronald heard the bugle-blast,
And on the floor at random cast,
   The untasted goblet fell.
But when the warder in his ear
Tells other news, his blither cheer
   Returns like sun of May,
When through a thunder-cloud it beams!—
Lord of two hundred isles, he seems
   As glad of brief delay
As some poor criminal might feel,
When from the gibbet or the wheel
   Respited for a day.

### VI.

"Brother of Lorn," with hurried voice
He said, "And you. fair lords, rejoice!
   Here, to augment our glee,

---

[1] [See Appendix, Note E.]

Come wandering knights from travel far,
Well proved, they say, in strife of war,
 And tempest on the sea.——
Ho! give them at your board such place
As best their presences may grace,
 And bid them welcome free!"
With solemn step, and silver wand,
The Seneschal the presence scann'd
Of these strange guests; and well he knew
How to assign their rank its due;[1]
 For though the costly furs
That erst had deck'd their caps were torn,
And their gay robes were over-worn,

---

[1] 'The Sewer, to whom, rather than the Seneschal, the office of arranging the guests of an island chief appertained, was an officer of importance in the family of a Hebridean chief.—— "Every family had commonly two stewards, which, in their language, were called Marischal Tach: the first of these served always at home, and was obliged to be versed in the pedigree of all the tribes in the isles, and in the highlands of Scotland; for it was his province to assign every man at table his seat according to his quality; and this was done without one word speaking, only by drawing a score with a white rod, which this Marischal had in his hand, before the person who was bid by him to sit down: and this was necessary to prevent disorder and contention; and though the Marischal might sometimes be mistaken, the master of the family incurred no censure by such an escape; but this custom has been laid aside of late. They had also cup-bearers, who always filled and carried the cup round the company, and he himself always drank off the first draught. They had likewise purse-masters, who kept their money. Both these officers had an hereditary right to their office in writing, and each of them had a town and land for his service: some of those rights I have seen fairly written on good parchment."—— MARTIN's *Western Isles.*

 5 *

And soil'd their gilded spurs,
Yet such a high commanding grace
Was in their mien and in their face,
As suited best the princely dais,[1]
    And royal canopy;
And there he marshall'd them their place,
    First of that company.

### VII.

Then lords and ladies spake aside,
And angry looks the error chide,
That gave to guests unnamed, unknown,
A place so near their prince's throne;
    But Owen Erraught said,
"For forty years a seneschal,
To marshal guests in bower and hall
    Has been my honour'd trade.
Worship and birth to me are known,
By look, by bearing, and by tone,
Not by furr'd robe or broider'd zone;
    And 'gainst an oaken bough
I'll gage my silver wand of state,
That these three strangers oft have sate
    In higher place than now."—

### VIII.

"I, too," the aged Ferrand said,
"Am qualified by minstrel trade
    Of rank and place to tell;—
Mark'd ye the younger stranger's eye,
My mates, how quick, how keen, how high,
    How fierce its flashes fell,

---

[1] *Dais*—the great hall-table—elevated a step or two above the rest of the room.

Glancing among the noble rout
As if to seek the noblest out,
Because the owner might not brook
On any save his peers to look?
    And yet it moves me more,
That steady, calm, majestic brow,
With which the elder chief even now
        Scann'd the gay presence o'er,
Like being of superior kind,
In whose high-toned impartial mind
Degrees of mortal rank and state
Seem objects of indifferent weight.
    The lady too — though closely tied
        The mantle veil both face and eye,
    Her motions' grace it could not hide,
        Nor could her form's fair symmetry."

### IX.

Suspicious doubt and lordly scorn
Lour'd on the haughty front of Lorn.
From underneath his brows of pride,
The stranger guests he sternly eyed,
    And whisper'd closely what the ear
    Of Argentine alone might hear;
        Then question'd, high and brief,
If, in their voyage, aught they knew
Of the rebellious Scottish crew,
Who to Rath-Erin's shelter drew,
        With Carrick's outlaw'd Chief?[1]

---

[1] It must be remembered by all who have read the Scottish
history, that after he had slain Comyn at Dumfries, and asserted
his right to the Scottish crown, Robert Bruce was reduced to the

And if, their winter's exile o'er,
They harbour'd still by Ulster's shore,

---

greatest extremity by the English and their adherents.  He was
crowned at Scone by the general consent of the Scottish barons,
but his authority endured but a short time.  According to the
phrase said to have been used by his wife, he was for that year
"a summer king, but not a winter one."  On the 29th March,
1306, he was crowned king at Scone.  Upon the 19th June, in
the same year, he was totally defeated at Methven, near Perth;
and his most important adherents, with few exceptions, were
either executed or compelled to embrace the English interest,
for safety of their lives and fortunes.  After this disaster, his life
was that of an outlaw, rather than a candidate for monarchy.
He separated himself from the females of his retinue, whom he
sent for safety to the Castle of Kildrummie, in Aberdeenshire,
where they afterward became captives to England.  From Aberdeenshire, Bruce retreated to the mountainous parts of Breadalbane, and approached the borders of Argyleshire.  There, as
mentioned in the Appendix, Note D, and more fully in Note F,
he was defeated by the Lord of Lorn, who had assumed arms
against him in revenge of the death of his relative, John the
Red Comyn.  Escaped from this peril, Bruce, with his few
attendants, subsisted by hunting and fishing, until the weather
compelled them to seek better sustenance and shelter than the
Highland mountains afforded.  With great difficulty they crossed, from Rowardennan probably, to the western banks of Loch-
lomond, partly in a miserable boat, and partly by swimming.  The
valiant and loyal Earl of Lennox, to whose territories they had
now found their way, welcomed them with tears, but was unable
to assist them to make an effectual head.  The Lord of the Isles,
then in possession of great part of Cantyre, received the fugitive
monarch and future restorer of his country's independence, in
his Castle of Dunnaverty, in that district.  But treason, says
Barbour, was so general, that the King durst not abide there.
Accordingly, with the remnant of his followers, Bruce embarked
for Rath-Erin, or Rachrine, the Recina of Ptolemy, a small
island, lying almost opposite to the shores of Ballycastle, on the

Or launch'd their galleys on the main,
To vex their native land again?

### X.

That younger stranger, fierce and high,
At once confronts the Chieftain's eye
    With look of equal scorn; —
"Of rebels have we nought to show;
But if of Royal Bruce thou'dst know,
    I warn thee he has sworn,
Ere thrice three days shall come and go,
His banner Scottish winds shall blow,
Despite each mean or mighty foe,
From England's every bill and bow,
    To Allaster of Lorn."
Kindled the mountain Chieftain's ire,
But Ronald quench'd the rising fire;
"Brother, it better suits the time
To chase the night with Ferrand's rhyme,
Than wake, 'midst mirth and wine, the jars
That flow from these unhappy wars."—
"Content," said Lorn; and spoke apart
With Ferrand, master of his art,
    Then whisper'd Argentine,—
"The lay I named will carry smart
To these bold strangers' haughty heart,
    If right this guess of mine."

---

coast of Ireland. The islanders at first fled from their new and
armed guests, but upon some explanation submitted themselves
to Bruce's sovereignty. He resided among them until the approach of spring, [1306,] when he again returned to Scotland,
with the desperate resolution to reconquer his kingdom, or perish
in the attempt. The progress of his success, from its commencement to its completion, forms the brightest period in Scottish
history

He ceased, and it was silence all,
Until the Minstrel waked the hall.

### XI.

#### 𝕿𝖍𝖊 𝕭𝖗𝖔𝖆𝖈𝖍 𝖔𝖋 𝕷𝖔𝖗𝖓.[1]

" Whence the broach of burning gold,
That clasps the Chieftain's mantle-fold,
Wrought and chased with rare device,
Studded fair with gems of price,[2]
On the varied tartans beaming,
As, through night's pale rainbow gleaming,
Fainter now, now seen afar,
Fitful shines the northern star?

" Gem! ne'er wrought on highland mountain.
Did the fairy of the fountain,
Or the mermaid of the wave,
Frame thee in some coral cave?
Did in Iceland's darksome mine
Dwarf's swart hands thy metal twine?

---

[1] [See Appendix, Note F.]

[2] Great art and expense was bestowed upon the *fibula*, or broach, which secured the plaid, when the wearer was a person of importance.   Martin mentions having seen a silver broach of a hundred marks value.  " It was broad as any ordinary pewter plate, the whole curiously engraven with various animals, &c. There was a lesser buckle, which was wore in the middle of the larger, and above two ounces weight; it had in the centre a large piece of crystal, or some finer stone, and this was set all round with several finer stones of a lesser size."— *Western Islands*.   Pennant has given an engraving of such a broach as Martin describes, and the workmanship of which is very elegant.   It is said to have belonged to the family of Lochbuy.— See PENNANT'S *Tour*, vol. iii. p. 14.

Or, mortal-moulded, comest thou here,
From England's love, or France's fear?

## XII.

### Song continued.

" No!—thy splendours nothing tell
Foreign art or faëry spell.
Moulded thou for Monarch's use,
By the overweening Bruce,
When the royal robe he tied
O'er a heart of wrath and pride;
Thence in triumph wert thou torn,
By the victor hand of Lorn!

" When the gem was won and lost,
Widely was the war-cry toss'd!
Rung aloud Bendourish fell,
Answer'd Douchart's sounding dell,
Fled the deer from wild Teyndrum,
When the homicide, o'ercome,
Hardly 'scaped with scathe and scorn,
Left the pledge with conquering Lorn!

## IX.

### Song concluded.

" Vain was then the Douglas brand,[1]
Vain the Campbell's vaunted hand,

---

[1] The gallant Sir James, called the Good Lord Douglas, the most faithful and valiant of Bruce's adherents, was wounded at the battle of Dalry. Sir Nigel, or Niel Campbell, was also in that unfortunate skirmish. He married Marjorie, sister to Robert Bruce, and was among his most faithful followers. In a manuscript account of the house of Argyle, supplied, it would

Vain Kirkpatrick's bloody·dirk,
Making sure of murder's work ;[1]
Barendown fled fast away,
Fled the fiery De la Haye,[2]

---

seem, as materials for Archbishop Spottiswoode's History of the
Church of Scotland, I find the following passage concerning Sir
Niel Campbell : — " Moreover, when all the nobles in Scotland
had left King Robert after his hard success, yet this noble knight
was most faithful, and shrinked not, as it is to be seen in an
indenture bearing these words : — *Memorandum quod cum ab
incarnatione Domini* 1308 *conventum fuit et concordatum inter
nobiles viros Dominum Alexandrum de Seatoun militem et
Dominum Gilbertum de Haye militem et Dominum Nigellum
Campbell militem apud monasterium de Cambuskenneth* 9° *Sep-
tembris qui tacta sancta eucharista, magnoque juramento facto,
jurarunt se debere libertatem regni et Robertum nuper regem
coronatum contra omnes mortales Francos Anglos Scotos defen-
dere usque ad ultimum terminum vitæ ipsorum.* Their sealles
are appended to the indenture in greene wax, togithir with the
seal of Gulfrid, Abbot of Cambuskenneth."

[1] [See Appendix, Note G.]

[2] These knights are enumerated by Barbour among the small
number of Bruce's adherents, who remained in arms with him
after the battle of Methven.

> " With him was a bold baron,
> Schyr William the Baroundoun,
>
> Schyr Gilbert de la Haye alsua."

There were more than one of the noble family of Hay engaged
in Bruce's cause ; but the principal was Gilbert de la Haye, Lord
of Errol, a stanch adherent to King Robert's interest, and whom
he rewarded by creating him hereditary Lord High Constable of
Scotland, a title which he used 16th March, 1308, where, in a
letter from the peers of Scotland to Philip the Fair of France,
he is designed *Gilbertus de Hay Constabularius Scotiæ.* He
was slain at the battle of Halidoun-hill. Hugh de la Haye, his
brother, was made prisoner at the battle of Methven.

When this broach, triumphant borne,
Beam'd upon the breast of Lorn.

'Farthest fled its former Lord,
Left his men to brand and cord,
Bloody brand of Highland steel,
English gibbet, axe, and wheel.
Let him fly from coast to coast,
Dogg'd by Comyn's vengeful ghost,
While his spoils, in triumph worn,
Long shall grace victorious Lorn!"

### XIV.

As glares the tiger on his foes,
Hemm'd in by hunters, spears, and bows,
And, ere he bounds upon the ring,
Selects the object of his spring,—
Now on the bard, now on his Lord,
So Edward glared and grasp'd his sword—
But stern his brother spoke,—" Be still.
What! art thou yet so wild of will,
After high deeds and sufferings long,
To chafe thee for a menial's song?—
Well hast thou framed, Old Man, thy strains,
To praise the hand that pays thy pains;[1]

---

[1] The character of the Highland bards, however high in an earlier period of society, seems soon to have degenerated. The Irish affirm, that in their kindred tribes severe laws became necessary to restrain their avarice. In the Highlands they seem gradually to have sunk into contempt, as well as the orators, or men of speech, with whose office that of family poet was often united.—" The orators, in their language called Isdane, were in high esteem both in these islands and the continent; until within these forty years, they sat always among the nobles and chiefs

Yet something might thy song have told
Of Lorn's three vassals, true and bold,
Who rent their Lord from Bruce's hold,
As underneath his knee he lay,
And died to save him in the fray.
I've heard the Bruce's cloak and clasp
Was clench'd within their dying grasp,

---

of families in the streah, or circle. Their houses and little villages were sanctuaries, as well as churches, and they took place
before doctors of physick. The orators, after the Druids were
extinct, were brought in to preserve the genealogy of families,
and to repeat the same at every succession of chiefs; and upon
the occasion of marriages and births, they made epithalamiums
and panegyricks, which the poet or bard pronounced. The orators, by the force of their eloquence, had a powerful ascendant
over the greatest men in their time; for if any orator did but ask
the habit, arms, horse, or any other thing belonging to the greatest man in these islands, it was readily granted them, sometimes
out of respect, and sometimes for fear of being exclaimed against
by a satyre, which, in those days, was reckoned a great dishonour. But these gentlemen becoming insolent, lost ever since
both the profit and esteem which was formerly due to their character; for neither their panegyricks nor satyres are regarded to
what they have been, and they are now allowed but a small
salary. I must not omit to relate their way of study, which is
very singular: They shut their doors and windows for a day's
time, and lie on their backs, with a stone upon their belly, and
plads about their heads, and their eyes being covered, they pump
their brains for rhetorical encomium or panegyrick; and indeed
they furnish such a style from this dark cell as is understood by
very few; and if they purchase a couple of horses as the reward
of their meditation, they think they have done a great matter.
The poet, or bard, had a title to the bridegroom's upper garb,
that is, the plad and bonnet; but now he is satisfyed with what
the bridegroom pleases to give him on such occasions."— MAR-
TIN's *Western Isles.*

What time a hundred foemen more
Rush'd in and back the victor bore,
Long after Lorn had left the strife,
Full glad to 'scape with limb and life.—
Enough of this—And, Minstrel, hold,
As minstrel-hire, this chain of gold,
For future lays a fair excuse,
To speak more nobly of the Bruce."—

### XV.

" Now, by Columba's shrine, I swear,
And every saint that's buried there,
'Tis he himself!" Lorn sternly cries,
" And for my kinsman's death he dies."
As loudly Ronald calls—" Forbear!
Not in my sight while brand I wear
O'ermatch'd by odds, shall warrior fall,
Or blood of stranger stain my hall!
This ancient fortress of my race
Shall be misfortune's resting-place,
Shelter and shield of the distress'd,
No slaughter-house for shipwreck'd guest "—
" Talk not to me," fierce Lorn replied,
" Of odds or match!— when Comyn died,
Three daggers clash'd within his side!
Talk not to me of sheltering hall,
The Church of God saw Comyn fall!
On God's own altar stream'd his blood,
While o'er my prostrate kinsman stood
The ruthless murderer — e'en as now —
With armed hand and scornful brow! —
Up, all who love me! blow on blow!
And lay the outlaw'd felons low!"

## XVI.

Then up sprung many a mainland Lord,
Obedient to their Chieftain's word.
Barcaldine's arm is high in air,
And Kinloch-Alline's blade is bare,
Black Murthok's dirk has left its sheath,
And clench'd is Dermid's hand of death.
Their mutter'd threats of vengeance swell
Into a wild and warlike yell;
Onward they press with weapons high,
The affrighted females shriek and fly,
And, Scotland, then thy brightest ray
Had darken'd ere its noon of day,
But every chief of birth and fame,
That from the Isles of Ocean came,
At Ronald's side that hour withstood
Fierce Lorn's relentless thirst for blood.

## XVII.

Brave Torquil from Dunvegan high,
Lord of the misty hills of Skye,
Mac-Niel, wild Bara's ancient thane,
Duart, of bold Clan Gillian's strain,
Fergus, of Canna's castled bay,
Mac-Duffith, Lord of Colonsay,
Soon as they saw the broadswords glance,
With ready weapons rose at once,
More prompt, that many an ancient feud,
Full oft suppress'd, full oft renew'd,
Glow'd 'twixt the chieftains of Argyle,
And many a lord of ocean's isle.
Wild was the scene—each sword was bare,
Back stream'd each chieftain's shaggy hair,

In gloomy opposition set,
Eyes, hands, and brandish'd weapons met;
Blue gleaming o'er the social board,
Flash'd to the torches many a sword;
And soon those bridal lights may shine
On purple blood for rosy wine.

### XVIII.

While thus for blows and death prepared,
Each heart was up, each weapon bared,
Each foot advanced,—a surly pause
Still reverenced hospitable laws.
All menaced violence, but alike
Reluctant each the first to strike,
(For aye accursed in minstrel line
Is he who brawls 'mid song and wine,)
And, match'd in numbers and in might,
Doubtful and desperate seem'd the fight.
Thus threat and murmur died away,
Till on the crowded hall there lay
Such silence, as the deadly still,
Ere bursts the thunder on the hill.
With blade advanced, each Chieftain bold
Show'd like the Sworder's form of old,
As wanting still the torch of life,
To wake the marble into strife.

### XIX.

That awful pause the stranger maid,
And Edith, seized to pray for aid.
As to De Argentine she clung,
Away her veil the stranger flung,
And, lovely 'mid her wild despair,
Fast stream'd her eyes, wide flow'd her hair.
   6 *

"O thou, of knighthood once the flower,
Sure refuge in distressful hour
Thou, who in Judah well hast fought
For our dear faith, and oft hast sought
Renown in knightly exercise,
When this poor hand has dealt the prize,
Say, can thy soul of honour brook
On the unequal strife to look,
When, butcher'd thus in peaceful hall,
Those once thy friends, my brethren, fall!"
To Argentine she turn'd her word,
But her eye sought the Island Lord.
A flush like evening's setting flame
Glow'd on his cheek; his hardy frame,
As with a brief convulsion, shook:
With hurried voice and eager look,—
"Fear not," he said, "my Isabel!
What said I—Edith!—all is well—
Nay, fear not—I will well provide
The safety of my lovely bride—
My bride?"—but there the accents clung
In tremor to his faltering tongue.

## XX.

Now rose De Argentine, to claim
The prisoners in his sovereign's name,
To England's crown, who, vassals sworn,
'Gainst their liege lord had weapon borne—
(Such speech, I ween, was but to hide
His care their safety to provide;
For knight more true in thought and deed
Than Argentine ne'er spurr'd a steed)—

And Ronald, who his meaning guess'd,
Seem'd half to sanction the request.
This purpose fiery Torquil broke;—
"Somewhat we've heard of England's yoke,"
He said, "and, in our islands, Fame
Hath whisper'd of a lawful claim,
That calls the Bruce fair Scotland's Lord,
Though dispossess'd by foreign sword.
This craves reflection — but though right
And just the charge of England's Knight,
Let England's crown her rebels seize
Where she has power;— in towers like these,
'Midst Scottish Chieftains summon'd here
To bridal mirth and bridal cheer,
Be sure, with no consent of mine,
Shall either Lorn or Argentine
With chains or violence, in our sight,
Oppress a brave and banish'd Knight."

## XXI.

Then waked the wild debate again,
With brawling threat and clamour vain.
Vassals and menials, thronging in,
Lent their brute rage to swell the din;
When, far and wide, a bugle-clang
From the dark ocean upward rang.
    "The Abbot comes!" they cry at once,
    "The holy man, whose favour'd glance
        Hath sainted visions known;
    Angels have met him on the way
    Beside the blessed martyrs' bay,
        And by Columba's stone.

His monks have heard their hymnings ligh
Sound from the summit of Dun-Y,
 To cheer his penance lone,
When at each cross, on girth and wold,
(Their number thrice a hundred-fold,)
His prayer he made, his beads he told,
 With Aves many a one —
He comes our feuds to reconcile,
A sainted man from sainted isle;
We will his holy doom abide,
The Abbot shall our strife decide."

### XXII.

Scarcely this fair accord was o'er,
When through the wide revolving door
 The black-stoled brethren wind;
Twelve sandall'd monks, who relics bore,
With many a torch-bearer before,
 And many a cross behind.
Then sunk each fierce uplifted hand,
And dagger bright and flashing brand
 Dropp'd swiftly at the sight;
They vanish'd from the Churchman's eye,
As shooting stars, that glance and die,
 Dart from the vault of night.

### XXIII.

The Abbot on the threshold stood,
And in his hand the holy rood;
Back on his shoulders flow'd his hood,
 The torch's glaring ray
Show'd, in its red and flashing light,
His wither'd cheek and amice white.

His blue eye glistening cold and bright,
 His tresses scant and grey.
" Fair Lords," he said, " Our Lady's love,
And peace be with you from above,
 And Benedicite !—
—But what means this ? no peace is here !—
Do dirks unsheathed suit bridal cheer ?
 Or are these naked brands
A seemly show for Churchman's sight,
When he comes summon'd to unite
Betrothed hearts and hands ?"

### XXIV.

Then, cloaking hate with fiery zeal,
Proud Lorn first answer'd the appeal ;—
 " Thou comest, O holy Man,
True sons of blessed church to greet,
But little deeming here to meet
 A wretch, beneath the ban
Of Pope and Church, for murder done
Even on the sacred altar-stone !—
Well mayst thou wonder we should know
Such miscreant here, nor lay him low,
Or dream of greeting, peace, or truce,
With excommunicated Bruce !
Yet well I grant, to end debate,
Thy sainted voice decide his fate."

### XXV.

Then Ronald pled the stranger's cause,
And knighthood's oath and honour's laws ;
 And Isabel, on bended knee,
Brought pray'rs and tears to back the plea.

And Edith lent her generous aid,
And wept, and Lorn for mercy pray'd.
" Hence," he exclaim'd, " degenerate maid!
Was't not enough to Ronald's bower
I brought thee, like a paramour,[1]
Or bond-maid at her master's gate,
His careless cold approach to wait?—
But the bold Lord of Cumberland,
The gallant Clifford, seeks thy hand;
His it shall be—Nay, no reply!
Hence! till those rebel eyes be dry."
With grief the Abbot heard and saw,
Yet nought relax'd his brow of awe.

### XXVI.

Then Argentine, in England's name,
So highly urged his sovereign's claim,
He waked a spark, that, long suppress'd,
Had smoulder'd in Lord Ronald's breast

---

[1] It was anciently customary in the Highlands to bring the
bride to the house of the husband. Nay, in some cases the com-
plaisance was stretched so far, that she remained there upon trial
for a twelvemonth; and the bridegroom, even after this period
of cohabitation, retained an option of refusing to fulfil his engagement. It is said that a desperate feud ensued between the clans
of Mac-Donald of Sleate and Mac-Leod, owing to the former
chief having availed himself of this license to send back to Dunvegan a sister, or daughter of the latter. Mac-Leod, resenting
the indignity, observed, that since there was no wedding bonfire,
there should be one to solemnize the divorce. Accordingly, he
burned and laid waste the territories of MacDonald, who retaliat-
ed, and a deadly feud, with all its accompaniments, took place

And now, as from the flint the fire,
Flash'd forth at once his generous ire.
" Enough of noble blood," he said,
" By English Edward had been shed,
Since matchless Wallace first had been
In mock'ry crown'd with wreaths of green.[1]

---

[1] Stow gives the following curious account of the trial and execution of this celebrated patriot :— " William Wallace, who had
oft-times set Scotland in great trouble, was taken and brought to
London, with great numbers of men and women wondering upon
him.   He was lodged in the house of William Delect, a citizen
of London, in Fenchurch-street.   On the morrow, being the eve
of St. Bartholomew, he was brought on horseback to Westminster.   John Legrave and Geffrey, knights, the mayor, sheriffs,
and aldermen of London, and many others, both on horseback
and on foot, accompanying him; and in the great hall at Westminster, he being placed on the south bench, crowned with laurel,
for that he had said in times past that he ought to bear a crown
in that hall, as it was commonly reported ; and being appeached
for a traitor by Sir Peter Malorie, the king's justice, he answered,
that he was never traitor to the King of England ; but for other
things whereof he was accused he confessed them ; and was
after headed and quartered."— STOW, *Chr.* p. 209.   There is
something singularly doubtful about the mode in which Wallace
was taken.   That he was betrayed to the English is indubitable ;
and popular fame charges Sir John Menteith with the indelible
infamy.   " Accursed," says Arnold Blair, " be the day of nativity
of John de Menteith, and may his name be struck out of the
book of life."   But John de Menteith was all along a zealous
favourer of the English interest, and was governor of Dumbarton
Castle by commission from Edward the First; and therefore, as
the accurate Lord Hailes has observed, could not be the friend
and confidant of Wallace, as tradition states him to be.   The
truth seems to be, that Menteith, thoroughly engaged in the
English interest, pursued Wallace closely, and made him prisoner through the treachery of an attendant, whom Peter Langtoft calls Jack Short.

And done to death by felon hand,
For guarding well his father's land.
Where's Nigel Bruce? and De la Haye,
And valiant Seton — where are they?
Where Somerville, the kind and free?
And Fraser, flower of chivalry?[1]
Have they not been on gibbet bound,
Their quarters flung to hawk and hound,
And hold we here a cold debate,
To yield more victims to their fate?
What! can the English Leopard's mood
Never be gorged with northern blood?
Was not the life of Athole shed,
To soothe the tyrant's sicken'd bed?[2]

---

" William Waleis is nomen that master was of theves,
    Tiding to the king is comen that robbery mischeives,
    Sir John of Menetest sued William so nigh,
    He tok him when he ween'd least, on night, his leman him by,
    That was through treason of *Jack Short* his man,
    He was the encheson that Sir John so him ran,
    Jack's brother had he slain, the Walleis that is said,
    The more Jack was fain to do William that braid "

From this it would appear that the infamy of seizing Wallace,
must rest between a degenerate Scottish nobleman, the vassal
of England, and a domestic, the obscure agent of his treachery;
between Sir John Menteith, son of Walter, Earl of Menteith,
and the traitor Jack Short.

[1] [See Appendix, Note H.]

[2] John de Strathbogie, Earl of Athole, had attempted to escape
out of the kingdom, but a storm cast him upon the coast, when
he was taken, sent to London, and executed, with circumstances
of great barbarity, being first half strangled, then let down from
the gallows while yet alive, barbarously dismembered, and his
body burnt. It may surprise the reader to learn, that this was a
*mitigated* punishment; for in respect that his mother was a
grand-daughter of King John, by his natural son Richard, he
was not drawn on a sledge to execution, " that point was for-

And must his word, till dying day,
Be nought but quarter, hang, and slay!—[1]

---

given," and he made the passage on horseback. Matthew of
Westminster tells us that King Edward, then extremely ill,
received great ease from the news that his relative was appre-
hended. "*Quo audito, Rex Angliæ, etsi gravissimo morbo tunc
langueret, levius tamen tulit dolorem.*" To this singular expression the text alludes.

[1] This alludes to a passage in Barbour, singularly expressive
of the vindictive spirit of Edward I. The prisoners taken at the
castle of Kildrummie had surrendered upon condition that they
should be at King Edward's disposal. "But his will," says Barbour, "was always evil towards Scottishmen." The news of the
surrender of Kildrummie arrived when he was in his mortal sickness at Burgh-upon-Sands.

> " And when he to the death was near,
> The folk that at Kyldromy wer
> Come with prisoners that they had tane,
> And syne to the king are gane.
> And for to comfort him they tauld
> How they the castell to them yauld;
> And how they till his will were brought,
> To do off that whatever he thought;
> And ask'd what men should off them do.
> Then look'd he angryly them to,
> He said, grinning, ' HANGS AND DRAWS.'
> That was wonder of sic saws,
> That he, that to the death was near,
> Should answer upon sic maner,
> Forouten moaning and mercy;
> How might he trust on him to cry,
> That sooth-fastly dooms all thing
> To have mercy for his crying,
> Off him that, throw his felony,
> Into sic point had no mercy?"

There was much truth in the Leonine couplet, with which Matthew of Westminster concludes his encomium on the first Edward:

> "Scotus Edwardus, dum vixit, suppeditavit,
> Tenuit, afflixit, depressit, dilaniavit."

Thou frown'st, De Argentine,—My gage
Is prompt to prove the strife I wage."—

### XXVII.

"Nor deem," said stout Dunvegan's knight,
"That thou shalt brave alone the fight!
By saints of isle and mainland both,
By Woden wild, (my grandsire's oath,)[1]
Let Rome and England do their worst,
Howe'er attainted or accursed,
If Bruce shall e'er find friends again,
Once more to brave a battle-plain,
If Douglas couch again his lance,
Or Randolph dare another chance,
Old Torquil will not be to lack
With twice a thousand at his back.—
Nay, chafe not at my bearing bold,
Good Abbot! for thou know'st of old,
Torquil's rude thought and stubborn will
Smack of the wild Norwegian still;
Nor will I barter Freedom's cause
For England's wealth, or Rome's applause."

### XXVIII.

The Abbot seem'd with eye severe
The hardy Chieftain's speech to hear;
Then on King Robert turn'd the Monk,
But twice his courage came and sunk,

---

[1] The MacLeods, and most other distinguished Hebridean families, were of Scandinavian extraction, and some were late or imperfect converts to Christianity. The family names of Torquil, Thormod, &c. are all Norwegian.

Confronted with the hero's look;
Twice fell his eye, his accents shook;
At length, resolved in tone and brow,
Sternly he questioned him —" And thou,
Unhappy! what hast thou to plead,
Why I denounce not on thy deed
That awful doom which canons tell
Shuts paradise, and opens hell;
Anathema of power so dread,
It blends the living with the dead,
Bids each good angel soar away,
And every ill one claim his prey;
Expels thee from the church's care,
And deafens Heaven against thy prayer;
Arms every hand against thy life,
Bans all who aid thee in the strife,
Nay, each whose succour, cold and scant
With meanest alms relieves thy want;
Haunts thee while living,—and, when dead,
Dwells on thy yet devoted head,
Rends Honour's scutcheon from thy hearse,
Stills o'er thy bier the holy verse,
And spurns thy corpse from hallow'd ground,
Flung like vile carrion to the hound;
Such is the dire and desperate doom
For sacrilege, decreed by Rome;
And such the well-deserved meed
Of thine unhallow'd, ruthless deed."—

### XXIX.

" Abbot!" The Bruce replied, "thy charge
It boots not to dispute at large.

This much, howe'er, I bid thee know,
No selfish vengeance dealt the blow,
For Comyn died his country's foe.
Nor blame I friends whose ill-timed speed
Fulfill'd my soon-repented deed,
Nor censure those from whose stern tongue
The dire anathema has rung.
I only blame mine own wild ire,
By Scotland's wrongs incensed to fire.
Heaven knows my purpose to atone,
Far as I may, the evil done,
And hears a penitent's appeal
From papal curse and prelate's zeal.
My first and dearest task achieved,
Fair Scotland from her thrall relieved,
Shall many a priest in cope and stole
Say requiem for Red Comyn's soul,
While I the blessed cross advance,
And expiate this unhappy chance,
In Palestine, with sword and lance.[1]
But, while content the church should know
My conscience owns the debt I owe,
Unto De Argentine and Lorn
The name of traitor I return,
Bid them defiance stern and high,
And give them in their throats the lie!

---

[1] Bruce uniformly professed, and probably felt, compunction for having violated the sanctuary of the church by the slaughter of Comyn; and finally, in his last hours, in testimony of his faith, penitence, and zeal, he requested James Lord Douglas to carry his heart to Jerusalem, to be there deposited in the Holy Sepulchre.

These brief words spoke, I speak no more:
Do what thou wilt; my shrift is o'er."

### XXX.

Like man by prodigy amazed,
Upon the King the Abbot gazed;
Then o'er his pallid features glance,
Convulsions of ecstatic trance.
His breathing came more thick and fast,
And from his pale blue eyes were cast
Strange rays of wild and wandering light;
Uprise his locks of silver white,
Flush'd is his brow, through every vein
In azure tide the currents strain,
And undistinguish'd accents broke
The awful silence ere he spoke.

### XXXI.

"De Bruce! I rose with purpose dread
To speak my curse upon thy head,[1]

---

[1] So soon as the notice of Comyn's slaughter reached Rome,
Bruce and his adherents were excommunicated.  It was published first by the Archbishop of York, and renewed at different
times, particularly by Lambyrton, Bishop of St. Andrews, in
1308; but it does not appear to have answered the purpose which
the English monarch expected.  Indeed, for reasons which it
may be difficult to trace, the thunders of Rome descended upon
the Scottish mountains with less effect than in more fertile countries.  Probably the comparative poverty of the benefices occasioned that fewer foreign clergy settled in Scotland; and the
interests of the native churchmen were linked with that of their
country.  Many of the Scottish prelates, Lambyrton the primate
particularly, declared for Bruce, while he was yet under the ban
of the church, although he afterwards again changed sides

7 *

And give thee as an outcast o'er
To him who burns to shed thy gore;—
But, like the Midianite of old,
Who stood on Zophim, heaven-controll'd,
I feel within mine aged breast
A power that will not be repress'd.[1]
It prompts my voice, it swells my veins,
It burns, it maddens, it constrains!—
De Bruce, thy sacrilegious blow
Hath at God's altar slain thy foe:
O'ermaster'd yet by high behest,
I bless thee, and thou shalt be bless'd!"
He spoke, and o'er the astonish'd throng
Was silence, awful, deep, and long.

## XXXII.

Again that light has fired his eye,
Again his form swells bold and high,
The broken voice of age is gone,
'T is vigorous manhood's lofty tone:—
" Thrice vanquish'd on the battle-plain,
Thy followers slaughter'd, fled, or ta'en.
A hunted wanderer on the wild,
On foreign shores a man exil'd,[2]
Disown'd, deserted, and distress'd,
I bless thee, and thou shalt be bless'd!
Bless'd in the hall and in the field,
Under the mantle as the shield.
Avenger of thy country's shame,
Restorer of her injured fame,

---

[1] [See Appendix, Note I.]        [2] [See Appendix, Note K.]

Bless'd in thy sceptre and thy sword,
De Bruce, fair Scotland's rightful Lord,
Bless'd in thy deeds and in thy fame,
What lengthen'd honours wait thy name!
In distant ages, sire to son
Shall tell thy tale of freedom won,
And teach his infants, in the use
Of earliest speech, to falter Bruce.
Go, then, triumphant! sweep along
Thy course, the theme of many a song!
The Power, whose dictates swell my breast,
Hath bless'd thee, and thou shalt be bless'd!—
Enough—my short-lived strength decays,
And sinks the momentary blaze.—
Heaven hath our destined purpose broke,
Not here must nuptial vow be spoke;
Brethren, our errand here is o'er,
Our task discharged.—Unmoor, unmoor!"—
His priests received the exhausted Monk,
As breathless in their arms he sunk.
Punctual his orders to obey,
The train refused all longer stay,
Embark'd, raised sail, and bore away.

# LORD OF THE ISLES

## CANTO THIRD.

THE

# LORD OF THE ISLES.

## CANTO THIRD.

Hast thou not mark'd, when o'er thy startled head
Sudden and deep the thunder-peal has roll'd,
How, when its echoes fell, a silence dead
Sunk on the wood, the meadow and the wold?
The rye-grass shakes not on the sod-built fold,
The rustling aspen's leaves are mute and still,
The wall-flower waves not on the ruin'd hold,
Till. murmuring distant first, then near and shrill,
The savage whirlwind wakes, and sweeps the groaning
　　hill!

### II.

Artornish! such a silence sunk
Upon thy halls, when that grey Monk
　　His prophet-speech had spoke;
And his obedient brethren's sail
Was stretch'd to meet the southern gale
　　Before a whisper woke.
Then murmuring sounds of doubt and fear,
Close pour'd in many an anxious ear,
　　The solemn stillness broke;
And still they gazed with eager guess,
Where, in an oriel's deep recess,
The Island Prince seem'd bent to press

What Lorn, by his impatient cheer,
And gesture fierce, scarce deign'd to hear.

### III.

Starting at length with frowning look,
His hand he clench'd, his head he shook,
  And sternly flung apart; —
" And deem'st thou me so mean of mood,
As to forget the mortal feud,
And clasp the hand with blood imbrued
  From my dear Kinsman's heart ?
Is this thy rede ? — a due return
For ancient league and friendship sworn!
But well our mountain proverb shows
The faith of Islesmen ebbs and flows.
Be it even so — believe, ere long,
He that now bears shall wreak the wrong.—
Call Edith — call the Maid of Lorn!
My sister, slaves ! — for further scorn,
Be sure nor she nor I will stay.—
Away, De Argentine, away ! —
We nor ally nor brother know,
In Bruce's friend, or England's foe."

### IV.

But who the Chieftain's rage can tell,
When, sought from lowest dungeon cell
To highest tower the castle round,
No Lady Edith was there found!
He shouted, " Falsehood ! — treachery ! —
Revenge and blood ! — a lordly meed
To him that will avenge the deed !

  A Baron s lands!"— His frantic mood
Was scarcely by the news withstood,
That Morag shared his sister's flight,
And that, in hurry of the night,
'Scaped noteless, and without remark,
Two strangers sought the Abbot's bark.—
" Man every galley!— fly— pursue!
The priest his treachery shall rue!
Ay, and the time shall quickly come,
When we shall hear the thanks that Rome
Will pay his feigned prophecy!"
Such was fierce Lorn's indignant cry;
And Cormac Doil in haste obey'd,
Hoisted his sail, his anchor weigh'd,
(For, glad of each pretext for spoil,
A pirate sworn was Cormac Doil.)[1]
But others, lingering, spoke apart,—
" The Maid has given her maiden heart
      To Ronald of the Isles,
And, fearful lest her brother's word
Bestow her on that English Lord,
      She seeks Iona's piles,

---

[1] A sort of persons common in the isles, as may be easily believed, until the introduction of civil polity. Witness the Dean of the Isles' account of Ronay. " At the north end of Raarsay, be half myle of sea frae it, layes ane ile callıt Ronay, maire then a myle in lengthe, full of wood and heddır, with ane havein for heiland galeys in the middis of it, and the same havein is guıd for fostering of theives, ruggairs and reivairs, till a naıl, upon the peilling and spulzeıng of poor pepıll. This ile perteins to M'Gıllychallan of Raarsay by force, and to the bishope of the iles be heritage."— SIR DONALD MONRO's *Description of the Western Islands of Scotland, Edinburgh,* 1805, p. 22.

And wisely deems it best to dwell
A votaress in the holy cell,
Until these feuds so fierce and fell
    The Abbot reconciles."

### V.

As, impotent of ire, the hall
Echoed to Lorn's impatient call,
"My horse, my mantle, and my train!
Let none who honours Lorn remain!"—
Courteous, but stern, a bold request
To Bruce De Argentine express'd.
"Lord Earl," he said,—"I cannot chuse
But yield such title to the Bruce,
Though name and earldom both are gone,
Since he braced rebel's armour on—
But, Earl or Serf—rude phrase was thine
Of late, and launch'd at Argentine;
Such as compels me to demand
Redress of honour at thy hand.
We need not to each other tell,
That both can wield their weapons well:
    Then do me but the soldier grace,
    This glove upon thy helm to place
      Where we may meet in fight;
    And I will say, as still I've said,
    Though by ambition far misled,
      Thou art a noble knight."—

### VI.

"And I," the princely Bruce replied,
"Might term it stain on knighthood's pride,
That the bright sword of Argentine
Should in a tyrant's quarrel shine;

But, for your brave request,
Be sure the honour'd pledge you gave
In every battle-field shall wave
    Upon my helmet-crest;
Believe, that if my hasty tongue
Hath done thine honour causeless wrong,
    It shall be well redress'd.
Not dearer to my soul was glove,
Bestow'd in youth by lady's love,
    Than this which thou hast given!
Thus, then, my noble foe I greet;
Health and high fortune till we meet,
    And then—what pleases Heaven.

### VII.

Thus parted they—for now, with sound
Like waves roll'd back from rocky ground,
    The friends of Lorn retire;
Each mainland chieftain, with his train,
Draws to his mountain towers again,
Pondering how mortal schemes prove vain,
    And mortal hopes expire.
But through the castle double guard,
By Ronald's charge, kept wakeful ward,
Wicket and gate were trebly barr'd,
    By beam and bolt and chain;
Then of the guests, in courteous sort,
He pray'd excuse for mirth broke short,
And bade them in Artornish fort
    In confidence remain.
Now torch and menial tendance led
Chieftain and knight to bower and bed
And beads were told, and aves said,

x

And soon they sunk away
Into such sleep, as wont to shed
Oblivion on the weary head,
    After a toilsome day.


### VIII.

But soon uproused, the Monarch cried
To Edward slumbering by his side,
    "Awake, or sleep for aye!
Even now there jarr'd a secret door—
A taper-light gleams on the floor—
    Up, Edward, up, I say!
Some one glides in like midnight ghost—
Nay, strike not! 'tis our noble Host."
Advancing then his taper's flame,
Ronald stept forth, and with him came
  Dunvegan's chief—each bent the knee
  To Bruce in sign of fealty,
    And proffer'd him his sword,
  And hail'd him, in a monarch's style,
  As king of mainland and of isle,
    And Scotland's rightful lord.
"And O," said Ronald, "Own'd of Heaven"
Say, is my erring youth forgiven,
By falsehood's arts from duty driven
    Who rebel falchion drew,
Yet ever to thy deeds of fame,
Even while I strove against thy claim,
    Paid homage just and true?"—
"Alas! dear youth, the unhappy time,"
Answer'd the Bruce, "must bear the crime,
    Since, guiltier far than you,

Even I"—he paused; for Falkirk's woes
Upon his conscious soul arose.[1]
The Chieftain to his breast he press'd,
And in a sigh conceal'd the rest.

---

[1] I have followed the vulgar and inaccurate tradition, that Bruce fought against Wallace, and the array of Scotland, at the fatal battle of Falkirk. The story, which seems to have no better authority than that of Blind Harry, bears, that having made much slaughter during the engagement, he sat down to dine with the conquerors without washing the filthy witness from his hands.

> "Fasting he was, and had been in great need,
> Blooded were all his weapons and his weed:
> Southeron lords scorn'd him in terms rude,
> And said, Behold yon Scot eats his own blood.

> "Then rued he sore, for reason bad be known,
> That blood and land alike should be his own;
> With them he long was, ere he got away,
> But contrair Scots he fought not from that day."

The account given by most of our historians, of the conversation between Bruce and Wallace over the Carron river, is equally apocryphal. There is full evidence that Bruce was not at that time on the English side, nor present at the battle of Falkirk; nay, that he acted as a guardian of Scotland, along with John Comyn, in the name of Baliol, and in opposition to the English. He was the grandson of the competitor, with whom he has been sometimes confounded. Lord Hailes has well described, and in some degree apologized for, the earlier part of his life.— " His grand-father, the competitor, had patiently acquiesced in the award of Edward. His father, yielding to the times, had served under the English banners. But young Bruce had more ambition, and a more restless spirit. In his earlier years he acted upon no regular plan. By turns the partisan of Edward, and the vicegerent of Baliol, he seems to have forgotten or stifled his pretensions to the crown. But his character developed itself by degrees, and in maturer age became firm and consistent "— *Annals of Scotland*, p. 290, *quarto, London*, 1776.

8 *

### IX.

They proffer'd aid, by arms and might,
To repossess him in his right;
But well their counsels must be weigh'd,
Ere banners raised and musters made,
For English hire and Lorn's intrigues
Bound many chiefs in southern leagues.
In answer, Bruce his purpose bold
To his new vassals frankly told.
"The winter worn in exile o'er,
I long'd for Carrick's kindred shore.
I thought upon my native Ayr,
And long'd to see the burly fare
That Clifford makes, whose lordly call
Now echoes through my father's hall.
But first my course to Arran led,
Where valiant Lennox gathers head,
And on the sea, by tempest toss'd,
Our barks dispersed, our purpose cross'd,
Mine own, a hostile sail to shun,
Far from her destined course had run,
When that wise will, which masters ours,
Compell'd us to your friendly towers."

### X.

Then Torquil spoke: "The time craves speed!
We must not linger in our deed,
But instant pray our Sovereign Liege,
To shun the perils of a siege.
The vengeful Lorn, with all his powers,
Lies but too near Artornish towers,
And England's light-armed vessels ride
Not distant far, the waves of Clyde,

Prompt at these tidings to unmoor,
And sweep each strait, and guard each shore.
Then, till this fresh alarm pass by,
Secret and safe my Liege must lie
In the far bounds of friendly Skye,
Torquil thy pilot and thy guide."—
"Not so, brave Chieftain," Ronald cried
"Myself will on my Sovereign wait,
And raise in arms the men of Sleate,
Whilst thou, renown'd where chiefs debate,
Shalt sway their souls by council sage,
And awe them by thy locks of age."—
—"And if my words in weight shall fail,
Tnis ponderous sword shall turn the scale."—

## XI.

"The scheme," said Bruce, "contents me well;
Meantime, 'twere best that Isabel,
For safety, with my bark and crew,
Again to friendly Erin drew.
There Edward, too, shall with her wend
In need to cheer her and defend,
And muster up each scatter'd friend."—
Here seem'd it as Lord Ronald's ear
Would other counsel gladlier hear;
But, all achieved as soon as plann'd,
Both barks, in secret arm'd and mann'd,
    From out the haven bore;
On different voyage forth they ply,
This for the coast of winged Skye,
    And that for Erin's shore.

## XII.

With Bruce and Ronald bides the tale.
To favouring winds they gave the sail,

Till Mull's dark headlands scarce they knew,
And Ardnamurchan's hills were blue.
But then the squalls blew close and hard,
And, fain to strike the galley's yard,
     And take them to the oar,
With these rude seas, in weary plight,
They strove the livelong day and night,
Nor till the dawning had a sight
     Of Skye's romantic shore.
Where Coolin stoops him to the west,
They saw upon his shiver'd crest
     The sun's arising gleam;
But such the labour and delay,
Ere they were moor'd in Scavigh bay,
(For calmer heaven compell'd to stay,)
     He shot a western beam.
Then Ronald said, "If true mine eye,
These are the savage wilds that lie
North of Strathnardill and Dunskye:[1]
     No human foot comes here,
And, since these adverse breezes blow,
If my good Liege love hunter's bow
What hinders that on land we go,
     And strike a mountain-deer?
Allan, my page, shall with us wend;
A bow full deftly can he bend,
And, if we meet a herd, may send
     A shaft shall mend our cheer."
Then each took bow and bolts in hand,
Their row-boat launch'd and leapt to land,
     And left their skiff and train,

---

[1] [See Appendix, Note L.]

Where a wild stream, with headlong shock,
Came brawling down its bed of rock,
 To mingle with the main.

### XIII.

A while their route they silent made,
 As men who stalk for mountain-deer,
Till the good Bruce to Ronald said,
 "St. Mary! what a scene is here!
I've traversed many a mountain-strand,
Abroad and in my native land,
And it has been my lot to tread
Where safety more than pleasure led;
 Thus, many a waste I've wander'd o'er,
 Clombe many a crag, cross'd many a moor,
  But, by my halidome,
A scene so rude, so wild as this,
Yet so sublime in barrenness,
Ne'er did my wandering footsteps press,
 Where'er I happ'd to roam."

### XIV.

No marvel thus the Monarch spake;
 For rarely human eye has known
A scene so stern as that dread lake,
 With its dark ledge of barren stone.
Seems that primeval earthquake's sway
Hath rent a strange and shatter'd way
 Through the rude bosom of the hill,
And that each naked precipice,
Sable ravine, and dark abyss,
 Tells of the outrage still.

The wildest glen, but this, can show
Some touch of Nature's genial glow;
On high Benmore green mosses grow,
And heath-bells bud in deep Glencroe,
    And copse on Cruchan-Ben;
But here,—above, around, below,
    On mountain or in glen
Nor tree, nor shrub, nor plant, nor flower,
Nor aught of vegetative power,
    The weary eye may ken.
For all is rocks at random thrown,
Black waves, bare crags, and banks of stone
    As if were here denied
The summer sun, the spring's sweet dew,
That clothe with many a varied hue
    The bleakest mountain-side.

## XV.

And wilder, forward as they wound,
Were the proud cliffs and lake profound.
Huge terraces of granite black
Afforded rude and cumber'd track;
    For from the mountain hoar,
Hurl'd headlong in some night of fear,
When yell'd the wolf and fled the deer,
    Loose crags had toppled o'er;
And some, chance-poised and balanced, lay,
So that a stripling arm might sway
    A mass no host could raise,
In Nature's rage at random thrown,
Yet trembling like the Druid's stone
    On its precarious base.

The evening mists, with ceaseless change,
Now clothed the mountains' lofty range,
 Now left their foreheads bare,
And round the skirts their mantle furl'd,
Or on the sable waters curl'd,
Or on the eddying breezes whirl'd,
 Dispersed in middle air.
And oft, condensed, at once they lower,
When, brief and fierce, the mountain shower
 Pours like a torrent down,
And when return the sun's glad beams,
Whiten'd with foam a thousand streams
 Leap from the mountain's crown.

### XVI.

" This lake," said Bruce, " whose barriers drear
Are precipices sharp and sheer,
Yielding no track for goat or deer,
 Save the black shelves we tread,
How term you its dark waves? and how
Yon northern mountain's pathless brow,
 And yonder peak of dread,
That to the evening sun uplifts
The griesly gulfs and slaty rifts,
 Which seam its shiver'd head?"—
" Coriskin call the dark lake's name,
Coolin the ridge, as bards proclaim,
From old Cuchullin, chief of fame.
But bards, familiar in our isles
Rather with Nature's frowns than smiles,
Full oft their careless humours please
By sportive names from scenes like these.
I would old Torquil were to show
His maidens with their breasts of snow,

Or that my noble Liege were nigh
To hear his Nurse sing lullaby!
(The Maids—tall cliffs with breakers white,
The Nurse—a torrent's roaring might,)
Or that your eye could see the mood
Of Corryvrekin's whirlpool rude,
When dons the Hag her whiten'd hood—
'Tis thus our islesmen's fancy frames,
For scenes so stern, fantastic names."

## XVII.

Answer'd the Bruce, "And musing mind
Might here a graver moral find.
These mighty cliffs, that heave on high
Their naked brows to middle sky,
Indifferent to the sun or snow,
Where nought can fade, and nought can blow,
May they not mark a Monarch's fate,—
Raised high 'mid storms of strife and state,
Beyond life's lowlier pleasures placed,
His soul a rock, his heart a waste?[1]
O'er hope and love and fear aloft
High rears his crowned head—But soft!
Look, underneath yon jutting crag
Are hunters and a slaughter'd stag.

---

[1] [" He who ascends to mountain-tops, shall find
    The loftiest peaks most wrapt in clouds and snow;
    He who surpasses or subdues mankind,
    Must look down on the hate of those below.
    Though high above the sun of glory glow,
    And far beneath the earth and ocean spread,
    Round him are icy rocks, and loudly blow
    Contending tempests on his naked head,
And thus reward the toils which to those summits led "
                          *Childe Harold*, Canto III.]

Who may they be? But late you said
No steps these desert regions tread?"—

## XVIII.

"So said I—and believed in sooth,"
Ronald replied, "I spoke the truth.
Yet now I spy, by yonder stone,
Five men—they mark us, and come on;
And by their badge on bonnet borne,
I guess them of the land of Lorn,
Foes to my Liege."—"So let it be;
I've faced worse odds than five to three—
—But the poor page can little aid;
Then be our battle thus array'd,
If our free passage they contest;
Cope thou with two, I'll match the rest."—
"Not so, my Liege—for, by my life,
This sword shall meet the treble strife;
My strength, my skill in arms, more small,
And less the loss should Ronald fall.
But islesmen soon to soldiers grow,
Allan has sword as well as bow,
And were my Monarch's order given,
Two shafts should make our number even."—
"No! not to save my life!" he said;
"Enough of blood rests on my head,
Too rashly spill'd—we soon shall know,
Whether they come as friend or foe."

## XIX.

Nigh came the strangers, and more nigh;—
Still less they pleased the Monarch's eye.

Men were they all of evil mien,
Down-look'd, unwilling to be seen;[1]
They moved with half-resolved pace,
And bent on earth each gloomy face.
The foremost two were fair array'd,
With brogue and bonnet, trews and plaid,
And bore the arms of mountaineers,
Daggers and broadswords, bows and spears.
The three, that lagg'd small space behind,
Seem'd serfs of more degraded kind;
Goat-skins or deer-hides o'er them cast,
Made a rude fence against the blast;
Their arms and feet and heads were bare,
Matted their beards, unshorn their hair;
For arms, the caitiffs bore in hand,
A club, as axe, a rusty brand.

### XX.

Onward, still mute, they kept the track;—
"Tell who ye be, or else stand back,"
Said Bruce; "In deserts when they meet,
Men pass not as in peaceful street."
Still, at his stern command, they stood,
And proffer'd greeting brief and rude,
But acted courtesy so ill,
As seem'd of fear, and not of will.
'Wanderers we are, as you may be;
Men hither driven by wind and sea,
Who, if you list to taste our cheer,
Will share with you this fallow deer."—
'If from the sea, where lies your bark?"—
'Ten fathom deep in ocean dark!

---

[1] [See Appendix, Note M.]

Wreck'd yesternight: but we are men,
Who little sense of peril ken.
The shades come down — the day is shut —
Will you go with us to our hut?"—
"Our vessel waits us in the bay;
Thanks for your proffer — have good-day."—
"Was that your galley, then, which rode
Not far from shore when evening glow'd?"—
"It was."—"Then spare your needless pain,
There will she now be sought in vain.
We saw her from the mountain head,
When with St. George's blazon red
A southern vessel bore in sight,
And yours raised sail, and took to flight."—

### XXI.

"Now, by the rood, unwelcome news!"
Thus with Lord Ronald communed Bruce;
"Nor rests there light enough to show
If this their tale be true or no.
The men seem bred of churlish kind,
Yet mellow nuts have hardest rind;
We will go with them — food and fire
And sheltering roof our wants require.
Sure guard 'gainst treachery will we keep,
And watch by turns our comrades' sleep.—
Good fellows, thanks; your guests we'll be,
And well will pay the courtesy.
Come, lead us where your lodging lies,—
—Nay, soft! we mix not companies.—
Show us the path o'er crag and stone,
And we will follow you — lead on."

### XXII.

They reach'd the dreary cabin, made
Of sails against a rock display'd,
  And there, on entering, found
A slender boy, whose form and mien
Ill suited with such savage scene,
In cap and cloak of velvet green,
  Low seated on the ground.
His garb was such as minstrels wear,
Dark was his hue, and dark his hair,
His youthful cheek was marr'd by care,
  His eyes in sorrow drown'd.
"Whence this poor boy?"—As Ronald spoke,
The voice his trance of anguish broke;
As if awaked from ghastly dream,
He raised his head with start and scream,
  And wildly gazed around;
Then to the wall his face he turn'd,
And his dark neck with blushes burn'd.

### XXIII.

"Whose is the boy?" again he said.
"By chance of war our captive made;
He may be yours, if you should hold
That music has more charms than gold;
For, though from earliest childhood mute,
The lad can deftly touch the lute,
  And on the rote and viol play,
  And well can drive the time away
   For those who love such glee;
For me, the favouring breeze, when loud
It pipes upon the galley's shroud,
   Makes blither melody."—

" Hath he, then, sense of spoken sound ?"—
　　" Aye ; so his mother bade us know,
A crone in our late shipwreck drown'd,
　　And hence the silly stripling's woe.
More of the youth I cannot say,
Our captive but since yesterday ;
When wind and weather wax'd so grim,
We little listed think of him.—
But why waste time in idle words ?
Sit to your cheer—unbelt your swords."
Sudden the captive turn'd his head,
And one quick glance to Ronald sped.
It was a keen and warning look,
And well the Chief the signal took.

## XXIV.

" Kind host," he said, " our needs require
A separate board and separate fire ;
For know, that on a pilgrimage
Wend I, my comrade, and this page.
And, sworn to vigil and to fast,
Long as this hallow'd task shall last,
We never doff the plaid or sword,
Or feast us at a stranger's board ;
And never share one common sleep,
But one must still his vigil keep.
Thus, for our separate use, good friend,
We 'll hold this hut's remoter end."—
" A churlish vow," the eldest said,
" And hard, methinks, to be obey'd.
How say you, if, to wreak the scorn
That pays our kindness harsh return,
　9 *

We should refuse to share our meal?"—
" Then say we, that our swords are steel!
And our vow binds us not to fast,
Where gold or force may buy repast."
Their host's dark brow grew keen and fell,
His teeth are clench'd, his features swell;
Yet sunk the felon's moody ire
Before Lord Ronald's glance of fire,
Nor could his craven courage brook
The Monarch's calm and dauntless look.
With laugh constrain'd,—"Let every man
Follow the fashion of his clan!
Each to his separate quarters keep,
And feed or fast, or wake or sleep."


## XXV.

Their fire at separate distance burns,
By turns they eat, keep guard by turns;
For evil seem'd that old man's eye,
Dark and designing, fierce yet shy.
Still he avoided forward look,
But slow and circumspectly took
A circling, never-ceasing glance,
By doubt and cunning mark'd at once.
Which shot a mischief-boding ray,
From under eyebrows shagg'd and grey.
The younger, too, who seem'd his son,
Had that dark look the timid shun;
The half-clad serfs behind them sate,
And scowl'd a glare 'twixt fear and hate—
Till all, as darkness onward crept,
Couch'd down, and seem'd to sleep. or slept.

Nor he, that boy, whose powerless tongue
Must trust his eyes to wail his wrong,
A longer watch of sorrow made,
But stretch'd his limbs to slumber laid.

### XXVI.

Not in his dangerous host confides
The King, but wary watch provides.
Ronald keeps ward till midnight past,
Then wakes the King, young Allan last;
Thus rank'd, to give the youthful page
The rest required by tender age.
What is Lord Ronald's wakeful thought,
To chase the languor toil had brought?—
(For deem not that he deign'd to throw
Much care upon such coward foe,)—
He thinks of lovely Isabel,
When at her foeman's feet she fell,
Nor less when, placed in princely selle,
She glanced on him with favouring eyes,
At Woodstocke when he won the prize
Nor, fair in joy, in sorrow fair,
In pride of place as 'mid despair,
Must she alone engross his care.
His thoughts to his betrothed bride,
To Edith, turn—O how decide,
When here his love and heart are given,
And there his faith stands plight to Heaven!
No drowsy ward 't is his to keep,
For seldom lovers long for sleep.
Till sung his midnight hymn the owl,
Answer'd the dog-fox with his howl,

Then waked the King—at his request,
Lord Ronald stretch'd himself to rest.

### XXVII.

What spell was good King Robert's, say,
To drive the weary night away?
His was the patriot's burning thought,
Of Freedom's battle bravely fought,
Of castles storm'd, of cities freed,
Of deep design and daring deed,
Of England's roses reft and torn,
And Scotland's cross in triumph worn,
Of rout and rally, war and truce,—
As heroes think, so thought the Bruce.
No marvel, 'mid such musings high,
Sleep shunn'd the monarch's thoughtful eye.
Now over Coolin's eastern head
The greyish light begins to spread,
The otter to his cavern drew,
And clamour'd shrill the wakening mew;
Then watch'd the page—to needful rest
The King resign'd his anxious breast.

### XXVIII.

To Allan's eyes was harder task,
The weary watch their safeties ask.
He trimm'd the fire, and gave to shine
With bickering light the splinter'd pine;
Then gazed awhile, where silent laid
Their hosts were shrouded by the plaid
But little fear waked in his mind,
For he was bred of martial kind,
And, if to manhood he arrive,
May match the boldest knight alive.

Then thought he of his mother's tower,
His little sisters' greenwood bower,
How there the Easter-gambols pass,
And of Dan Joseph's lengthen'd mass.
But still before his weary eye
In rays prolong'd the blazes die—
Again he roused him—on the lake
Look'd forth, where now the twilight-flake
Of pale cold dawn began to wake.
On Coolin's cliffs the mist lay furl'd,
The morning breeze the lake had curl'd,
The short dark waves, heaved to the land,
With ceaseless plash kiss'd cliff or sand;—
It was a slumbrous sound—he turn'd
To tales at which his youth had burn'd,
Of pilgrim's path by demon cross'd,
Of sprightly elf or yelling ghost,
Of the wild witch's baneful cot,
And mermaid's alabaster grot,
Who bathes her limbs in sunless well
Deep in Strathaird's enchanted cell.[1]

---

[1] Imagination can hardly conceive any thing more beautiful than the extraordinary grotto discovered not many years since upon the estate of Alexander Mac-Allister, Esq. of Strathaird. It has since been much and deservedly celebrated, and a full account of its beauties has been published by Dr. Mac-Leay of Oban. The general impression may perhaps be gathered from the following extract from a journal, which, written under the feelings of the moment, is likely to be more accurate than any attempt to recollect the impressions then received.—"The first entrance to this celebrated cave is rude and unpromising; but the light of the torches, with which we were provided, was soon reflected from the roof, floor, and walls, which seem as if they were sheeted with marble, partly smooth, partly rough with frost-

Thither in fancy rapt he flies,
And on his sight the vaults arise;

---

work and rustic ornaments, and partly seeming to be wrought
into statuary. The floor forms a steep and difficult ascent, and
might be fancifully compared to a sheet of water, which, while
it rushed whitening and foaming down a declivity, had been suddenly arrested and consolidated by the spell of an enchanter.
Upon attaining the summit of this ascent, the cave opens into a
splendid gallery, adorned with the most dazzling crystallizations,
and finally descends with rapidity to the brink of a pool, of the
most limpid water, about four or five yards broad. There opens
beyond this pool a portal arch, formed by two columns of white
spar, with beautiful chasing upon the sides, which promises a
continuation of the cave. One of our sailors swam across, for
there is no other mode of passing, and informed us (as indeed we
partly saw by the light he carried) that the enchantment of
Maccalister's cave terminates with this portal, a little beyond
which there was only a rude cavern, speedily choked with stones
and earth. But the pool, on the brink of which we stood, surrounded by the most fanciful mouldings, in a substance resem-
bling white marble, and distinguished by the depth and purity
of its waters, might have been the bathing grotto of a naiad.
The groups of combined figures projecting, or embossed, by
which the pool is surrounded, are exquisitely elegant and fanciful. A statuary might catch beautiful hints from the singular
and romantic disposition of those stalactites. There is scarce a
form, or group, on which active fancy may not trace figures or
grotesque ornaments, which have been gradually moulded in this
cavern by the dropping of the calcareous water hardening into
petrifactions. Many of those fine groups have been injured by
the senseless rage of appropriation of recent tourists; and the
grotto has lost, (I am informed,) through the smoke of torches
something of that vivid silver tint which was originally one of
its chief distinctions. But enough of beauty remains to compen-
sate for all that may be lost."—Mr. Mac-Allister of Straithaird
has, with great propriety, built up the exterior entrance to this
cave, in order that strangers may enter properly attended by a

That hut's dark walls he sees no more,
His foot is on the marble floor,
And o'er his head the dazzling spars
Gleam like a firmament of stars!
—Hark! hears he not the sea-nymph speak
Her anger in that thrilling shriek!—
No! all too late, with Allan's dream
Mingled the captive's warning scream.
As from the ground he strives to start,
A ruffian's dagger finds his heart!
Upward he casts his dizzy eyes, . . .
Murmurs his master's name, . . . and dies!

### XXIX.

Not so awoke the King! his hand
Snatch'd from the flame a knotted brand,
The nearest weapon of his wrath;
With this he cross'd the murderer's path,
    And venged young Allan well!
The spatter'd brain and bubbling blood
Hiss'd on the half-extinguish'd wood,
    The miscreant gasp'd and fell!
Nor rose in peace the Island Lord;
One caitiff died upon his sword,
And one beneath his grasp lies prone,
In mortal grapple overthrown.
But while Lord Ronald's dagger drank
The life-blood from his panting flank,
The Father-ruffian of the band
Behind him rears a coward hand!

---

guide, to prevent any repetition of the wanton and selfish injury
which this singular scene has already sustained.

—O for a moment's aid,
Till Bruce, who deals no double blow,[1]
Dash to the earth another foe,
 Above his comrade laid!—
And it is gain'd—the captive sprung
On the raised arm, and closely clung,
 And, ere he shook him loose,
The master'd felon press'd the ground,
And gasp'd beneath a mortal wound,
 While o'er him stands the Bruce.

## XXX.

"Miscreant! while lasts thy flitting spark,
Give me to know the purpose dark,
That arm'd thy hand with murderous knife,
Against offenceless stranger's life?"—
"No stranger thou!" with accent fell,
Murmur'd the wretch; "I know thee well;
And know thee for the foeman sworn
Of my high chief, the mighty Lorn."—
"Speak yet again, and speak the truth
For thy soul's sake!—from whence this youth?
His country, birth, and name declare,
And thus one evil deed repair."—
—"Vex me no more!... my blood runs cold...
No more I know than I have told.

---

[1] ["On witnessing the disinterment of Bruce's remains at Dunfermline, in 1822," says Sir Walter, "many people shed tears; for there was the wasted skull, which once was the head that thought so wisely and boldly for his country's deliverance; and there was the dry bone, which had once been the sturdy arm that killed Sir Henry de Bohun, between the two armies, *at a single blow*, on the evening before the battle of Bannockburn."— *Tales of a Grandfather. First Series*, vol. i. p. 255.]

We found him in a bark we sought
With different purpose ... and I thought" ..
Fate cut him short; in blood and broil,
As he had lived, died Cormac Doil.

### XXXI.

Then resting on his bloody blade,
The valiant Bruce to Ronald said,
"Now shame upon us both! — that boy
  Lifts his mute face to heaven,
And clasps his hands, to testify
His gratitude to God on high,
  For strange deliverance given.
His speechless gesture thanks hath paid,
Which our free tongues have left unsaid!"
He raised the youth with kindly word,
But mark'd him shudder at the sword:
He cleansed it from its hue of death,
And plunged the weapon in its sheath.
"Alas, poor child! unfitting part
Fate doom'd, when with so soft a heart,
  And form so slight as thine,
She made thee first a pirate's slave,
Then, in his stead, a patron gave
  Of wayward lot like mine;
A landless prince, whose wandering life
Is but one scene of blood and strife —
Yet scant of friends the Bruce shall be,
But he'll find resting-place for thee. —
Come, noble Ronald! o'er the dead
Enough thy generous grief is paid,
And well has Allan's fate been wroke;
Come, wend we hence — the day has broke.
 Vol. V. —— 10

Seek we our bark — I trust the tale
Was false, that she had hoisted sail."

### XXXII.

Yet, ere they left that charnel-cell,
The Island Lord bade sad farewell
To Allan: — "Who shall tell this tale,"
He said, "in halls of Donagaile!
Oh, who his widow'd mother tell,
That, ere his bloom, her fairest fell! —
Rest thee, poor youth! and trust my care
For mass and knell and funeral prayer;
While o'er those caitiffs, where they lie,
The wolf shall snarl, the raven cry!"
And now the eastern mountain's head
On the dark lake threw lustre red;
Bright gleams of gold and purple streak
Ravine and precipice and peak —
(So earthly power at distance shows;
Reveals his splendour, hides his woes.)
O'er sheets of granite, dark and broad,
Rent and unequal, lay the road.
In sad discourse the warriors wind,
And the mute captive moves behind.

THE

# LORD OF THE ISLES

## CANTO FOURTH.

THE

# LORD OF THE ISLES.

## CANTO FOURTH.

----

STRANGER! if e'er thine ardent step hath traced
The northern realms of ancient Caledon,
Where the proud Queen of Wilderness hath placed.
By lake and cataract, her lonely throne;
Sublime but sad delight thy soul hath known,
Gazing on pathless glen and mountain high,
Listing where from the cliffs the torrents thrown
Mingle their echoes with the eagle's cry,
And with the sounding lake, and with the moaning
    sky.

Yes! 'twas sublime, but sad.—The loneliness
Loaded thy heart, the desert tired thine eye;
And strange and awful fears began to press
Thy bosom with a stern solemnity.
Then hast thou wish'd some woodman's cottage
    nigh,
Something that show'd of life, though low and mean;
Glad sight, its curling wreath of smoke to spy,
Glad sound, its cock's blithe carol would have been,
Or children whooping wild beneath the willows
    green.

z    10 *

Such are the scenes, where savage grandeur wakes
An awful thrill that softens into sighs;
Such feelings rouse them by dim Rannoch's lakes,
In dark Glencoe such gloomy raptures rise:
Or farther, where, beneath the northern skies,
Chides wild Loch-Eribol his caverns hoar—
But, be the minstrel judge, they yield the prize
Of desert dignity to that dread shore,
That sees grim Coolin rise, and hears Coriskin roar.

### II.

Through such wild scenes the champion pass'd,
When bold halloo and bugle-blast
Upon the breeze came loud and fast.
"There." said the Bruce, "rung Edward's horn!
What can have caused such brief return?
And see, brave Ronald,—see him dart
O'er stock and stone like hunted hart,
Precipitate, as is the use,
In war or sport, of Edward Bruce.
—He marks us, and his eager cry
Will tell his news ere he be nigh."

### III.

Loud Edward shouts, "What make ye here,
Warring upon the mountain deer,
     When Scotland wants her King?
A bark from Lennox cross'd our track,
With her in speed I hurried back.
     These joyful news to bring—
The Stuart stirs in Teviotdale,
And Douglas wakes his native vale;
Thy storm-toss'd fleet hath won its way
With little loss to Brodick-Bay,

And Lennox, with a gallant band,
Waits but thy coming and command
To waft them o'er to Carrick strand.
There are blithe news!—but mark the close!
Edward, the deadliest of our foes,
As with his host he northward pass'd,
Hath on the Borders breathed his last."

### IV.

Still stood the Bruce—his steady cheek
Was little wont his joy to speak,
    But then his colour rose:
"Now, Scotland! shortly shalt thou see,
With God's high will, thy children free,
    And vengeance on thy foes!
Yet to no sense of selfish wrongs,
Bear witness with me, Heaven, belongs
    My joy o'er Edward's bier;[1]

---

[1] The generosity which does justice to the character of an enemy, often marks Bruce's sentiments, as recorded by the faithful Barbour. He seldom mentions a fallen enemy without praising such good qualities as he might possess. I shall only take one instance. Shortly after Bruce landed in Carrick, in 1306, Sir Ingram Bell, the English governor of Ayr, engaged a wealthy yeoman, who had hitherto been a follower of Bruce, to undertake the task of assassinating him. The King learned this treachery, as he is said to have done other secrets of the enemy, by means of a female with whom he had an intrigue. Shortly after he was possessed of this information, Bruce, resorting to a small thicket at a distance from his men, with only a single page to attend him, met the traitor, accompanied by two of his sons. They approached him with their wonted familiarity, but Bruce, taking his page's bow and arrow, commanded them to keep at a distance. As they still pressed forward with professions of zeal for his person and service, he, after a second warning, shot the

I took my knighthood at his hand,
And lordship held of him, and land,
　　And well may vouch it here,
That, blot the story from his page,
Of Scotland ruin'd in his rage,
You read a monarch brave and sage,
　　And to his people dear."—
" Let London's burghers mourn her Lord,
And Croydon monks his praise record,"
　　The eager Edward said ;
" Eternal as his own, my hate
Surmounts the bounds of mortal fate,
　　And dies not with the dead !
Such hate was his on Solway's strand,
When vengeance clench'd his palsied hand,
That pointed yet to Scotland's land,[1]
　　As his last accents pray'd

---

father with the arrow ; and being assaulted successively by the
two sons, despatched first one, who was armed with an axe, then
as the other charged him with a spear, avoided the thrust, struck
the head from the spear, and cleft the skull of the assassin with
a blow of his two-handed sword.

| | |
|---|---|
| 'He rushed down of blood all red, | |
| And when the king saw they were dead, | |
| All three lying, he wiped his brand. | |
| With that his boy came fast running, | |
| And said, 'Our lord might lowyt* be, | *Lauded. |
| That granted you might and poweste† | †Power |
| To fell the felony and the pride, | |
| Of three in so little tide.' | |
| The king said, 'So our lord me see, | |
| They have been worthy men all three, | |
| Had they not been full of treason: | |
| But that made their confusion.' "—Barbour's *Bruce*, b. v. p. 159 | |

[1] [See Appendix, Note N.]

Disgrace and curse upon his heir,
If he one Scottish head should spare,
Till stretch'd upon the bloody lair
  Each rebel corpse was laid!
Such hate was his, when his last breath
Renounced the peaceful house of death,
And bade his bones to Scotland's coast
Be borne by his remorseless host,
As if his dead and stony eye
Could still enjoy her misery!
Such hate was his—dark, deadly, long;
Mine,—as enduring, deep, and strong!"—

### V.

"Let women, Edward, war with words,
With curses monks, but men with swords:
Nor doubt of living foes, to sate
Deepest revenge and deadliest hate.
Now, to the sea! behold the beach,
And see the galleys' pendants stretch
Their fluttering length down favouring gale!
Aboard, aboard! and hoist the sail.
Hold we our way for Arran first,
Where meet in arms our friends dispersed;
Lennox the loyal, De la Haye,
And Boyd the bold in battle fray.
I long the hardy band to head,
And see once more my standard spread.—
Does noble Ronald share our course,
Or stay to raise his island force?"—
"Come weal, come woe, by Bruce's side,"
Replied the Chief, "will Ronald bide.
And since two galleys yonder ride.

Be mine, so please my liege, dismiss'd
To wake to arms the clans of Uist,
And all who hear the Minche's roar,
On the Long Island's lonely shore.
The nearer Isles, with slight delay,
Ourselves may summon in our way;
And soon on Arran's shore shall meet,
With Torquil's aid, a gallant fleet,
If aught avails their Chieftain's hest
Among the islesmen of the west."

### VI.

Thus was their venturous council said.
But, ere their sails the galleys spread.
Coriskin dark and Coolin high
Echoed the dirge's doleful cry.
Along that sable lake pass'd slow,—
Fit scene for such a sight of woe,—
The sorrowing islesmen, as they bore
The murder'd Allan to the shore.
At every pause, with dismal shout,
Their coronach of grief rung out,
And ever, when they moved again,
The pipes resumed their clamorous strain,
And, with the pibroch's shrilling wail,
Mourn'd the young heir of Donagaile.
Round and around, from cliff and cave,
His answer stern old Coolin gave,
Till high upon his misty side
Languish'd the mournful notes, and died.
For never sounds, by mortal made,
Attain'd his high and haggard head,
That echoes but the tempest's moan,
Or the deep thunder's rending groan.

## VII.

Merrily, merrily bounds the bark,
    She bounds before the gale,
The mountain breeze from Ben-na-darch
    Is joyous in her sail!
With fluttering sound like laughter hoarse
    The cords and canvas strain,
The waves, divided by her force,
In rippling eddies chased her course,
    As if they laugh'd again.
Not down the breeze more blithely blew,
Skimming the wave, the light sea-mew,
    Than the gay galley bore
Her course upon that favouring wind,
And Coolin's crest has sunk behind,
    And Slapin's cavern'd shore.
'T was then that warlike signals wake
Dunscaith's dark towers and Eisord's lake,
And soon, from Cavilgarrigh's head,
Thick wreaths of eddying smoke were spread;
A summons these of war and wrath
To the brave clans of Sleat and Strath,
    And, ready at the sight,
Each warrior to his weapons sprung,
And targe upon his shoulder flung,
    Impatient for the fight.
Mac-Kinnon's chief, in warfare grey,
Had charge to muster their array,
And guide their barks to Brodick-Bay.

## VIII.

Signal of Ronald's high command,
A beacon gleam'd o'er sea and land,

From Canna's tower, that, steep and grey,
Like falcon-nest o'erhangs the bay.[1]
Seek not the giddy crag to climb,
To view the turret scathed by time;
It is a task of doubt and fear
To aught but goat or mountain-deer.
    But rest thee on the silver beach,
    And let the aged herdsman teach
        His tale of former day;
    His cur's wild clamour he shall chide,
    And for thy seat by ocean's side,
        His varied plaid display;
    Then tell, how with their Chieftain came,
    In ancient times, a foreign dame
        To yonder turret grey.
Stern was her Lord's suspicious mind,
Who in so rude a jail confined
        So soft and fair a thrall!
And oft when moon on ocean slept,
That lovely lady sate and wept
        Upon the castle-wall,
And turn'd her eye to southern climes,
And thought perchance of happier times,

---

[1] The little island of Canna, or Cannay, adjoins to those of Rum and Muick, with which it forms one parish. In a pretty bay opening towards the east, there is a lofty and slender rock detached from the shore. Upon the summit are the ruins of a very small tower, scarcely accessible by a steep and precipitous path. Here it is said one of the kings, or Lords of the Isles, confined a beautiful lady, of whom he was jealous. The ruins are of course haunted by her restless spirit, and many romantic stories are told by the aged people of the island concerning her fate in life, and her appearances after death.

And touch'd her lute by fits, and sung
Wild ditties in her native tongue.
And still, when on the cliff and bay
Placid and pale the moonbeams play,
    And every breeze is mute,
Upon the lone Hebridean's ear,
Steals a strange pleasure mix'd with fear,
While from that cliff he seems to hear
    The murmur of a lute,
And sounds, as of a captive lone,
That mourns her woes in tongue unknown.—
Strange is the tale—but all too long
Already hath it staid the song—
    Yet who may pass them by,
That crag and tower in ruins grey,
Nor to their hapless tenant pay
    The tribute of a sigh!

### IX.

Merrily, merrily bounds the bark
    O'er the broad ocean driven,
Her path by Ronin's mountains dark
    The steersman's hand hath given.
And Ronin's mountains dark have sent
    Their hunters to the shore,[1]

---

[1] Ronin (popularly called Rum, a name which a poet may be pardoned for avoiding if possible) is a very rough and mountainous island, adjacent to those of Eigg and Cannay. There is almost no arable ground upon it, so that, except in the plenty of the deer, which of course are now nearly extirpated, it still deserves the description bestowed by the archdean of the Isles. "Ronin, sixteen myle north-wast from the ile of Coll, lyes ane ile callit Ronin Ile, of sixteen myle long, and six in bredthe in the narrowest,

And each his ashen bow unbent,
   And gave his pastime o'er,
And at the Island Lord's command,
For hunting spear took warrior's bran
On Scooreigg next a warning light
Summon'd her warriors to the fight;
A numerous race, ere stern Macleod
O'er their bleak shores in vengeance strode,[1]
When all in vain the ocean-cave
Its refuge to his victims gave.
The Chief, relentless in his wrath,
With blazing heath blockades the path;
In dense and stifling volumes roll'd,
The vapour fill'd the cavern'd hold!
The warrior-threat, the infant's plain,
The mother's screams, were heard in vain;
The vengeful Chief maintains his fires,
Till in the vault a tribe expires!
The bones which strew that cavern's gloom,
Too well attest their dismal doom.

### X.

Merrily, merrily goes the bark[2]
   On a breeze from the northward free,

---

ane forest of heigh mountains, and abundance of little deir in it.
quhilk deir will never be slane dounewith, but the principal sait-
tis man be in the height of the hill, because the deir will be callit
upwart ay be the tainchell, or without tynchel they will pass
upwart perforce. In this ile will be gotten about Britane als
many wild nests upon the plane mure as men pleasis to gadder.
and yet by resson the fowls hes few to start them except deir.
This ile lyes from the west to the eist in lenth, and pertains to
M'Kenabrey of Colla. Many solan geese are in this ile."—
Monro's *Description of the Western Isles*, p. 18.

  [1] [See Appendix, Note O.]     [2] [See Appendix, Note E.]

So shoots through the morning sky the lark,
　Or the swan through the summer sea.
The shores of Mull on the eastward lay,
And Ulva dark and Colonsay,
And all the group of islets gay
　That guard famed Staffa round.
Then all unknown its columns rose,
Where dark and undisturb'd repose
　The cormorant had found,
And the shy seal had quiet home,
And welter'd in that wondrous dome,
Where, as to shame the temples deck'd
By skill of earthly architect,
Nature herself, it seem'd, would raise
A Minster to her Maker's praise![1]

---

[1] It would be unpardonable to detain the reader upon a wonder
so often described, and yet so incapable of being understood by
description. This palace of Neptune is even grander upon a
second than the first view. The stupendous columns which form
the sides of the cave, the depth and strength of the tide which
rolls its deep and heavy swell up to the extremity of the vault
—the variety of tints formed by white, crimson, and yellow
stalactites, or petrifactions, which occupy the vacancies between
the base of the broken pillars which form the roof, and intersect
them with a rich, curious, and variegated chasing, occupying
each interstice—the corresponding variety below water, where
the ocean rolls over a dark-red or violet-coloured rock, from
which, as from a base, the basaltic columns arise—the tremendous noise of the swelling tide, mingling with the deep-toned
echoes of the vault,—are circumstances elsewhere unparalleled.

Nothing can be more interesting than the varied appearance
of the little archipelago of islets, of which Staffa is the most
remarkable. This group, called in Gaelic Tresharnish, affords
a thousand varied views to the voyager, as they appear in different positions with reference to his course. The variety of their
shape contributes much to the beauty of these effects.

Not for a meaner use ascend
Her columns, or her arches bend;
Nor of a theme less solemn tells
That mighty surge that ebbs and swells,
And still, between each awful pause,
From the high vault an answer draws,
In varied tone prolong'd and high,
That mocks the organ's melody.
Nor doth its entrance front in vain
To old Iona's holy fane,
That Nature's voice might seem to say,
"Well hast thou done, frail Child of clay!
Thy humble powers that stately shrine
Task'd high and hard—but witness mine!"

### XI.

Merrily, merrily goes the bark,
    Before the gale she bounds;
So darts the dolphin from the shark,
    Or the deer before the hounds.
They left Loch-Tua on their lee,
And they waken'd the men of the wild Tiree,
    And the Chief of the sandy Coll;
They paused not at Columba's isle,
Though peal'd the bells from the holy pile
    With long and measured toll;[1]

---

[1] ["We were now treading that illustrious island, which was once the luminary of the Caledonian regions, whence savage clans and roving barbarians derived the benefits of knowledge, and the blessings of religion. To abstract the mind from all local emotion would be impossible, if it were endeavoured, and would be foolish, if it were possible. Whatever withdraws us from the power of our senses; whatever makes the past, the distant, or the future predominate over the present, advances us in the dignity

No time for matin or for mass,
And the sounds of the holy summons pass
     Away in the billows' roll.
Lochbuie's fierce and warlike Lord
Their signal saw, and grasp'd his sword
And verdant Ilay call'd her host,
And the clans of Jura's rugged coast
     Lord Ronald's call obey,
And Scarba's isle, whose tortured shore
Still rings to Corrievreken's roar,
     And lonely Colonsay;
—Scenes sung by him who sings no more
His bright and brief career is o'er,
     And mute his tuneful strains;
Quench'd is his lamp of varied lore,
That loved the light of song to pour
A distant and a deadly shore
     Has LEYDEN's cold remains![1]

---

of thinking beings. Far from me and from my friends be such frigid philosophy, as may conduct us indifferent and unmoved over any ground which has been dignified by wisdom, bravery, or virtue. That man is little to be envied, whose patriotism would not gain force upon the plain of Marathon, or whose piety would not grow warmer among the ruins of Iona."—JOHNSON.]

[1] The ballad, entitled "Macphail of Colonsay, and the Mermaid of Corrievrekin," [See Border Minstrelsy, vol. iv. p. 285,] was composed by John Leyden, from a tradition which he found while making a tour through the Hebrides about 1801, soon before his fatal departure for India, where, after having made farther progress in Oriental literature than any man of letters who had embraced those studies, he died a martyr to his zeal for knowledge, in the island of Java, immediately after the landing of our forces near Batavia, in August, 1811.

## XII.

Ever the breeze blows merrily,
But the galley ploughs no more the sea.
Lest, rounding wild Cantire, they meet
The southern foeman's watchful fleet,
  They held unwonted way; —
Up Tarbat's western lake they bore,
Then dragg'd their bark the isthmus o'er,[1]
As far as Kilmaconnel's shore,
  Upon the eastern bay.
It was a wondrous sight to see
Topmast and pennon glitter free,
High raised above the greenwood tree,
As on dry land the galley moves,
By cliff and copse and alder groves.
Deep import from that selcouth sign,
Did many a mountain Seer divine,
For ancient legends told the Gael,
That when a royal bark should sail
  O'er Kilmaconnel moss,
Old Albyn should in fight prevail,
And every foe should faint and quail
  Before her silver Cross.

## XIII.

Now launch'd once more, the inland sea
They furrow with fair augury,
  And steer for Arran's isle;
The sun, ere yet he sunk behind
Ben-Ghoil, "the Mountain of the Wind,
Gave his grim peaks a greeting kind,
  And bade Loch Ranza smile.[2]

---

[1] [See Appendix, Note P.]
[2] Loch Ranza is a beautiful bay, on the northern extremity of

Thither their destined course they drew;
It seem'd the isle her monarch knew,
So brilliant was the landward view,
 The ocean so serene;
Each puny wave in diamonds roll'd
O'er the calm deep, where hues of gold
 With azure strove and green.
The hill, the vale, the tree, the tower,
Glow'd with the tints of evening's hour,
 The beach was silver sheen,
The wind breathed soft as lover's sigh,
And, oft renew'd, seem'd oft to die,
 With breathless pause between.
O who, with speech of war and woes,
Would wish to break the soft repose
 Of such enchanting scene!

### XIV.

Is it of war Lord Ronald speaks?
The blush that dyes his manly cheeks,
The timid look, and downcast eye,
And faltering voice the theme deny.

---

Arran, opening towards East Tarbat Loch. It is well described by Pennant:—"The approach was magnificent; a fine bay in front, about a mile deep, having a ruined castle near the lower end, on a low far projecting neck of land, that forms another harbour, with a narrow passage; but within has three fathom of water, even at the lowest ebb. Beyond is a little plain watered by a stream, and inhabited by the people of a small village. The whole is environed with a theatre of mountains; and in the background the serrated crags of Grianan-Athol soar above."— Pennant's *Tour to the Western Isles*, p. 191–2. Ben-Ghaoil, "the mountain of the winds," is generally known by its English, and less poetical name, of Goatfield.

And good King Robert's brow express'd.
He ponder'd o'er some high request,
   As doubtful to approve;
Yet in his eye and lip the while,
Dwelt the half-pitying glance and smile,
Which manhood's graver mood beguile,
   When lovers talk of love.
Anxious his suit Lord Ronald pled;
—"And for my bride betroth'd," he said,
"My Liege has heard the rumour spread
Of Edith from Artornish fled.
Too hard her fate—I claim no right
To blame her for her hasty flight;
Be joy and happiness her lot!—
But she hath fled the bridal-knot,
And Lorn recall'd his promised plight.
In the assembled chieftains' sight.—
   When, to fulfil our fathers' band,
I proffer'd all I could—my hand—
   I was repulsed with scorn;
Mine honour I should ill assert,
And worse the feelings of my heart,
If I should play a suitor's part
   Again, to pleasure Lorn."—

## XV.

"Young Lord," the Royal Bruce replied,
"That question must the Church decide
Yet seems it hard, since rumours state
Edith takes Clifford for her mate,
The very tie, which she hath broke,
To thee should still be binding yoke.

But, for my sister Isabel—
The mood of woman who can tell?
I guess the Champion of the Rock,
Victorious in the tourney shock,
That knight unknown, to whom the prize
She dealt,—had favour in her eyes;
But since our brother Nigel's fate,
Our ruin'd house and hapless state,
From worldly joy and hope estranged,
Much is the hapless mourner changed.
Perchance," here smiled the noble King,
" This tale may other musings bring.
Soon shall we know—yon mountains hide
The little convent of Saint Bride;
There, sent by Edward, she must stay,
Till fate shall give more prosperous day;
And thither will I bear thy suit,
Nor will thine advocate be mute."

### XVI.

As thus they talk'd in earnest mood,
That speechless boy beside them stood.
He stoop'd his head against the mast.
And bitter sobs came thick and fast,
A grief that would not be repress'd,
But seem'd to burst his youthful breast.
His hands, against his forehead held,
As if by force his tears repell'd,
But through his fingers, long and slight,
Fast trill'd the drops of crystal bright.
Edward, who walk'd the deck apart,
First spied this conflict of the heart.
Thoughtless as brave, with bluntness kind
He sought to cheer the sorrower's mind;

By force the slender hand he drew
From those poor eyes that stream'd with dew.
As in his hold the stripling strove,—
('Twas a rough grasp, though meant in love,)
Away his tears the warrior swept
And bade shame on him that he wept.
"I would to heaven, thy helpless tongue
Could tell me who hath wrought thee wrong;
For, were he of our crew the best,
The insult went not unredress'd.
Come, cheer thee; thou art now of age
To be a warrior's gallant page;
Thou shalt be mine!—a palfrey fair
O'er hill and holt my boy shall bear,
To hold my bow in hunting grove,
Or speed on errand to my love;
For well I wot thou wilt not tell
The temple where my wishes dwell."


XVII.

Bruce interposed,—"Gay Edward, no,
This is no youth to hold thy bow,
To fill thy goblet, or to bear
Thy message light to lighter fair.
Thou art a patron all too wild
And thoughtless, for this orphan child.
See'st thou not how apart he steals,
Keeps lonely couch, and lonely meals?
Fitter by far in yon calm cell
To tend our sister Isabel,
With father Augustin to share
The peaceful change of convent prayer,

Than wander wild adventures through,
With such a reckless guide as you."—
"Thanks, brother!" Edward answer'd gay,
"For the high laud thy words convey!
But we may learn, some future day,
If thou or I can this poor boy
Protect the best, or best employ.
Meanwhile, our vessel nears the strand;
Launch we the boat, and seek the land."

## XVIII.

To land King Robert lightly sprung,
And thrice aloud his bugle rung
With note prolong'd and varied strain,
Till bold Ben-ghoil replied again.
Good Douglas then, and De la Haye,
Had in a glen a hart at bay,
And Lennox cheer'd the laggard hounds,
When waked that horn the greenwood bounds.
"It is the foe!" cried Boyd, who came
In breathless haste with eye on flame,—
"It is the foe!—Each valiant lord
Fling by his bow, and grasp his sword!"—
"Not so," replied the good Lord James,
"That blast no English bugle claims.
Oft have I heard it fire the fight,
Cheer the pursuit, or stop the flight.
Dead were my heart, and deaf mine ear,
If Bruce should call, nor Douglas hear!
Each to Loch Ranza's margin spring;
That blast was winded by the King!"[1]

---

[1] The passage in Barbour, describing the landing of Bruce, and

## XIX.

Fast to their mates the tidings spread,
And fast to shore the warriors sped.

---

his being recognised by Douglas and those of his followers who
had preceded him, by the sound of his horn, is in the original
singularly simple and affecting.—The king arrived in Arran with
thirty-three small row-boats.  He interrogated a female if there
had arrived any warlike men of late in that country.  " Surely,
sir," she replied, " I can tell you of many who lately came hither,
discomfited the English governor, and blockaded his castle of
Brodick.  They maintain themselves in a wood at no great distance."  The king, truly conceiving that this must be Douglas
and his followers, who had lately set forth to try their fortune in
Arran, desired the woman to conduct him to the wood.  She
obeyed.

> "The king then blew his horn on high;
> And girt his men that were him by,
> Hold them still, and all privy:
> And syne again his horne blew he.
> James of Dowglas heard him blow,
> And at the last alone gan know,
> And said, ' Soothly yon is the king;
> I know long while since his blowing.'
> The third time therewithall he blew,
> And then Sir Robert Boid it knew;
> And said, ' Yon is the king, but dread,
> Go we forth till him, better speed.'
> Then went they till the king in hye,
> And him inclined courteously.
> And blithly welcomed the king,
> And was joyful of their meeting,
> And kissed them; and speared * syne          * *Asked.*
> How they had fared in hunting?
> And they him told all, but lesing: †          † *Without lying*
> Syne laud they God of their meeting.
> Syne with the king till his harbourye
> Went both joyfu' and jolly."

BARBOUR's *Bruce*, Book v. p 115, 116,

Bursting from glen and greenwood tree.
High waked their loyal jubilee!
Around the royal Bruce they crowd,
And clasp'd his hands, and wept aloud.
Veterans of early fields were there,
Whose helmets press'd their hoary hair,
Whose swords and axes bore a stain
From life-blood of the red-hair'd Dane;
And boys, whose hands scarce brook'd to wield
The heavy sword or bossy shield.
Men too were there, that bore the scars
Impress'd in Albyn's woful wars,
At Falkirk's fierce and fatal fight,
Teyndrum's dread rout and Methven's flight.
The might of Douglas there was seen,
There Lennox with his graceful mien;
Kirkpatrick, Closeburn's dreaded Knight;
The Lindsay, fiery, fierce, and light;
The Heir of murder'd De la Haye,
And Boyd the grave, and Seton gay.
Around their King regain'd they press'd,
Wept, shouted, clasp'd him to their breast,
And young and old, and serf and lord,
And he who ne'er unsheathed a sword,
And he in many a peril tried,
Alike resolved the brunt to bide,
And live or die by Bruce's side!

### XX.

Oh, War! thou hast thy fierce delight,
Thy gleams of joy, intensely bright!
Such gleams, as from thy polish'd shield
Fly dazzling o'er the battle-field!

Such transports wake, severe and high,
Amid the pealing conquest-cry;
Scarce less, when, after battle lost,
Muster the remnants of a host,
And as each comrade's name they tell,
Who in the well-fought conflict fell,
Knitting stern brow o'er flashing eye,
Vow to avenge them or to die!—
Warriors!—and where are warriors found,
If not on martial Britain's ground?
And who, when waked with note of fire,
Love more than they the British lyre?—
Know ye not,—hearts to honour dear!
That joy, deep-thrilling, stern, severe,
At which the heart-strings vibrate high,
And wake the fountains of the eye?[1]
And blame ye, then, the Bruce, if trace
Of tear is on his manly face,
When, scanty relics of the train
That hail'd at Scone his early reign,
This patriot band around him hung,
And to his knees and bosom clung?—
Blame ye the Bruce?—his brother blamed.
But shared the weakness, while ashamed,
With haughty laugh his head he turn'd,
And dash'd away the tear he scorn'd.[2]

---

[1] ["Ours are the tears, though few, sincerely shed,
When Ocean shrouds and sepulchres our dead.
For us, even banquets fond regret supply
In the red cup that crowns our memory:
And the brief epitaph in danger's day,
When those who win at length divide the prey,
And cry, Remembrance saddening o'er each brow,
How had the brave who fell exulted *now!*"

BYRON'S *Corsair.*]

The kind, and yet fiery character of Edward Bruce, is well

## XXI.

'Tis morning, and the Convent bell
Long time had ceased its matin knell
     Within thy walls, Saint Bride!
An aged Sister sought the cell
Assign'd to Lady Isabel,
     And hurriedly she cried,
" Haste, gentle Lady, haste — there waits
A noble stranger at the gates;
Saint Bride's poor vot'ress ne'er has seen
A Knight of such a princely mien;

---

painted by Barbour, in the account of his behaviour after the battle
of Bannockburn. Sir Walter Ross, one of the very few Scottish
nobles who fell in that battle, was so dearly beloved by Edward,
that he wished the victory had been lost, so Ross had lived.

> " Out-taken him, men has not seen
> Where he for any men made moaning.'

And here the venerable Archdeacon intimates a piece of scandal.
Sir Edward Bruce, it seems, loved Ross's sister, *par amours*, to
the neglect of his own lady, sister to David de Strathbogie, Earl
of Athole. This criminal passion had evil consequences; for, in
resentment of the affront done to his sister, Athole attacked the
guard which Bruce had left at Cambuskenneth, during the battle
of Bannockburn, to protect his magazine of provisions, and slew
Sir William Keith, the commander. For which treason he was
forfeited.

In like manner, when in a sally from Carrickfergus, Neil Fle-
ming, and the guards whom he commanded, had fallen, after the
protracted resistance which saved the rest of Edward Bruce's
army, he made such moan as surprised his followers:

> " Sic moan he made men had ferly,*          * *Wonder.*
> For he was not customably
> Wont for to moan men any thing,
> Nor would not hear men make moaning "

Such are the nice traits of character so often lost in general history

His errand, as he bade me tell.
Is with the Lady Isabel."
The princess rose,— for on her knee
Low bent she told her rosary,—
"Let him by thee his purpose teach;
I may not give a stranger speech."—
"Saint Bride forefend, thou royal Maid!"
The portress cross'd herself, and said,—
"Not to be prioress might I
Debate his will, his suit deny."—
"Has earthly show then, simple fool,
Power o'er a sister of thy rule,
And art thou, like the worldly train,
Subdued by splendours light and vain?"—

### XXII.

"No, Lady! in old eyes like mine,
Gauds have no glitter, gems no shine;
Nor grace his rank attendants vain,
One youthful page is all his train.
It is the form, the eye, the word,
The bearing of that stranger Lord;
His stature, manly, bold, and tall,
Built like a castle's battled wall,
Yet moulded in such just degrees,
His giant-strength seems lightsome ease.
Close as the tendrils of the vine
His locks upon his forehead twine,
Jet-black, save where some touch of grey
Has ta'en the youthful hue away.
Weather and war their rougher trace
Have left on that majestic face;—
But 't is his dignity of eye!
There, if a suppliant, would I fly,

Secure, 'mid danger, wrongs, and grief,
Of sympathy, redress, relief—
That glance, if guilty, would I dread
More than the doom that spoke me dead!"—
"Enough, enough," the princess cried,
"'T is Scotland's hope, her joy, her pride!
To meaner front was ne'er assign'd
Such mastery o'er the common mind—
Bestow'd thy high designs to aid,
How long, O Heaven! how long delay'd!—
Haste, Mona, haste, to introduce
My darling brother, royal Bruce!"

### XXIII.

They met like friends who part in pain,
And meet in doubtful hope again.
But when subdued that fitful swell,
The Bruce survey'd the humble cell;—
"And this is thine, poor Isabel!—
That pallet-couch, and naked wall,
For room of state, and bed of pall;
For costly robes and jewels rare,
A string of beads and zone of hair;
And for the trumpet's sprightly call
To sport or banquet, grove or hall,
The bell's grim voice divides thy care,
'Twixt hours of penitence and prayer!—
O ill for thee, my royal claim
From the First David's sainted name!
O woe for thee, that while he sought
His right, thy brother feebly fought!"—

b b   12 *

### XXIV.

"Now lay these vain regrets aside,
And be the unshaken Bruce!" she cried.
"For more I glory to have shared
The woes thy venturous spirit dared,
When raising first thy valiant band
In rescue of thy native land,
Than had fair Fortune set me down
The partner of an empire's crown.
And grieve not that on Pleasure's stream
No more I drive in giddy dream,
For Heaven the erring pilot knew,
And from the gulf the vessel drew.
Tried me with judgments stern and great,
My house's ruin, thy defeat,
Poor Nigel's death, till, tamed, I own,
My hopes are fixed on Heaven alone;
Nor e'er shall earthly prospects win
My heart to this vain world of sin."—

### XXV.

"Nay, Isabel, for such stern choice,
First wilt thou wait thy brother's voice;
Then ponder if in convent scene
No softer thoughts might intervene—
Say they were of that unknown Knight,
Victor in Woodstock's tourney-fight—
Nay, if his name such blush you owe,
Victorious o'er a fairer foe!"
Truly his penetrating eye
Hath caught that blush's passing dye,—
Like the last beam of evening thrown
On a white cloud,—just seen and gone.

Soon with calm cheek and steady eye,
The princess made composed reply:—
"I guess my brother's meaning well;
For not so silent is the cell,
But we have heard the islesmen all
Arm in thy cause at Ronald's call,
And mine eye proves that Knight unknown
And the brave Island Lord are one.—
Had then his suit been earlier made,
In his own name, with thee to aid,
(But that his plighted faith forbade,)
I know not . . . . . . But thy page so near?—
This is no tale for menial's ear."

### XXVI.

Still stood that page, as far apart
    As the small cell would space afford;
With dizzy eye and bursting heart,
    He leant his weight on Bruce's sword,
The monarch's mantle too he bore,
And drew the fold his visage o'er.
"Fear not for him—in murderous strife,"
Said Bruce, "his warning saved my life;
Full seldom parts he from my side,
And in his silence I confide,
Since he can tell no tale again.
He is a boy of gentle strain,
And I have purposed he shall dwell
In Augustin the chaplain's cell,
And wait on thee, my Isabel.—
Mind not his tears; I've seen them flow,
As in the thaw dissolves the snow.

'Tis a kind youth, but fanciful,
Unfit against the tide to pull,
And those that with the Bruce would sail,
Must learn to strive with stream and gale.-
But forward, gentle Isabel —
My answer for Lord Ronald tell."—

### XXVII.

"This answer be to Ronald given —
The heart he asks is fix'd on heaven
My love was like a summer flower,
That wither'd in the wintry hour,
Born but of vanity and pride,
And with these sunny visions died.
If further press his suit—then say,
He should his plighted troth obey,
Troth plighted both with ring and word,
And sworn on crucifix and sword.—
Oh, shame thee, Robert! I have seen
Thou hast a woman's guardian been!
Even in extremity's dread hour,
When press'd on thee the Southern power,
And safety, to all human sight,
Was only found in rapid flight,
Thou heard'st a wretched female plain
In agony of travail-pain,
And thou didst bid thy little band
Upon the instant turn and stand,
And dare the worst the foe might do,
Rather than, like a knight untrue,
Leave to pursuers merciless
A woman in her last distress.—[1]

---

[1] This incident, which illustrates so happily the chivalrous

And wilt thou now deny thine aid
To an oppress'd and injured maid,
Even plead for Ronald's perfidy,
And press his fickle faith on me?—
So witness Heaven, as true I vow,
Had I those earthly feelings now,
Which could my former bosom move
Ere taught to set its hopes above,
I'd spurn each proffer he could bring,
Till at my feet he laid the ring,
The ring and spousal contract both,
And fair acquittal of his oath,

---

generosity of Bruce's character, is one of the many simple and natural traits recorded by Barbour. It occurred during the expedition which Bruce made to Ireland, to support the pretensions of his brother Edward to the throne of that kingdom. Bruce was about to retreat, and his host was arrayed for moving.

> "The king has heard a woman cry,
> He asked what that was in hy.[1]                     [1] *Haste.*
> 'It is the layndar,[2] sir,' sai ane,               [2] *Laundress*
> 'That her child-ill[3] right now has ta'en:         [3] *Child-bed.*
> And must leave now behind us here.
> Therefore she makes an evil cheer.'[4]              [4] *Stop.*
> The king said, 'Certes,[5] it were pity             [5] *Certainly.*
> That she in that point left should be.
> For certes I trow there is no man
> That he no will rue[6] a woman than;                [6] *Pity.*
> His hosts all there arested he,
> And gert[7] a tent soon stintit[8] be,   [7] *Caused.*   [8] *Pitched.*
> And gert her gang in hastily,
> And other women to be her by.
> While she was delivered he bade;
> And syne forth on his ways rade.
> And how she forth should carried be,
> Or he forth fure,[9] ordained he.                   [9] *Moved*
> This was a full great courtesy,
> That swilk a king and so mighty,
> Gart his men dwell on this manner,
> But for a poor lavender."

BARBOUR's *Bruce*, Book xvi. pp. 39, 40

By her who brooks his perjured scorn,
The ill-requited Maid of Lorn!"

### XXVIII.

With sudden impulse forward sprung
The page, and on her neck he hung;
Then, recollected instantly,
His head he stoop'd, and bent his knee,
Kiss'd twice the hand of Isabel,
Arose, and sudden left the cell.—
The princess, loosen'd from his hold,
Blush'd angry at his bearing bold;
     But good King Robert cried,
"Chafe not—by signs he speaks his mind,
He heard the plan my care design'd,
     Nor could his transports hide.—
But, sister, now bethink thee well;
No easy choice the convent cell;
Trust, I shall play no tyrant part,
Either to force thy hand or heart,
Or suffer that Lord Ronald scorn,
Or wrong for thee, the Maid of Lorn.
But think,—not long the time has been,
That thou wert wont to sigh unseen,
And wouldst the ditties best approve,
That told some lay of hapless love.
Now are thy wishes in thy power,
And thou art bent on cloister bower!
O! if our Edward knew the change,
How would his busy satire range,
With many a sarcasm varied still
On woman's wish, and woman's will!"—

## XXIX.

"Brother, I well believe," she said,
"Even so would Edward's part be play'd.
Kindly in heart, in word severe,
A foe to thought, and grief, and fear,
He holds his humour uncontroll'd;
But thou art of another mould.
Say then to Ronald, as I say,
Unless before my feet he lay
The ring which bound the faith he swore,
By Edith freely yielded o'er,
He moves his suit to me no more.
Nor do I promise, even if now
He stood absolved of spousal vow,
That I would change my purpose made,
To shelter me in holy shade.—
Brother, for little space, farewell!
To other duties warns the bell."—

## XXX.

"Lost to the world," King Robert said,
When he had left the royal maid,
"Lost to the world by lot severe,
O what a gem lies buried here,
Nipp'd by misfortune's cruel frost,
The buds of fair affection lost!—
But what have I with love to do?
Far sterner cares my lot pursue.
—Pent in this isle we may not lie,
Nor would it long our wants supply.
Right opposite, the mainland towers
Of my own Turnberry court our powers—

—Might not my father's beadsman hoar,
Cuthbert, who dwells upon the shore,
Kindle a signal-flame, to show
The time propitious for the blow?
It shall be so — some friend shall bear
Our mandate with despatch and care;
—Edward shall find the messenger.
That fortress ours, the island fleet
May on the coast of Carrick meet.—
O Scotland! shall it e'er be mine
To wreak thy wrongs in battle-line,
To raise my victor-head, and see
Thy hills, thy dales, thy people free,—
That glance of bliss is all I crave,
Betwixt my labours and my grave!"
Then down the hill he slowly went,
Oft pausing on the steep descent,
And reach'd the spot where his bold train
Held rustic camp upon the plain.

THE

# LORD OF THE ISLES

## CANTO FIFTH.

THE

# LORD OF THE ISLES.

## CANTO FIFTH.

On fair Loch-Ranza stream'd the early day,
Thin wreaths of cottage-smoke are upward curl'd
From the lone hamlet, which her inland bay
And circling mountains sever from the world.
And there the fisherman his sail unfurl'd,
The goat-herd drove his kids to steep Ben-Ghoil,
Before the hut the dame her spindle twirl'd,
Courting the sunbeam as she plied her toil,—
For, wake where'er he may, Man wakes to care and
    coil.

But other duties call'd each convent maid,
Roused by the summons of the moss-grown bell;
Sung were the matins, and the mass was said,
And every sister sought her separate cell,
Such was the rule, her rosary to tell.
And Isabel has knelt in lonely prayer;
The sunbeam, through the narrow lattice, fell
Upon the snowy neck and long dark hair,
As stoop'd her gentle head in meek devotion there

## II.

She raised her eyes, that duty done,
When glanced upon the pavement-stone.

Gemm'd and enchased, a golden ring,
Bound to a scroll with silken string,
With few brief words inscribed to tell,
" This for the Lady Isabel."
Within, the writing farther bore,—
" 'Twas with this ring his plight he swore,
With this his promise I restore ;
To her who can the heart command,
Well may I yield the plighted hand.
And O ! for better fortune born,
Grudge not a passing sigh to mourn
Her who was Edith once of Lorn !"
One single flash of glad surprise
Just glanced from Isabel's dark eyes,
But vanish'd in the blush of shame,
That, as its penance, instant came.
" O thought unworthy of my race !
Selfish, ungenerous, mean, and base,
A moment's throb of joy to own,
That rose upon her hopes o'erthrown !—
Thou pledge of vows too well believed,
Of man ingrate and maid deceived,
Think not thy lustre here shall gain
Another heart to hope in vain !
For thou shalt rest, thou tempting gaud,
Where worldly thoughts are overawed,
And worldly splendours sink debased."
Then by the cross the ring she placed.

### III.

Next rose the thought,—its owner far
How came it here through bolt and bar ? —
But the dim lattice is ajar.—

She looks abroad — the morning dew
A light short step had brush'd anew,
   And there were foot-prints seen
On the carved buttress rising still,
Till on the mossy window-sill
   Their track effaced the green.
The ivy twigs were torn and fray'd,
As if some climber's steps to aid.—
But who the hardy messenger,
Whose venturous path these signs infer?—
"Strange doubts are mine!—Mona, draw nigh;
—Nought 'scapes old Mona's curious eye—
What strangers, gentle mother, say,
Have sought these holy walls to-day?"—
"None, Lady, none of note or name;
Only your brother's foot-page came,
At peep of dawn — I pray'd him pass
To chapel where they said the mass;
But like an arrow he shot by,
And tears seem'd bursting from his eye."

#### IV.

The truth at once on Isabel,
As darted by a sunbeam, fell.—
"'Tis Edith's self! — her speechless woe,
Her form, her looks, the secret show!
—Instant, good Mona, to the bay,
And to my royal brother say,
I do conjure him seek my cell,
With that mute page he loves so well."—
"What! know'st thou not his warlike host
At break of day has left our coast?
   13 *

My old eyes saw them from the tower.
At eve they couch'd in greenwood bower,
At dawn a bugle-signal, made
By their bold Lord, their ranks array'd;
Up sprung the spears through bush and tree,
No time for benedicite!
Like deer, that, rousing from their lair,
Just shake the dewdrops from their hair,
And toss their armed crests aloft,
Such matins theirs!"—"Good mother, soft—
Where does my brother bend his way?"—
"As I have heard, for Brodick-Bay,
Across the isle—of barks a score
Lie there, 'tis said, to waft them o'er,
On sudden news, to Carrick-shore."—
"If such their purpose, deep the need,"
Said anxious Isabel, "of speed!
Call Father Augustine, good dame."
The nun obey'd, the Father came.

## V.

"Kind Father, hie without delay,
Across the hills to Brodick-Bay.
This message to the Bruce be given;
I pray him, by his hopes of Heaven,
That, till he speak with me, he stay!
Or, if his haste brook no delay,
That he deliver, on my suit,
Into thy charge that stripling mute.
Thus prays his sister Isabel,
For causes more than she may tell—
Away, good father!—and take heed,
That life and death are on thy speed."

His cowl the good old priest did on,
Took his piked staff and sandall'd shoon,
And, like a palmer bent by eld,
O'er moss and moor his journey held.

## VI.

Heavy and dull the foot of age,
And rugged was the pilgrimage;
But none was there beside, whose care
Might such important message bear.
Through birchen copse he wander'd slow,
Stunted and sapless, thin and low;
By many a mountain stream he pass'd,
From the tall cliffs in tumult cast,
Dashing to foam their waters dun,
And sparkling in the summer sun.
Round his grey head the wild curlew
In many a fearless circle flew.
O'er chasms he pass'd, where fractures wide
Craved wary eye and ample stride;[1]
He cross'd his brow beside the stone,
Where Druids erst heard victims groan,

---

[1] The interior of the island of Arran abounds with beautiful highland scenery. The hills, being very rocky and precipitous, afford some cataracts of great height, though of inconsiderable breadth. There is one pass over the river Machrai, renowned for the dilemma of a poor woman, who, being tempted by the narrowness of the ravine to step across, succeeded in making the first movement, but took fright when it became necessary to move the other foot, and remained in a posture equally ludicrous and dangerous, until some chance passenger assisted her to extricate herself. It is said she remained there some hours.

C C

And at the cairns upon the wild,
O'er many a heathen hero piled,[1]
He breathed a timid prayer for those
Who died ere Shiloh's sun arose.
Beside Macfarlane's Cross he staid,
There told his hours within the shade,
And at the stream his thirst allay'd.
Thence onward journeying slowly still,
As evening closed he reach'd the hill,
Where, rising through the woodland green,
Old Brodick's gothic towers were seen.
From Hastings, late their English lord,
Douglas had won them by the sword.[2]

---

[1] The isle of Arran, like those of Man and Anglesea, abounds
with many relics of heathen, and probably Druidical, superstition.
There are high erect columns of unhewn stone, the most early
of all monuments, the circles of rude stones, commonly entitled
Druidical, and the cairns, or sepulchral piles, within which are
usually found urns enclosing ashes. Much doubt necessarily
rests upon the history of such monuments, nor is it possible to
consider them as exclusively Celtic, or Druidical. By much the
finest circles of standing stones, excepting Stonehenge, are those
of Stenhouse, at Stennis, in the island of Pomona, the principal
isle of the Orcades. These, of course, are neither Celtic nor
Druidical; and we are assured that many circles of the kind
occur both in Sweden and Norway.

[2] Brodick or Brathwick Castle, in the Isle of Arran, is an
ancient fortress, near an open roadstead called Brodick-Bay, and
not far distant from a tolerable harbour, closed in by the island
of Lamlash. This important place had been assailed a short
time before Bruce's arrival in the island. James Lord Douglas,
who accompanied Bruce to his retreat in Rachrine, seems, in the
spring of 1306, to have tired of his abode there, and set out
accordingly, in the phrase of the times, to see what adventure
God would send him. Sir Robert Boyd accompanied him; and

The sun that sunk behind the isle,
Now tinged them with a parting smile.

### VII.

But though the beams of light decay,
'Twas bustle all in Brodick-Bay.
The Bruce's followers crowd the shore,
And boats and barges some unmoor,
Some raise the sail, some seize the oar;
Their eyes oft turn'd where glimmer'd far
What might have seem'd an early star
On heaven's blue arch, save that its light
Was all too flickering, fierce, and bright.
  Far distant in the south, the ray
  Shone pale amid retiring day,
      But as, on Carrick shore,
  Dim seen in outline faintly blue,
  The shades of evening closer drew,
      It kindled more and more.

---

his knowledge of the localities of Arran appears to have directed his course thither.   They landed in the island privately, and
appear to have laid an ambush for Sir John Hastings, the English governor of Brodwick, and surprised a considerable supply
of arms and provisions, and nearly took the castle itself.   Indeed,
that they actually did so, has been generally averred by historians, although it does not appear from the narrative of Barbour.
On the contrary, it would seem that they took shelter within a
fortification of the ancient inhabitants, a rampart called *Tor an
Schian*.   When they were joined by Bruce, it seems probable
that they had gained Brodick Castle.   At least tradition says,
that from the battlements of the tower he saw the supposed signal-fire on Turnberry-nook. . . . The castle is now much mod-
ernized, but has a dignified appearance, being surrounded by
flourishing plantations.

The monk's slow steps now press the sands,
And now amid a scene he stands,
   Full strange to churchman's eye;
Warriors, who, arming for the fight,
Rivet and clasp their harness light,
And twinkling spears, and axes bright,
   And helmets flashing high.
Oft, too, with unaccustom'd ears,
A language much unmeet he hears,[1]
   While, hastening all on board,
As stormy as the swelling surge
That mix'd its roar, the leaders urge
Their followers to the ocean verge,
   With many a haughty word.

### VIII.

Through that wild throng the Father pass'd,
And reach'd the Royal Bruce at last.
He leant against a stranded boat,
That the approaching tide must float,

---

[1] Barbour, with great simplicity, gives an anecdote, from which it would seem that the vice of profane swearing, afterwards too general among the Scottish nation, was, at this time, confined to military men. As Douglas, after Bruce's return to Scotland, was roving about the mountainous country of Tweeddale, near the water of Line, he chanced to hear some persons in a farm-house say "*the devil.*" Concluding, from this hardy expression, that the house contained warlike guests, he immediately assailed it, and had the good fortune to make prisoners Thomas Randolph, afterwards the famous Earl of Murray, and Alexander Stuart, Lord Bonkle. Both were then in the English interest, and had come into that country with the purpose of driving out Douglas. They afterwards ranked among Bruce's most zealous adherents.

And counted every rippling wave,
As higher yet her sides they lave,
And oft the distant fire he eyed,
And closer yet his hauberk tied,
And loosen'd in its sheath his brand.
Edward and Lennox were at hand,
Douglas and Ronald had the care
The soldiers to the barks to share.—
The Monk approach'd and homage paid;
"And art thou come," King Robert said,
"So far to bless us ere we part?"—
—"My Liege, and with a loyal heart!—
But other charge I have to tell,"—
And spoke the hest of Isabel.
—"Now by Saint Giles," the monarch cried,
"This moves me much!—this morning tide,
I sent the stripling to Saint Bride,
With my commandment there to bide."—
—"Thither he came the portress show'd,
But there, my Liege, made brief abode."—

IX.

"'Twas I," said Edward, "found employ
Of nobler import for the boy.
Deep pondering in my anxious mind,
A fitting messenger to find,
To bear thy written mandate o'er
To Cuthbert on the Carrick shore,
I chanced, at early dawn, to pass
The chapel gate to snatch a mass.
I found the stripling on a tomb
Low-seated, weeping for the doom
That gave his youth to convent gloom.

I told my purpose, aud his eyes
Flash'd joyful at the glad surprise.
He bounded to the skiff, the sail
Was spread before a prosperous gale,
And well my charge he hath obey'd;
For, see! the ruddy signal made,
That Clifford, with his merry-men all,
Guards carelessly our father's hall." [1]

## X.

" O wild of thought, and hard of heart
Answer'd the Monarch, " on a part
Of such deep danger to employ
A mute, an orphan, and a boy!
Unfit for flight, unfit for strife,
Without a tongue to plead for life!
Now, were my right restored by Heaven
Edward, my crown I would have given,
Ere, thrust on such adventure wild,
I peril'd thus the helpless child."—
—Offended half, and half submiss,
" Brother and Liege, of blame like this,"
Edward replied, " I little dream'd.
A stranger messenger, I deem'd,
Might safest seek the beadsman's cell,
Where all thy squires are known so well.
Noteless his presence, sharp his sense,
His imperfection his defence.
If seen, none can his errand guess;
If ta'en, no words his tale express—

---

[1] [See Appendix, Note Q.]

Methinks, too, yonder beacon's shine
Might expiate greater fault than mine."—
"Rash," said King Robert, "was the deed—
But it is done.—Embark with speed!—
Good Father, say to Isabel
How this unhappy chance befell;
If well we thrive on yonder shore,
Soon shall my care her page restore.
Our greeting to our sister bear,
And think of us in mass and prayer."—

## XI.

"Ay!" said the Priest,—"while this poor hand
Can chalice raise or cross command,
While my old voice has accents' use,
Can Augustine forget the Bruce!"
Then to his side Lord Ronald press'd,
And whisper'd, "Bear thou this request,
That when by Bruce's side I fight,
For Scotland's crown and freedom's right,
The princess grace her knight to bear
Some token of her favouring care;
It shall be shown where England's best
May shrink to see it on my crest.
And for the boy—since weightier care
For royal Bruce the times prepare,
The helpless youth is Ronald's charge,
His couch my plaid, his fence my targe."
He ceased; for many an eager hand
Had urged the barges from the strand.
Their number was a score and ten,
They bore thrice threescore chosen men.

With such small force did Bruce at last
The die for death or empire cast!

## XII.

Now on the darkening main afloat,
Ready and mann'd rocks every boat;
Beneath their oars the ocean's might
Was dash'd to sparks of glimmering light.
Faint and more faint, as off they bore,
Their armour glanced against the shore,
And, mingled with the dashing tide,
Their murmuring voices distant died.—
" God speed them!" said the Priest, as dark
On distant billows glides each bark;
"O Heaven! when swords for freedom shine,
And monarch's right, the cause is thine!
Edge doubly every patriot blow!
Beat down the banners of the foe!
And be it to the nations known,
That Victory is from God alone!"
As up the hill his path he drew,
He turn'd his blessings to renew,
Oft turn'd, till on the darken'd coast
All traces of their course were lost;
Then slowly bent to Brodick tower,
To shelter for the evening hour.

## XIII.

In night the fairy prospects sink,
Where Cumray's isles with verdant link
Close the fair entrance of the Clyde;
The woods of Bute, no more descried,
Are gone—and on the placid sea
The rowers ply their task with glee,

While hands that knightly lances bore
Impatient aid the labouring oar.
The half-faced moon shone dim and pale,
And glanced against the whiten'd sail;
But on that ruddy beacon-light
Each steersman kept the helm aright,
And oft, for such the King's command,
That all at once might reach the strand,
From boat to boat loud shout and hail
Warn'd them to crowd or slacken sail.
South and by west the armada bore,
And near at length the Carrick shore.
As less and less the distance grows,
High and more high the beacon rose;
The light, that seem'd a twinkling star,
Now blazed portentous, fierce, and far.
Dark-red the heaven above it glow'd,
Dark-red the sea beneath it flow'd,
Red rose the rocks on ocean's brim,
In blood-red light her islets swim;
Wild scream the dazzled sea-fowl gave,
Dropp'd from their crags on plashing wave
The deer to distant covert drew,
The black-cock deem'd it day, and crew.
Like some tall castle given to flame,
O'er half the land the lustre came.
"Now, good my Liege, and brother sage,
What think ye of mine elfin page?"—
"Row on!" the noble King replied,
"We'll learn the truth whate'er betide;
Yet sure the beadsman and the child
Could ne'er have waked that beacon wild."

## XIV.

With that the boats approach'd the land,
But Edward's grounded on the sand;
The eager knight leap'd in the sea
Waist-deep, and first on shore was he,
Though every barge's hardy band
Contended which should gain the land,
When that strange light, which, seen afar,
Seem'd steady as the polar star,
Now, like a prophet's fiery chair,
Seem'd travelling the realms of air.
Wide o'er the sky the splendour glows,
As that portentous meteor rose;
Helm, axe, and falchion glitter'd bright,
And in the red and dusky light
His comrade's face each warrior saw,
Nor marvell'd it was pale with awe.
Then high in air the beams were lost,
And darkness sunk upon the coast.—
Ronald to Heaven a prayer address'd,
And Douglas cross'd his dauntless breast;
"Saint James protect us!" Lennox cried,
But reckless Edward spoke aside,
"Deem'st thou, Kirkpatrick, in that flame
Red Comyn's angry spirit came,
Or would thy dauntless heart endure
Once more to make assurance sure?"—
"Hush!" said the Bruce; "we soon shall know.
If this be sorcerer's empty show,
Or stratagem of Southern foe.
The moon shines out—upon the sand
Let every leader rank his band."

## XV.

Faintly the moon's pale beams supply
That ruddy light's unnatural dye;
The dubious cold reflection lay
On the wet sands and quiet bay.
Beneath the rocks King Robert drew
His scatter'd files to order due,
Till shield compact and serried spear
In the cool light shone blue and clear.
Then down a path that sought the tide,
That speechless page was seen to glide;
He knelt him lowly on the sand,
And gave a scroll to Robert's hand.
"A torch," the Monarch cried, "What, ho!
Now shall we Cuthbert's tidings know."
But evil news the tidings bare,
The Clifford's force was strong and ware,
Augmented, too, that very morn,
By mountaineers who came with Lorn.
Long harrow'd by oppressor's hand,
Courage and faith had fled the land,
And over Carrick, dark and deep,
Had sunk dejection's iron sleep.——
Cuthbert had seen that beacon-flame,
Unwitting from what source it came.
Doubtful of perilous event,
Edward's mute messenger he sent,
If Bruce deceived should venture o'er,
To warn him from the fatal shore.

## XVI.

As round the torch the leaders crowd,
Bruce read these chilling news aloud.
　　14 *

" What council, nobles, have we now?—
To ambush us in greenwood bough,
And take the chance which fate may send
To bring our enterprise to end,
Or shall we turn us to the main
As exiles, and embark again?"—
Answer'd fierce Edward, " Hap what may,
In Carrick, Carrick's Lord must stay.
I would not minstrels told the tale,
Wildfire or meteor made us quail."
Answer'd the Douglas, " If my liege
May win yon walls by storm or siege,
Then were each brave and patriot heart
Kindled of new for loyal part."—
Answer'd Lord Ronald, " Not for shame
Would I that aged Torquil came,
And found, for all our empty boast,
Without a blow we fled the coast.
I will not credit that this land,
So famed for warlike heart and hand,
The nurse of Wallace and of Bruce,
Will long with tyrants hold a truce."—
" Prove we our fate — the brunt we'll bide !"
So Boyd and Haye and Lennox cried;
So said, so vow'd, the leaders all;
So Bruce resolved: " And in my hall
Since the bold Southern make their home,
The hour of payment soon shall come,
When with a rough and rugged host
Clifford may reckon to his cost.
Meantime, through well-known bosk and dell,
I'll lead where we may shelter well."

## XVII.

Now ask you whence that wondrous light,
Whose fairy glow beguiled their sight?—
It ne'er was known[1]—yet grey-hair'd eld
A superstitious credence held,
That never did a mortal hand
Wake its broad glare on Carrick strand;

---

[1] The following are the words of an ingenious correspondent, to whom I am obliged for much information respecting Turnberry and its neighbourhood. "The only tradition now remembered of the landing of Robert the Bruce in Carrick, relates to the fire seen by him from the Isle of Arran. It is still generally reported, and religiously believed by many, that this fire was really the work of supernatural power, unassisted by the hand of any mortal being; and it is said, that, for several centuries, the flame rose yearly on the same hour of the same night of the year, on which the king first saw it from the turrets of Brodick castle; and some go so far as to say, that if the exact time were known, it would be still seen. That this superstitious notion is very ancient, is evident from the place where the fire is said to have appeared, being called the Bogles' Brae, beyond the remembrance of man. In support of this curious belief, it is said that the practice of burning heath for the improvement of land was then unknown; that a spunkie (Jack o'lanthorn) could not have been seen across the breadth of the Forth of Clyde, between Ayrshire and Arran; and that the courier of Bruce was his kinsman, and never suspected of treachery."— Letter from Mr. Joseph Train, of Newton Stuart, author of an ingenious Collection of Poems, illustrative of many ancient Traditions in Galloway and Ayrshire, Edinburgh, 1814. [Mr. Train made a journey into Ayrshire at Sir Walter Scott's request, on purpose to collect accurate information for the Notes to this poem; and the reader will find more of the fruits of his labours in the Appendix, Note R. This is the same gentleman whose friendly assistance is so often acknowledged in the Notes and Introductions of the Waverley Novels.]

d d

Nay, and that on the self-same night
When Bruce cross'd o'er, still gleams the light.
Yearly it gleams o'er mount and moor,
And glittering wave and crimson'd shore—
But whether beam celestial, lent
By Heaven to aid the King's descent,
Or fire hell-kindled from beneath,
To lure him to defeat and death,
Or were it but some meteor strange,
Of such as oft through midnight range,
Startling the traveller late and lone,
I know not—and it ne'er was known.


## XVIII.

Now up the rocky pass they drew,
And Ronald, to his promise true,
Still made his arm the stripling's stay,
To aid him on the rugged way.
"Now cheer thee, simple Amadine!
Why throbs that silly heart of thine?"—
— That name the pirates to their slave
(In Gaelic 'tis the Changeling) gave —
"Dost thou not rest thee on my arm?
Do not my plaid-folds hold thee warm?
Hath not the wild bull's treble hide
This targe for thee and me supplied?
Is not Clan-Colla's sword of steel?
And, trembler, canst thou terror feel?
Cheer thee, and still that throbbing heart;
From Ronald's guard thou shalt not part."
—O! many a shaft, at random sent,
Finds mark the archer little meant!

And many a word, at random spoken,
May soothe or wound a heart that's broken!
Half soothed, half grieved, half terrified,
Close drew the page to Ronald's side;
A wild delirious thrill of joy
Was in that hour of agony,
As up the steepy pass he strove,
Fear, toil, and sorrow, lost in love!

### XIX.

The barrier of that iron shore,
The rock's steep ledge, is now climb'd o'er;
And from the castle's distant wall,
From tower to tower the warders call:
The sound swings over land and sea,
And marks a watchful enemy.—
They gain'd the Chase, a wide domain
Left for the Castle's sylvan reign,
(Seek not the scene — the axe, the plough,
The boor's dull fence, have marr'd it now,)[1]

---

[1] The Castle of Turnberry, on the coast of Ayrshire, was the property of Robert Bruce, in right of his mother. Lord Hailes mentions the following remarkable circumstance concerning the mode in which he became proprietor of it:—" Martha, Countess of Carrick in her own right, the wife of Robert Bruce, Lord of Annandale, bare him a son, afterwards Robert I. (11th July, 1274.) The circumstances of her marriage were singular: happening to meet Robert Bruce in her domains, she became enamoured of him, and with some violence led him to her castle of Turnberry. A few days after she married him, without the knowledge of the relations of either party, and without the requisite consent of the king. The king instantly seized her castle and whole estates. She afterwards atoned by a fine for her feudal delinquency. Little did Alexander foresee, that, from

But then, soft swept in velvet green
The plain with many a glade between,
Whose tangled alleys far invade
The depth of the brown forest shade.
Here the tall fern obscured the lawn,
Fair shelter for the sportive fawn;
There, tufted close with copsewood green,
Was many a swelling hillock seen;

---

this union, the restorer of the Scottisn monarcny was to arise."—
*Annals of Scotland*, vol. ii. p. 180.  The same obliging correspondent, whom I have quoted in the preceding note, gives me
the following account of the present state of the ruins of Turnberry:—"Turnberry Point is a rock projecting into the sea; the
top of it is about eighteen feet above high-water mark.  Upon
this rock was built the castle.  There is about twenty-five feet
high of the wall next to the sea yet standing.  Upon the land-
side the wall is only about four feet high; the length has been
sixty feet, and the breadth forty-five.  It was surrounded by a
ditch, but that is now nearly filled up.  The top of the ruin,
rising between forty and fifty feet above the water, has a majestic
appearance from the sea.  There is not much local tradition in
the vicinity connected with Bruce or his history.  In front,
however, of the rock, upon which stands Culzean Castle, is the
mouth of a romantic cavern, called the Cove of Colean, in which
it is said Bruce and his followers concealed themselves immediately after landing, till they arranged matters for their farther
enterprises.  Burns mentions it in the poem of Hallowe'en.  The
only place to the south of Turnberry worth mentioning, with
reference to Bruce's history, is the Weary Nuik, a little romantic
green hill, where he and his party are said to have rested, after
assaulting the castle."

Around the Castle of Turnberry was a level plain of about
two miles in extent, forming the castle park.  There could be
nothing, I am informed, more beautiful than the copsewood and
verdure of this extensive meadow, before it was invaded by the
ploughshare

And all around was verdure meet
For pressure of the fairies' feet.
The glossy holly loved the park,
The yew-tree lent its shadow dark,
And many an old oak, worn and bare,
With all its shiver'd boughs, was there.
Lovely between, the moonbeams fell
On lawn and hillock, glade and dell.
The gallant Monarch sigh'd to see
These glades so loved in childhood free,
Bethinking that, as outlaw now,
He ranged beneath the forest bough.

## XX.

Fast o'er the moonlight Chase they sped.
Well knew the band that measured tread,
When, in retreat or in advance,
The serried warriors move at once;
And evil were the luck, if dawn
Descried them on the open lawn.
Copses they traverse, brooks they cross,
Strain up the bank and o'er the moss.
From the exhausted page's brow
Cold drops of toil are streaming now;
With effort faint and lengthen'd pause,
His weary step the stripling draws.
"Nay, droop not yet!" the warrior said;
"Come, let me give thee ease and aid!
Strong are mine arms, and little care
A weight so slight as thine to bear.—
What! wilt thou not?—capricious boy!—
Then thine own limbs and strength employ.
Pass but this night, and pass thy care,
I'll place thee with a lady fair,

Where thou shalt tune thy lute to tell
How Ronald loves fair Isabel!"
Worn out, dishearten'd, and dismay'd,
Here Amadine let go the plaid;
His trembling limbs their aid refuse,
He sunk among the midnight dews!

## XXI.

What may be done?—the night is gone—
The Bruce's band moves swiftly on—
Eternal shame, if at the brunt
Lord Ronald grace not battle's front!—
'See yonder oak, within whose trunk
Decay a darken'd cell hath sunk;
Enter, and rest thee there a space,
Wrap in my plaid thy limbs, thy face.
I will not be, believe me, far;
But must not quit the ranks of war.
Well will I mark the bosky bourne,
And soon, to guard thee hence, return.—
Nay, weep not so, thou simple boy!
But sleep in peace, and wake in joy."
In sylvan lodging close bestow'd,
He placed the page, and onward strode
With strength put forth, o'er moss and brook,
And soon the marching band o'ertook.

## XXII.

Thus strangely left, long sobb'd and wept
The page, till, wearied out, he slept—
A rough voice waked his dream—"Nay, here,
Here by this thicket, pass'd the deer—

Beneath that oak old Ryno staid —
What have we here? — a Scottish plaid,
And in its folds a stripling laid? —
Come forth! thy name and business tell! —
What, silent? — then I guess thee well,
The spy that sought old Cuthbert's cell,
Wafted from Arran yester morn —
Come, comrades, we will straight return.
Our Lord may choose the rack should teach
To this young lurcher use of speech.
Thy bow-string, till I bind him fast." —
"Nay, but he weeps and stands aghast;
Unbound we 'll lead him, fear it not;
'T is a fair stripling, though a Scot."
The hunters to the castle sped,
And there the hapless captive led.

## XXIII.

Stout Clifford in the castle-court
Prepared him for the morning sport;
And now with Lorn held deep discourse,
Now gave command for hound and horse.
War-steeds and palfreys paw'd the ground,
And many a deer-dog howl'd around.
To Amadine, Lorn's well-known word
Replying to that Southern Lord,
Mix'd with this clanging din, might seem
The phantasm of a fever'd dream.
The tone upon his ringing ears
Came like the sounds which fancy hears,
When in rude waves or roaring winds
Some words of woe the muser finds,

Until more loudly and more near,
Their speech arrests the page's ear.

### XXIV.

" And was she thus," said Clifford, " lost ?
The priest should rue it to his cost !
What says the monk ?"—" The holy Sire
Owns, that in masquer's quaint attire,
She sought his skiff, disguised, unknown
To all except to him alone.
But, says the priest, a bark from Lorn
Laid them aboard that very morn,
And pirates seized her for their prey.
He proffer'd ransom-gold to pay,
And they agreed—but ere told o'er,
The winds blow loud, the billows roar;
They sever'd, and they met no more.
He deems—such tempest vex'd the coast—
Ship, crew, and fugitive, were lost.
So let it be, with the disgrace
And scandal of her lofty race !
Thrice better she had ne'er been born,
Than brought her infamy on Lorn !"

### XXV.

Lord Clifford now the captive spied ;—
" Whom, Herbert, hast thou there ?" he cried,
" A spy we seized within the Chase,
A hollow oak his lurking place."—
" What tidings can the youth afford?"—
" He plays the mute."—" Then noose a cord—
Unless brave Lorn reverse the doom
For his plaid's sake."—" Clan-Colla's loom,"

Said Lorn, whose careless glances trace
Rather the vesture than the face,
" Clan-Colla's dames such tartans twine ;
Wearer nor plaid claim care of mine.
Give him, if my advice you crave,
His own scathed oak ; and let him wave
In air, unless, by terror wrung,
, frank confession find his tongue.—
Nor shall he die without his rite ;
—Thou, Angus Roy, attend the sight,
And give Clan-Colla's dirge thy breath,
As they convey him to his death."—
" O brother ! cruel to the last ! "
Through the poor captive's bosom pass'd
The thought, but, to his purpose true,
He said not, though he sigh'd, " Adieu ! "

### XXVI.

And will he keep his purpose still,
In sight of that last closing ill,
When one poor breath, one single word,
May freedom, safety, life, afford ?
Can he resist the instinctive call,
For life that bids us barter all ?—
Love, strong as death, his heart hath steel'd,
His nerves hath strung—he will not yield !
Since that poor breath, that little word,
May yield Lord Ronald to the sword.—
Clan-Colla's dirge is pealing wide,
The grisly headsman 's by his side ;
Along the greenwood Chase they bend,
And now their march has ghastly end !
That old and shatter'd oak beneath,
They destine for the place of death

—What thoughts are his, while all in vain
His eye for aid explores the plain?
What thoughts, while, with a dizzy ear,
He hears the death-prayer mutter'd near?
And must he die such death accurst,
Or will that bosom-secret burst?
Cold on his brow breaks terror's dew,
His trembling lips are livid blue;
The agony of parting life
Has nought to match that moment's strife!

### XXVII.

But other witnesses are nigh,
Who mock at fear, and death defy!
Soon as the dire lament was play'd,
It waked the lurking ambuscade.
The Island Lord look'd forth, and spied
The cause, and loud in fury cried,
" By Heaven they lead the page to die,
And mock me in his agony!
They shall abye it!"—On his arm
Bruce laid strong grasp, " They shall not harm
A ringlet of the stripling's hair ;
But, till I give the word, forbear.
—Douglas, lead fifty of our force
Up yonder hollow water-course,
And couch thee midway on the wold,
Between the flyers and their hold:
A spear above the copse display'd,
Be signal of the ambush made.
—Edward, with forty spearmen, straight
Through yonder copse approach the gate,
And, when thou hear'st the battle-din,
Rush forward, and the passage win,

Secure the drawbridge — storm the port,
And man and guard the castle-court.—
The rest move slowly forth with me,
In shelter of the forest-tree,
Till Douglas at his post I see."

### XXVIII.

Like war-horse eager to rush on,
Compell'd to wait the signal blown,
Hid, and scarce hid, by greenwood bough,
Trembling with rage, stands Ronald now,
And in his grasp his sword gleams blue,
Soon to be dyed with deadlier hue.—
Meanwhile the Bruce, with steady eye,
Sees the dark death-train moving by,
And heedful measures oft the space,
The Douglas and his band must trace,
Ere they can reach their destined ground.
Now sinks the dirge's wailing sound,
Now cluster round the direful tree
That slow and solemn company,
While hymn mistuned and mutter'd prayer
The victim for his fate prepare.—
What glances o'er the greenwood shade?
The spear that marks the ambuscade!—
"Now, noble Chief! I leave thee loose;
Upon them, Ronald!" said the Bruce.

### XXIX.

"The Bruce, the Bruce!" to well-known cry
His native rocks and woods reply.
"The Bruce, the Bruce!" in that dread word
The knell of hundred deaths was heard.

15 *

The astonish'd Southern gazed at first,
Where the wild tempest was to burst,
That waked in that presaging name.
Before, behind, around it came!
Half-arm'd, surprised, on every side
Hemm'd in, hew'd down, they bled and died.
Deep in the ring the Bruce engaged,
And fierce Clan-Colla's broadsword raged!
Full soon the few who fought were sped,
Nor better was their lot who fled,
And met, 'mid terror's wild career,
The Douglas's redoubted spear!
Two hundred yeomen on that morn
The castle left, and none return.

## XXX.

Not on their flight press'd Ronald's brand,
A gentler duty claim'd his hand.
He raised the page, where on the plain
His fear had sunk him with the slain:
And twice, that morn, surprise well near
Betray'd the secret kept by fear;
Once, when, with life returning, came
To the boy's lip Lord Ronald's name,
And hardly recollection drown'd
The accents in a murmuring sound;
And once, when scarce he could resist
The Chieftain's care to loose the vest,
Drawn tightly o'er his labouring breast.
But then the Bruce's bugle blew,
For martial work was yet to do.

## XXXI.

A harder task fierce Edward waits.
Ere signal given, the castle gates
 His fury had assail'd;
Such was his wonted reckless mood,
Yet desperate valour oft made good,
Even by its daring, venture rude,
 Where prudence might have fail'd.
Upon the bridge his strength he threw,
And struck the iron chain in two,
 By which its planks arose;
The warder next his axe's edge
Struck down upon the threshold ledge,
'Twixt door and post a ghastly wedge!
 The gate they may not close.
Well fought the Southern in the fray,
Clifford and Lorn fought well that day,
But stubborn Edward forced his way
 Against a hundred foes.
Loud came the cry, "The Bruce, the Bruce!"
No hope or in defence or truce,
 Fresh combatants pour in;
Mad with success, and drunk with gore,
They drive the struggling foe before
 And ward on ward they win.
Unsparing was the vengeful sword,
And limbs were lopp'd and life-blood pour'd,
The cry of death and conflict roar'd,
 And fearful was the din!
The startling horses plunged and flung,
Clamour'd the dogs till turrets rung
 Nor sunk the fearful cry,

e e

Till not a foeman was there found
Alive, save those who on the ground
    Groan'd in their agony![1]

### XXXII.

The valiant Clifford is no more;[2]
On Ronald's broadsword stream'd his gore.
But better hap had he of Lorn,
Who, by the foemen backward borne,
Yet gain'd with slender train the port,
Where lay his bark beneath the fort,
    And cut the cable loose.
Short were his shrift in that debate,
That hour of fury and of hate,
    If Lorn encounter'd Bruce!
Then long and loud the victor shout
From turret and from tower rung out,
    The rugged vaults replied;
And from the donjon tower on high,
The men of Carrick may descry
Saint Andrew's cross, in blazonry
    Of silver, waving wide!

---

[1] [The concluding stanza of "The Siege of Corinth" contains an obvious, though, no doubt, an unconscious imitation of the preceding nine lines, magnificently expanded through an extent of about thirty couplets: —

    "All the living things that heard
    That deadly earth-shock disappear'd;
    The wild birds flew; the wild dogs fled,
    And howling left the unburied dead;
    The camels from their keepers broke;
    The distant steer forsook the yoke—
    The nearer steed plunged o'er the plain,
    And burst his girth, and tore his rein," &c.]

[In point of fact, Clifford fell at Bannockburn.]

### XXXIII.

The Bruce hath won his father's hall![1]
—"Welcome, brave friends and comrades all,
   Welcome to mirth and joy!
The first, the last, is welcome here,
From lord and chieftain, prince and peer,
   To this poor speechless boy.
Great God! once more my sire's abode
Is mine—behold the floor I trode
   In tottering infancy!
And there the vaulted arch, whose sound
Echoed my joyous shout and bound
In boyhood, and that rung around
   To youth's unthinking glee!
O first, to thee, all-gracious Heaven,
Then to my friends, my thanks be given!"—
He paused a space, his brow he cross'd—
Then on the board his sword he toss'd,
Yet steaming hot; with Southern gore
From hilt to point 'twas crimson'd o'er.

### XXXIV.

"Bring here," he said, "the mazers four,
My noble fathers loved of yore.[2]
Thrice let them circle round the board,
The pledge, fair Scotland's rights restored!
And he whose lip shall touch the wine,
Without a vow as true as mine,
To hold both lands and life at nought,
Until her freedom shall be bought,—

---

[1] [See Appendix, Note R.]      [2] [See Appendix, Note S.]

Be brand of a disloyal Scot,
And lasting infamy his lot!
Sit, gentle friends! our hour of glee
Is brief, we 'll spend it joyously!
Blithest of all the sun's bright beams,
When betwixt storm and storm he gleams.
Well is our country's work begun,
But more, far more, must yet be done.
Speed messengers the country through;
Arouse old friends, and gather new;[1]
Warn Lanark's knights to gird their mail,
Rouse the brave sons of Teviotdale,
Let Ettrick's archer  sharp their darts,
The fairest forms, the truest hearts![2]

---

[1] As soon as it was known in Kyle, says ancient tradition, that Robert Bruce had landed in Carrick, with the intention of recovering the crown of Scotland, the Laird of Craigie, and forty-eight men in his immediate neighbourhood, declared in favour of their legitimate prince.  Bruce granted them a tract of land, still retained by the freemen of Newton to this day.  The original charter was lost when the pestilence was raging at Ayr; but it was renewed by one of the Jameses, and is dated at Faulkland. The freemen of Newton were formerly officers by rotation.  The Provost of Ayr at one time was a freeman of Newton, and it happened to be his turn, while provost in Ayr, to be officer in Newton, both of which offices he discharged at the same time.

[2] The forest of Selkirk, or Ettrick, at this period, occupied all the district which retains that denomination, and embraced the neighbouring dales of Tweeddale, and at least the Upper Ward of Clydesdale.  All that tract was probably as waste as it is mountainous, and covered with the remains of the ancient Caledonian Forest, which is supposed to have stretched from Cheviot Hills as far as Hamilton, and to have comprehended even a part of Ayrshire.  At the fatal battle of Falkirk, Sir John Stewart of Bonkill, brother to the Steward of Scotland  commanded the

Call all, call all! from Reedswair-Path,
To the wild confines of Cape-Wrath;
Wide let the news through Scotland ring,
The Northern Eagle claps his wing!"

---

archers of Selkirk Forest, who fell around the dead body of their leader.   The English historians have commemorated the tall and stately persons, as well as the unswerving faith, of these forest-ers.   Nor has their interesting fall escaped the notice of an elegant modern poetess, whose subject led her to treat of that calamitous engagement.

> "The glance of the morn had sparkled bright
> On their plumage green and their actons light;
> The bugle was strung at each hunter's side,
> As they had been bound to the chase to ride;
> But the bugle is mute, and the shafts are spent,
> The arm unnerved and the bow unbent,
> And the tired forester is laid
> Far, far from the clustering greenwood shade!
> Sore have they toil'd—they are fallen asleep,
> And their slumber is heavy, and dull, and deep!
> When over their bones the grass shall wave,
> When the wild winds over their tombs shall rave,
> Memory shall lean on their graves, and tell
> How Selkirk's hunters bold around old Stewart fell!"
>
> WALLACE, *or the Fight of Falkirk,* [by Miss HOLFORD,
> Lond. 4to, 1809, pp. 170, 1.

# LORD OF THE ISLES

## CANTO SIXTH.

THE

# LORD OF THE ISLES.

## CANTO SIXTH.

O WHO, that shared them, ever shall forget
The emotions of the spirit-rousing time,
When breathless in the mart the couriers met.
Early and late, at evening and at prime;
When the loud cannon and the merry chime
Hail'd news on news, as field on field was won,
When Hope, long doubtful, soar'd at length sublime,
And our glad eyes, awake as day begun,
Watch'd Joy's broad banner rise, to meet the rising
    sun!

O these were hours, when thrilling joy repaid
A long, long course of darkness, doubts, and fears!
The heart-sick faintness of the hope delay'd,
The waste, the woe, the bloodshed, and the tears,
That track'd with terror twenty rolling years,
All was forgot in that blithe jubilee!
Her downcast eye even pale Affliction rears,
To sigh a thankful prayer, amid the glee,
That hail'd the Despot's fall, and peace and liberty!

Such news o'er Scotland's hills triumphant rode,
When 'gainst the invaders turn'd the battle's scale,
When Bruce's banner had victorious flow'd

O'er Loudoun's mountain, and in Ury's vale;[1]
When English blood oft deluged Douglas-dale[2]
And fiery Edward routed stout St. John,[3]
When Randolph's war-cry swell'd the southern gale,[4]

---

[1] The first important advantage gained by Bruce, after landing
at Turnberry, was over Aymer de Valence, Earl of Pembroke,
the same by whom he had been defeated near Methven. They
met, as has been said, by appointment, at Loudonhill, in the west
of Scotland. Pembroke sustained a defeat; and from that time
Bruce was at the head of a considerable flying army. Yet he
was subsequently obliged to retreat into Aberdeenshire, and was
there assailed by Comyn, Earl of Buchan, desirous to avenge the
death of his relative, the Red Comyn, and supported by a body
of English troops under Philip de Moubray. Bruce was ill at
the time of a scrofulous disorder, but took horse to meet his enemies, although obliged to be supported on either side. He was
victorious, and it is said that the agitation of his spirits restored
his health.

[2] [See Appendix, Note T.]

[3] "John de St. John, with 15,000 horsemen, had advanced to
oppose the inroad of the Scots. By a forced march he endeavoured to surprise them, but intelligence of his motions was
timeously received. The courage of Edward Bruce, approaching to temerity, frequently enabled him to achieve what men of
more judicious valour would never have attempted. He ordered
the infantry, and the meaner sort of his army, to intrench themselves in strong narrow ground. He himself, with fifty horsemen well harnessed, issued forth under cover of a thick mist,
surprised the English on their march, attacked and dispersed
them."— DALRYMPLE'S *Annals of Scotland, quarto, Edinburgh,*
1779, p. 25.

[4] Thomas Randolph, Bruce's sister's son, a renowned Scottish
chief, was in the early part of his life not more remarkable for
consistency than Bruce himself. He espoused his uncle's party
when Bruce first assumed the crown, and was made prisoner at
the fatal battle of Methven, in which his relative's hopes appeared to be ruined. Randolph accordingly not only submitted to the

And many a fortress, town, and tower, was won,
And Fame still sounded forth fresh deeds of glory done.

### II.

Blithe tidings flew from baron's tower,
To peasant's cot, to forest-bower,
And waked the solitary cell,
Where lone Saint Bride's recluses dwell.
Princess no more, fair Isabel,
   A vot'ress of the order now,
Say, did the rule that bid thee wear,
Dim veil and woollen scapulare,
And reft thy locks of dark-brown hair,
   That stern and rigid vow,
Did it condemn the transport high,
Which glisten'd in thy watery eye,
When minstrel or when palmer told
Each fresh exploit of Bruce the bold?—
And whose the lovely form that shares
Thy anxious hopes, thy fears, thy prayers?
No sister she of convent shade;
So say these locks in lengthen'd braid,

---

English, but took an active part against Bruce, appeared in arms
against him, and in the skirmish where he was so closely pursued by the bloodhound, it is said his nephew took his standard
with his own hand.   But Randolph was afterwards made prisoner
by Douglas in Tweeddale, and brought before King Robert.
Some harsh language was exchanged between the uncle and
nephew, and the latter was committed for a time to close custody.
Afterwards, however, they were reconciled, and Randolph was
created Earl of Moray about 1312.   After this period he emi-
nently distinguished himself, first by the surprise of Edinburgh
Castle, and afterwards by many similar enterprises, conducted
with equal courage and ability.

16 *

So say the blushes and the sighs,
The tremors that unbidden rise,
When, mingled with the Bruce's fame,
The brave Lord Ronald's praises came.

### III.

Believe, his father's castle won,
And his bold enterprise begun,
That Bruce's earliest cares restore
The speechless page to Arran's shore:
Nor think that long the quaint disguise
Conceal'd her from a sister's eyes;
And sister-like in love they dwell
In that lone convent's silent cell.
There Bruce's slow assent allows
Fair Isabel the veil and vows;
And there, her sex's dress regain'd,
The lovely Maid of Lorn remain'd,
Unnamed, unknown, while Scotland far
Resounded with the din of war;
And many a month, and many a day,
In calm seclusion wore away.

### IV.

These days, these months, to years had worn,
When tidings of high weight were borne
        To that lone island's shore;
Of all the Scottish conquests made
By the first Edward's ruthless blade,
        His son retain'd no more,
Northward of Tweed, but Stirling's towers,
Beleaguer'd by King Robert's powers;
        And they took term of truce,[1]

---

[1] When a long train of success, actively improved by Robert

If England's King should not relieve
The siege ere John the Baptist's eve,
   To yield them to the Bruce.
England was roused—on every side
Courier and post and herald hied,
   To summon prince and peer,
At Berwick-bounds to meet their Liege,[1]
Prepared to raise fair Stirling's siege,
   With buckler, brand, and spear.

---

Bruce, had made him master of almost all Scotland, Stirling
Castle continued to hold out. The care of the blockade was
committed by the king to his brother Edward, who concluded a
treaty with Sir Philip Mowbray, the governor, that he should
surrender the fortress, if it were not succoured by the King of
England before St. John the Baptist's day. The King severely
blamed his brother for the impolicy of a treaty, which gave time
to the King of England to advance to the relief of the castle with
all his assembled forces, and obliged himself either to meet them
in battle with an inferior force, or to retreat with dishonour.
" Let all England come," answered the reckless Edward, " we
will fight them were they more." The consequence was, of
course, that each kingdom mustered its strength for the expected
battle ; and as the space agreed upon reached from Lent to Mid-
summer, full time was allowed for that purpose.

  [1] There is printed in Rymer's Fœdera the summons issued
upon this occasion to the sheriff of York ; and he mentions eighteen
other persons to whom similar ordinances were issued. It seems
to respect the infantry alone, for it is entitled, *De peditibus ad
recussum Castri de Stryvelin a Scotis obsessi, properare facien-
dis.* This circumstance is also clear from the reasoning of the
writ, which states: " We have understood that our Scottish enemies and rebels are endeavouring to collect as strong a force as
possible of infantry, in strong and marshy grounds, where the
approach of cavalry would be difficult, between us and the castle
of Stirling."—It then sets forth Mowbray's agreement to surrender the castle, if not relieved before St. John the Baptist's day,

The term was nigh—they muster'd fast,
By beacon and by bugle-blast
   Forth marshall'd for the field;
There rode each knight of noble name,
There England's hardy archers came,
The land they trode seem'd all on flame,
   With banner, blade, and shield!
And not famed England's powers alone,
Renown'd in arms, the summons own;
   For Neustria's knights obey'd,
Gascogne hath lent her horsemen good,
And Cambria, but of late subdued,
Sent forth her mountain-multitude,[1]

---

and the king's determination, with divine grace, to raise the
siege. "Therefore," the summons further bears, "to remove
our said enemies and rebels from such places as above mentioned, it is necessary for us to have a strong force of infantry fit
for arms." And accordingly the sheriff of York is commanded
to equip and send forth a body of four thousand infantry, to be
assembled at Werk, upon the tenth day of June first, under pain
of the royal displeasure, &c.

[1] Edward the First, with the usual policy of a conqueror, employed the Welsh, whom he had subdued, to assist him in his
Scottish wars, for which their habits, as mountaineers, particularly fitted them. But this policy was not without its risks.
Previous to the battle of Falkirk, the Welsh quarrelled with the
English men-at-arms, and after bloodshed on both parts, separated
themselves from his army, and the feud between them, at so dangerous and critical a juncture, was reconciled with difficulty.
Edward II. followed his father's example in this particular, and
with no better success. They could not be brought to exert
themselves in the cause of their conquerors. But they had an
indifferent reward for their forbearance. Without arms, and clad
only in scanty dresses of linen cloth, they appeared naked in the
eyes even of the Scottish peasantry; and after the rout of Ban-

And Connoght pour'd from waste and wood
Her hundred tribes, whose sceptre rude
    Dark Eth O'Connor sway'd.[1]

### V.

Right to devoted Caledon
The storm of war rolls slowly on,
    With menace deep and dread;
So the dark clouds, with gathering power,
Suspend awhile the threaten'd shower,
Till every peak and summit lower
    Round the pale pilgrim's head.
Not with such pilgrim's startled eye
King Robert mark'd the tempest nigh!
    Resolved the brunt to bide,
His royal summons warn'd the land,
That all who own'd their King's command
Should instant take the spear and brand,
    To combat at his side.
O who may tell the sons of fame,
That at King Robert's bidding came,
    To battle for the right!
From Cheviot to the shores of Ross,
From Solway-Sands to Marshal's-Moss,
    All boun'd them for the fight.
Such news the royal courier tells,
Who came to rouse dark Arran's dells;
But farther tidings must the ear
Of Isabel in secret hear.

---

nockburn, were massacred by them in great numbers, as they
retired in confusion towards their own country. They were
under command of Sir Maurice de Berkeley.

    [1][See Appendix, Note U.]
f f

These in her cloister walk, next morn,
Thus shared she with the Maid of Lorn.

### VI.

" My Edith, can I tell how dear
Our intercourse of hearts sincere
    Hath been to Isabel? —
Judge then the sorrow of my heart,
When I must say the words, We part!
    The cheerless convent-cell
Was not, sweet maiden, made for thee;
Go thou where thy vocation free
    On happier fortunes fell.
Nor, Edith, judge thyself betray'd,
Though Robert knows that Lorn's high Maid
And his poor silent page were one.
Versed in the fickle heart of man,
Earnest and anxious hath he look'd
How Ronald's heart the message brook'd
That gave him, with her last farewell,
The charge of Sister Isabel,
To think upon thy better right,
And keep the faith his promise plight.
Forgive him for thy sister's sake,
At first if vain repinings wake —
    Long since that mood is gone:
Now dwells he on thy juster claims,
And oft his breach of faith he blames —
    Forgive him for thine own!"—

### VII.

" No! never to Lord Ronald's bower
Will I again as paramour"——

" Nay, hush thee, too impatient maid,
Until my final tale be said! —
The good King Robert would engage
Edith once more his elfin page,
By her own heart, and her own eye,
Her lover's penitence to try —
Safe in his royal charge, and free,
Should such thy final purpose be,
Again unknown to seek the cell,
And live and die with Isabel."
Thus spoke the maid—King Robert's eye
Might have some glance of policy;
Dunstaffnage had the monarch ta'en,
And Lorn had own'd King Robert's reign:
Her brother had to England fled,
And there in banishment was dead;
Ample, through exile, death, and flight,
O'er tower and land was Edith's right;
This ample right o'er tower and land
Were safe in Ronald's faithful hand.

### VIII.

Embarrass'd eye and blushing cheek
Pleasure and shame, and fear bespeak!
Yet much the reasoning Edith made:
" Her sister's faith she must upbraid,
Who gave such secret, dark and dear,
In council to another's ear.
Why should she leave the peaceful cell? —
How should she part with Isabel? —
How wear that strange attire agen?
How risk herself 'midst martial men? —

And how be guarded on the way?—
At least she might entreat delay."
Kind Isabel, with secret smile,
Saw and forgave the maiden's wile.
Reluctant to be thought to move
At the first call of truant love.

### IX.

Oh, blame her not!—when zephyrs wake,
The aspen's trembling leaves must shake;
When beams the sun through April's shower,
It needs must bloom, the violet flower;
And Love, howe'er the maiden strive,
Must with reviving hope revive!
A thousand soft excuses came,
To plead his cause 'gainst virgin shame.
Pledged by their sires in earliest youth,
He had her plighted faith and truth—
Then, 'twas her Liege's strict command,
And she, beneath his royal hand,
A ward in person and in land:—
And, last, she was resolved to stay
Only brief space—one little day—
Close hidden in her safe disguise
From all, but most from Ronald's eyes—
But once to see him more!—nor blame
Her wish—to hear him name her name!—
Then, to bear back to solitude
The thought, he had his falsehood rued!
But Isabel, who long had seen
Her pallid cheek and pensive mien,
And well herself the cause might know,
Though innocent, of Edith's woe,

Joy'd, generous, that revolving time
Gave means to expiate the crime.
High glow'd her bosom as she said,
" Well shall her sufferings be repaid ! "
Now came the parting hour—a band
From Arran's mountains left the land;
Their chief, Fitz-Louis,[1] had the care
The speechless Amadine to bear
To Bruce, with honour, as behoved
To page the monarch dearly loved.

### X.

The King had deem'd the maiden bright
Should reach him long before the fight,
But storms and fate her course delay:
It was on eve of battle-day,
When o'er the Gillie's-hill she rode.
The landscape like a furnace glow'd,
And far as e'er the eye was borne,
The lances waved like autumn-corn.
In battles four beneath their eye,
The forces of King Robert lie.[2]
And one below the hill was laid,
Reserved for rescue and for aid;

---

[1] Fitz-Louis, or Mac-Louis, otherwise called Fullarton, is a family of ancient descent in the Isle of Arran. They are said to be of French origin, as the name intimates. They attached themselves to Bruce upon his first landing; and Fergus Mac-Louis, or Fullarton, received from the grateful monarch a charter, dated 26th November, in the second year of his reign (1307), for the lands of Kilmichel, and others, which still remain in this very ancient and respectable family.

[2] [See Appendix, Note V.]

And three, advanced, form'd vaward-line,
'Twixt Bannock's brook and Ninian's shrine.
Detach'd was each, yet each so nigh
As well might mutual aid supply.
Beyond, the Southern host appears,[1]
A boundless wilderness of spears,
Whose verge or rear the anxious eye
Strove far, but strove in vain, to spy.
Thick flashing in the evening beam,
Glaives, lances, bills, and banners gleam;
And where the heaven join'd with the hill,
Was distant armour flashing still,
So wide, so far, the boundless host
Seem'd in the blue horizon lost.

---

[1] Upon the 23d June, 1314, the alarm reached the Scottish army of the approach of the enemy. Douglas and the Marshal were sent to reconnoitre with a body of cavalry;

> " And soon the great host have they seen,
> Where shields shining were so sheen,
> And basinets burnished bright,
> That gave against the sun great light.
> They saw so fele* brawdyne† baners,    *Many.* †*Displayed*
> Standards and pennons and spears,
> And so fele knights upon steeds,
> All flaming in their weeds.
> And so fele bataills, and so broad,
> And too so great room as they rode,
> That the maist host, and the stoutest
> Of Christendom, and the greatest,
> Should be abaysit for to see
> Their foes into such quantity."

*The Bruce,* vol ii. p. 111.

The two Scottish commanders were cautious in the account which they brought back to their camp. To the king in private they told the formidable state of the enemy; but in public reported that the English were indeed a numerous host, but ill commanded and worse disciplined.

## XI.

Down from the hill the maiden pass'd,
At the wild show of war aghast;
And traversed first the rearward host,
Reserved for aid where needed most.
The men of Carrick and of Ayr,
Lennox and Lanark too, were there,
  And all the western land;
With these the valiant of the Isles
Beneath their chieftains rank'd their files,
  In many a plaided band.
There, in the centre, proudly raised,
The Bruce's royal standard blazed,
And there Lord Ronald's banner bore
A galley driven by sail and oar.
A wild, yet pleasing contrast, made
Warriors in mail and plate array'd,
With the plumed bonnet and the plaid
  By these Hebrideans worn;
But O! unseen for three long years,
Dear was the garb of mountaineers
  To the fair maid of Lorn!
For one she look'd — but he was far
Busied amid the ranks of war —
Yet with affection's troubled eye
She mark'd his banner boldly fly,
Gave on the countless foe a glance,
And thought on battle's desperate chance.

## XII.

To centre of the vaward line
Fitz-Louis guided Amadine.

---

[1] [See Appendix, Note W.]

Arm'd all on foot, that host appears
A serried mass of glimmering spears.
There stood the Marchers' warlike band,
The warriors there of Lodon's land;
Ettrick and Liddell bent the yew,
A band of archers fierce, though few;
The men of Nith and Annan's vale,
And the bold spears of Teviotdale; —
The dauntless Douglas these obey,
And the young Stuart's gentle sway.
North-eastward by Saint Ninian's shrine,
Beneath fierce Randolph's charge, combine
The warriors whom the hardy North
From Tay to Sutherland sent forth.
The rest of Scotland's war-array
With Edward Bruce to westward lay,
Where Bannock, with his broken bank
And deep ravine, protects their flank.
Behind them, screen'd by sheltering wood,
The gallant Keith, Lord Marshal, stood
His men-at-arms bear mace and lance,
And plumes that wave, and helms that glance.
Thus fair divided by the King,
Centre, and right, and left-ward wing,
Composed his front; nor distant far
Was strong reserve to aid the war.
And 'twas to front of this array,
Her guide and Edith made their way.

### XIII.

Here must they pause; for, in advance
As far as one might pitch a lance,

The Monarch rode along the van,[1]
The foe's approaching force to scan,
His line to marshal and to range,
And ranks to square, and fronts to change.
Alone he rode—from head to heel
Sheathed in his ready arms of steel;
Nor mounted yet on war-horse wight,
But, till more near the shock of fight,
Reining a palfrey low and light.
A diadem of gold was set
Above his bright steel basinet,
And clasp'd within its glittering twine
Was seen the glove of Argentine;
Truncheon or leading staff he lacks
Bearing, instead, a battle-axe.
He ranged his soldiers for the fight,
Accoutred thus, in open sight
Of either host.—Three bowshots far,
Paused the deep front of England's war,
And rested on their arms awhile,
To close and rank their warlike file,
And hold high council, if that night
Should view the strife, or dawning light.

### XIV.

O gay, yet fearful to behold,
Flashing with steel and rough with gold,
    And bristled o'er with bills and spears,
With plumes and pennons waving fair,
Was that bright battle-front! for there
    Rode England's King and peers:

---

[1] [See Appendix, Note X.]

17 *

And who, that saw that monarch ride,
His kingdom battled by his side,
Could then his direful doom foretell!—
Fair was his seat in knightly selle,
And in his sprightly eye was set
Some spark of the Plantagenet.
Though light and wandering was his glance,
It flash'd at sight of shield and lance.
"Know'st thou," he said, "De Argentine,
Yon knight who marshals thus their line?"—
"The tokens on his helmet tell
The Bruce, my Liege: I know him well."—
"And shall the audacious traitor brave
The presence where our banners wave?"—
"So please my Liege," said Argentine,
"Were he but horsed on steed like mine,
To give him fair and knightly chance,
I would adventure forth my lance."—
"In battle-day," the King replied,
"Nice tourney rules are set aside.
—Still must the rebel dare our wrath?
Set on him—sweep him from our path!"
And, at King Edward's signal, soon
Dash'd from the ranks Sir Henry Boune.

### XV.

Of Hereford's high blood he came,
A race renown'd for knightly fame.
He burn'd before his Monarch's eye
To do some deed of chivalry.
He spurr'd his steed, he couch'd his lance,
And darted on the Bruce at once.
—As motionless as rocks, that bide
The wrath of the advancing tide,

The Bruce stood fast.—Each breast beat high,
And dazzled was each gazing eye—
The heart had hardly time to think,
The eyelid scarce had time to wink,
While on the King, like flash of flame,
Spurr'd to full speed the war-horse came!
The partridge may the falcon mock,
If that slight palfrey stand the shock—
But, swerving from the Knight's career,
Just as they met, Bruce shunn'd the spear.
Onward the baffled warrior bore
His course—but soon his course was o'er!—
High in his stirrups stood the King,
And gave his battle-axe the swing.
Right on De Boune, the whiles he pass'd,
Fell that stern dint—the first—the last!—
Such strength upon the blow was put,
The helmet crash'd like hazel-nut;
The axe-shaft, with its brazen clasp,
Was shiver'd to the gauntlet grasp.
Springs from the blow the startled horse,
Drops to the plain the lifeless corse;
—First of that fatal field, how soon,
How sudden, fell the fierce De Boune!

### XVI.

One pitying glance the Monarch sped,
Where on the field his foe lay dead;
Then gently turn'd his palfrey's head,
And, pacing back his sober way,
Slowly he gain'd his own array.
There round their King the leaders crowd,
And blame his recklessness aloud.

That risk'd 'gainst each adventurous spear
A life so valued and so dear.
His broken weapon's shaft survey'd
The King, and careless answer made,—
" My loss may pay my folly's tax;
I've broke my trusty battle-axe."
'Twas then Fitz-Louis, bending low,
Did Isabel's commission show;
Edith, disguised, at distance stands,
And hides her blushes with her hands.
The monarch's brow has changed its hue,
Away the gory axe he threw,
While to the seeming page he drew,
　　Clearing war's terrors from his eye.
Her hand with gentle ease he took,
With such a kind protecting look,
　　As to a weak and timid boy
Might speak, that elder brother's care
And elder brother's love were there.

### XVII.

" Fear not," he said, " young Amadine !"
Then whisper'd, " Still that name be thine.
Fate plays her wonted fantasy,
Kind Amadine, with thee and me,
And sends thee here in doubtful hour.
But soon we are beyond her power;
For on this chosen battle-plain,
Victor or vanquish'd, I remain.
Do thou to yonder hill repair;
The followers of our host are there,
And all who may not weapons bear.—
Fitz-Louis, have him in thy care.—

Joyful we meet, if all go well;
If not, in Arran's holy cell
Thou must take part with Isabel;
For brave Lord Ronald, too, hath sworn,
Not to regain the Maid of Lorn,
(The bliss on earth he covets most,)
Would he forsake his battle-post,
Or shun the fortune that may fall
To Bruce, to Scotland, and to all.—
But, hark! some news these trumpets tell;
Forgive my haste—farewell—farewell."—
And in a lower voice he said,
" Be of good cheer—farewell, sweet maid!".—

### XVIII.

" What train of dust, with trumpet-sound
And glimmering spears, is wheeling round
Our leftward flank?"[1]—the Monarch cried,
To Moray's Earl who rode beside.
" Lo! round thy station pass the foes!
Randolph, thy wreath has lost a rose."
The Earl his visor closed, and said,
" My wreath shall bloom, or life shall fade.—
Follow, my household!"—And they go
Like lightning on the advancing foe.
" My Liege," said noble Douglas then,
" Earl Randolph has but one to ten:
Let me go forth his band to aid!"—
—" Stir not. The error he hath made,
Let him amend it as he may;
I will not weaken mine array."

---

[1] [See Appendix, Note Y.]

g g

Then loudly rose the conflict-cry,
And Douglas's brave heart swell'd high,—
"My Liege," he said, "with patient ear
I must not Moray's death-knell hear!"—
Forth sprung the Douglas with his train.
But when they won a rising hill,
He bade his followers hold them still.—
"See, see! the routed Southern fly!
The Earl hath won the victory.
Lo! where yon steeds run masterless,
His banner towers above the press.
Rein up; our presence would impair
The fame we come too late to share."
Back to the host the Douglas rode,
And soon glad tidings are abroad,
That, Dayncourt by stout Randolph slain,
His followers fled with loosen'd rein.—
That skirmish closed the busy day,
And couch'd in battle's prompt array,
Each army on their weapons lay.

### XIX.

It was a night of lovely June,
High rode in cloudless blue the moon,
 Demayet smiled beneath her ray;
Old Stirling's towers arose in light,
And, twined in links of silver bright,
 Her winding river lay.
Ah, gentle planet! other sight
Shall greet thee, next returning night,
Of broken arms and banners tore,
And marshes dark with human gore,
And piles of slaughter'd men and horse,
And Forth that floats the frequent corse.

And many a wounded wretch to plain
Beneath thy silver light in vain!
But now, from England's host, the cry
Thou hear'st of wassail revelry,
While from the Scottish legions pass
The murmur'd prayer, the early mass!—
Here, numbers had presumption given;
There, bands o'er-match'd sought aid from Heaven.

### XX.

On Gillie's-hill, whose height commands
The battle-field, fair Edith stands,
With serf and page unfit for war,
To eye the conflict from afar.
O! with what doubtful agony
She sees the dawning tint the sky!—
Now on the Ochils gleams the sun,
And glistens now Demayet dun;
    Is it the lark that carols shrill,
    Is it the bittern's early hum?
No!—distant, but increasing still,
    The trumpet's sound swells up the hill,
    With the deep murmur of the drum.
Responsive from the Scottish host,
Pipe-clang and bugle-sound were toss'd,[1]
His breast and brow each soldier cross'd,

---

[1] There is an old tradition, that the well-known Scottish tune of "Hey, tutti taitti," was Bruce's march at the battle of Bannockburn. The late Mr. Ritson, no granter of propositions, doubts whether the Scots had any martial music, quotes Froissart's account of each soldier in the host bearing a little horn, on which, at the onset, they would make such a horrible noise, as if all the devils of hell had been among them. He observes, that

And started from the ground;
Arm'd and array'd for instant fight,
Rose archer, spearman, squire and knight,
And in the pomp of battle bright
    The dread battalia frown'd.


## XXI.

Now onward, and in open view,
The countless ranks of England drew,[1]

---

these horns are the only music mentioned by Barbour, and concludes, that it must remain a moot point whether Bruce's army
were cheered by the sound even of a solitary bagpipe.—*Historical Essay prefixed to Ritson's Scottish Songs.* It may be
observed in passing, that the Scottish of this period certainly
observed some musical cadence, even in winding their horns,
since Bruce was at once recognised by his followers from his
mode of blowing. See note X. on canto iv. But the tradition,
true or false, has been the means of securing to Scotland one of
the finest lyrics in the language, the celebrated war-song of
Burns,—" Scots, wha hae wi' Wallace bled."

[1] Upon the 24th of June, the English army advanced to the
attack. The narrowness of the Scottish front, and the nature of
the ground, did not permit them to have the full advantage of
their numbers, nor is it very easy to find out what was their proposed order of battle. The vanguard, however, appeared a dis-
tinct body, consisting of archers and spearmen on foot, and commanded, as already said, by the Earls of Gloucester and Hereford.
Barbour, in one place, mentions that they formed nine BATTLES,
or divisions; but from the following passage, it appears that there
was no room or space for them to extend themselves, so that,
except the vanguard, the whole army appeared to form one solid
and compact body : —

> "The English men, on either party,
> That as angels shone brightly,
> Were not arrayed on such manner,
> For all their battles samyn[1] were
> [1] Together.

Dark rolling like the ocean-tide,
When the rough west hath chafed his pride,
And his deep roar sends challenge wide
    To all that bars his way!
In front the gallant archers trode,
The men-at-arms behind them rode,
And midmost of the phalanx broad
    The Monarch held his sway.
Beside him many a war-horse fumes,
Around him waves a sea of plumes,

---

> In a schiltrum.[1]  But whether it was
> Through the great straitness of the place
> That they were in, to bide fighting;
> Or that it was for abaysing;[2]
> I wete not.  But in a schiltrum
> It seemed they were all and some;
> Out ta'en the vaward anerly,[3]
> That right with a great company,
> Be them selwyn, arrayed were.
> Who had been by, might have seen there
> That folk ourtake a mekill feild
> On breadth, where many a shining shield,
> And many a burnished bright armour,
> And many a man of great valour,
> Might in that great schiltrum be seen:
> And many a bright banner and sheen."
>
> > BARBOUR'S *Bruce*, vol ii. p. 137.

[1] *Schiltrum.*—This word has been variously limited or extended in its signification  In geneial, it seems to imply a large body of men drawn up very closely together.  But it has been limited to imply a round or circular body of men so drawn up.  I cannot understand it with this limitation in the present case.  The schiltrum of the Scottish army at Falkirk was undoubtedly of a circular form, in order to resist the attacks of the English cavalry, on whatever quarter they might be charged  But it does not appear how, or why, the English advancing to the attack at Bannockburn, should have arrayed themselves in a circular form.  It seems more probable, that, by *Schiltrum* in the present case, Barbour means to express an irregular mass into which the English army was compressed by the unwieldiness of its numbers, and the carelessness or ignorance of its leaders.

[2] Frightening                                    [3] Alone.

Where many a knight in battle known,
And some who spurs had first braced on,
And deem'd that fight should see them won,
    King Edward's hests obey.
De Argentine attends his side,
With stout De Valence, Pembroke's pride,
Selected champions from the train,
To wait upon his bridle-rein.
Upon the Scottish foe he gazed—
—At once, before his sight amazed,
    Sunk banner, spear, and shield;
Each weapon-point is downward sent,
Each warrior to the ground is bent.
" The rebels, Argentine, repent!
    For pardon they have kneel'd."—
" Ay!—but they bend to other powers,
And other pardon sue than ours!
See where yon barefoot Abbot stands,
And blesses them with lifted hands![1]
Upon the spot where they have kneel'd,
These men will die, or win the field."—
—" Then prove we if they die or win!
Bid Gloster's Earl the fight begin."

---

[1] " Maurice, abbot of Inchaffray, placing himself on an eminence, celebrated mass in sight of the Scottish army. He then passed along the front, bare-footed, and bearing a crucifix in his hands, and exhorting the Scots in few and forcible words, to combat for their rights and their liberty. The Scots kneeled down. ' They yield,' cried Edward; ' see, they implore mercy.'—' They do,' answered Ingelram de Umfraville, ' but not ours. On that field they will be victorious, or die.' " — *Annals of Scotland,* vol. II. p. 47.

## XXII.

Earl Gilbert waved his truncheon high,
 Just as the Northern ranks arose,
Signal for England's archery
 To halt and bend their bows.
Then stepp'd each yeoman forth a pace,
Glanced at the intervening space,
 And raised his left hand high;
To the right ear the cords they bring—
—At once ten thousand bow-strings ring,
 Ten thousand arrows fly!
Nor paused on the devoted Scot
The ceaseless fury of their shot;
 As fiercely and as fast,
Forth whistling came the grey-goose wing
As the wild hailstones pelt and ring
 Adown December's blast.
Nor mountain targe of tough bull-hide,
Nor lowland mail, that storm may bide;
Woe, woe to Scotland's banner'd pride,
 If the fell shower may last!
Upon the right, behind the wood,
Each by his steed dismounted, stood
 The Scottish chivalry;—
—With foot in stirrup, hand on mane,
Fierce Edward Bruce can scarce restrain
His own keen heart, his eager train,
Until the archers gain'd the plain;
 Then, " Mount, ye gallants free!"
He cried; and, vaulting from the ground,
His saddle every horseman found.
On high their glittering crests they toss,
As springs the wild-fire from the moss;

The shield hangs down on every breast,
Each ready lance is in the rest,
 And loud shouts Edward Bruce,—
"Forth, Marshal, on the peasant foe!
We'll tame the terrors of their bow,
 And cut the bow-string loose!"[1]

### XXIII.

Then spurs were dash'd in chargers' flanks,
They rush'd among the archer ranks.
No spears were there the shock to let,
No stakes to turn the charge were set,
And how shall yeoman's armour slight
Stand the long lance and mace of might?
Or what may their short swords avail,
'Gainst barbed horse and shirt of mail?
Amid their ranks the chargers sprung,
High o'er their heads the weapons swung,
And shriek and groan and vengeful shout
Give note of triumph and of rout!
Awhile, with stubborn hardihood,
Their English hearts the strife made good:
Borne down at length on every side,
Compell'd to flight they scatter wide.—
Let stags of Sherwood leap for glee,
And bound the deer of Dallom-Lee!
The broken bows of Bannock's shore
Shall in the greenwood ring no more!
Round Wakefield's merry may-pole now,
The maids may twine the summer bough,
May northward look with longing glance,
For those that wont to lead the dance,

---

[1] [See Appendix, Note Z.]

For the blithe archers look in vain!
Broken, dispersed, in flight o'erta'en,
Pierced through, trod down, by thousands slain,
They cumber Bannock's bloody plain.

### XXIV.

The King with scorn beheld their flight.
"Are these," he said, "our yeomen wight?
Each braggart churl could boast before,
Twelve Scottish lives his baldric bore![1]
Fitter to plunder chase or park,
Than make a manly foe their mark.—
Forward, each gentleman and knight!
Let gentle blood show generous might
And chivalry redeem the fight!"
To rightward of the wild affray,
The field show'd fair and level way;
   But, in mid-space, the Bruce's care

---

[1] Roger Ascham quotes a similar Scottish proverb, "whereby they give the whole praise of shooting honestly to Englishmen, saying thus, 'that every English archer beareth under his girdle twenty-four Scottes.' Indeed Toxophilus says before, and truly of the Scottish nation, 'The Scottes surely be good men of warre in theyre owne feates as can be; but as for shootinge, they can neither use it to any profite, nor yet challenge it for any praise.'" —*Works of Ascham, edited by Bennet*, 4to, p. 110.

It is said, I trust incorrectly, by an ancient English historian, that the "good Lord James of Douglas" dreaded the superiority of the English archers so much, that when he made any of them prisoner, he gave him the option of losing the forefinger of his right hand, or his right eye, either species of mutilation rendering him incapable to use the bow. I have mislaid the reference to this singular passage.

18 *

Had bored the earth with many a pit,
With turf and brushwood hidden yet,
    That form'd a ghastly snare.
Rushing, ten thousand horsemen came,
With spears in rest, and hearts on flame,
    That panted for the shock!
With blazing crests and banners spread,
And trumpet-clang and clamour dread,
The wide plain thunder'd to their tread,
    As far as Stirling rock.
Down! down! in headlong overthrow,
Horseman and horse, the foremost go,[1]
    Wild floundering on the field!
The first are in destruction's gorge,
Their followers wildly o'er them urge;—
    The knightly helm and shield,
The mail, the acton, and the spear,
Strong hand, high heart, are useless here!
Loud from the mass confused the cry
Of dying warriors swells on high,
And steeds that shriek in agony![2]

---

[1] It is generally alleged by historians, that the English men-at-arms fell into the hidden snare which Bruce had prepared for them. Barbour does not mention the circumstance. According to his account, Randolph, seeing the slaughter made by the cavalry on the right wing among the archers, advanced courageously against the main body of the English, and entered into close combat with them. Douglas and Stuart, who commanded the Scottish centre, led their division also to the charge, and the battle becoming general along the whole line, was obstinately maintained on both sides for a long space of time; the Scottish archers doing great execution among the English men-at-arms, after the bowmen of England were dispersed.

[2] I have been told that this line requires an explanatory note;

They came like mountain-torrent red,
That thunders o'er its rocky bed;
They broke like that same torrent's wave,[1]
When swallow'd by a darksome cave.
Billows on billows burst and boil,
Maintaining still the stern turmoil,
And to their wild and tortured groan
Each adds new terrors of his own!

### XXV.

Too strong in courage and in might
Was England yet, to yield the fight.
   Her noblest all are here;
Names that to fear were never known,
Bold Norfolk's Earl De Brotherton,
   And Oxford's famed De Vere.
There Gloster plied the bloody sword,
And Berkley, Grey, and Hereford,

---

and, indeed, those who witness the silent patience with which horses submit to the most cruel usage, may be permitted to doubt, that, in moments of sudden or intolerable anguish, they utter a most melancholy cry. Lord Erskine, in a speech made in the House of Lords, upon a bill for enforcing humanity towards animals, noticed this remarkable fact, in language which I will not mutilate by attempting to repeat it. It was my fortune, upon one occasion, to hear a horse, in a moment of agony, utter a thrilling scream, which I still consider the most melancholy sound I ever heard.

[1] [It is impossible not to recollect our author's own lines —

"As Bracklinn's chasm, so black and steep,
  Receives her roaring linn,
As the dark caverns of the deep
  Suck the wild whirlpool in;
So did the deep and darksome pass
Devour the battle's mingled mass."
      *Lady of the Lake*, Canto vi. stanza 18.]

Bottetourt and Sanzavere,
Ross, Montague, and Mauley, came,
And Courtenay's pride, and Percy's fame—
Names known too well in Scotland's war,
At Falkirk, Methven, and Dunbar,
Blazed broader yet in after years,
At Cressy red and fell Poitiers.
Pembroke with these, and Argentine,
Brought up the rearward battle-line.
With caution o'er the ground they tread,
Slippery with blood and piled with dead,
Till hand to hand in battle set,
The bills with spears and axes met,
And, closing dark on every side,
Raged the full contest far and wide.
Then was the strength of Douglas tried,
Then proved was Randolph's generous pride,
And well did Stewart's actions grace
The sire of Scotland's royal race!
    Firmly they kept their ground;
As firmly England onward press'd,
And down went many a noble crest,
And rent was many a valiant breast,
    And Slaughter revell'd round.

### XXVI.

Unflinching foot 'gainst foot was set,
Unceasing blow by blow was met;
    The groans of those who fell
Were drown'd amid the shriller clang,
That from the blades and harness rang,
    And in the battle-yell.
Yet fast they fell, unheard, forgot,
Both Southern fierce and hardy Scot;

And O! amid that waste of life,
What various motives fired the strife!
The aspiring Noble bled for fame,
The Patriot for his country's claim;
This Knight his youthful strength to prove,
And that to win his lady's love;
Some fought from ruffian thirst of blood,
From habit some, or hardihood.
But ruffian stern, and soldier good,
 The noble and the slave,
From various cause the same wild road,
On the same bloody morning, trode,
 To that dark inn, the Grave![1]

## XXVII.

The tug of strife to flag begins,
Though neither loses yet nor wins.
High rides the sun, thick rolls the dust,
And feebler speeds the blow and thrust.
Douglas leans on his war-sword now,
And Randolph wipes his bloody brow;
Nor less had toil'd each Southern knight,
From morn till mid-day in the fight.
Strong Egremont for air must gasp,
Beauchamp undoes his visor clasp,
And Montague must quit his spear,
And sinks thy falchion, bold De Vere!
The blow of Berkley fall less fast,
And gallant Pembroke's bugle-blast
 Hath lost its lively tone;

---

[1] [" All these, life's rambling journey done,
 Have found their home, the grave."—
      Cowper.]

h h

Sinks, Argentine, thy battle-word,
And Percy's shout was fainter heard,
 "My merry-men, fight on!"

### XXVIII.

Bruce, with the pilot's wary eye,
The slackening of the storm could spy.
 "One effort more, and Scotland's free!
Lord of the Isles, my trust in thee
  Is firm as Ailsa Rock;
Rush on with Highland sword and targe,
I, with my Carrick spearmen, charge;[1]
  Now, forward to the shock!"
At once the spears were forward thrown,
Against the sun the broadswords shone:
The pibroch lent its maddening tone,
And loud King Robert's voice was known—
"Carrick, press on—they fail, they fail!
Press on, brave sons of Innisgail,
  The foe is fainting fast!
Each strike for parent, child, and wife,
For Scotland, liberty, and life,—
  The battle cannot last!"

---

[1] When the engagement between the main bodies had lasted some time, Bruce made a decisive movement, by bringing up the Scottish reserve. It is traditionally said, that at this crisis, he addressed the Lord of the Isles in a phrase used as a motto by some of his descendants, "My trust is constant in thee." Barbour intimates, that the reserve "assembled on one field," that is, on tne same line with the Scottish forces already engaged; which leads Lord Hailes to conjecture that the Scottish ranks must have been much thinned by slaughter, since, in that circumscribed ground, there was room for the reserve to fall into the line. But the advance of the Scottish cavalry must have contributed a good deal to form the vacancy occupied by the reserve.

## XXIX.

The fresh and desperate onset bore
The foes three furlongs back and more,
Leaving their noblest in their gore.
 Alone, De Argentine
Yet bears on high his red-cross shield,
Gathers the relics of the field,
Renews the ranks where they have reel'd,
 And still makes good the line.
Brief strife, but fierce, his efforts raise,
A bright but momentary blaze.
Fair Edith heard the Southern shout,
Beheld them turning from the rout,
Heard the wild call their trumpets sent,
In notes 'twixt triumph and lament.
That rallying force, combined anew,
Appear'd in her distracted view,
 To hem the Islesmen round;
"O God! the combat they renew,
 And is no rescue found!
And ye that look thus tamely on,
And see your native land o'erthrown
O! are your hearts of flesh or stone?"

## XXX.

The multitude that watch'd afar,
Rejected from the ranks of war,
Had not unmoved beheld the fight,
When strove the Bruce for Scotland's right;
Each heart had caught the patriot spark,
Old man and stripling, priest and clerk,
Bondsman and serf; even female hand
Stretch'd to the hatchet or the brand:

But, when mute Amadine they heard
Give to their zeal his signal-word,
        A frenzy fired the throng;
" Portents and miracles impeach
Our sloth—the dumb our duties teach—
And he that gives the mute his speech,
        Can bid the weak be strong.
To us, as to our lords, are given
A native earth, a promised heaven;
To us, as to our lords, belongs
The vengeance for our nation's wrongs;
The choice, 'twixt death or freedom, warms
Our breasts as theirs—To arms, to arms!"
To arms they flew,—axe, club, or spear,—
And mimic ensigns high they rear,[1]
And, like a banner'd host afar,
Bear down on England's wearied war.

## XXXI.

Already scatter'd o'er the plain,
Reproof, command, and counsel vain,
The rearward squadrons fled amain,
        Or made but doubtful stay;—
But when they mark'd the seeming show
Of fresh and fierce and marshall'd foe,
        The boldest broke array.
O give their hapless prince his due![2]
In vain the royal Edward threw
        His person 'mid the spears,
Cried " Fight!" to terror and despair,
Menaced, and wept, and tore his hair,

[See Appendix, Note A 2.]        [2][See Appendix, Note B 2.]

And cursed their caitiff fears;
Till Pembroke turn'd his bridle rein,
And forced him from the fatal plain.
With them rode Argentine, until
They gain'd the summit of the hill,
But quitted there the train:—
"In yonder field a gage I left,—
I must not live of fame bereft;
 I needs must turn again.
Speed hence, my Liege, for on your trace
The fiery Douglas takes the chase,
 I know his banner well.
God send my Sovereign joy and bliss,
And many a happier field than this!—
 Once more, my Liege, farewell."

## XXXII.

Again he faced the battle-field,—
Wildly they fly, are slain, or yield.
"Now then," he said, and couch'd his spear
"My course is run, the goal is near;
One effort more, one brave career,
 Must close this race of mine."
Then in his stirrups rising high,
He shouted loud his battle-cry,
 "Saint James for Argentine!"
And, of the bold pursuers, four
The gallant knight from saddle bore;
But not unharm'd — a lance's point
Has found his breastplate's loosen'd joint,
 An axe has razed his crest;
Yet still on Colonsay's fierce lord,
Who press'd the chase with gory sword,

He rode with spear in rest,
And through his bloody tartans bored,
And through his gallant breast.
Nail'd to the earth, the mountaineer
Yet writhed him up against the spear,
And swung his broadsword round!
— Stirrup, steel-boot, and cuish gave way,
Beneath that blow's tremendous sway,
The blood gush'd from the wound;
And the grim Lord of Colonsay
Hath turn'd him on the ground,
And laugh'd in death-pang, that his blade
The mortal thrust so well repaid.

### XXXIII.

Now toil'd the Bruce, the battle done,
To use his conquest boldly won;
And gave command for horse and spear
To press the Southern's scatter'd rear,
Nor let his broken force combine;
—When the war-cry of Argentine
Fell faintly on his ear;
"Save, save his life," he cried, " O save
The kind, the noble, and the brave!"
The squadrons round free passage gave,
The wounded knight drew near;
He raised his red-cross shield no more,
Helm, cuish, and breastplate stream'd with gore
Yet, as he saw the King advance,
He strove even then to couch his lance—
The effort was in vain!
The spur-stroke fail'd to rouse the horse;
Wounded and weary, in mid course
He stumbled on the plain.

Then foremost was the generous Bruce
To raise his head, his helm to loose;—
　　"Lord Earl, the day is thine!
My Sovereign's charge, and adverse fate,
Have made our meeting all too late:
　　Yet this may Argentine,
As boon from ancient comrade, crave—
A Christian's mass, a soldier's grave."

### XXXIV.

Bruce press'd his dying hand—its grasp
Kindly replied; but, in his clasp,
　　It stiffen'd and grew cold—
"And, O farewell!" the victor cried,
"Of chivalry the flower and pride,
　　The arm in battle bold,
The courteous mien, the noble race,
The stainless faith, the manly face!—
Bid Ninian's convent light their shrine,
For late-wake of De Argentine.
O'er better knight on death-bier laid,
Torch never gleam'd nor mass was said!"

### XXXV.

Nor for De Argentine alone,
Through Ninian's church these torches shone,
And rose the death-prayer's awful tone.[1]
That yellow lustre glimmer'd pale,
On broken plate and bloodied mail,
Rent crest and shatter'd coronet,
Of Baron, Earl, and Banneret;
And the best names that England knew,
Claim'd in the death-prayer dismal due.

---

[1] [See Appendix, Note C 2.]

Yet mourn not, Land of Fame!
Though ne'er the leopards on thy shield
Retreated from so sad a field,
    Since Norman William came.
Oft may thine annals justly boast
Of battles stern by Scotland lost;
    Grudge not her victory,
When for her freeborn rights she strove;
Rights dear to all who freedom love,
    To none so dear as thee!

### XXXVI.

Turn we to Bruce, whose curious ear
Must from Fitz-Louis tidings hear;
With him, a hundred voices tell
Of prodigy and miracle,
    "For the mute page had spoke."—
"Page!" said Fitz-Louis, "rather say,
An angel sent from realms of day,
    To burst the English yoke.
I saw his plume and bonnet drop,
When hurrying from the mountain top;
A lovely brow, dark locks that wave,
To his bright eyes new lustre gave,
A step as light upon the green,
As if his pinions waved unseen!"—
"Spoke he with none?"—"With none—one word
Burst when he saw the Island Lord,
Returning from the battle-field."—
"What answer made the Chief?"—"He kneel'd,
Durst not look up, but mutter'd low
Some mingled sounds that none might know,
And greeted him, 'twixt joy and fear,
As being of superior sphere."

## XXXVII.

Even upon Bannock's bloody plain,
Heap'd then with thousands of the slain,
'Mid victor monarch's musings high,
Mirth laugh'd in good King Robert's eye.
" And bore he such angelic air,
Such noble front, such waving hair?
Hath Ronald kneel'd to him?" he said,
" Then must we call the church to aid—
Our will be to the Abbot known,
Ere these strange news are wider blown,
To Cambuskenneth straight ye pass,
And deck the church for solemn mass,
To pay for high deliverance given,
A nation's thanks to gracious Heaven.
Let him array, besides, such state,
As should on princes' nuptials wait.
Ourself the cause, through fortune's spite,
That once broke short that spousal rite,
Ourself will grace, with early morn,
The bridal of the Maid of Lorn."[1]

---

[1] [" *To Mr. James Ballantyne.*—Dear Sir,—You have now the whole affair, excepting two or three concluding stanzas. As your taste for bride's cake may induce you to desire to know more of the wedding, I will save you some criticism by saying, I have settled to stop short as above.—Witness my hand,

19 *                                              " W. S."]

# CONCLUSION.

Go forth, my Song, upon thy venturous way;
Go boldly forth; nor yet thy master blame,
Who chose no patron for his humble lay,
And graced thy numbers with no friendly name,
Whose partial zeal might smooth thy path to fame.
*There was* — and O! how many sorrows crowd
Into these two brief words!—*there was* a claim
By generous friendship given — had fate allow'd,
It well had bid thee rank the proudest of the proud!

All angel now—yet little less than all,
While still a pilgrim in our world below!
What 'vails it us that patience to recall,
Which hid its own to soothe all other woe;
What 'vails to tell, how Virtue's purest glow
Shone yet more lovely in a form so fair:[1]
And, least of all, what 'vails the world should know,
That one poor garland, twined to deck thy hair,
Is hung upon thy hearse, to droop and wither there!

---

[1] [The reader is referred to Mr. Hogg's "Pilgrims of the Sun"
for some beautiful lines, and a highly interesting note, on the
death of the Duchess of Buccleuch. See *ante*, p. 10.]

# APPENDIX

## TO THE

# LORD OF THE ISLES

# APPENDIX.

---

## NOTE A.

*Thy rugged halls, Artornish! rung.*— P. 21.

THE ruins of the Castle of Artornish are situated upon a promontory, on the Morven, or mainland side of the Sound of Mull, a name given to the deep arm of the sea, which divides that island from the continent. The situation is wild and romantic in the highest degree, having on the one hand a high and precipitous chain of rocks overhanging the sea, and on the other the narrow entrance to the beautiful salt-water lake, called Loch Alline, which is in many places finely fringed with copsewood. The ruins of Artornish are not now very considerable, and consist chiefly of the remains of an old keep, or tower, with fragments of outward defences. But, in former days, it was a place of great consequence, being one of the principal strongholds which the Lords of the Isles, during the period of their stormy independence, possessed upon the mainland of Argyleshire. Here they assembled what popular tradition calls their parliaments, meaning, I suppose, their *cour pléniere*, or assembly of feudal and patriarchal vassals and dependants. From this Castle of Artornish, upon the 19th day of October, 1461, John de Yle, designing himself Earl of Ross and Lord of the Isles, granted, in the style of an independent sovereign, a commission to his trusty and well-beloved cousins, Ronald of the Isles, and Duncan, Arch-Dean of the Isles, for empowering them to enter into a treaty with the most excellent Prince Edward, by the grace of God, King of France and England, and Lord of Ireland. Edward IV., on his part, named Laurence, Bishop of Durham, the Earl of Worcester, the Prior of St. John's, Lord Wenlock, and Mr. Robert Stillington, keeper of the privy seal, his deputies and commissioners, to confer with those named by the Lord of the Isles. The conference terminated in a treaty, by which the Lord of the Isles

agreed to become a vassal to the crown of England, and to assist
Edward IV. and James Earl of Douglas, then in banishment, in
subduing the realm of Scotland.

The first article provides, that John de Isle, Earl of Ross, with
his son Donald Balloch, and his grandson John de Isle, with all
their subjects, men, people, and inhabitants, become vassals and
liegemen to Edward IV. of England, and assist him in his wars
in Scotland or Ireland; and then follow the allowances to be made
to the Lord of the Isles, in recompense of his military service,
and the provisions for dividing such conquests as their united
arms should make upon the mainland of Scotland among the con-
federates. These appear such curious illustrations of the period,
that they are here subjoined:

" *Item*, The seid John Erle of Rosse shall, from the seid fest
of Whittesontyde next comyng, yerely, during his lyf, have and
take, for fees and wages in tyme of peas, of the seid most high
and Christien prince c. mark sterlyng of Englysh money; and in
tyme of werre, as long as he shall entende with his myght and
power in the said werres, in manner and fourm abovesaid, he
shall have wages of cc. lb. sterlyng of English money yearly,
and after the rate of the tyme that he shall be occupied in the
seid werres.

" *Item*, The seid Donald shall, from the seid feste of Whittesontyde, have and take, during his lyf, yerly, in tyme of peas,
for his fees and wages, xx l. sterlyng of Englysh money; and,
when he shall be occupied and intend to the werre, with his
myght and power, and in manner and fourme aboveseid, he shall
have and take, for his wages yearly, xl l. sterlynge of Englysh
money; or for the rate of the tyme of werre ——

" *Item*, The seid John, sonn and heire apparant of the said
Donald, shall have and take, yerely, from the seid fest, for his
fees and wages, in the tyme of peas, x l. sterlynge of Englysh
money; and for tyme of werre, and his intendyng thereto, in
manner and fourme aboveseid, he shall have, for his fees and
wages, yearly xx l. sterlynge of English money; or after the
rate of the tyme that he shall be occupied in the werre: And
the seid John, th' Erle Donald and John, and eche of them, shall
have good and sufficiaunt paiment of the seid fees and wages,
as wel for tyme of peas as of werre, accordyng to thees articules

and appoyntements. *Item*, it is appointed, accorded, concluded.
and finally determined, that, if it be so that hereafter the seid
reaume of Scotlande, or the more part thereof, be conquered,
subdued, and brought to the obeissance of the seid most high and
Christien prince, and his heires, or successoures, of the seid
Lionell, in fourme aboveseid descendyng, be the assistance, helpe,
and aide of the seid John Erle of Rosse, and Donald, and of James
Erle of Douglas, then, the seid fees and wages for the tyme of
peas cessying, the same erles and Donald shall have, by the
graunte of the same most Christien prince, all the possessions
of the seid reaume beyonde Scottishe see, they to be departed
equally betwix them : eche of them, his heires and successours,
to hold his parte of the seid most Christien prince, his heires and
successours, for evermore, in right of his croune of England, by
homage and feaute to be done therefore.

"*Item*, If so be that, by th' aide and assistence of the seid
James Erle of Douglas, the saide reaume of Scotlande be conquered and subdued as above, then he shall have, enjoie, and
inherite all his own possessions, landes, and inheritance, on this
syde the Scottish see ; that is to saye, betwixt the seid Scottishe
see and Englande, such he hath rejoiced and be possessed of before this ; there to holde them of the seid most high and Christien prince, his heires, and successours, as is abovesaid, for evermore, in right of the coroune of Englonde, as weel the seid
Erle of Douglas, as his heires and successours, by homage and
feaute to be done therefore." — RYMER's *Fœdera Conventiones
Literæ et cujuscunque generis Acta Publica*, fol. vol. v., 1741.

Such was the treaty of Artornish ; but it does not appear that
the allies ever made any very active effort to realize their ambi-
tious designs. It will serve to show both the power of these
reguli, and their independence upon the crown of Scotland.

It is only farther necessary to say of the Castle of Artornish,
that it is almost opposite to the Bay of Aros, in the Island of
Mull, where there was another castle, the occasional residence
of the Lord of the Isles.

## Note B.

*—— Mingarry sternly placed,*
*O'erawes the woodland and the waste.* — P. 27.

The Castle of Mingarry is situated on the sea-coast of the district of Ardnamurchan. The ruins, which are tolerably entire, are surrounded by a very high wall, forming a kind of polygon, for the purpose of adapting itself to the projecting angles of a precipice overhanging the sea, on which the castle stands. It was anciently the residence of the Mac-Ians, a clan of Mac-Donalds, descended from Ian, or John, a grandson of Angus Og, Lord of the Isles. The last time that Mingarry was of military importance, occurs in the celebrated Leabhar dearg, or Red-book of Clanronald, a MS. renowned in the Ossianic controversy. Allaster Mac-Donald, commonly called Colquitto, who commanded the Irish auxiliaries, sent over by the Earl of Antrim during the great civil war to the assistance of Montrose, began his enterprise in 1644, by taking the castles of Kinloch-Alline, and Mingarry, the last of which made considerable resistance, as might, from the strength of the situation, be expected. In the meanwhile, Allaster Mac-Donald's ships, which had brought him over, were attacked in Loch Eisord, in Skye, by an armament sent round by the covenanting parliament, and his own vessel was taken. This circumstance is said chiefly to have induced him to continue in Scotland, where there seemed little prospect of raising an army in behalf of the king. He had no sooner moved eastward to join Montrose, a junction which he effected in the braes of Athole, than the Marquis of Argyle besieged the castle of Mingarry, but without success. Among other warriors and chiefs whom Argyle summoned to his camp to assist upon this occasion, was John of Moidart, the Captain of Clanronald. Clanronald appeared; but, far from yielding effectual resistance to Argyle, he took the opportunity of being in arms to lay waste the district of Sunart, then belonging to the adherents of Argyle, and sent part of the spoil to relieve the Castle of Mingarry. Thus the castle was maintained until relieved by Allaster Mac-Donald (Colquitto), who had been detached for the purpose by Montrose. These particulars are hardly worth mentioning, were they not connected with the memorable successes of Montrose, related by an eyewitness, and hitherto unknown to Scottish historians.

## Note C.

### *Lord of the Isles.* — P. 28.

The representative of this independent principality, for such it seems to have been, though acknowledging occasionally the preeminence of the Scottish crown, was, at the period of the poem, Angus, called Angus Og; but the name has been, *euphoniæ gratia*, exchanged for that of Ronald, which frequently occurs in the genealogy. Angus was a protector of Robert Bruce, whom he received in his Castle of Dunnaverty, during the time of his greatest distress. As I shall be equally liable to censure for attempting to decide a controversy which has long existed between three distinguished chieftains of this family, who have long disputed the representation of the Lord of the Isles, or for leaving a question of such importance altogether untouched, I choose, in the first place, to give such information as I have been able to derive from Highland genealogists, and which, for those who have patience to investigate such subjects, really contains some curious information concerning the history of the Isles. In the second place, I shall offer a few remarks upon the rules of succession at that period, without pretending to decide their bearing upon the question at issue, which must depend upon evidence which I have had no opportunity to examine.

"Angus Og," says an ancient manuscript translated from the Gaelic, "son of Angus Mor, son of Donald, son of Ronald, son of Somerled, high chief and superior Lord of Innisgall, (or the Isles of the Gael, the general name given to the Hebrides,) he married a daughter of Cunbui, namely, Cathan; she was mother to John, son of Angus, and with her came an unusual portion from Ireland, viz. twenty-four clans, of whom twenty-four families in Scotland are descended. Angus had another son, namely, young John Fraoch, whose descendants are called Clan-Ean of Glencoe, and the M'Donalds of Fraoch. This Angus Og died in Isla, where his body was interred. His son John succeeded to the inheritance of Innisgall. He had good descendants, namely, three sons procreate of Ann, daughter of Rodric, high chief of Lorn, and one daughter, Mary, married to John Maclean, Laird of Duart, and Lauchlan, his brother, Laird of Coll; she was

interred in the church of the Black Nuns.   The eldest sons of
John were Ronald, Godfrey, and Angus.  .  .  .  .  He gave
Ronald a great inheritance.   These were the lands which he
gave him, viz. from Kilcumin in Abertarf to the river Seil, and
from thence to Beilli, north of Eig and Rum, and the two Uists,
and from thence to the foot of the river Glaichan, and threescore
long ships.  John married afterwards Margaret Stewart, daughter
to Robert Stewart, King of Scotland, called John Fernyear; she
bore him three good sons, Donald of the Isles, the heir, John the
Tainister, (*i. e.* Thane,) the second son, and Alexander Carrach.
John had another son called Marcus, of whom the clan Macdonald
of Cnoc. in Tirowen, are descended.   This John lived long, and
made donations to Icolumkill; he covered the chapel of Eorsay-
Elan, the chapel of Finlagam, and the chapel of the Isle of
Tsuibhne, and gave the proper furniture for the service of God,
upholding the clergy and monks; he built or repaired the church
of the Holy Cross immediately before his death.   He died at his
own castle of Ardtornish, many priests and monks took the
sacrament at his funeral, and they embalmed the body of this
dear man, and brought it to Icolumkill; the abbot, monks, and
vicar, came as they ought to meet the King of Piongal,[1] and out
of great respect to his memory mourned eight days and nights
over it, and laid it in the same grave with his father, in the
church of Oran, 1380.

"Ronald, son of John, was chief ruler of the Isles in his father's
lifetime, and was old in the government at his father's death.

"He assembled the gentry of the Isles, brought the sceptre
from Kildonan in Eig, and delivered it to his brother Donald, who
was thereupon called M'Donald, and Donald Lord of the Isles,[2]
contrary to the opinion of the men of the Isles.

"Ronald, son of John, son of Angus Og, was a great supporter
of the church and clergy; his descendants are called Clanronald.
He gave the lands of Tiruma, in Uist, to the minister of it for
ever, for the honour of God and Columkill; he was proprietor of
all the lands of the north along the coast and the isles; he died
in the year of Christ 1386, in his own mansion of Castle Tirim,
leaving five children.   Donald of the Isles, son of John, son of

---

[1] Western Isles and adjacent coast.                [2] Innisgal

Angus Og, the brother of Ronald, took possession of Inisgall by the consent of his brother and the gentry thereof; they were all obedient to him; he married Mary Lesley, daughter to the Earl of Ross, and by her came the earldom of Ross to the M'Donalds. After his succession to that earldom, he was called M'Donald, Lord of the Isles and Earl of Ross. There are many things written of him in other places.

"He fought the battle of Garioch (*i. e.*) Harlaw) against Duke Murdoch, the governor, the Earl of Mar commanded the army, in support of his claim to the earldom of Ross: which was ceded to him by King James the First, after his release from the King of England, and Duke Murdoch, his two sons and retainers, were beheaded: he gave lands in Mull and Isla to the minister of Hi, and every privilege which the minister of Iona had formerly, besides vessels of gold and silver to Columkill for the monastery, and became himself one of the fraternity. He left issue, a lawful heir to Innisgall and Ross, namely, Alexander, the son of Donald: he died in Isla, and his body was interred in the south side of the temple of Oran. Alexander, called John of the Isles, son of Alexander of the Isles, son of Donald of the Isles. Angus, the third son of John, son of Angus Og, married the daughter of John, the son of Allan, which connexion caused some disagreement betwixt the two families about their marches and division of lands, the one party adhering to Angus, and the other to John: the differences increased so much, that John obtained from Allan all the lands betwixt *Abhan Fahda* (*i. e.* the long river) and *old na sionnach* (*i. e.* the fox-burn brook), in the upper part of Cantyre. Allan went to the king to complain of his son-in-law; in a short time thereafter, there happened to be a great meeting about this young Angus's lands to the north of Inverness, where he was murdered by his own harper Mac-Cairbre, by cutting his throat with a long knife. He [1] lived a year thereafter, and many of those concerned were delivered up to the king. Angus's wife was pregnant at the time of his murder, and she bore him a son who was named Donald, and called Donald Du. He was kept in confinement until he was thirty years of age, when he was released by the men of Glenco, by the strong hand. After this

---

[1] The murderer, I presume, not the man who was murdered

enlargement, he came to the Isles, and convened the gentry thereof. There happened great feuds betwixt these families while Donald Du was in confinement, insomuch that Mac-Cean of Ardnamurchan destroyed the greatest part of the posterity of John Mor of the Isles and Cantyre. For John Cathanach, son of John, son of Donald Balloch, son of John Mor, son of John, son of Angus Og (the chief of the descendants of John Mor), and John Mor, son of John Cathanach, and young John, son of John Cathanach, and young Donald Balloch, son of John Cathanach, were treacherously taken by Mac-Cean in the island of Finlagan, in Isla, and carried to Edinburgh, where he got them hanged at the Burrow-muir, and their bodies were buried in the church of St. Anthony, called the New Church. There were none left alive at that time of the children of John Cathanach, except Alexander, the son of John Cathanach, and Agnes Flach, who concealed themselves in the glens of Ireland. Mac-Cean, hearing of their hiding-places, went to cut down the woods of these glens, in order to destroy Alexander, and extirpate the whole race. At length M'Cean and Alexander met, were reconciled, and a marriage alliance took place; Alexander married Mac-Cean's daughter, and she brought him good children. The Mac-Donalds of the north had also descendants; for, after the death of John, Lord of the Isles, and Earl of Ross, and the murder of Angus, Alexander, the son of Archibald, the son of Alexander of the Isles, took possession, and John was in possession of the earldom of Ross, and the north bordering country; he married a daughter of the Earl of Moray, of whom some of the men of the north had descended. The Mac-Kenzies rose against Alexander, and fought the battle called *Blar na Pairc*. Alexander had only a few of the men of Ross at the battle. He went after that battle to take possession of the Isles, and sailed in a ship to the south to see if he could find any of the posterity of John Mor alive, to rise along with him; but Mac-Cean of Ardnamurchan watched him as he sailed past, followed him to Oransay and Colonsay, went to the house where he was, and he and Alexander. son of John Cathanach, murdered him there.

" A good while after these things fell out, Donald Galda, son of Alexander, son of Archibald, became major; he, with the advice and direction of the Earl of Moray, came to the Isles, and

Mac-Leod of the Lewis, and many of the gentry of the Isles, rose with him: they went by the promontory of Ardnamurchan, where they met Alexander, the son of John Cathanach, were reconciled to him, he joined his men with theirs against Mac-Cean of Ardnamurchan, came upon him at a place called the Silver Craig, where he and his three sons, and a great number of his people, were killed, and Donald Galda was immediately declared Mac-Donald: And, after the affair of Ardnamurchan, all the men of the Isles yielded to him, but he did not live above seven or eight weeks after it; he died at Carnaborg, in Mull, without issue. He had three sisters' daughters of Alexander, son of Archibald, who were portioned in the north upon the continent, but the earldom of Ross was kept for them. Alexander, the son of Archibald, had a natural son, called John Cam, of whom is descended Achnacoichan, in Ramoeh, and Donald Gorm, son of Ronald, son of Alexander Duson, of John Cam. Donald Du, son of Angus, son of John of the Isles, son of Alexander of the Isles, son of Donald of the Isles, son of John of the Isles, son of Angus Og, namely, the true heir of the Isles and Ross, came after his release from captivity to the Isles, and convened the men thereof, and he and the Earl of Lennox agreed to raise a great army for the purpose of taking possession, and a ship came from England with a supply of money to carry on the war, which landed at Mull, and the money was given to Mac-Lean of Duart to be distributed among the commanders of the army, which they not receiving in proportion as it should have been distributed among them, caused the army to disperse, which, when the Earl of Lennox heard, he disbanded his own men, and made it up with the King. Mac-Donald went to Ireland to raise men, but he died on his way to Dublin, at Drogheda, of a fever, without issue of either sons or daughters."

In this history may be traced, though the Bard, or Seannachie, touches such a delicate discussion with a gentle hand, the point of difference between the three principal septs descended from the Lords of the Isles. The first question, and one of no easy solution, where so little evidence is produced, respects the nature of the connexion of John, called by the Archdean of the Isles "the Good John of Ila," and "the last Lord of the Isles," with Anne, daughter of Roderick Mac-Dougal, high-chief of Lorn

In the absence of positive evidence, presumptive must be resorted to, and I own it appears to render it in the highest degree improbable that this connexion was otherwise than legitimate. In the wars between David II. and Edward Baliol, John of the Isles espoused the Baliol interest, to which he was probably determined by his alliance with Roderick of Lorn, who was, from every family predilection, friendly to Baliol and hostile to Bruce. It seems absurd to suppose, that between two chiefs of the same descent, and nearly equal power and rank, (though the Mac-Dougals had been much crushed by Robert Bruce,) such a connexion should have been that of concubinage; and it appears more likely that the tempting offer of an alliance with the Bruce family, when they had obtained the decided superiority in Scotland, induced " the good John of Ila" to disinherit, to a certain extent, his eldest son Ronald, who came of a stock so unpopular as the Mac-Dougals, and to call to his succession his younger family, born of Margaret Stuart, daughter of Robert, afterwards King of Scotland. The setting aside of this elder branch of his family, was most probably a condition of his new alliance, and his being received into favour with the dynasty he had always opposed. Nor were the laws of succession at this early period so clearly understood as to bar such transactions. The numerous and strange claims set up to the crown of Scotland, when vacant by the death of Alexander III., make it manifest how very little the indefeasible hereditary right of primogeniture was valued at that period. In fact, the title of the Bruces themselves to the crown, though justly the most popular, when assumed with the determination of asserting the independence of Scotland, was, upon pure principle, greatly inferior to that of Baliol. For Bruce, the competitor, claimed as son of Isabella, *second* daughter of David, Earl of Huntingdon; and John Baliol, as grandson of Margaret, the elder daughter of that same earl. So that the plea of Bruce was founded upon the very loose idea, that as the great grandson of David I., King of Scotland, and the nearest collateral relation of Alexander III.. he was entitled to succeed in exclusion of the great great grandson of the same David, though by an elder daughter. This maxim savoured of the ancient practice of Scotland, which often called a brother to succeed to the crown as nearer in blood than a grand-child, or even a son of a deceased monarch. But, in truth, the maxims of inheritance in Scotland were sometimes departed from at periods when they were much more distinctly understood. Such a transposition took place in the family of Hamilton, in 1513, when the descendants of James, third Lord, by Lady Janet Home, were set aside, with an appanage of great value indeed, in order to call to the succession those which he had by a subsequent marriage with Janet Beatoun. In short, many other examples might be quoted to show that the question of legitimacy is not always determined by the fact of succession; and there seems reason to believe that Ronald, descendant of "John of Ila," by Ann of Lorn, was legitimate, and therefore Lord of the Isles *de jure*, though *de facto* his younger half-brother Donald, son of his father's second marriage with the Princess of Scotland, superseded him in his right, and apparently by his own consent. From this Donald so preferred is descended the family of Sleat, now Lords Mac-Donald. On the other hand, from Ronald, the excluded heir, upon whom a very large appanage was settled, descended the chiefs of Glengary and Clanronald, each of whom had large possessions, and a numerous vassalage, and boasted a long descent of warlike ancestry. Their common ancestor Ronald was murdered by the Earl of Ross, at the Monastery of Elcho, A.D. 1346. I believe it has been subject of fierce dispute, whether Donald, who carried on the line of Glengary, or Allan of Moidart, the ancestor of the captains of Clanronald, was the eldest son of Ronald, the son of John of Isla. A humble Lowlander may be permitted to waive the discussion, since a Sennachie of no small note, who wrote in the sixteenth century, expresses himself upon this delicate topic in the following words: —

"I have now given you an account of every thing you can expect of the descendants of the clan Colla, (*i. e.* the Mac-Donalds,) to the death of Donald Du at Drogheda, namely, the true line of those who possessed the Isles, Ross, and the mountainous countries of Scotland. It was Donald, the son of Angus, that was killed at Inverness, by his own harper (Mac-i'Cairbre,) son of John of the Isles, son of Alexander, son of Donald, son of John, son of Angus Og. And I know not which of his kindred or relations is the true heir, except these five sons of John, the son of Angus Og, whom I here set down for you, namely, Ronald

and Godfrey, the two sons of the daughter of Mac-Donald of
Lorn, and Donald and John Mor, and Alexander Carrach, the
three sons of Margaret Stewart, daughter of Robert Stewart,
King of Scotland."—*Leabhar Dearg*.

## Note D.

#### —— *The House of Lorn.*—P. 31.

The House of Lorn, as we observed in a former note, was, like
the Lord of the Isles, descended from a son of Somerled, slain at
Renfrew, in 1164.  This son obtained the succession of his mainland territories, comprehending the greater part of the three
districts of Lorn, in Argyleshire, and of course might rather be
considered as petty princes than feudal barons.  They assumed
the patronymic appellation of Mac-Dougal, by which they are
distinguished in the history of the middle ages.  The Lord of
Lorn, who flourished during the wars of Bruce, was Allaster (or
Alexander) Mac-Dougal, called Allaster of Argyle.  He had
married the third daughter of John, called the Red Comyn,[1] who
was slain by Bruce in the Dominican Church at Dumfries, and
hence he was a mortal enemy of that prince, and more than once
reduced him to great straits during the early and distressed period
of his reign, as we shall have repeated occasion to notice.
Bruce, when he began to obtain an ascendency in Scotland, took
the first opportunity in his power to requite these injuries.  He
marched into Argyleshire to lay waste the country.  John of
Lorn, son of the chieftain, was posted with his followers in the
formidable pass between Dalmally and Bunawe.  It is a narrow
path along the verge of the huge and precipitous mountain, called
Cruachan Ben, and guarded on the other side by a precipice over-

---

[1] The aunt, according to Lord Hailes.  But the genealogy is distinctly
given by Wyntoun:—

> " The thryd douchtyr of Red Cwmyn,
> Alysawndyr of Argayle syne
> Tuk, and weddyt til hys wyf,
> And on hyr he gat in-til hys lyfe
> Jhon of Lorne, the quhilk gat
> Ewyn of Lorne eftyr that."
>
> Wyntoun's *Chronicles*, Book viii., Chap. vi., line 206.

hanging Loch Awe. The pass seems to the eye of a soldier as strong, as it is wild and romantic to that of an ordinary traveller. But the skill of Bruce had anticipated this difficulty. While his main body, engaged in a skirmish with the men of Lorn, detained their attention to the front of their position, James of Douglas, with Sir Alexander Fraser, Sir William Wiseman, and Sir Andrew Grey, ascended the mountain with a select body of archery, and obtained possession of the heights which commanded the pass. A volley of arrows descending upon them directly warned the Argyleshire men of their perilous situation, and their resistance, which had hitherto been bold and manly, was changed into a precipitate flight. The deep and rapid river of Awe was then (we learn the fact from Barbour with some surprise,) crossed by a bridge. This bridge the mountaineers attempted to demolish. But Bruce's followers were too close upon their rear; they were, therefore, without refuge and defence, and were dispersed with great slaughter. John of Lorn, suspicious of the event, had early betaken himself to the galleys which he had upon the lake; but the feelings which Barbour assigns to him, while witnessing the rout and slaughter of his followers, exculpate him from the charge of cowardice.

> "To Jhone off Lorne it suld displese
> I trow, quhen he his men mycht se,
> Owte off his schippis fra the se,
> Be slayne and chassyt in the hill,
> That he mycht set na help thar till
> Bot it angrys als gretumly,
> To gud hartis that ar worthi,
> To se thair fayis fulfill thair will
> As to thaim selff to thole the ill."—B. vii., v. 394.

After this decisive engagement, Bruce laid waste Argyleshire, and besieged Dunstaffnage Castle, on the western shore of Lorn, compelled it to surrender, and placed in that principal stronghold of the Mac-Dougals a garrison and governor of his own. The elder Mac-Dougal, now wearied with the contest, submitted to the victor; but his son, " rebellious," says Barbour, " as he wont o be," fled to England by sea. When the wars between the Bruce and Baliol factions again broke out in the reign of David II., the Lords of Lorn were again found upon the losing side.

owing to their hereditary enmity to the house of Bruce. Accordingly, upon the issue of that contest, they were deprived by David II. and his successor of by far the greater part of their extensive territories, which were conferred upon Stewart, called the Knight of Lorn. The house of Mac-Dougal continued, however, to survive the loss of power, and affords a very rare, if not a unique, instance of a family of such unlimited power, and so distinguished during the middle ages, surviving the decay of their grandeur, and flourishing in a private station. The Castle of Dunolly, near Oban, with its dependencies, was the principal part of what remained to them, with their right of chieftainship over the families of their name and blood. These they continued to enjoy until the year 1715, when the representative incurred the penalty of forfeiture, for his accession to the insurrection of that period; thus losing the remains of his inheritance, to replace upon the throne the descendants of those princes, whose accession his ancestors had opposed at the expense of their feudal grandeur. The estate was, however, restored about 1745, to the father of the present proprietor, whom family experience had taught the hazard of interfering with the established government, and who remained quiet upon that occasion. He therefore regained his property when many Highland chiefs lost theirs.

Nothing can be more wildly beautiful than the situation of Dunolly. The ruins are situated upon a bold and precipitous promontory, overhanging Loch Etive, and distant about a mile from the village and port of Oban. The principal part which remains is the donjon or keep; but fragments of other buildings, overgrown with ivy, attest that it had been once a place of importance, as large apparently as Artornish or Dunstaffnage. These fragments enclose a courtyard, of which the keep probably formed one side; the entrance being by a steep ascent from the neck of the isthmus, formerly cut across by a moat, and defended doubtless by outworks and a drawbridge. Beneath the castle stands the present mansion of the family, having on the one hand Loch Etive, with its islands and mountains, on the other two romantic eminences tufted with copsewood. There are other accompaniments suited to the scene; in particular, a huge upright pillar, or detached fragment of that sort of rock called plum-pudding

stone, upon the shore, about a quarter of a mile from the castle.
It is called *Clachna-cau,* or the Dog's Pillar, because Fingal is
said to have used it as a stake to which he bound his celebrated
dog Bran. Others say, that when the Lord of the Isles came
upon a visit to the Lord of Lorn, the dogs brought for his sport
were kept beside this pillar. Upon the whole, a more delightful
and romantic spot can scarce be conceived; and it receives a
moral interest from the considerations attached to the residence
of a family once powerful enough to confront and defeat Robert
Bruce, and now sunk into the shade of private life. It is at present possessed by Patrick Mac-Dougal, Esq., the lineal and undis-
puted representative of the ancient Lords of Lorn. The heir
of Dunolly fell lately in Spain, fighting under the Duke of Wellington,—a death well becoming his ancestry.

## Note E.

*" Fill me the mighty cup," he said,*
*" Erst own'd by royal Somerled."*—P. 52.

A Hebridean drinking cup, of the most ancient and curious
workmanship, has been long preserved in the Castle of Dunvegan,
in Skye, the romantic seat of Mac-Leod of Mac-Leod, the chief
of that ancient and powerful clan. The horn of Rorie More,
preserved in the same family, and recorded by Dr. Johnson, is not
to be compared with this piece of antiquity, which is one of the
greatest curiosities in Scotland. The following is a pretty accurate description of its shape and dimensions, but cannot, I fear,
be perfectly understood without a drawing.

This very curious piece of antiquity is nine inches and three
quarters in inside depth, and ten and a half in height on the out-
side, the extreme measure over the lips being four inches and a
half. The cup is divided into two parts by a wrought ledge,
beautifully ornamented, about three-fourths of an inch in breadth.
Beneath this ledge the shape of the cup is rounded off, and terminates in a flat circle, like that of a tea-cup; four short feet
support the whole. Above the projecting ledge the shape of the
cup is nearly square, projecting outward at the brim. The cup
is made of wood, (oak to all appearance,) but most curiously

wrought and embossed with silver work, which projects from the vessel. There are a number of regular projecting sockets, which appear to have been set with stones; two or three of them still hold pieces of coral, the rest are empty. At the four corners of the projecting ledge, or cornice, are four sockets, much larger, probably for pebbles or precious stones. The workmanship of the silver is extremely elegant, and appears to have been highly gilded. The ledge, brim, and legs of the cup, are of silver. The family tradition bears that it was the property of Neil Ghlune-dhu, or Black-knee. But who this Neil was, no one pretends to say. Around the edge of the cup is a legend, perfectly legible, in the Saxon black-letter, which seems to run thus:

𝔘𝔣𝔬: 𝔍𝔬𝔥𝔦𝔰: 𝔐𝔦𝔠𝔥: ‖ 𝔐𝔤𝔫: 𝔓𝔫𝔠𝔦𝔭𝔦𝔰: 𝔇𝔢: ‖ 𝔥𝔯: 𝔐𝔞𝔫𝔞𝔢: 𝔘𝔦𝔠𝔥: ‖
𝔏𝔦𝔞𝔥𝔦𝔞: 𝔐𝔤𝔯𝔶𝔫𝔢𝔦𝔩: ‖ 𝔈𝔱: 𝔖𝔭𝔞𝔱: 𝔇𝔬: 𝔈𝔥𝔲: 𝔇𝔞: ‖ 𝔈𝔩𝔢𝔞: 𝔈𝔩𝔩𝔬𝔯𝔞
𝔈𝔭𝔞: ‖ 𝔉𝔢𝔠𝔦𝔱: 𝔄𝔫𝔬: 𝔇𝔦: 𝔎𝔯: 93𝔤 𝔒𝔫𝔦𝔩𝔦: 𝔒𝔦𝔪𝔦: ‖

The inscription may run thus at length: *Ufo Johanis Mich Magni Principis de Hr Manae Vich Liahia Magryneil et sperat Domino Ihesu dari clementiam illorum opera. Fecit Anno Domini 993 Onili Oimi.* Which may run in English: Ufo, the son of John, the son of Magnus, Prince of Man, the grandson of Liahia Macgryneil, trusts in the Lord Jesus that their works (*i. e.* his own and those of his ancestors) will obtain mercy. Oneil Oimi made this in the year of God nine hundred and ninety-three.

But this version does not include the puzzling letters ʜʀ before the word Manae. Within the mouth of the cup the letters 𝔌𝔥𝔰. (Jesus) are repeated four times. From this and other circumstances it would seem to have been a chalice. This circumstance may perhaps account for the use of the two Arabic numerals 93. These figures were introduced by Pope Sylvester, A. D. 991, and might be used in a vessel formed for church service so early as 993. The workmanship of the whole cup is extremely elegant, and resembles, I am told, antiques of the same nature preserved in Ireland.

The cups, thus elegantly formed, and highly valued, were by no means utensils of mere show. Martin gives the following account of the festivals of his time, and I have heard similar instances of brutality in the Lowlands at no very distant period.

" The manner of drinking used by the chief men of the Isles is called in their language Streah, *i. e.* a Round; for the company sat in a circle, the cup-bearer fill'd the drink round to them, and all was drank out, whatever the liquor was, whether strong or weak; they continued drinking sometimes twenty-four, sometimes forty-eight hours: It was reckoned a piece of manhood to drink until they became drunk, and there were two men with a barrow attending punctually on such occasions. They stood at the door until some became drunk, and they carry'd them upon the barrow to bed, and returned again to their post as long as any continued fresh, and so carried off the whole company, one by one, as they became drunk. Several of my acquaintance have been witnesses to this custom of drinking, but it is now abolished."

This savage custom was not entirely done away within this last generation. I have heard of a gentleman who happened to be a water-drinker, and was permitted to abstain from the strong potations of the company. The bearers carried away one man after another, till no one was left but this Scottish Mirglip. They then came to do him the same good office, which, however, he declined as unnecessary, and proposed to walk to his bedroom. It was a permission he could not obtain. Never such a thing had happened, they said, in the castle! that it was impossible but he must require their assistance, at any rate he must submit to receive it; and carried him off in the barrow accordingly. A classical penalty was sometimes imposed on those who baulked the rules of good fellowship by evading their share of the banquet. The same author continues: —

" Among persons of distinction it was reckoned an affront put upon any company to broach a piece of wine, ale, or aquavitæ, and not to see it all drank out at one meeting. If any man chance to go out from the company, though but for a few minutes, he is obliged, upon his return, and before he take his seat, to make an apology for his absence in rhyme; which if he cannot perform, he is liable to such a share of the reckoning as the company thinks fit to impose: which custom obtains in many places still, and is called Bianchiz Bard, which, in their language, signifies the poet's congratulating the company."

Few cups were better, at least more actively, employed in the rude hospitality of the period, than those of Dunvegan; one of which we have just described. There is in the Leabhar Dearg, a song, intimating the overflowing gratitude of a bard of Clan-Ronald, after the exuberance of a Hebridean festival at the patriarchal fortress of Mac-Leod. The translation being obviously very literal, has greatly flattened, as I am informed, the enthusiastic gratitude of the ancient bard; and it must be owned that the works of Homer or Virgil, to say nothing of Mac-Vuirich, might have suffered by their transfusion through such a medium. It is pretty plain, that when the tribute of poetical praise was bestowed, the horn of Rorie More had not been inactive.

*Upon Sir Roderic Mor Macleod, by Niall Mor Mac Vuirich.*

" The six nights I remained in the Dunvegan, it was not a show of hospitality I met with there, but a plentiful feast in thy fair hall among thy numerous host of heroes.

" The family placed all around under the protection of their great chief, raised by his prosperity and respect for his warlike feats, now enjoying the company of his friends at the feast,—Amidst the sound of harps, overflowing cups, and happy youth unaccustomed to guile, or feud, partaking of the generous fare by a flaming fire.

" Mighty Chief, liberal to all in your princely mansion, filled with your numerous warlike host, whose generous wine would overcome the hardiest heroes, yet we continued to enjoy the feast, so happy our host, so generous our fare."—*Translated by D. MacIntosh.*

It would be unpardonable in a modern bard, who has experienced the hospitality of Dunvegan Castle in the present day, to omit paying his own tribute of gratitude for a reception more elegant indeed, but not less kindly sincere, than Sir Roderick More himself could have afforded. But Johnson has already described a similar scene in the same ancient patriarchal residence of the Lords of Mac-Leod:—" Whatever is imaged in the wildest tales, if giants, dragons, and enchantment be excepted, would be felt by him, who, wandering in the mountains without a guide, or upon the sea without a pilot, should be carried, amidst his terror and uncertainty, to the hospitality and elegance of Raasay or Dunvegan."

## NOTE F.

### *The Broach of Lorn.*— P. 58.

It has been generally mentioned in the preceding notes, that Robert Bruce, after his defeat at Methven, being hard pressed by the English, endeavoured, with the dispirited remnant of his followers, to escape from Breadalbane and the mountains of Perthshire into the Argyleshire Highlands. But he was encountered and repulsed, after a very severe engagement, by the Lord of Lorn. Bruce's personal strength and courage were never displayed to greater advantage than in this conflict. There is a tradition in the family of the Mac-Dougals of Lorn, that their chieftain engaged in personal battle with Bruce himself, while the latter was employed in protecting the retreat of his men ; that Mac-Dougal was struck down by the king, whose strength of body was equal to his vigour of mind, and would have been slain on the spot, had not two of Lorn's vassals, a father and son, whom tradition terms M'Keoch, rescued him, by seizing the mantle of the monarch, and dragging him from above his adversary. Bruce rid himself of these foes by two blows of his redoubted battle-axe, but was so closely pressed by the other followers of Lorn, that he was forced to abandon the mantle, and broach which fastened it, clasped in the dying grasp of the Mac-Keochs. A studded broach, said to have been that which King Robert lost upon this occasion, was long preserved in the family of Mac-Dougal, and was lost in a fire which consumed their temporary residence.

The metrical history of Barbour throws an air of credibility upon the tradition, although it does not entirely coincide either in the names or number of the vassals by whom Bruce was assailed, and makes no mention of the personal danger of Lorn, or of the loss of Bruce's mantle. The last circumstance, indeed, might be warrantably omitted.

According to Barbour, the King, with his handful of followers, not amounting probably to three hundred men, encountered Lorn with about a thousand Argyleshire men, in Glen-Douchart, at the head of Breadalbane, near Teyndrum. The place of action

is still called Dalry, or the King's Field. The field of battle
was unfavourable to Bruce's adherents, who were chiefly men-
at-arms. Many of the horses were slain by the long pole-axe
of which the Argyleshire Scottish had learned the use from the
Norwegians. At length Bruce commanded a retreat up a narrow and difficult pass, he himself bringing up the rear, and
repeatedly turning and driving back the more venturous assailants. Lorn, observing the skill and valour used by his enemy in
protecting the retreat of his followers, " Methinks, Murthokson,"
said he, addressing one of his followers, " he resembles Gol
Mak-morn, protecting his followers from Fingal."— " A most
unworthy comparison," observes the Archdeacon of Aberdeen,
unsuspicious of the future fame of these names; " he might with
more propriety have compared the King to Sir Gaudefer de
Layrs, protecting the foragers of Gadyrs against the attacks of
Alexander." [1] Two brothers, the strongest among Lorn's followers, whose names Barbour calls Mackyn-Drosser, (interpreted
Durward, or Porterson,) resolved to rid their chief of this for
midable foe. A third person (perhaps the Mac-Keoch of the
family tradition) associated himself with them for this purpose.
They watched their opportunity until Bruce's party had entered
a pass between a lake (Loch Dochart probably) and a precipice,
where the King, who was the last of the party, had scarce room
to manage his steed. Here his three foes sprung upon him at
once. One seized his bridle, but received a wound which hewed
off his arm; a second grasped Bruce by the stirrup and leg, and
endeavoured to dismount him, but the King, putting spurs to his
horse, threw him down, still holding by the stirrup. The third,
taking advantage of an acclivity, sprung up behind him upon
his horse. Bruce, however, whose personal strength is uniformly mentioned as exceeding that of most men, extricated himself

---

[1] This is a very curious passage, and has been often quoted in the Ossianic
controversy. That it refers to ancient Celtic tradition, there can be no doubt,
and as little that it refers to no incident in the poems published by Mr. Mac-
pherson as from the Gaelic The hero of romance, whom Barbour thinks a
more proper prototype for the Bruce, occurs in the romance of Alexander, of
which there is a unique translation into Scottish verse, in the library of the
Honourable Mr. Maule of Panmure "— See WEBER's *Romances*, vol. i. Appen
dix to Introduction, p lxxiii.

from his grasp, threw him to the ground, and cleft his skull with his sword. By similar exertion he drew the stirrup from his grasp whom he had overthrown, and killed him also with his sword as he lay among the horse's feet. The story seems romantic, but this was the age of romantic exploit; and it must be remembered that Bruce was armed cap-a-pie, and the assailants were half-clad mountaineers. Barbour adds the following circumstance, highly characteristic of the sentiments of chivalry. Mac-Naughton, a Baron of Cowal, pointed out to the Lord of Lorn the deeds of valour which Bruce performed in this memorable retreat, with the highest expressions of admiration. "It seems to give thee pleasure," said Lorn, "that he makes such havoc among our friends."—"Not so, by my faith," replied Mac-Naughton; "but be he friend or foe who achieves high deeds of chivalry, men should bear faithful witness to his valour; and never have I heard of one, who, by his knightly feats, has extricated himself from such dangers as have this day surrounded Bruce."

## Note G.

*Vain Kirkpatrick's bloody dirk,*
*Making sure of murder's work.*—P. 60.

Every reader must recollect that the proximate cause of Bruce's asserting his right to the crown of Scotland, was the death of John, called the Red Comyn. The causes of this act of violence, equally extraordinary from the high rank both of the perpetrator and sufferer, and from the place where the slaughter was committed, are variously related by the Scottish and English historians, and cannot now be ascertained. The fact that they met at the high altar of the Minorites, or Greyfriars Church in Dumfries, that their difference broke out into high and insulting language, and that Bruce drew his dagger and stabbed Comyn, is certain. Rushing to the door of the church, Bruce met two powerful barons, Kirkpatrick of Closeburn, and James de Lindsay, who eagerly asked him what tidings? "Bad tidings," answered Bruce, "I doubt I have slain Comyn."—"Doubtest thou?" said Kirkpatrick; "I make sicker," (*i. e.* sure). With these words, he and Lindsay rushed into the church, and despatched

21 *

the wounded Comyn. The Kirkpatricks of Closeburn assumed, in memory of this deed, a hand holding a dagger, with the memorable words, "I make sicker." Some doubt having been started by the late Lord Hailes as to the identity of the Kirkpa trick who completed this day's work with Sir Roger, then representative of the ancient family of Closeburn, my kind and ingenious friend, Mr. Charles Kirkpatricke Sharpe, has furnished me with the following memorandum, which appears to fix the deed with his ancestor : —

"The circumstances of the Regent Cummin's murder, from which the family of Kirkpatrick, in Nithsdale, is said to have derived its crest and motto, are well known to all conversant with Scottish history; but Lord Hailes has started a doubt as to the authenticity of this tradition, when recording the murder of Roger Kirkpatrick, in his own Castle of Caerlaverock, by Sir James Lindsay. 'Fordun,' says his Lordship, 'remarks that Lindsay and Kirkpatrick were the heirs of the two men who accompanied Robert Brus at the fatal conference with Comyn. If Fordun was rightly informed as to this particular, an argument arises, in support of a notion which I have long entertained, that the person who struck his dagger in Comyn's heart, was *not* the representative of the honourable family of Kirkpatrick in Nithsdale. Roger de K. was made prisoner at the battle of Durham, in 1346. Roger de Kirkpatrick was alive on the 6th of August, 1357; for, on that day, Humphry, the son and heir of Roger de K., is proposed as one of the young gentlemen who were to be hostages for David Bruce. Roger de K. Miles was present at the Parliament held at Edinburgh, 25th September, 1357, and he is mentioned as alive 3d October, 1357, (*Fœdera ;*) it follows, of necessary consequence, that Roger de K., murdered in June, 1357, must have been a different person.'— *Annals of Scotland*, vol. ii. p. 242.

" To this it may be answered, that at the period of the regent's murder, there were only *two* families of the name of Kirkpatrick (nearly allied to each other) in existence—Stephen Kirkpatrick, styled in the Chartulary of Kelso (1278) *Dominus villæ de Closc-burn, Filius et hæres Domini Ade de Kirkpatrick, Militis,* (whose father, Ivone de Kirkpatrick, witnesses a charter of Robert Brus, Lord of Annandale, before the year 1141,) had two sons, Sir Roger, who carried on the line of Closeburn, and Duncan, who married Isobel, daughter and heiress of Sir David Torthorwald of that Ilk; they had a charter of the lands of Torthorwald from King Robert Brus, dated 10th August, the year being omitted—Umphray, the son of Duncan and Isobel, got a charter of Torthorwald from the king, 16th July, 1322—his son, Roger of Torthorwald, got a charter from John the Grahame, son of Sir John Grahame of Mosskessen, of an annual rent of 40 shillings, out of the lands of Overdryft, 1355—his son, William Kirkpatrick, grants a charter to John of Garroch, of the twa merk land of Glengip and Garvellgill, within the tenement of Wamphray, 22d April, 1372. From this, it appears that the Torthorwald branch was not concerned in the affair of Comyn's murder, and the inflictions of Providence which ensued: Duncan Kirkpatrick, if we are to believe the Blind Minstrel, was the firm friend of Wallace, to whom he was related:—

> 'Ane Kyrk Patrick, that cruel was and keyne,
> In Esdaill wod that half yer he had beyne;
> With Ingliss men he couth nocht weyll accord,
> Off Torthorowald he Barron was and Lord,
> Off kyn he was, and Wallace modyr ner;'—&c.
>
> B. v, v. 920.

But this Baron seems to have had no share in the adventures of King Robert; the crest of his family, as it still remains on a carved stone built into a cottage wall, in the village of Torthorwald, bears some resemblance, says Grose, to a rose.

"Universal tradition, and all our later historians, have attributed the regent's death-blow to Sir Roger K. of Closeburn. The author of the MS. History of the Presbytery of Penpont, in the Advocates' Library, affirms, that the crest and motto were given by the king on that occasion; and proceeds to relate some circumstances respecting a grant to a cottager and his wife in the vicinity of Closeburn Castle, which are certainly authentic, and strongly vouch for the truth of the other report.—'The steep hill,' (says he,) 'called the Dune of Tynron, of a considerable height, upon the top of which there hath been some habitation or fort. There have been in ancient times, on all hands of it, very thick woods, and great about that place, which made it the more inaccessible, into which K. Ro. Bruce is said to have been conducted by Roger Kirkpatrick of Closeburn, after they had killed the Cumin at Dumfriess, which is nine miles from this place, whereabout it is probable that he did abide for some time thereafter; and it is reported, that during his abode there, he did often divert to a poor man's cottage, named Brownrig, situate in a small parcel of stoney ground, incompassed with thick woods, where he was content sometimes with such mean accommodation as the place could afford.  The poor man's wife being advised to petition the king for somewhat, was so modest in her desires, that she sought no more but security for the croft in her husband's possession, and a liberty of pasturage for a very few cattle of different kinds on the hill, and the rest of the bounds.  Of which priviledge that ancient family, by the injury of time, hath a long time been, and is, deprived: but the croft continues in the possession of the heirs and successours lineally descended of this Brownrig and his wife; so that this family, being more ancient than rich, doth yet continue in the name, and, as they say, retains the old charter."— *MS. History of the Presbytery of Penpont, in the Advocates' Library of Edinburgh.*

## NOTE H.

> *Where's Nigel Bruce? and De la Haye,*
> *And valiant Seton — where are they?*
> *Where Somerville, the kind and free?*
> *And Fraser, flower of chivalry?*— P. 72.

When these lines were written, the author was remote from the means of correcting his indistinct recollection concerning the individual fate of Bruce's followers, after the battle of Methven. Hugh de la Haye, and Thomas Somerville of Lintoun and Cowdally, ancestor of Lord Somerville, were both made prisoners at that defeat, but neither was executed.

Sir Nigel Bruce was the younger brother of Robert, to whom he committed the charge of his wife and daughter, Marjorie, and the defence of his strong castle of Kildrummie, near the head of the Don, in Aberdeenshire.  Kildrummie long resisted the arms of the Earls of Lancaster and Hereford, until the magazine was treacherously burnt.  The garrison was then compelled to surrender at discretion, and Nigel Bruce, a youth remarkable for personal beauty, as well as for gallantry, fell into the hands of the unrelenting Edward. He was tried by a special commission at Berwick, was condemned, and executed.

Christopher Seatoun shared the same unfortunate fate. He also was distinguished by personal valour, and signalized himself in the fatal battle of Methven. Robert Bruce adventured his person in that battle like a knight of romance. He dismounted Aymer de Valence, Earl of Pembroke, but was in his turn dismounted by Sir Philip Mowbray. In this emergence Seatoun came to his aid, and remounted him. Langtoft mentions, that in this battle the Scottish wore white surplices, or shirts, over their armour, that those of rank might not be known. In this manner both Bruce and Seatoun escaped. But the latter was afterwards betrayed to the English, through means, according to Barbour, of one Mac-Nab, "a disciple of Judas," in whom the unfortunate knight reposed entire confidence. There was some peculiarity respecting his punishment; because, according to Matthew of Westminster, he was considered not as a Scottish subject, but an Englishman. He was therefore taken to Dumfries, where he was tried, condemned, and executed, for the murder of a soldier slain by him. His brother, John de Seton, had the same fate at Newcastle; both were considered as accomplices in the slaughter of Comyn, but in what manner they were particularly accessary to that deed does not appear.

The fate of Sir Simon Frazer, or Frizel, ancestor of the family of Lovat, is dwelt upon at great length, and with savage exultation, by the English historians. This knight, who was renowned for personal gallantry, and high deeds of chivalry, was also made prisoner, after a gallant defence, in the battle of Methven. Some stanzas of a ballad of the times, which, for the sake of rendering it intelligible, I have translated out of its rude orthography, give minute particulars of his fate. It was written immediately at the period, for it mentions the Earl of Athole as not yet in custody. It was first published by the indefatigable Mr. Ritson, but with so many contractions and peculiarities of character, as to render it illegible, excepting by antiquaries.

* This was before saint Bartholomew's mass,
That Frizel was y-taken, were it more other less,

To Sir Thomas of Multon, gentil baron and free,
And to Sir Johan Jose be-take tho was he
                                To hand
                    He was y-fettered wele
                    Both with iron and with steel
                                To bringen of Scotland.

"Soon thereafter the tiding to the king come,
He sent him to London, with mony armed groom,
He came in at Newgate, I tell you it on a-plight,
A garland of leaves on his head y-dight
                                Of green,
                    For he should be y-know
                    Both of high and of low,
                                For traitour I ween.

"Y-fettered were his legs under his horse's wombe,
Both with iron and with steel mancled were his hond,
A garland of pervynk¹ set upon his heved,²
Much was the power that him was bereved,
                                In land.
                    So God me amend,
                    Little he ween'd
                                So to be brought in hand.

"This was upon our lady's even, forsooth I understand,
The justices sate for the knights of Scotland,
Sir Thomas of Multon, an kinde knyght and wise,
And Sir Ralph of Sandwich that mickle is told in price
                                And Sir Johan Abel,
                    Moe I might tell by tale
                    Both of great and of small
                                Ye know sooth well

"Then said the justice, that gentil is and free,
Sir Simond Frizel the king's traiter hast thou be,
In water and in land that mony mighten see,
What sayst thou thereto, how will thou quite thee,
                                Do say,
                    So foul he him wist,
                    Nede war on trust
                                For to say nay.

---

¹ Periwinckle.                                    ² Head.

"With fetters and with gives[1] y-hot he was to-draw
From the tower of London that many men might know,
In a kirtle of burel, a selcouth wise,
And a garland on his head of the new guise.
    Through Cheape
   Many men of England
   For to see Symond
    Thitherward can leap.

"Though he cam to the gallows first he was on hung,
All quick beheaded that him thought long;
Then he was y-opened, his bowels y-brend,[2]
The heved to London-bridge was send
    To shende.
   So evermore mote I the,
   Some while weened he
    Thus little to stand.[3]

"He rideth through the city, as I tell may,
With gamen and with solace that was their play,
To London-bridge he took the way,
Mony was the wives child that thereon lacketh a day,[4]
    And said, alas!
   That he was y-born
   And so vilely forlorn,
    So fair man he was.[5]

"Now standeth the heved above the tu-brigge,
Fast by Wallace sooth for to segge;
After succour of Scotland long may he pry,
And after help of France what halt it to lie,
    I ween,
   Better him were in Scotland,
   With his axe in his hand,
    To play on the green," &c.

The preceding stanzas contain probably as minute an account
as can be found of the trial and execution of state criminals of
the period. Superstition mingled its horrors with those of a fero-
cious state policy, as appears from the following singular narrative.

---

[1] He was condemned to be drawn. — [2] Burned. — [3] Meaning at one time he
little thought to stand thus. — [4] viz. Saith Lack-a-day. — [5] T  rallant knight,
like others in the same situation, was pitied by the female  ctators as " a
proper young man."

" The Friday next, before the assumption of Our Lady, King Edward met Robert the Bruce at Saint Johnstoune, in Scotland, and with his company, of which company King Edward quelde seven thousand.   When Robert the Bruce saw this mischief, and gan to flee, and hov'd him that men might not him find; but S. Simond Frisell pursued was so sore, so that he turned again and abode bataille, for he was a worthy knight and a bolde of bodye, and the Englishmen pursuede him sore on every side, and quelde the steed that Sir Simon Frisell rode upon, and then toke him and led him to the host.   And S. Symond began for to flatter and speke fair, and saide, Lordys, I shall give you four thousand markes of silver, and myne horse and harness, and all my armoure and income.   Tho' answered Thobaude of Pevenes, that was the kinges archer, Now, God me so helpe, it is for nought that thou speakest, for all the gold of England I would not let thee go without commandment of King Edward.   And tho' he was led to the King, and the King would not see him, but commanded to lead him away to his doom in London, on Our Lady's even nativity.   And he was hung and drawn, and his head smitten off and hanged again with chains of iron upon the gallows, and his head was set at London-bridge upon a spear, and against Christmas the body was burnt, for encheson (*reason*) that the men tha keeped the body saw many devils ramping with iron crooks, running upon the gallows, and horribly tormenting the body.   And many that them saw, anon thereafter died for dread, or waxen mad, or sore sickness they had."— *MS. Chronicle in the British Museum, quoted by Ritson.*

## Note I.

*I feel within mine aged breast*
*A power that will not be repress'd.*—P. 78.

Bruce, like other heroes, observed omens, and one is recorded by tradition.   After he had retreated to one of the miserable places of shelter, in which he could venture to take some repose after his disasters, he lay stretched upon a handful of straw, and abandoned himself to his melancholy meditations.   He had now been defeated four times, and was upon the point of resolving to

abandon all hopes of further opposition to his fate, and to go to
the Holy Land. It chanced his eye, while he was thus pondering, was attracted by the exertions of a spider, who, in order to
fix his web, endeavoured to swing himself from one beam to
another above his head. Involuntarily he became interested in
the pertinacity with which the insect renewed his exertions,
after failing six times; and it occurred to him that he would
decide his own course according to the success or failure of the
spider. At the seventh effort the insect gained his object; and
Bruce, in like manner, persevered and carried his own. Hence
it has been held unlucky or ungrateful, or both, in one of the
name of Bruce to kill a spider.

The archdeacon of Aberdeen, instead of the abbot of this tale,
introduces an Irish Pythoness, who not only predicted his good
fortune as he left the island of Rachrin, but sent her two sons
along with him, to ensure her own family a share in it.

> "Then in schort time men mycht thaim se
> Schute all thair galayis to the se,
> And ber to se baith ayr and ster,
> And othyr thingis that mystir[1] wer.
> And as the king apon the sand
> Wes gangand wp and doun, bidand[2]
> Till that his menye redy war,
> His ost come rycht till him thar.
> And quhen that scho him halyst had,
> And priwé spek till him scho made;
> And said, 'Takis gud kep till my saw
> For or ye pass I sall yow schaw,
> Off your fortoun a gret party.
> Bot our all speceally
> A wyttring her I sall yow ma,
> Quhat end that your purpos sall ta.
> For in this land is nane trewly
> Wate thingis to cum sa weill as I.
> Ye pass now furth on your wiage,
> To wenge the harme, and the owtrag,
> That Ingliss men has to yow done;
> Bot ye wat nocht quhatkyne forton
> Ye mon drey in your werraying.
> Bot wyt ye weill, with outyn lesing,

---

[1] Need.      [2] Abiding.

That fra ye now haiff takyn land,
Nane sa mychty, na sa strength thi of hand,
Sall ger yow pass owt of your countré
Till all to yow abendonnyt be.
With in schort tyme ye sall be king,
And haiff the land at your liking,
And ourcum your fayis all.
Bot fele anoyis thole ye sall,
Or that your purpose end haiff tane :
Bot ye sall thaim ourdryve ilkane.
And, that ye trow this sekyrly,
My twa sonnys with yow sall I
Send to tak part of your trawaill ;
For I wate weill thai sall nocht faill
To be rewardyt weill at rycht,
Quhen ye ar heyit to yowr mycht.' "

BARBOUR'S *Bruce,* Book iii., v. 856.

## NOTE K.

*A hunted wanderer on the wild,*
*On foreign shores a man exiled.* — P. 78.

This is not metaphorical. The echoes of Scotland did actually

———— " ring
With the bloodhounds that bayed for her fugitive king."

A very curious and romantic tale is told by Barbour upon this
subject, which may be abridged as follows : —

When Bruce had again got footing in Scotland in the spring
of 1306, he continued to be in a very weak and precarious condition, gaining, indeed, occasional advantages, but obliged to fly
before his enemies whenever they assembled in force.  Upon one
occasion, while he was lying with a small party in the wilds of
Cumnock, in Ayrshire, Aymer de Valence, Earl of Pembroke,
with his inveterate foe John of Lorn, came against him suddenly
with eight hundred Highlanders, besides a large body of men-at-
arms.  They brought with them a slough-dog, or bloodhound,
which, some say, had been once a favourite with the Bruce himself, and therefore was least likely to lose the trace.

Bruce, whose force was under four hundred men, continued to
make head against the cavalry, till the men of Lorn had nearly

cut off his retreat. Perceiving the danger of his situation, he
acted as the celebrated and ill-requited Mina is said to have done
in similar circumstances. He divided his force into three parts,
appointed a place of rendezvous, and commanded them to retreat
by different routes. But when John of Lorn arrived at the spot
where they divided, he caused the hound to be put upon the
trace, which immediately directed him to the pursuit of that party
which Bruce headed. This, therefore, Lorn pursued with his
whole force, paying no attention to the others. The king again
subdivided his small body into three parts, and with the same
result, for the pursuers attached themselves exclusively to that
which he led in person. He then caused his followers to disperse,
and retained only his foster-brother in his company. The slough-
dog followed the trace, and, neglecting the others, attached himself and his attendants to pursuit of the king. Lorn became
convinced that his enemy was nearly in his power, and detached
five of his most active attendants to follow him, and interrupt his
flight. They did so with all the agility of mountaineers. "What
aid wilt thou make?" said Bruce to his single attendant, when
he saw the five men gain ground on him. "The best I can,"
replied his foster-brother. "Then," said Bruce, "here I make
my stand." The five pursuers came up fast. The king took
three to himself, leaving the other two to his foster-brother. He
slew the first who encountered him; but observing his foster-
brother hard pressed, he sprung to his assistance, and despatched
one of his assailants. Leaving him to deal with the survivor, he
returned upon the other two, both of whom he slew before his
foster-brother had despatched his single antagonist. When this
hard encounter was over, with a courtesy, which in the whole
work marks Bruce's character, he thanked his foster-brother for
his aid. "It likes you to say so," answered his follower; "but
you yourself slew four of the five."—"True," said the king, "but
only because I had better opportunity than you. They were not
apprehensive of me when they saw me encounter three, so I had
a moment's time to spring to thy aid, and to return equally unex-
pectedly upon my own opponents."

In the meanwhile Lorn's party approached rapidly, and the
king and his foster-brother betook themselves to a neighbouring
wood. Here they sat down, for Bruce was exhausted by fatigue,

until the cry of the slough-hound came so near, that his foster-brother entreated Bruce to provide for his safety by retreating further. "I have heard," answered the king, "that whosoever will wade a bowshot length down a running stream, shall make the slough-hound lose scent.— Let us try the experiment, for were yon devilish hound silenced, I should care little for the rest."

Lorn in the meanwhile advanced, and found the bodies of his slain vassals, over whom he made his moan, and threatened the most deadly vengeance. Then he followed the hound to the side of the brook, down which the king had waded a great way. Here the hound was at fault, and John of Lorn, after long attempting in vain to recover Bruce's trace, relinquished the pursuit.

"Others," says Barbour, "affirm, that upon this occasion the king's life was saved by an excellent archer who accompanied him, and who perceiving they would be finally taken by means of the blood-hound, hid himself in a thicket, and shot him with an arrow. In which way," adds the metrical biographer, "this escape happened I am uncertain, but at that brook the king escaped from his pursuers."

> "Quhen the chasseris relyit war,
> And Jhon of Lorn had met thaim thar,
> He tauld Schyr Aymer all the cass
> How that the king eschapyt wass;
> And how that he his five men slew,
> And syne to the wode him drew.
> Quhen Schyr Aymer herd this, in hy
> He sanyt him for the ferly:
> And said; 'He is gretly to pryss;
> For I knaw nane that liffand is,
> That at myscheyff gan help him swa.
> I trow he suld be hard to sla,
> And he war bodyn [1] ewynly.'
> On this wiss spak Schyr Aymery."

BARBOUR'S *Bruce*, Book v., v. 391

The English historians agree with Barbour as to the mode in which the English pursued Bruce and his followers, and the dex-

[1] Matched

terity with which he evaded them.   The following is the testimony of Harding, a great enemy to the Scottish nation: —

> "The King Edward with hoost hym sought full sore,
> But ay he fled into woodes and strayte forest,
> And slewe his men at staytes and daungers thore,
> And at marreys and mires was ay full prest
> Englyshmen to kyll withoutyn any rest;
> In the mountaynes and cragges he slew ay where,
> And in the nyght his foes he frayed full sere:
>
> " The King Edward with hornes and houndes him soght,
> With menne on fote, through marris, mosse, and myre,
> Through wodes also, and mountens (wher thei fought,)
> And euer the Kyng Edward hight men greate hyre,
> Hym for to take and by myght conquere;
> But thei might hym not gette by force ne by train,
> He satte by the fyre when thei went in the rain."

HARDYNG's Chronicle, p. 303–4.

Peter Langtoft has also a passage concerning the extremities to which King Robert was reduced, which he entitles

De Roberto Brus et fuga circum circa fit.

> "And wele I understode that the Kyng Robyn
> Has drunken of that blode the drink of Dan Waryn.
> Dan Waryn he les tounes that he held,
> With wrong he mad a res, and misberyng of scheld,
> Sithen into the forest he yede naked and wode,
> Als a wild beast, ete of the gres that stode,
> Thus of Dan Waryn in his boke men rede,
> God gyf the King Robyn, that alle his kynde so spede,
> Sir Robynet the Brus he durst noure abide,
> That thei mad him restus, both in more and wod-side,
> To while he mad this train, and did umwhile outrage," &c.

PETER LANGTOFT's Chronicle, vol. ii., p. 335,<br>8vo, London, 1810.

## Note L.

These are the savage wilds that lie<br>North of Strathnardill and Dunskye.—P. 108.

The extraordinary piece of scenery which I have here attempted to describe, is, I think, unparalleled in any part of Scotland,

22 *

at least in any which I have happened to visit. It lies just upon the frontier of the Laird of Mac-Leod's country, which is thereabouts divided from the estate of Mr. Maccallister of Strath-Aird, called Strathnardill by the Dean of the Isles. The following account of it is extracted from a journal[1] kept during a tour through the Scottish islands: —

"The western coast of Sky is highly romantic, and at the same time displays a richness of vegetation in the lower grounds to which we have hitherto been strangers. We passed three salt-water lochs, or deep embayments, called Loch Bracadale. Loch Einort, and Loch ——, and about 11 o'clock opened Loch Slavig. We were now under the western termination of the high ridge of mountains called Cuillen, or Quillin, or Coolin, whose weather-beaten and serrated peaks we had admired at a distance from Dunvegan. They sunk here upon the sea, but with the same bold and peremptory aspect which their distant appearance indicated. They appeared to consist of precipitous sheets of naked rock, down which the torrents were leaping in a hundred lines of foam. The tops of the ridge, apparently inaccessible to human foot, were rent and split into the most tremendous pinnacles. Towards the base of these bare and precipitous crags, the ground, enriched by the soil washed down from them, is comparatively verdant and productive. Where we passed within the small isle of Soa, we entered Loch Slavig, under the shoulder of one of these grisly mountains, and observed that the opposite side of the loch was of a milder character, the mountains being softened down into steep green declivities. From the bottom of the bay advanced a headland of high rocks, which divided its depth into two recesses, from each of which a brook issued. Here it had been intimated to us we would find some romantic scenery; but we were uncertain up which inlet we should proceed in search of it. We chose, against our better judgment, the southerly dip of the bay, where we saw a house which might afford us information. We found, upon enquiry, that there is a lake adjoining to each branch of the bay; and walked a couple of miles to see that near the farmhouse, merely because the honest highlander seemed jealous of

---

[1] [This is the Poet's own journal.—ED.]

the honour of his own loch, though we were speedily convinced
it was not that which we were recommended to examine. It
had no particular merit, excepting from its neighbourhood to a
very high cliff, or precipitous mountain, otherwise the sheet of
water had nothing differing from any ordinary low-country lake.
We returned and re-embarked in our boat, for our guide shook
his head at our proposal to climb over the peninsula, or rocky
headland which divided the two lakes. In rowing round the
headland, we were surprised at the infinite number of sea-fowl,
then busy apparently with a shoal of fish.

"Arrived at the depth of the bay, we found that the discharge
from this second lake forms a sort of waterfall, or rather a rapid
stream, which rushes down to the sea with great fury and pre-
cipitation. Round this place were assembled hundreds of trouts
and salmon, struggling to get up into the fresh water: with a
net we might have had twenty salmon at a haul; and a sailor,
with no better hook than a crooked pin, caught a dish of trouts
during our absence. Advancing up this huddling and riotous
brook, we found ourselves in a most extraordinary scene; we
lost sight of the sea almost immediately after we had climbed
over a low ridge of crags, and were surrounded by mountains of
naked rock, of the boldest and most precipitous character. The
ground on which we walked was the margin of a lake, which
seemed to have sustained the constant ravage of torrents from
these rude neighbours. The shores consisted of huge strata of
naked granite, here and there intermixed with bogs, and heaps
of gravel and sand piled in the empty water-courses. Vegetation there was little or none; and the mountains rose so perpen-
dicularly from the water edge, that Borrowdale, or even Glencoe,
is a jest to them. We proceeded a mile and a half up this deep,
dark, and solitary lake, which was about two miles long, half a
mile broad, and is, as we learned, of extreme depth. The murky
vapours which enveloped the mountain ridges, obliged us by
assuming a thousand varied shapes, changing their drapery into
all sorts of forms, and sometimes clearing off all together. It is
true, the mist made us pay the penalty by some heavy and down-
right showers, from the frequency of which a Highland boy,
whom we brought from the farm, told us the lake was popularly
called the Water-kettle. The proper name is Loch Corriskin,

from the deep corrie, or hollow, in the mountains of Cuilin, which affords the basin for this wonderful sheet of water. It is as exquisite a savage scene as Loch Katrine is a scene of romantic beauty. After having penetrated so far as distinctly to observe the termination of the lake under an immense precipice, which rises abruptly from the water, we returned, and often stopped to admire the ravages which storms must have made in these recesses, when all human witnesses were driven to places of more shelter and security. Stones, or rather large masses and fragments of rocks of a composite kind, perfectly different from the strata of the lake, were scattered upon the bare rocky beach, in the strangest and most precarious situations, as if abandoned by the torrents which had borne them down from above. Some lay loose and tottering upon the ledges of the natural rock, with so little security, that the slightest push moved them, though their weight might exceed many tons. These detached rocks, or stones, were chiefly what is called plum-pudding stones. The bare rocks, which formed the shore of the lakes, were a species of granite. The opposite side of the lake seemed quite pathless and inaccessible, as a huge mountain, one of the detached ridges of the Cuillen hills, sinks in a profound and perpendicular precipice down to the water. On the left-hand side, which we traversed, rose a higher and equally inaccessible mountain, the top of which strongly resembled the shivered crater of an exhausted volcano. I never saw a spot in which there was less appearance of vegetation of any kind. The eye rested on nothing but barren and naked crags, and the rocks on which we walked by the side of the loch, were as bare as the pavements of Cheapside. There are one or two small islets in the loch, which seem to bear juniper, or some such low bushy shrub. Upon the whole, though I have seen many scenes of more extensive desolation, I never witnessed any in which it pressed more deeply upon the eye and the heart than at Loch Corrisken; at the same time that its grandeur elevated and redeemed it from the wild and dreary character of utter barrenness."

## Note M.

*Men were they all of evil mien,*
*Down-look'd, unwilling to be seen.* — P. 115.

The story of Bruce's meeting the banditti is copied, with such
alterations as the fictitious narrative rendered necessary, from a
striking incident in the monarch's history, told by Barbour, and
which I shall give in the words of the hero's biographer. It is
the sequel to the adventure of the bloodhound, narrated in Note
K. It will be remembered that the narrative broke off, leaving
the Bruce escaped from his pursuers, but worn out with fatigue,
and having no other attendant but his foster-brother.

> And the gud king held forth his way,
> Betuix him and his man, quhill thai
> Passyt owt throw the forest war,
> Syne in the more thai entryt thar,
> It wes bathe hey, and lang, and braid;
> And or thai haiff it passyt had,
> Thai saw on syd three men cummand,
> Lik to lycht men and wauerand.
> Swerdis thai had, and axys als;
> And ane off thaim, apon his hals,[1]
> A mekill boundyn wethir bar.
> Thai met the king, and halist[2] him thar:
> And the king thaim thar hailsing yauld;[3]
> And askyt thaim quethir thai wauld
> Thai said, Robert the Bruyss thai soucht;
> For mete with him giff that thai moucht,
> Thar duelling with him wauld thai ma[4]
> The king said, 'Gif that ye will swa
> Haldys furth your way with me,
> And I sall ger yow sone him se'
>   "Thai persawyt, be his speking,
> That he wes the selwyn Robert king.
> And chaungyt contenance and late;[5]
> And held nocht in the fyrst state.
> For thai war fayis to the king:
> And thoucht to cum in to sculking
> And duell with him, quhill that thai saw
> Thar poynt, and bring him than off daw[6]

---

[1] Neck —[2] Saluted.—[3] Returned their salute.—[4] Make —[5] Gesture or manner —
[6] Kill him.

Thai grantyt till his spek forthi.[1]
Bot the king, that wes witty,
Persawyt weill, by thar hawing,
That thai luffyt him na thing:
And said, 'Falowis, ye mon, all thre,
Forthir aqwent till that we be,
All be your selwyn furth ga;
And, on the samyn wyss, we twa
Sall folow behind weill ner.'
Quoth thai, 'Schyr, it is na myster[2]
To trow in ws ony ill.'
'Nane do I,' said he; 'bot I will,
That yhe ga fourth thus, quhill we
Better with othyr knawin be.'
'We grant,' thai said, 'sen ye will swa.
And furth apon thair gate gan ga.

  "Thus yeid thai till the nycht wes ner
And than the formast cummyn wer
Till a waist housband houss;[3] and thar
They slew the wethir that thai bar:
And slew fyr for to rost thar mete;
And askyt the king giff he wald ete,
And rest him till the mete war dycht.
The king, that hungry was, Ik hycht,
Assentyt till thair spek in hy.
Bot he said, he wald anerly[4]
At a fyr; and thai all thre
On na wyss with thaim till gyddre be.
In the end off the houss thai suld na
Ane othyr fyr: and thai did swa.
Thai drew thaim in the houss end,
And halff the wethir till him send.
And thai rostyt in hy thair mete;
And fell rycht freschly for till ete.
For the king weill lang fastyt had;
And had rycht mekill trawaill mad:
Tharfor he eyt full egrely
And quhen he had etyn hastily,
He had to slep sa mekill will,
That he moucht set na let thar till.
For quhen the wanys[5] fillyt ar
Men worthys[6] hewy euirmar;

---

[1] Therefore.—[2] There is no need.—[3] Husbandman's house, cottage.—[4] Alone.
—[5] Bellies.—[6] Becomes.

And tu slepe drawys hewynes,
The king, that all fortrawaillyt [1] wes,
Saw that him worthtyt slep nedwayis.
Till his fostyr-brodyr he sayis;
'May I traist in the, me to waik,
Till Ik a litill sleping tak ?'
'Ya, Schyr,' he said, till I may drey [2]
The king then wynkyt a litill wey;
And slepyt nocht full encrely;
Bot gliffnyt wp oft sodanly.
For he had dreid off thai thre men.
That at the tothyr fyr war then.
That thai his fais war he wyst;
Tharfor he slepyt as foule on twyst

  "The king slepyt bot a litill than;
Quhen sic slep fell on this man,
That he mycht nocht hald wp his ey,
Bot fell in slep, and rowtyt hey.
Now is the king in gret perile.
For slep he swa a litill quhile,
He sall be ded, for owtyn dreid.
For the thre tratouris tuk gud heid,
That he on slep wes, and his man
In full gret hy thai raiss wp than,
And drew thair suerdis hastily;
And went towart the king in hy,
Quhen that thai saw him sleip swa,
And slepand thoucht thai wald him sla.
The king wp blenkit hastily,
And saw his man slepand him by;
And saw cummand the tothyr thre.
Deliuerly on fute gat he;
And drew his suerd owt, and thaim mete.
And, as he yude, his fute he set
Apon his man, weill hewyly.
He waknyt, and raiss disily:
For the slep maistryt hym sway,
That or he gat wp, ane off thai,
That com for to sla the king,
Gaiff hym a strak in his rysing,
Swa that he mycht help him no mar.
The king sa straitly stad [4] wes thar,

---

[1] Fatigued. — [2] Endure. — [3] Bird on bough. — [4] So dangerously situated.

Thet he wes neuir yeyt sa stad.
Ne war the armyng [1] that he had,
He had bene dede, for owtyn wer.
But nocht for thi [2] on sic maner
He helpyt him, in that bargayne,[3]
That thai thre tratowris he has slan,
Throw Goddis grace, and his manheid.
His fostyr-brothyr thar was dede
Then wes he wondre will of wayn,[4]
Quhen he saw him left allane.
His fostyr-brodyr menyt he;
And waryit [5] all the tothyr thre.
And syne hys way tuk him allane,
And rycht towart his tryst [6] is gane."

                              *The Bruce*, Book v., v  405.

## Note N.

*Such hate was his on Solway's strand,*
*When vengeance clench'd his palsied hand,*
*That pointed yet to Scotland's land.* — P. 116.

To establish his dominion in Scotland had been a favourite
object of Edward's ambition, and nothing could exceed the pertinacity with which he pursued it, unless his inveterate resentment
against the insurgents, who so frequently broke the English yoke
when he deemed it most firmly riveted. After the battles of Falkirk and Methven, and the dreadful examples which he had made
of Wallace and other champions of national independence, he
probably concluded every chance of insurrection was completely
annihilated. This was in 1306, when Bruce, as we have seen,
was utterly expelled from Scotland: yet, in the conclusion of the
same year, Bruce was again in arms and formidable; and in 1307,
Edward, though exhausted by a long and wasting malady, put
himself at the head of the army destined to destroy him utterly.
This was, perhaps, partly in consequence of a vow which he had
taken upon him, with all the pomp of chivalry, upon the day in
which he dubbed his son a knight, for which see a subsequent
note.   But even his spirit of vengeance was unable to restore his

---

[1] Had it not been for the armour he wore.—[2] Nevertheless.—[3] Fray, or dis
pute.—[4] Much afflicted.—[5] Cursed.—[6] The place of rendezvous appointed for his
soldiers.

exhausted strength. He reached Burgh-upon-Sands, a petty village of Cumberland, on the shores of the Solway Firth, and there, 6th July, 1307, expired in sight of the detested and devoted country of Scotland. His dying injunctions to his son required him to continue the Scottish war, and never to recall Gaveston. Edward II. disobeyed both charges. Yet more to mark his animosity, the dying monarch ordered his bones to be carried with the invading army. Froissart, who probably had the authority of eye-witnesses, has given us the following account of this remarkable charge : —

" In the said forest, the old King Robert of Scotland dyd kepe hymselfe, whan King Edward the Fyrst conquered nygh all Scotland ; for he was so often chased, that none durst loge him in castell, nor fortresse, for feare of the said Kyng.

" And ever whan the King was returned into Ingland, than he would gather together agayn his people, and conquere townes, castells, and fortresses, iuste to Berwick, some by battle, and some by fair speech and love: and when the said King Edward heard thereof, than would he assemble his power, and wyn the realme of Scotland again ; thus the chance went between these two foresaid Kings. It was shewed me, how that this King Robert wan and lost his realme v. times. So this continued till the said King Edward died at Berwick: and when he saw that he should die, he called before him his eldest son, who was King after him, and there, before all the barones, he caused him to swear, that as soon as he were dead, that he should take his body, and boyle it in a cauldron, till the flesh departed clean from the bones, and than to bury the flesh, and keep still the bones, and that as often as the Scotts should rebell against him, he should assemble the people against them, and carry with him the bones of his father ; for he believed verily, that if they had his bones with them, that the Scotts should never attain any victory against them. The which thing was not accomplished, for when the King died his son carried him to London."— BERNERS' FROISSART'S *Chronicle*, London, 1812, pp. 39, 40.

Edward's commands were not obeyed, for he was interred in Westminster Abbey, with the appropriate inscription : —

" EDWARDUS PRIMUS SCOTORUM MALLEUS HIC EST.

PACTUM SERVA."

Yet some steps seem to have been taken towards rendering his body capable of occasional transportation, for it was exquisitely embalmed, as was ascertained when his tomb was opened some years ago. Edward II. judged wisely in not carrying the dead body of his father into Scotland, since he would not obey his living counsels.

It ought to be observed, that though the order of the incidents is reversed in the poem, yet, in point of historical accuracy, Bruce had landed in Scotland, and obtained some successes of consequence, before the death of Edward I.

## NOTE O.

*On Scooreigg next a warning light*
*Summon'd her warriors to the fight ;*
*A numerous race, ere stern Macleod*
*O'er their black shores in vengeance strode.* — P. 146.

These, and the following lines of the stanza, refer to a dreadful tale of feudal vengeance, of which unfortunately there are relics that still attest the truth. Scoor-Eigg is a high peak in the centre of the small Isle of Eigg, or Egg. It is well known to mineralogists, as affording many interesting specimens, and to others whom chance or curiosity may lead to the island, for the astonishing view of the mainland and neighbouring isles, which it commands. I shall again avail myself of the journal I have quoted.[1]

" 26*th August*, 1814.—At seven this morning we were in the Sound which divides the Isle of Rum from that of Egg. The latter, although hilly and rocky, and traversed by a remarkably high and barren ridge, called Scoor-Rigg, has, in point of soil, a much more promising appearance. Southward of both lies the Isle of Muich, or Muck, a low and fertile island, and though the least, yet probably the most valuable of the three. We manned the boat, and rowed along the shore of Egg in quest of a cavern, which had been the memorable scene of a horrid feudal vengeance. We had rounded more than half the island, admiring the entrance

---

[1] [See note to p 258, *arte* ]

of many a bold natural cave, which its rocks exhibited, without
finding that which we sought, until we procured a guide. Nor,
indeed, was it surprising that it should have escaped the search
of strangers, as there are no outward indications more than might
distinguish the entrance of a fox-earth. This noted cave has a
very narrow opening, through which one can hardly creep on his
knees and hands. It rises steep and lofty within, and runs into
the bowels of the rock to the depth of 255 measured feet; the
height at the entrance may be about three feet, but rises within
to eighteen or twenty, and the breadth may vary in the same proportion. The rude and stony bottom of this cave is strewed with
the bones of men, women, and children, the sad relics of the
ancient inhabitants of the island, 200 in number, who were slain
on the following occasion:—The Mac-Donalds of the Isle of Egg,
a people dependent on Clan-Ranald, had done some injury to the
Laird of Mac-Leod. The tradition of the isle says, that it was
by a personal attack on the chieftain, in which his back was broken. But that of the other isles bears, more probably, that the
injury was offered to two or three of the Mac-Leods, who, landing upon Eigg, and using some freedom with the young women,
were seized by the islanders, bound hand and foot, and turned
adrift in a boat, which the winds and waves safely conducted to
Skye. To avenge the offence given, Mac-Leod sailed with such
a body of men, as rendered resistance hopeless. The natives,
fearing his vengeance, concealed themselves in this cavern, and,
after a strict search, the Mac-Leods went on board their galleys,
after doing what mischief they could, concluding the inhabitants
had left the isle, and betaken themselves to the Long Island, or
some of Clan-Ranald's other possessions. But next morning
they espied from the vessels a man upon the island, and immediately landing again, they traced his retreat by the marks of his
footsteps, a light snow being unhappily on the ground. Mac-
Leod then surrounded the cavern, summoned the subterranean
garrison, and demanded that the individuals who had offended him
should be delivered up to him. This was peremptorily refused.
The chieftain then caused his people to divert the course of a rill
of water, which, falling over the entrance of the cave, would
have prevented his purposed vengeance. He then kindled at the
entrance of the cavern a huge fire, composed of turf and fern,

and maintained it with unrelenting assiduity, until all within were destroyed by suffocation. The date of this dreadful deed must have been recent, if one may judge from the fresh appearance of those relics. I brought off, in spite of the prejudice of our sailors, a skull from among the numerous specimens of mortality which the cavern afforded. Before re-embarking we visited another cave, opening to the sea, but of a character entirely different, being a large open vault as high as that of a cathedral, and running back a great way into the rock at the same height. The height and width of the opening give ample light to the whole. Here, after 1745, when the Catholic priests were scarcely tolerated, the priest of Eigg used to perform the Roman Catholic service, most of the islanders being of that persuasion. A huge ledge of rocks rising about half-way up one side of the vault, served for altar and pulpit; and the appearance of a priest and Highland congregation in such an extraordinary place of worship, might have engaged the pencil of Salvator."

## Note P.

*Up Tarbat's western lake they bore,*
*Then dragg'd their bark the isthmus o'er.* — P. 126.

The peninsula of Cantire is joined to South Knapdale by a very narrow isthmus, formed by the western and eastern Loch of Tarbat. These two salt-water lakes, or bays, encroach so far upon the land, and the extremities come so near to each other, that there is not above a mile of land to divide them.

" It is not long," says Pennant, " since vessels of nine or ten tons were drawn by horses out of the west loch into that of the east, to avoid the dangers of the Mull of Cantyre, so dreaded and so little known was the navigation round that promontory. It is the opinion of many, that these little isthmuses, so frequently styled Tarbat in North Britain, took their name from the above circumstance; Tarruing, signifying to draw, and Bata, a boat. This too might be called, by way of pre-eminence, the Tarbat, from a very singular circumstance related by Torfœus. When Magnus, the barefooted king of Norway, obtained from Donald-bane of Scotland the cession of the Western Isles, or all those places that could be surrounded in a boat, he added to them the peninsula of Cantyre by this fraud: he placed himself in the stern of a boat, held the rudder, was drawn over this narrow track, and by this species of navigation wrested the country from his brother monarch." — PENNANT's *Scotland, London*, 1790, p. 190.

But that Bruce also made this passage, although at a period two or three years later than in the poem, appears from the evidence of Barbour, who mentions also the effect produced upon the minds of the Highlanders, from the prophecies current amongst them : —

> "Bot to King Robert will we gang,
> That we haff left wnspokyn of lang.
> Quhen he had conwoyit to the se
> His brodyr Eduuard, and his menye,
> And othyr men off gret noblay.
> To Tarbart thai held thair way,
> In galayis ordanyt for thair far.
> Bot thaim worthyt [1] draw thair schippis thar
> And a myle wes betux the seys:
> Bot that wes lompnyt [2] all with treis.
> The King his schippis thar gert [3] draw.
> And for the wynd couth [4] stoutly blaw
> Apon thair bak, as thai wald ga,
> He gert men rapys and mastis ta,
> And set thaim in the schippis hey,
> And sayllis to the toppis tey;
> And gert men gang thar by drawand.
> The wynd thaim helpyt, that was blawand
> Swa that, in a litill space,
> Thair flote all our drawin was.
>
> "And quhen thai, that in the Ilis war,
> Hard tell how the gud King had thar
> Gert hys schippis with saillis ga
> Owt our betuix [the] Tarbart[is] twa,
> Thai war abaysit [5] sa wtrely.
> For thai wyst, throw auld prophecy,
> That he that suld ger [6] schippis sua
> Betuix thai seis with saillis ga,

---

[1] Were obliged to.— [2] Laid with trees.— [3] Caused. — [4] Could.— [5] Confounded. — [6] Make.

23 *

> Suld wyne the Ilis sua till hand,
> That nane with strength suld him withstand.
> Tharfor thai come all to the King.
> Wes nane withstud his bidding,
> Owtakyn[1] Jhone of Lorne allayne.
> Bot weill sone eftre wes he tayne;
> And present rycht to the King.
> And thai that war of his leding,
> That till the King had brokyn fay,[2]
> War all dede, and destroyit away."
>
> BARBOUR'S *Bruce*, Book x., v. 821.

## NOTE Q.

*For, see ! the ruddy signal made,*
*That Clifford, with his merry-men all,*
*Guards carelessly our father's hall.*— P. 156.

The remarkable circumstances by which Bruce was induced to enter Scotland, under the false idea that a signal-fire was lighted upon the shore near his maternal castle of Turnberry— the disappointment which he met with, and the train of success which arose out of that very disappointment, are too curious to be passed over unnoticed. The following is the narrative of Barbour. The introduction is a favourable specimen of his style, which seems to be in some degree the model for that of Gawain Douglas : —

> "This wes in ver,[3] quhen wynter tid,
> With his blastis hidwyss to bid,
> Was our drywyn: and byrdis smale,
> As turturis and the nychtyngale,
> Begouth[4] rycht sariely[5] to syng;
> And for to mak in thair singyng
> Swete notis, and sownys ser,[6]
> And melodys plesand to her.
> And the treis begouth to ma[7]
> Burgeans,[8] and brycht blomys alsua,
> To wyn the helyng[9] off thair hewid,
> That wykkyt wyntir had thaim rewid.[10]

---

[1] Excepting.— [2] Faith.— [3] Spring.— [4] Began.— [5] Loftily.— [6] Several.— [7] Make.
— [8] Buds.— [9] Covering.— [10] Bereaved.

And all gressys beguth to spryng
In to that tyme the nobill king,
With his flote, and a few menye,[1]
Thre hundyr I trow that mycht be,
Is to the se, owte off Arane
A litill forouth,[2] ewyn gane.

"Thai rowit fast, with all their mycht,
Till that apon thaim fell the nycht,
That woux myrk[3] apon gret maner
Swa that thai wyst nocht quhar thai wer.
For thai na nedill had, na stane;
But rowyt alwayis in till ane,
Sterand all tyme apon the fyr,
That thai saw brynnand lycht and schyr.[4]
It wes bot auentur[5] thaim led:
And thai in schort tyme sa thaim sped,
That at the fyr arywyt thai;
And went to land bot mar delay.
And Cuthbert, that has sene the fyr,
Was full off angyr, and off ire:
For he durst nocht do it away;
And wes alsua dowtand ay
That his lord suld pass to se.
Tharfor thair cummyn waytit he;
And met thaim at thair arywing.
He wes wele sone broucht to the King,
That speryt at him how he had done.
And he with sar hart tauld him sone,
How that he fand nane weill luffand;
Bot all war fayis, that he fand:
And that the lord the Persy,
With ner thre hundre in cumpany,
Was in the castell thar besid,
Fulfillyt off dispyt and prid.
But ma than twa partis off his rowt
War herberyt in the toune without;
And dyspytyt yow mar, Schir King
Than men may dispyt ony thing.'
Than said the King, in full gret ire;
'Tratour, quhy maid thow than the fyr?'
'A! Schyr,' said he, 'sa God me se!
The fyr wes newyr maid for me.
Na, or the nycht, I wyst it nocht;
Bot fra I wyst it, weill I thocht

---

[1] Men.—[2] Before.—[3] Dark.—[4] Clear.—[5] Adventure.

That ye, and haly your menye,
In hy¹ suld put yow to the se,
For thi I cum to mete yow her,
To tell perellys that may aper.'

  "The King wes off his spek angry,
And askyt his prywé men, in hy,
Quhat at thaim thoucht wes best to do.
Schyr Edward fryst answert thar to,
His brodyr that wes swa hardy,
And said; 'I say yow sekyrly
Thar sall na perell, that may be,
Dryve me eftsonys² to the se.
Myne auentur her tak will I,
Quhethir it be esfull or angry.'
'Brothyr,' he said, 'sen thou will sua,
It is gud that we samyn ta
Dissese or ese, or payne or play,
Eftyr as God will ws purway.³
And sen men sayis that the Persy
Myn heretage will occupy;
And his menye sa ner ws lyis,
That ws dispytis mony wyss;
Ga we and wenge⁴ sum off the dispyte
And that may we haiff done alss tite;⁵
For thai ly traistly,⁶ but dreding
Off ws, or off our her cummyng.
And thoucht we slepand slew thaim all,
Repruff tharof na man sall.
For werrayour na forss suld ma,
Quhethir he mycht ourcum his fa
Throw strenth, or throw sutelté;
But that gud faith ay haldyn be.' "
                    BARBOUR'S *Bruce*, Book iv., v. 1.

## NOTE R.

*The Bruce hath won his father's hall !* — P. 177.

I have followed the flattering and pleasing tradition, that the Bruce, after his descent upon the coast of Ayrshire, actually gained possession of his maternal castle.  But the tradition is not accurate.  The fact is, that he was only strong enough to alarm and drive in the outposts of the English garrison, then com-

¹ Haste.—² Soon after.—³ Prepare.—⁴ Avenge.—⁵ Quickly.—⁶ Confidently.

manded, not by Clifford, as assumed in the text, but by Percy. Neither was Clifford slain upon this occasion, though he had several skirmishes with Bruce. He fell afterwards in the battle of Bannockburn. Bruce, after alarming the castle of Turnberry, and surprising some part of the garrison, who were quartered without the walls of the fortress, retreated into the mountainous part of Carrick, and there made himself so strong, that the English were obliged to evacuate Turnberry, and at length the Castle of Ayr. Many of his benefactions and royal gifts attest his attachment to the hereditary followers of his house, in this part of the country.

It is generally known, that Bruce, in consequence of his dis tresses after the battle of Methven, was affected by a scorbutic disorder, which was then called a leprosy. It is said he experi- enced benefit from the use of a medicinal spring, about a' mile north of the town of Ayr, called from that circumstance King's Ease.[1] The following is the tradition of the country, collected by Mr. Train :—" After Robert ascended the throne, he founded the priory of Dominican monks, every one of whom was under the obligation of putting up to Heaven a prayer once every week-day, and twice in holydays, for the recovery of the king; and, after his death, these masses were continued for the saving of his soul. The ruins of this old monastery are now nearly level with the ground. Robert likewise caused houses to be built round the well of King's Ease, for eight lepers, and allow- ed eight bolls of oatmeal, and 28l. Scotch money, per annum, to each person. These donations were laid upon the lands of Fullarton, and are now payable by the Duke of Portland. The farm of Shiels, in the neighbourhood of Ayr, has to give, if required, a certain quantity of straw for the lepers' beds, and so much to thatch their houses annually. Each leprous person had a drinking-horn provided him by the king, which continued to be hereditary in the house to which it was first granted. One of those identical horns, of very curious workmanship, was in the possession of the late Colonel Fullarton of that Ilk."

---

[1] [Sir Walter Scott had misread Mr. Train's MS., which gave not *King's Ease*, but *King's Case*, i e *Casa Regis*, the name of the royal foundation described below Mr. Train's kindness enables the Editor to make this correc- tion. 1833 ]

My correspondent proceeds to mention some curious remnants of antiquity respecting this foundation. " In compliment to Sir William Wallace, the great deliverer of his country, King Robert Bruce invested the descendants of that hero with the right of placing all the lepers upon the establishment of King's Case. This patronage continued in the family of Craigie, till it was sold along with the lands of the late Sir Thomas Wallace. The burgh of Ayr then purchased the right of applying the donations of King's Case to the support of the poor-house of Ayr. The lepers' charter-stone was a basaltic block, exactly the shape of a sheep's kidney, and weighing an Ayrshire boll of meal. The surface of this stone being as smooth as glass, there was not any other way of lifting it than by turning the hollow to the ground, there extending the arms along each side of the stone, and clasping the hands in the cavity. Young lads were always considered as deserving to be ranked among men, when they could lift the blue stone of King's Case. It always lay beside the well, till a few years ago, when some English dragoons encamped at that place wantonly broke it, since which the fragments have been kept by the freemen of Prestwick in a place of security. There is one of these charter-stones at the village of Old Daily, in Carrick, which has become more celebrated by the following event, which happened only a very few years ago:— The village of New Daily being now larger than the old place of the same name, the inhabitants insisted that the charter-stone should be removed from the old town to the new, but the people of Old Daily were unwilling to part with their ancient right. Demands and remonstrances were made on each side without effect, till at last man, woman, and child, of both villages, marched out, and by one desperate engagement put an end to a war, the commencement of which no person then living remembered. Justice and victory, in this instance, being of the same party, the villagers of the old town of Daily now enjoy the pleasure of keeping the *blue-stane* unmolested. Ideal privileges are often attached to some of these stones. In Girvan, if a man can set his back against one of the above description, he is supposed not liable to be arrested for debt, nor can cattle, it is imagined, be poinded as long as they are fastened to the same stone. That stones were often used as symbols to denote the right of possess-

ing land, before the use of written documents became general in
Scotland, is, I think, exceedingly probable. The charter-stone
of Inverness is still kept with great care, set in a frame, and
hooped with iron, at the market-place of that town. It is called
by the inhabitants of that district Clack na Couldin. I think it
is very likely that Carey has mentioned this stone in his poem of
Craig Phaderick. This is only a conjecture, as I have never seen
that work. While the famous marble chair was allowed to
remain at Scoon, it was considered as the charter-stone of the
kingdom of Scotland."

## NOTE S.

> " *Bring here,*" *he said,* " *the mazers four,*
> *My noble fathers loved of yore.*"—P. 177.

These mazers were large drinking-cups, or goblets. Mention
of them occurs in a curious inventory of the treasure and jewels
of James III., which will be published, with other curious documents of antiquity, by my friend, Mr. Thomas Thomson, D. Register of Scotland, under the title of "A Collection of Invento-
ries, and other Records of the Royal Wardrobe, Jewel-House,"
&c. I copy the passage, in which mention is made of the mazers, and also of a habiliment, called "King Robert Bruce's serk,"
i. e. *shirt,* meaning, perhaps, his shirt of mail; although no other
arms are mentioned in the inventory. It might have been a relic
of more sanctified description, a penance shirt perhaps.

*Extract from* " *Inventare of ane Parte of the Gold and Silver*
*conyeit and unconyeit, Jowellis, and uther Stuff perteining to*
*Umquhile oure Soverane Lords Fader, that he had in Depois*
*the Tyme of his Deceis, and that come to the Handis of oure*
*Soverane Lord that now is,* M.CCCC.LXXXVIII."

"Memorandum fundin a bandit kist like a gardeviant,[1] in the
fyrst the grete chenye[2] of gold, contenand sevin score sex linkis.
*Item,* thre platis of silver.
*Item,* tuelf salfatis.[3]
*Item,* fyftene discheis[4] ouregilt.

---

[1] Gard-vin, or wine-cooler.—[2] Chain.—[3] Salt-cellars, anciently the object of
much curious workmanship.—[4] Dishes.

*Item*, a grete gilt plate.

*Item*, twa grete bassingis[1] ouregilt.

*Item*, FOUR MASARIS, CALLED KING ROBERT THE BROCIS, with a cover.

*Item*, a grete cok maid of silver.

*Item*, the hede of silver of ane of the coveris of masar.

*Item*, a fare dialle.[2]

*Item*, twa kasis of knyffis.[3]

*Item*, a pare of auld kniffis.

*Item*, takin be the smyth that opinnit the lokkis, in gold fourty demyis.

*Item*, in Inglys grotis[4] - - - - - - - - - xxiii li. and the said silver given again to the takaris of hym.

*Item*, ressavit in the cloissat of Davidis tour, ane haly water-fat of silver, twa boxis, a cageat tume, a glas with rois-water, a dosoune of torchis, KING ROBERT BRUCIS SERK."

The real use of the antiquarian's studies, is to bring the minute information which he collects to bear upon points of history. For example, in the inventory I have just quoted, there is given the contents of the *black kist*, or chest, belonging to James III., which was his strong box, and contained a quantity of treasure, in money and jewels, surpassing what might have been at the period expected of " poor Scotland's gear." This illustrates and authenticates a striking passage in the history of the house of Douglas, by Hume of Godscroft. The last Earl of Douglas (of the elder branch) had been reduced to monastic seclusion in the Abbey of Lindores, by James II. James III., in his distresses, would willingly have recalled him to public life, and made him his lieutenant. " But he," says Godscroft, " laden with years and old age, and weary of troubles, refused, saying, Sir, you have kept mee, and your *black coffer* in Sterling, too long, neither of us can doe you any good: I, because my friends have forsaken me, and my followers and dependers are fallen from me, betaking themselves to other masters; and your black trunk is too farre from you, and your enemies are between you and it: or (as others say) because there was in it a sort of black coyne, that the king had caused to

---

be coyned by the advice of his courtiers; which moneyes (saith he) sir. if you had put out at the first, the people would have taken it; and if you had employed mee in due time I might have done you service. But now there is none that will take notice of me, nor meddle with your money."—HUME's *History of the House of Douglas*, fol. Edin. 1644, p. 206.

## NOTE T.

*When English blood oft deluged Douglas-dale.*—P. 184.

The "good Lord James of Douglas," during these commotions, often took from the English his own castle of Douglas, but being unable to garrison it, contented himself with destroying the fortifications, and retiring into the mountains. As a reward to his patriotism, it is said to have been prophesied, that how often soever Douglas Castle should be destroyed, it should always again arise more magnificent from its ruins. Upon one of these occasions he used fearful cruelty, causing all the store of provisions, which the English had laid up in his castle, to be heaped together, bursting the wine and beer-casks among the wheat and flour, slaughtering the cattle upon the same spot, and upon the top of the whole cutting the throats of the English prisoners. This pleasantry of the "good Lord James" is commemorated under the name of the *Douglas's Larder*. A more pleasing tale of chivalry is recorded by Godscroft. "By this means, and such other exploits, he so affrighted the enemy, that it was counted a matter of great jeopardie to keep this castle, which began to be called the *adventurous* (or hazardous) *Castle of Douglas*; whereupon Sir John Walton being in suit of an English lady, she wrote to him, that when he had kept the adventurous Castle of Douglas seven years, then he might think himself worthy to be a suitor to her. Upon this occasion Walton took upon him the keeping of it, and succeeded to Thruswall, but he ran the same fortune with the rest that were before him. For Sir James, having first dressed an ambuscado near unto the place, he made fourteen of his men take so mary sacks, and fill them with grass, as though it had been corn, which they carried in the way to Lanark, the chief market town in that county : so hoping to draw forth the captain by that bait, and either to take him or the castle, or both. Neither was this expectation frustrated, for the captain did bite, and came forth to have taken this victual (as he supposed.) But ere he could reach these carriers, Sir James, with his company, had gotten between the castle and him; and these disguised carriers, seeing the captain following after them, did quickly cast off their sacks, mounted themselves on horseback, and met the captain with a sharp encounter, being so much the more amazed, as it was unlooked for: wherefore, when he saw these carriers metamorphosed into warriors, and ready to assault him, fearing that which was, that there was some train laid for them, he turned about to have retired to his castle, but there he also met with his enemies; between which two companies he and his whole followers were slain, so that none escaped: the captain afterwards being searched, they found (as it is reported) his mistress's letter about him."— HUME'S *History of the House of Douglas*, fol. pp. 29, 30.[1]

## NOTE U.

*And Connoght pour'd from waste and wood*
*Her hundred tribes, whose sceptre rude*
*Dark Eth O'Connor sway'd.*—P. 189.

There is in the Fœdera an invitation to Eth O'Connor, chief of the Irish of Connaught, setting forth that the king was about to move against his Scottish rebels, and therefore requesting the attendance of all the force he could muster, either commanded by himself in person, or by some nobleman of his race. These auxiliaries were to be commanded by Richard de Burgh, Earl of Ulster. Similar mandates were issued to the following Irish chiefs, whose names may astonish the unlearned, and amuse the antiquary.

" Eth O Donnuld, Duci Hibernicorum de Tyconil;
Demod O Kahan, Duci Hibernicorum de Fernetrew;
Doneval O Neel, Duci Hibernicorum de Trowyn;
Neel Macbreen, Duci Hibernicorum de Kynallewan;
Eth. Offyn, Duci Hibernicorum de Turtery;
Admely Mac Anegus, Duci Hibernicorum de Onehagh;

---

[This is the foundation of the Author's last romance, *Castle Dangerous.*—ED.]

Neel O Hanlan, Duci Hibernicorum de Erthere,
Bien Mac Mahun, Duci Hibernicorum de Uriel;
Lauercagh Mac Wyr, Duci Hibernicorum de Lougherin;
Gillys O Railly, Duci Hibernicorum de Bresfeny;
Geffrey O Fergy, Duci Hibernicorum de Montiragwil;
Felyn O Honughur, Duci Hibernicorum de Connach;
Donethuth O Bien, Duci Hibernicorum de Tothmund;
Dermod Mac Arthy, Duci Hibernicorum de Dessemound;
Denenol Carbragh;
Maur. Kenenagh Mac Murgh;
Murghugh O Bryn;
David O Tothvill;
Dermod O Tonoghur, Doffaly;
Fyn O Dymsy;
Souethuth Mac Gillephatrick;
Leyssagh O Morth;
Gilbertus Ekelly, Duci Hibernicorum de Omany;
Mac Ethelau;
Omalan Helyn, Duci Hibernicorum Midie."

RYMER'S *Fœdera*, vol. iii., pp. 476 477.

## NOTE V.

*In battles four beneath their eye,*
*The forces of King Robert lie.* — P. 193.

The arrangements adopted by King Robert for the decisive
battle of Bannockburn, are given very distinctly by Barbour, and
form an edifying lesson to tacticians.    Yet, till commented upon
by Lord Hailes, this important passage of history has been generally and strangely misunderstood by historians.    I w·ll here
endeavour to detail it fully.

Two days before the battle, Bruce selected the field of action,
and took post there with his army, consisting of about 30,000
disciplined men, and about half the number of disorderly attendants upon the camp.    The ground was called the New Park of
Stirling; it was partly open, and partly broken by copses of wood
and marshy ground.    He divided his regular forces into four
divisions.    Three of these occupied a front line, separated from
each other, yet sufficiently near for the purposes of communica

tion. The fourth division formed a reserve. The line extended in a north-easterly direction from the brook of Bannock, which was so rugged and broken as to cover the right flank effectually to the village of Saint Ninian's, probably in the line of the present road from Stirling to Kilsyth. Edward Bruce commanded the right wing, which was strengthened by a strong body of cavalry under Keith, the Mareschal of Scotland, to whom was committed the important charge of attacking the English archers; Douglas, and the young Steward of Scotland, led the central wing; and Thomas Randolph, Earl of Moray, the left wing. The King himself commanded the fourth division, which lay in reserve behind the others. The royal standard was pitched, according to tradition, in a stone, having a round hole for its reception, and thence called the Bore-stone. It is still shown on the top of a small eminence, called Brock's-brae, to the south-west of St. Ninian's. His main body thus disposed, King Robert sent the followers of the camp, fifteen thousand and upwards in number, to the eminence in rear of his army, called from that circumstance the *Gillies'* (*i. e.* the servants') *Hill.*

The military advantages of this position were obvious. The Scottish left flank, protected by the brook of Bannock, could not be turned; or, if that attempt were made, a movement by the reserve might have covered it. Again, the English could not pass the Scottish army, and move towards Stirling, without exposing their flank to be attacked while in march.

If, on the other hand, the Scottish line had been drawn up east and west, and facing to the southward, as affirmed by Buchanan, and adopted by Mr. Nimmo, the author of the History of Stirlingshire, there appears nothing to have prevented the English approaching upon the carse, or level ground, from Falkirk, either from turning the Scottish left flank, or from passing their position, if they preferred it, without coming to an action, and moving on to the relief of Stirling. And the Gillie's Hill, if this less probable hypothesis be adopted, would be situated, not in the rear, as allowed by all the historians, but upon the left flank of Bruce's army. The only objection to the hypothesis above laid down, is, that the left flank of Bruce's army was thereby exposed to a sally from the garrison of Stirling. But, 1st, the garrison were bound to neutrality by terms of Mowbray's treaty; and Barbour even seems to censure, as a breach of faith, some secret assistance which they rendered their countrymen upon the eve of battle, in placing temporary bridges of doors and spars over the pools of water in the carse, to enable them to advance to the charge.[1]  2dly, Had this not been the case, the strength of the garrison was probably not sufficient to excite apprehension.  3dly, The adverse hypothesis leaves the rear of the Scottish army as much exposed to the Stirling garrison, as the left flank would be in the case supposed.

It only remains to notice the nature of the ground in front of Bruce's line of battle.  Being part of a park, or chase, it was considerably interrupted with trees; and an extensive marsh, still visible, in some places rendered it inaccessible, and in all of difficult approach.  More to the northward, where the natural impediments were fewer, Bruce fortified his position against cavalry, by digging a number of pits so close together, says Barbour, as to resemble the cells in a honey-comb.  They were a foot in breadth, and between two and three feet deep, many rows of them being placed one behind the other.  They were slightly covered with brushwood and green sods, so as not to be obvious to an impetuous enemy.

All the Scottish army were on foot, except a select body of cavalry stationed with Edward Bruce on the right wing, under the immediate command of Sir Robert Keith, the Marshal of Scotland, who were destined for the important service of charging and dispersing the English archers.

Thus judiciously posted, in a situation fortified both by art and nature, Bruce awaited the attack of the English.

## NOTE W.

*With these the valiant of the Isles*
*Beneath their chieftains rank'd their files. — P. 195.*

The men of Argyle, the islanders, and the Highlanders in general, were ranked in the rear.  They must have been nume-

---

[1] An assistance which (by the way) could not have been rendered. had not the English approached from the south-east; since, had their march been due north, the whole Scottish army must have been between them and the garrison.

24 *

rous, for Bruce had reconciled himself with almost all their chieftains, excepting the obnoxious Mac-Dougals of Lorn. The follow
ing deed, containing the submission of the potent Earl of Ross to
the King, was never before published. It is dated in the third
year of Robert's reign, that is, 1309.

### "Obligacio Comitis Rossensis per Homagium Fidelitatem et Scriptum.

" Universis christi fidelibus ad quorum noticiam presentes
litere peruenerint Willielmus Comes de Ross salutem in domino
sempiternam. Quia magnificus princeps Dominus Robertus dei
gracia Rex Scottorum Dominus meus ex innata sibi bonitate,
inspirataque clemencia, et gracia speciali remisit michi pure ran-
corem animi sui, et relaxauit ac condonauit michi omnimodas
transgressiones seu offensas contra ipsum et suos per me et meos
vsque ad confeccionem literarum presencium perpetratas: Et
terras meas et tenementa mea omnia graciose concessit. Et me
nichilominus de terra de Dingwal et ferncroskry infra comitatum
de Suthyrland de benigna liberalitate sua heriditarie infeodare
curauit. Ego tantam principis beneuolenciam efficaciter attend-
ens, et pro tot graciis michi factis, vicem sibi gratitudinis meis
pro viribus de cetero digne - - - - - - - - - - - - - vite cupiens exhi-
bere, subicio et obligo me et heredes meos et homines meos
vniuersos dicto Domino meo Regi per omnia - - - - - - - - - - - - - - -
erga suam regiam dignitatem, quod erimus de cetero fideles sibi
et heredibus suis et fidele sibi seruicium auxilium et concilium
- - - - - - - - - - - - - contra omnes homines et feminas qui vivere
poterint aut mori, et super h - - - Ego Willielmus pro me - - - - -
- - - - - - - - hominibus meis vniuersis dicto domino meo Regi - -
- - - - - - manibus homagium sponte feci et super dei ewangelia
sacramentum prestiti - - - - - - - - - - - - In quorum omnium testi-
monium sigillum meum, et sigilla Hugonis filii et heredis et
Johannis filii mei vna cum sigillis venerabilium patrum Domino-
rum Dauid et Thome Moraviensis et Rossensis dei gracia episcoporum presentibus literis sunt appensa. Acta scripta et data apud
Aldern in Morauia vltimo die mensis Octobris, Anno Regni dicti
domini nostri Regis Roberti Tertio. Testibus venerabilibus
patribus supradictis, Domino Bernardo Cancellario Regis, Dominis
Willielmo de Haya, Johanne de Striuelyn, Willielmo Wysman.

Johanne de Ffenton, Dauid de Berkeley, et Waltero de Berkeley
militibus, magistro Waltero Heroc, Decano ecclesie Morauie,
magistro Willielmo de Creswel eiusdem ecclesie precentore et
multis aliis nobilibus clericis et laicis dictis die et loco con-
gregatis."

The copy of this curious document was supplied by my friend,
Mr. Thomson, Deputy Register of Scotland, whose researches
into our ancient records are daily throwing new and important
light upon the history of the country.

## Note X.

### The Monarch rode along the van. — P. 197.

The English vanguard, commanded by the Earls of Gloucester
and Hereford, came in sight of the Scottish army upon the evening of the 23d of June. Bruce was then riding upon a little
palfrey, in front of his foremost line, putting his host in order. It
was then that the personal encounter took place betwixt him and
Sir Henry de Bohun, a gallant English knight, the issue of which
had a great effect upon the spirits of both armies. It is thus
recorded by BARBOUR : —

> " And quhen Glosyster and Herfurd war
> With thair bataill, approchand ner,
> Befor thaim all thar come rydand,
> With helm on heid, and sper in hand,
> Schyr Henry the Boune, the worthi,
> That wes a wycht knycht, and a hardy ;
> And to the Erle off Herfurd cusyne :
> Armyt in armys gud and fyne ;
> Come on a sted, a bow schote ner,
> Befor all othyr that thar wer :
> And knew the King, for that he saw
> Him swa rang his men on raw ;
> And by the croune, that wes set
> Alsua apon his bassynet.
> And towart him he went in hy.
> And [quhen] the King sua apertly
> Saw him cum, forouth all his feris,[1]
> In hy[2] till him the hors he steris.

---

[1] Comrades. — [2] Haste.

And quhen Schyr Henry saw the King
Cum on, for owtyn abaysing,[1]
Till him he raid in full gret hy.
He thoucht that he suld weill lychtly
Wyn him, and haf him at his will
Sen he him horsyt saw sa ill.
Sprent[2] thai samyn in till a ling.[3]
Schyr Henry myssit the noble king.
And he, that in his sterapys stud,
With the ax that wes hard and gud,
With sa gret mayne[4] raucht him a dynt,
That nothyr hat, na helm, mycht stynt
The hewy[5] dusche[6] that he him gave,
That ner the heid till the harnys clave.
The hand ax schaft fruschit[7] in twa;
And he doune to the erd gan ga
All flatlynys,[8] for him faillyt mycht.
This wes the fryst strak off the fycht."

BARBOUR's *Bruce*, Book viii., v 684.

The Scottish leaders remonstrated with the King upon his temerity. He only answered, "I have broken my good battle-axe."—The English vanguard retreated after witnessing this single combat. Probably their generals did not think it advisable to hazard an attack, while its unfavourable issue remained upon their minds.

## NOTE Y.

*What train of dust, with trumpet-sound,*
*And glimmering spears, is wheeling round*
*Our leftward flank?* ———— P. 201.

While the van of the English army advanced, a detached body attempted to relieve Stirling. Lord Hailes gives the following account of this manœuvre and the result, which is accompanied by circumstances highly characteristic of the chivalrous manners of the age, and displays that generosity which reconciles us even to their ferocity upon other occasions.

Bruce had enjoined Randolph, who commanded the left wing

---

[1] Without shrinking —[2] Spurred. —[3] Line. —[4] Strength, or force. —[5] Heavy —[6] Clash.—[7] Broke —[8] Flat.

of his army, to be vigilant in preventing any advanced parties of the English from throwing succours into the castle of Stirling.

"Eight hundred horsemen, commanded by Sir Robert Clifford. were detached from the English army; they made a circuit by the low grounds to the east, and approached the castle. The king perceived their motions, and coming up to Randolph, angrily exclaimed, 'Thoughtless man! you have suffered the enemy to pass.' Randolph hasted to repair his fault, or perish. As he advanced, the English cavalry wheeled to attack him. Randolph drew up his troops in a circular form, with their spears resting on the ground, and protended on every side. At the first onset, Sir William Daynecourt, an English commander of distinguished note, was slain. The enemy, far superior in numbers to Randolph, environed him, and pressed hard on his little band. Douglas saw his jeopardy, and requested the king's permission to go and succour him. 'You shall not move from your ground,' cried the king; 'let Randolph extricate himself as he best may. I will not alter my order of battle, and lose the advantage of my position.'—'In truth,' replied Douglas, 'I cannot stand by and see Randolph perish; and, therefore, with your leave, I must aid him.' The king unwillingly consented, and Douglas flew to the assistance of his friend. While approaching, he perceived that the English were falling into disorder, and that the perseverance of Randolph had prevailed over their impetuous courage. 'Halt,' cried Douglas, 'those brave men have repulsed the enemy; let us not diminish their glory by sharing it.'"— DALRYMPLE's *Annals of Scotland*, 4to, Edinburgh, 1779, pp. 44, 45.

Two large stones erected at the north end of the village of Newhouse, about a quarter of a mile from the south part of Stirling, ascertain the place of this memorable skirmish. The cir cumstance tends, were confirmation necessary, to support the opinion of Lord Hailes, that the Scottish line had Stirling on its left flank. It will be remembered, that Randolph commanded infantry, Daynecourt cavalry. Supposing, therefore, according to the vulgar hypothesis, that the Scottish line was drawn up, facing to the south, in the line of the brook of Bannock, and consequently that Randolph was stationed with his left flank resting upon Milntown bog, it is morally impossible that his infantry, moving from that position, with whatever celerity, could cut off from Stirling a body of cavalry who had already passed St. Nini ans,[1] or, in other words, were already between them and the town. Whereas, supposing Randolph's left to have approached St. Ninians, the short movement to Newhouse could easily be executed, so as to intercept the English in the manner described.

## Note Z.

*Forth, Marshal, on the peasant foe!*
*We'll tame the terrors of their bow,*
*And cut the bow-string loose!*— P. 208.

The English archers commenced the attack with their usual bravery and dexterity. But against a force, whose importance he had learned by fatal experience, Bruce was provided. A small but select body of cavalry were detached from the right, under command of Sir Robert Keith. They rounded, as I conceive, the marsh called Milntown bog, and, keeping the firm ground, charged the left flank and rear of the English archers. As the bowmen had no spears, nor long weapons, fit to defend themselves against horse, they were instantly thrown into disorder, and spread through the whole English army a confusion, from which they never fairly recovered.

> " The Inglis archeris schot sa fast,
> That mycht thair schot haff ony last,
> It had bene hard to Scottis men.
> Bot King Robert, that wele gan ken [2]
> That thair archeris, war peralouss,
> And thair schot rycht hard and grewouss,
> Ordanyt, forouth [3] the assemblé,
> Hys marschell with a gret menye,
> Fyve hundre armyt in to stele,
> That on lycht horss war horsyt welle,
> For to pryk [4] amang the archeris;
> And swa assaile thaim with thair speris,
> That thai na layser haiff to schute.
> This marschell that Ik of mute, [5]

---

[1] Barbour says expressly, they avoided the New Park, (where Bruce's army lay,) and held " well neath the Kirk," which can only mean St. Ninians.

[2] Know.—[3] Disjoined from the main body —[4] Spur.—[5] That I speak of

> That Schyr Robert of Keyth was cauld,
> As Ik befor her has yow tauld,
> Quhen he saw the bataillis sua
> Assembill, and to gidder ga,
> And saw the archeris schoyt stoutly;
> With all thaim off his cumpany,
> In hy apon thaim gan he rid;
> And our tuk thaim at a sid;[1]
> And ruschyt amang thaim sa rudly,
> Stekand thaim sa dispitously,
> And in sic fusoun[2] berand doun,
> And slayand thaim, for owtyn ransoun;[3]
> That thai thaim scalyt[4] euirilkane.[5]
> And fra that tyme furth thar wes nane
> That assemblyt schot to ma.[6]
> Quhen Scottis archeris saw that thai sua
> War rebutyt,[7] thai woux hardy,
> And with all thair mycht schot egrely
> Amang the horss men, that thair raid;
> And woundis wid to thaim thai maid;
> And slew of thaim a full gret dele."
>
> BARBOUR'S *Bruce*, Book ix., v. 218.

Although the success of this manœuvre was evident, it is very remarkable that the Scottish generals do not appear to have profited by the lesson. Almost every subsequent battle which they lost against England, was decided by the archers, to whom the close and compact array of the Scottish phalanx afforded an exposed and unresisting mark. The bloody battle of Halidoun-hill, fought scarce twenty years afterwards, was so completely gained by the archers, that the English are said to have lost only one knight, one esquire, and a few foot-soldiers. At the battle of Neville's Cross, in 1346, where David II. was defeated and made prisoner, John de Graham, observing the loss which the Scots sustained from the English bowmen, offered to charge and disperse them, if a hundred men-at-arms were put under his command. " *But*, to confess the truth," says Fordun, " he could not procure a single horseman for the service proposed." Of such little use is experience in war, where its results are opposed by habit or prejudice.

---

[1] Set upon their flank. — [2] Numbers. — [3] Ransom. — [4] Dispersed. — [5] Every one.
[6] Make. — [7] Driven back.

## Note A 2.

*To arms they flew,—axe, club, or spear,—*
*And mimic ensigns high they rear.* — P. 216.

The followers of the Scottish camp observed, from the Gillie's Hill in the rear, the impression produced upon the English army by the bringing up of the Scottish reserve, and, prompted by the enthusiasm of the moment, or the desire of plunder, assumed, in a tumultuary manner, such arms as they found nearest, fastened sheets to tent-poles and lances, and showed themselves like a new army advancing to battle.

> " Yomen, and swanys,[1] and pitaill,[2]
> That in the Park yemyt wictaill,[3]
> War left; quhen thai wyst but lesing,[4]
> That thair lordis, with fell fechtyng,
> On thair fayis assemblyt wer;
> Ane off thaim selwyn[5] that war thar
> Capitane of thaim all thai maid
> And schetis, that war sumedele[6] brad,
> Thai festnyt in stoid off baneris,
> Apon lang treys and speris :
> And said that thai wald se the fycht;
> And help thair lordis at thair mycht.
> Quhen her till all assentyt wer,
> In a rout assemblit er;[7]
> Fyftene thowsand thai war, or ma.
> And than in gret hy gan thai ga,
> With thair baneris, all in a rout,
> As thai had men bene styth[8] and stout.
> Thai come, with all that assemblé,
> Rycht quhill thai mycht the bataill se;
> Than all at anys thai gave a cry,
> ' Sla! Sla! Apon thaim hastily !' "
> BARBOUR'S *Bruce*, Book ix., v. 410.

The unexpected apparition, of what seemed a new army, completed the confusion which already prevailed among the English, who fled in every direction, and were pursued with immense slaughter. The brook of Bannock, according to Barbour, was so

---

[1] Swains.—[2] Rabble.—[3] Kept the provisions —[4] Lying.—[5] Selves.—[6] Somewhat Are —[8] Stiff.

choked with the bodies of men and horses, that it might have been passed dry-shod. The followers of the Scottish camp fell upon the disheartened fugitives, and added to the confusion and slaughter. Many were driven into the Forth, and perished there, which, by the way, could hardly have happened, had the armies been drawn up east and west, since, in that case, to get at the river, the English fugitives must have fled through the victorious army. About a short mile from the field of battle is a place called the Bloody Folds. Here the Earl of Gloucester is said to have made a stand, and died gallantly at the head of his own military tenants and vassals. He was much regretted by both sides; and it is said the Scottish would gladly have saved his life, but, neglecting to wear his surcoat with armorial bearings over his armour, he fell unknown, after his horse had been stabbed with spears.

Sir Marmaduke Twenge, an English knight, contrived to conceal himself during the fury of the pursuit, and when it was somewhat slackened, approached King Robert. "Whose prisoner are you, Sir Marmaduke?" said Bruce, to whom he was personally known. "Yours, sir," answered the knight. "I receive you," answered the king, and, treating him with the utmost courtesy, loaded him with gifts, and dismissed him without ransom. The other prisoners were all well treated. There might be policy in this, as Bruce would naturally wish to acquire the good opinion of the English barons, who were at this time at great variance with their king. But it also well accords with his high chivalrous character.

## Note B 2.

*O! give their hapless prince his due.* — P. 216.

Edward II., according to the best authorities, showed, in the fatal field of Bannockburn, personal gallantry not unworthy of his great sire and greater son. He remained on the field till forced away by the Earl of Pembroke, when all was lost. He then rode to the Castle of Stirling, and demanded admittance: but the governor, remonstrating upon the imprudence of shutting himself up in that fortress, which must so soon surrender, he assembled around his person five hundred men-at-arms, and, avoiding the field of battle and the victorious army, fled towards Linlithgow, pursued by Douglas with about sixty horse. They were augmented by Sir Lawrence Abernethy with twenty more, whom Douglas met in the Torwood upon their way to join the English army, and whom he easily persuaded to desert the defeated monarch, and to assist in the pursuit. They hung upon Edward's flight as far as Dunbar, too few in number to assail him with effect, but enough to harass his retreat so constantly, that whoever fell an instant behind was instantly slain, or made prisoner. Edward's ignominious flight terminated at Dunbar, where the Earl of March, who still professed allegiance to him, "received him full gently." From thence, the monarch of so great an empire, and the late commander of so gallant and numerous an army, escaped to Bamborough in a fishing vessel.

Bruce, as will appear from the following document, lost no time in directing the thunders of parliamentary censure against such part of his subjects as did not return to their natural allegiance after the battle of Bannockburn.

APUD MONASTERIUM DE CAMBUSKENNETH,

VI DIE NOVEMBRIS, M,CCC,XIV.

*Judicium Reditum apud Kambuskinet contra omnes illos qui tunc fuerunt contra fidem et pacem Domini Regis.*

Anno gracie millesimo tricentisimo quarto decimo sexto die Novembris tenente parliamentum suum Excellentissimo principe Domino Roberto Dei gracia Rege Scottorum Illustri in monasterio de Cambuskyneth concordatum fuit finaliter Judicatum [ac super] hoc statutum de Concilio et Assensu Episcoporum et ceterorum Prelatorum Comitum Baronum et aliorum nobilium regni Scocie nec non et tocius communitatis regni predicti quod omnes qui contra fidem et pacem dicti domini regis in bello seu alibi mortui sunt [vel qui dic] to die ad pacem ejus et fidem non venerant licet sepius vocati et legitime expectati fuissent de terris et tenementis et omni alio statu infra regnum Scocie perpetuo sint exheredati et habeantur de cetero tanquam inimici Regis et Regni ab omni vendicacione juris hereditarii vel juris alterius cujuscunque in posterum pro se et heredibus suis in perpetuum privati Ad perpetuam igitur rei memoriam et evidentem probacionem hujus

Judicii et Statuti sigilla Episcoporum et aliorum Prelatorum nec non et comitum Baronum ac ceterorum nobilium dicti Regni precenti ordinacioni Judicio et statuto sunt appensa.

Sigillum Domini Regis

Sigillum Willelmi Episcopi Sancti Andree

Sigillum Roberti Episcopi Glascuensis

Sigillum Willelmi Episcopi Dunkeldensis

. . . Episcopi . . . . . . . .

. . . Episcopi . . . . . . . .

. . . Episcopi . . . . . . . .

Sigillum Alani Episcopi Sodorensis

Sigillum Johannis Episcopi Brechynensis

Sigillum Andree Episcopi Ergadiensis

Sigillum Frechardi Episcopi Cathanensis

Sigillum Abbatis de Scona

Sigillum Abbatis de Calco

Sigillum Abbatis de Abirbrothok

Sigillum Abbatis de Sancta Cruce

Sigillum Abbatis de Londoris

Sigillum Abbatis de Newbotill

Sigillum Abbatis de Cupro

Sigillum Abbatis de Paslet

Sigillum Abbatis de Dunfermelyn

Sigillum Abbatis de Lincluden

Sigillum Abbatis de Insula Missarum

Sigillum Abbatis de Sancto Columba

Sigillum Abbatis de Deer

Sigillum Abbatis de Dulce Corde

Sigillum Prioris de Coldinghame

Sigillum Prioris de Rostynot

Sigillum Prioris Sancte Andree

Sigillum Prioris de Pettinwem

Sigillum Prioris de Insula de Lochlevin

Sigillum Senescalli Scocie

Sigillum Willelmi Comitis de Ros

. . . . . . . . . . . . .

. . . . . . . . . . . . .

. . . . . . . . . . . . .

Sigillum Gilberti de la Haya Constabularii Scocie

Sigillum Roberti de Keth Mariscalli Scocie
Sigillum Hugonis de Ros
Sigillum Jacobi de Duglas
Sigillum Johannis de Sancto Claro
Sigillum Thome de Ros
Sigillum Alexandri de Settone
Sigillum Walteri Haliburtone
Sigillum Davidis de Balfour
Sigillum Duncani de Wallays
Sigillum Thome de Dischingtone
Sigillum Andree de Moravia
Sigillum Archibaldi de Betun
Sigillum Ranulphi de Lyill
Sigillum Malcomi de Balfour
Sigillum Normanni de Lesley
Sigillum Nigelli de Campo bello
Sigillum Morni de Musco Campo

. . . . . . . . . . . . . .
. . . . . . . . . . . .

## Note C 2.

*Nor for De Argentine alone,*
*Through Ninian's church these torches shone,*
*And rose the death-prayer's awful tone.* — P. 219.

The remarkable circumstances attending the death of De Argentine have been already noticed (p. 51.) Besides this renowned
warrior, there fell many representatives of the noblest houses in
England, which never sustained a more bloody and disastrous
defeat. Barbour says that two hundred pairs of gilded spurs
were taken from the field of battle; and that some were left the
author can bear witness, who has in his possession a curious antique spur, dug up in the morass, not long since.

> " It wes forsuth a gret ferly,
> To se samyn [1] sa fele dede lie.
> Twa hundre payr of spurris reid, [2]
> War tane of knichtis that war deid."

I am now to take my leave of Barbour, not without a sincere
wish that the public may encourage the undertaking of my friend

---

[1] Together. — [2] Red, or gilded.

Dr. Jamieson, who has issued proposals for publishing an accurate edition of his poem, and of Blind Harry's Wallace.* The only good edition of The Bruce was published by Mr. Pinkerton, in 3 vols., in 1790; and, the learned editor having had no personal access to consult the manuscript, it is not without errors; and it has besides become scarce. Of Wallace there is no tolerable edition; yet these two poems do no small honour to the early state of Scottish poetry, and The Bruce is justly regarded as containing authentic historical facts.

The following list of the slain at Bannockburn, extracted from the continuator of Trivet's Annals, will show the extent of the national calamity.

### LIST OF THE SLAIN.

*Barons and Knights Bannerets.*

Gilbert de Clare, Earl of Gloucester,
Robert de Clifford,
Payan Tybetot,
William Le Mareschal,
John Comyn,
William de Vescey,
John de Montfort,
Nicolas de Hasteleigh,
William Dayncourt,
Ægidius de Argenteyne,
Edmond Comyn,
John Lovel, (the rich,)
Edmund de Hastynge,
Milo de Stapleton,
Simon Ward,
Robert de Felton,
Michael Poyning,
Edmund Maulley.

*Knights.*

Henry de Boun,
Thomas de Ufford,
John de Elsingfelde,
John de Harcourt,
Walter de Hakelut,
Philip de Courtenay,
Hugo de Scales,
Radulph de Beauchamp,
John de Penbrigge,
With thirty-three others of the same rank, not named.

### PRISONERS.

*Barons and Baronets.*

Henry de Boun, Earl of Hereford,
Lord John Giffard,
William de Latimer,
Maurice de Berkley,
Ingelram de Umfraville,
Marmaduke de Twenge,
John de Wyletone,
Robert de Maulee,
Henry Fitz-Hugh,
Thomas de Gray,
Walter de Beauchamp,

---

* [The extracts from Barbour in this edition of Sir Walter Scott's poems have been uniformly corrected by the text of Dr Jamieson's Bruce, published along with Blind Harry's Wallace, Edin 1820. 2 vols. 4to — ED.]

Richard de Charon,
John de Wevelmton,
Robert de Nevil,
John de Segrave,
Gilbert Peeche,
John de Clavering,
Antony de Lucy,
Radulph de Camys,
John de Evere,
Andrew de Abremhyn.
*Knights.*
Thomas de Berkeley,
The son of Roger Tyrrel,
Anselm de Mareschal,
Giles de Beauchamp,
John de Cyfrewast,
John Bluwet,
Roger Corbet,
Gilbert de Boun,

Bartholomew de Enefeld,
Thomas de Ferrers,
Radulph and Thomas Bottetort,
John and Nicholas de Kingstone,
(brothers,)
William Lovel,
Henry de Wileton,
Baldwin de Frevill,
John de Clivedon,[1]
Adomar la Zouche,
John de Merewode,
John Maufe,[2]
Thomas and Odo Lele Ercede-
kene,
Robert Beaupel, (the son,)
John Mautravers, (the son,)
William and William Giffard,
and thirty-four other knights,
not named by the historian.

And in sum there were there slain, along with the Earl of Gloucester, forty-two barons and bannerets. The number of earls,
barons, and bannerets made captive, was twenty-two, and sixty-
eight knights. Many clerks and esquires were also there slain
or taken. Roger de Northburge, keeper of the king's signet,
(*Custos Targiæ Domini Regis,*) was made prisoner with his two
clerks, Roger de Wakenfelde and Thomas de Switon, upon
which the king caused a seal to be made, and entitled it his *privy
seal,* to distinguish the same from the signet so lost. The Earl
of Hereford was exchanged against Bruce's queen, who had been
detained in captivity ever since the year 1306. The *Targia,* or
signet, was restored to England through the intercession of Ralph
de Monthermer, ancestor of Lord Moira, who is said to have
found favour in the eyes of the Scottish king.—*Continuation of
Trivet's Annals, Hall's edit. Oxford,* 1712, vol. ii., p. 14.

Such were the immediate consequences of the field of Bannockburn. Its more remote effects, in completely establishing
the national independence of Scotland, afford a boundless field
for speculation.

---

[1] Supposed Clinton.                    [2] Maule.

# THE

# FIELD OF WATERLOO.

## A POEM.

"Though Valois braved young Edward's gentle hand,
And Albert rush'd on Henry's way-worn band,
With Europe's chosen sons, in arms renown'd,
Yet not on Vere's bold archers long they look'd,
Nor Audley's squires nor Mowbray's yeomen brook'd,—
They saw their standard fall, and left their monarch bound.

AKENSIDE.

# ADVERTISEMENT.

It may be some apology for the imperfections of this poem, that it was composed hastily, and during a short tour upon the Continent, when the Author's labours were liable to frequent interruption; but its best apology is, that it was written for the purpose of assisting the Waterloo Subscription.

ABBOTSFORD, 1815.

THE

# FIELD OF WATERLOO.

## I.

FAIR Brussels, thou art far behind,
Though, lingering on the morning wind,
    We yet may hear the hour
Peal'd over orchard and canal,
With voice prolong'd and measured fall,
    From proud St. Michael's tower;
Thy wood, dark Soignies, holds us now,[1]
Where the tall beeches' glossy bough
    For many a league around,
With birch and darksome oak between
Spreads deep and far a pathless screen,
    Of tangled forest ground.
Stems planted close by stems defy
The adventurous foot—the curious eye
    For access seeks in vain:
And the brown tapestry of leaves,
Strew'd on the blighted ground, receives
    Nor sun, nor air, nor rain.

---

[1] ["The wood of Soignies is supposed to be a remnant of the
forest of Ardennes, famous in Boiardo's Orlando, and immortal in
Shakspeare's 'As you Like it.' It is also celebrated in Tacitus
as being the spot of successful defence by the Germans against
the Roman encroachments."—BYRON.]

t t

No opening glade dawns on our way,
No streamlet, glancing to the ray,
    Our woodland path has cross'd;
And the straight causeway which we tread,
Prolongs a line of dull arcade,
Unvarying through the unvaried shade
    Until in distance lost.

## II.

A brighter, livelier scene succeeds:[1]
In groups the scattering wood recedes,
Hedge-rows, and huts, and sunny meads,
    And corn-fields, glance between;
The peasant, at his labour blithe,
Plies the hook'd staff and shorten'd scythe:—[2]

---

[1] ["Southward from Brussels lies the field of blood,
    Some three hours' journey for a well-girt man;
A horseman who in haste pursued his road
    Would reach it as the second hour began.
The way is through a forest deep and wide,
Extending many a mile on either side.

"No cheerful woodland this of antique trees,
    With thickets varied and with sunny glade;
Look where he will, the weary traveller sees
    One gloomy, thick, impenetrable shade
Of tall straight trunks, which move before his sight,
With interchange of lines of long green light.

"Here, where the woods receding from the road
    Have left on either hand an open space
For fields and gardens, and for man's abode,
    Stands Waterloo; a little lowly place
Obscure till now, when it hath risen to fame,
And given the victory its English name."

             SOUTHEY'S *Pilgrimage to Waterloo.*]

[2] The reaper in Flanders carries in his left hand a stick with an
iron hook, with which he collects as much grain as he can cut at
one sweep with a short scythe, which he holds in his right hand.
They carry on this double process with great spirit and dexterity.

But when these ears were green,
Placed close within destruction's scope,
Full little was that rustic's hope
  Their ripening to have seen!
And, lo, a hamlet and its fane:—
Let not the gazer with disdain
  Their architecture view;
For yonder rude ungraceful shrine,
And disproportioned spire, are thine,
  Immortal WATERLOO![1]

### III.

Fear not the heat, though full and high
The sun has scorch'd the autumn sky,
And scarce a forest straggler now
To shade us spreads a greenwood bough;
These fields have seen a hotter day
Than e'er was fired by sunny ray.
Yet one mile on—yon shatter'd hedge
Crests the soft hill whose long smooth ridge
  Looks on the fields below,
And sinks so gently on the dale,
That not the folds of Beauty's veil
  In easier curves can flow.

---

[1] [" What time the second Carlos ruled in Spain,
 Last of the Austrian line by fate decreed,
Here Castanaza rear'd a votive fane,
 Praying the patron saints to bless with seed
His childless sovereign. Heaven denied an heir,
And Europe mourn'd in blood the frustrate prayer."

           SOUTHEY.

To the original chapel of the Marquis of Castanaza has now
been added a building of considerable extent, the whole interior
of which is filled with monumental inscriptions for the heroes who
fell in the battle.]

Brief space from thence, the ground again
Ascending slowly from the plain,
  Forms an opposing screen,
Which, with its crest of upland ground,
Shuts the horizon all around.
  The soften'd vale between
Slopes smooth and fair for courser's tread.
Not the most timid maid need dread
To give her snow-white palfrey head
  On that wide stubble-ground;[1]
Nor wood, nor tree, nor bush, are there,
Her course to intercept or scare,
  Nor fosse nor fence are found,
Save where, from out her shatter'd bowers,
Rise Hougomont's dismantled towers.

### IV.

Now, see'st thou aught in this lone scene
Can tell of that which late hath been? —
  A stranger might reply,
" The bare extent of stubble-plain
Seems lately lighten'd of its grain;
And yonder sable tracks remain
Marks of the peasant's ponderous wain,
  When harvest-home was nigh.[2]

---

[1] [" As a plain, Waterloo seems marked out for the scene of
some great action, though this may be mere imagination.  I have
viewed with attention those of Platea, Troy, Mantinea, Leuctra,
Chæronea, and Marathon; and the field around Mont St. Jean
and Hougomont appears to want little but a better cause, and
that indefinable but impressive halo which the lapse of ages
throws around a consecrated spot, to vie in interest with any or
all of these, except, perhaps, the last mentioned."—BYRON.]

 [2] [' Is the spot mark'd with no colossal bust,
  Nor column trophied for triumphal show?

On these broad spots of trampled ground,
Perchance the rustics danced such round
    As Teniers loved to draw;
And where the earth seems scorch'd by flame,
To dress the homely feast they came,
And toil'd the kerchief'd village dame
    Around her fire of straw."

### V.

So deem'st thou—so each mortal deems,
Of that which is from that which seems:—
    But other harvest here,
Than that which peasant's scythe demands.
Was gather'd in by sterner hands,
    With bayonet, blade, and spear.
No vulgar crop was theirs to reap,
No stinted harvest thin and cheap!
Heroes before each fatal sweep
    Fell thick as ripen'd grain;—

---

None: But the moral's truth tells simpler so,
As the ground was before, thus let it be;—
How that red rain hath made the harvest grow!
And is this all the world has gain'd by thee,
Thou first and last of fields! king-making Victory?"

BYRON.

---

"Was it a soothing or a mournful thought,
    Amid this scene of slaughter as we stood,
Where armies had with recent fury fought,
    To mark how gentle Nature still pursued
Her quiet course, as if she took no care
For what her noblest work had suffer'd there.

The pears had ripen'd on the garden wall;
    Those leaves which on the autumnal earth were spread,
The trees, though pierced and scared with many a ball,
    Had only in their natural season shed;
Flowers were in seed, whose buds to swell began
When such wild havoc here was made by man."

SOUTHEY]

And ere the darkening of the day,
Piled high as autumn shocks, there lay
The ghastly harvest of the fray,
    The corpses of the slain.[1]

## VI.

Ay, look again—that line so black
And trampled marks the bivouack,
Yon deep-graved ruts the artillery's track
    So often lost and won;
And close beside, the harden'd mud
Still shows where, fetlock-deep in blood,
The fierce dragoon, through battle's flood,
    Dash'd the hot war-horse on.
These spots of excavation tell
The ravage of the bursting shell—
And feel'st thou not the tainted steam,
That reeks against the sultry beam,
    From yonder trenched mound?
The pestilential fumes declare
That Carnage has replenish'd there
    Her garner-house profound.

---

[1] [" Earth had received into her silent womb
  Her slaughter'd creatures; horse and man they lay,
And friend and foe, within the general tomb.
  Equal had been their lot; one fatal day
For all, .. one labour, .. and one place of rest
They found within their common parent's breast.

The passing seasons had not yet effaced
  The stamp of numerous hoofs impress'd by force
Of cavalry, whose path might still be traced.
  Yet nature everywhere resumed her course;
Low pansies to the sun their purple gave,
And the soft poppy blossom'd on the grave."

                                 SOUTHEY.

## VII.

Far other harvest-home and feast,
Than claims the boor from scythe released,
   On these scorch'd fields were known!
Death hover'd o'er the maddening rout,
And, in the thrilling battle-shout,
Sent for the bloody banquet out
   A summons of his own.
Through rolling smoke the Demon's eye
Could well each destined guest espy,
Well could his ear in ecstasy
   Distinguish every tone
That fill'd the chorus of the fray—
From cannon-roar and trumpet-bray,
From charging squadrons' wild hurra,
From the wild clang that mark'd their way,—
   Down to the dying groan,
And the last sob of life's decay,
   When breath was all but flown.

## VIII.

Feast on, stern foe of mortal life,
Feast on!—but think not that a strife,
With such promiscuous carnage rife,
   Protracted space may last;
The deadly tug of war at length
Must limits find in human strength,
   And cease when these are past.
Vain hope!—that morn's o'erclouded sun
Heard the wild shout of fight begun
   Ere he attain'd his height,
And through the war-smoke, volumed high,
Still peals that unremitted cry,
   Though now he stoops to night.

26 *

For ten long hours of doubt and dread,
Fresh succours from the extended head
Of either hill the contest fed;
    Still down the slope they drew,
The charge of columns paused not,
Nor ceased the storm of shell and shot;
    For all that war could do
Of skill and force was proved that day,
And turn'd not yet the doubtful fray
    On bloody Waterloo.

## IX.

Pale Brussels! then what thoughts were thine,[1]
When ceaseless from the distant line
    Continued thunders came!
Each burgher held his breath, to hear
These forerunners of havoc near,
    Of rapine and of flame.
What ghastly sights were thine to meet,
When rolling through thy stately street,
The wounded show'd their mangled plight
In token of the unfinish'd fight,
And from each anguish-laden wain
The blood-drops laid thy dust like rain![2]

---

[1] It was affirmed by the prisoners of war, that Bonaparte had promised his army, in case of victory, twenty-four hours' plunder of the city of Brussels.

[2] ["Within those walls there linger'd at that hour
  Many a brave soldier on the bed of pain,
Whom aid of human art should ne'er restore
  To see his country and his friends again;
And many a victim of that fell debate,
Whose life yet waver'd in the scales of fate.

How often in the distant drum
Heard'st thou the fell Invader come,
While Ruin, shouting to his band,
Shook high her torch and gory brand!—
Cheer thee, fair City! From yon stand,
Impatient, still his outstretch'd hand

    Points to his prey in vain,
While maddening in his eager mood,
And all unwont to be withstood,

    He fires the fight again.

## X.

"On! On!" was still his stern exclaim,
"Confront the battery's jaws of flame!

    Rush on the levell'd gun!
My steel-clad cuirassiers, advance!
Each Hulan forward with his lance,

---

"Others in wagons borne abroad I saw,
  Albeit recovering, still a mournful sight;
Languid and helpless, some were stretch'd on straw,
  Some more advanced, sustain'd themselves upright,
And with bold eye and careless front, methought,
Seem'd to set wounds and death again at nought.

"What had it been, then, in the recent days
  Of that great triumph, when the open wound
Was festering, and along the crowded ways,
  Hour after hour was heard the incessant sound
Of wheels, which o'er the rough and stony road
Convey'd their living agonizing load!

"Hearts little to the melting mood inclined,
  Grew sick to see their sufferings; and the thought
Still comes with horror to the shuddering mind
  Of those sad days, when Belgian ears were taught
The British soldier's cry, half groan, half prayer,
Breathed when his pain is more than he can bear."

                SOUTHEY.]

My Guard — my Chosen — charge for France,
    France and Napoleon!"[1]
Loud answer'd their acclaiming shout,
Greeting the mandate which sent out
Their bravest and their best to dare
The fate their leader shunn'd to share.[2]

---

[1] The characteristic obstinacy of Napoleon was never more
fully displayed than in what we may be permitted to hope will
prove the last of his fields. He would listen to no advice, and
allow of no obstacles. An eyewitness has given the following
account of his demeanour towards the end of the action:—

"It was near seven o'clock; Bonaparte, who till then had
remained upon the ridge of the hill whence he could best behold
what passed, contemplated with a stern countenance, the scene
of this horrible slaughter. The more that obstacles seemed to
multiply, the more his obstinacy seemed to increase. He became
indignant at these unforeseen difficulties; and, far from fearing
to push to extremities an army whose confidence in him was
boundless, he ceased not to pour down fresh troops, and to give
orders to march forward—to charge with the bayonet—to carry
by storm. He was repeatedly informed, from different points,
that the day went against him, and that the troops seemed to be
disordered; to which he only replied,—' *En-avant! En-avant!*'

"One general sent to inform the Emperor that he was in a
position which he could not maintain, because it was commanded
by a battery, and requested to know, at the same time, in what
way he should protect his division from the murderous fire of the
English artillery. ' Let him storm the battery!' replied Bonaparte, and turned his back on the aide-de-camp who brought the
message."— *Relatione de la Bataille de Mont-St-Jean. Par un
Témoin Oculaire.* Paris, 1815, 8vo, p. 51.

[2] It has been reported that Bonaparte charged at the head of
his guards, at the last period of this dreadful conflict. This,
however, is not accurate. He came down indeed to a hollow
part of the high road, leading to Charleroi, within less than a
quarter of a mile of the farm of La Haye Sainte, one of the
points most fiercely disputed. Here he harangued the guards,

But HE, his country's sword and shield,
Still in the battle-front reveal'd,
Where danger fiercest swept the field,
    Came like a beam of light,
In action prompt, in sentence brief—
" Soldiers, stand firm," exclaim'd the Chief,
    " England shall tell the fight!"[1]

---

and informed them that his preceding operations had destroyed
the British infantry and cavalry, and that they had only to support the fire of the artillery, which they were to attack with the
bayonet. This exhortation was received with shouts of *Vive
l'Empereur*, which were heard over all our line, and led to an
idea that Napoleon was charging in person. But the guards
were led on by Ney; nor did Bonaparte approach nearer the
scene of action than the spot already mentioned, which the rising
banks on each side rendered secure from all such balls as did not
come in a straight line. He witnessed the earlier part of the
battle from places yet more remote, particularly from an observatory which had been placed there by the King of the Netherlands, some weeks before, for the purpose of surveying the country.* It is not meant to infer from these particulars that Napoleon showed, on that memorable occasion, the least deficiency in
personal courage; on the contrary, he evinced the greatest com-
posure and presence of mind during the whole action. But it is
no less true that report has erred in ascribing to him any desperate efforts of valour for recovery of the battle; and it is remarkable, that during the whole carnage, none of his suite were either
killed or wounded, whereas scarcely one of the Duke of Wellington's personal attendants escaped unhurt.

[1] In riding up to a regiment which was hard pressed, the Duke
called to the men, " Soldiers, we must never be beat,—what will
they say in England?" It is needless to say how this appeal was
answered.

* The mistakes concerning this observatory have been mutual. The English
supposed it was erected for the use of Bonaparte: and a French writer affirms
it was constructed by the Duke of Wellington.

## XI.

On came the whirlwind—like the last
But fiercest sweep of tempest-blast—
On came the whirlwind—steel-gleams broke
Like lightning through the rolling smoke;
 The war was waked anew,
Three hundred cannon-mouths roar'd loud,
And from their throats, with flash and cloud,
 Their showers of iron threw.
Beneath their fire, in full career,
Rush'd on the ponderous cuirassier,
The lancer couch'd his ruthless spear,
And hurrying as to havoc near,
 The cohorts' eagles flew.
In one dark torrent, broad and strong,
The advancing onset roll'd along,
Forth harbinger'd by fierce acclaim,
That, from the shroud of smoke and flame,
Peal'd wildly the imperial name.

## XII.

But on the British heart were lost
The terrors of the charging host;
For not an eye the storm that view'd
Changed its proud glance of fortitude,
Nor was one forward footstep staid,
As dropp'd the dying and the dead.
Fast as their ranks the thunders tear,
Fast they renew'd each serried square;
And on the wounded and the slain
Closed their diminish'd files again,
Till from their line scarce spears' lengths three.
Emerging from the smoke they see

Helmet, and plume, and panoply,—
    Then waked their fire at once!
Each musketeer's revolving knell,
As fast, as regularly fell,
As when they practise to display
Their discipline on festal day.
    Then down went helm and lance,
Down were the eagle banners sent,
Down reeling steeds and riders went,
Corslets were pierced, and pennons rent;
    And, to augment the fray,
Wheel'd full against their staggering flanks,
The English horsemen's foaming ranks
    Forced their resistless way.
Then to the musket-knell succeeds
The clash of swords — the neigh of steeds —
As plies the smith his clanging trade,[1]
Against the cuirass rang the blade:[2]
And while amid their close array
The well-served cannon rent their way,
And while amid their scatter'd band
Raged the fierce rider's bloody brand,
Recoil'd in common rout and fear,
Lancer and guard and cuirassier,
Horsemen and foot, — a mingled host,
Their leaders fall'n, their standards lost.

---

[1] A private soldier of the 95th regiment compared the sound which took place immediately upon the British cavalry mingling with those of the enemy, to "*a thousand tinkers at work mending pots and kettles.*"

[2] ["I heard the broadswords' deadly clang,
    As if an hundred anvils rang!'"
                    *Lady of the Lake.*]

## XIII.

Then, WELLINGTON! thy piercing eye
This crisis caught of destiny —
   The British host had stood
That morn 'gainst charge of sword and lance [1]
As their own ocean-rocks hold stance,
But when thy voice had said, "Advance!"
   They were their ocean's flood.—
O Thou, whose inauspicious aim
Hath wrought thy host this hour of shame,
Think'st thou thy broken bands will bide
The terrors of yon rushing tide?
Or will thy chosen brook to feel
The British shock of levell'd steel, [2]

---

[1] [The cuirassiers continued their dreadful onset, and rode up to the squares in the full confidence, apparently, of sweeping every thing before the impetuosity of their charge. Their onset and reception was like a furious ocean pouring itself against a chain of insulated rocks. The British squares stood unmoved, and never gave fire until the cavalry were within ten yards, when men rolled one way, horses galloped another, and the cuirassiers were in every instance driven back." — *Life of Bonaparte*, vol. viii. p. 487.]

[2] No persuasion or authority could prevail upon the French troops to stand the shock of the bayonet. The Imperial Guards, in particular, hardly stood till the British were within thirty yards of them, although the French author, already quoted, has put into their mouths the magnanimous sentiment, "The Guards never yield—they die." The same author has covered the plateau, or eminence, of St. Jean, which formed the British position, with redoubts and intrenchments which never had an existence. As the narrative, which is in many respects curious, was written by an eyewitness, he was probably deceived by the appearance of a road and ditch which run along part of the hill. It may be also mentioned, in criticising this work, that the writer mentions the

Or dost thou turn thine eye
Where coming squadrons gleam afar,
And fresher thunders wake the war,
    And other standards fly?—
Think not that in yon columns, file
Thy conquering troops from distant Dyle—
    Is Blucher yet unknown?
Or dwells not in thy memory still,
(Heard frequent in thine hour of ill,)
What notes of hate and vengeance thrill
    In Prussia's trumpet tone?—
What yet remains?—shall it be thine
To head the relics of thy line
    In one dread effort more?—
The Roman lore thy leisure loved,
And thou canst tell what fortune proved
    That Chieftain, who, of yore,
Ambition's dizzy paths essay'd,
And with the gladiators' aid
    For empire enterprised—
He stood the cast his rashness play'd,
Left not the victims he had made,

---

Chateau of Hougomont to have been carried by the French, although it was resolutely and successfully defended during the whole action. The enemy, indeed, possessed themselves of the wood by which it is surrounded, and at length set fire to the house itself; but the British (a detachment of the Guards, under the command of Colonel Macdonnell, and afterwards of Colonel Home) made good the garden, and thus preserved, by their desperate resistance, the post which covered the return of the Duke of Wellington's right flank.

Dug his red grave with his own blade,
And on the field he lost was laid,
        Abhorr'd—but not despised.[1]

### XIV.

But if revolves thy fainter thought
On safety—howsoever bought,
Then turn thy fearful rein and ride,
Though twice ten thousand men have died
        On this eventful day,
To gild the military fame
Which thou, for life, in traffic tame
        Wilt barter thus away.
Shall future ages tell this tale
Of inconsistence faint and frail?

---

[1] [" When the engagement was ended, it evidently appeared with what undaunted spirit and resolution Catiline's army had been fired; for the body of every one was found on that very spot which, during the battle, he had occupied; those only excepted who were forced from their posts by the Prætorian cohort; and even they, though they fell a little out of their ranks, were all wounded before. Catiline himself was found, far from his own men, amidst the dead bodies of the enemy, breathing a little, with an air of that fierceness still in his face which he had when alive. Finally, in all his army, there was not so much as one free citizen taken prisoner, either in the engagement or in flight; for they spared their own lives as little as those of the enemy. The army of the republic obtained the victory, indeed, but it was neither a cheap nor a joyful one, for their bravest men were either slain in battle or dangerously wounded. As there were many, too, who went to view the field, either out of curiosity or a desire of plunder, in turning over the dead bodies, some found a friend, some a relation, and some a guest; others there were likewise who discovered their enemies; so that, through the whole army, there appeared a mixture of gladness and sorrow, joy and mourning."—SALLUST.]

And art thou He of Lodi's bridge,
Marengo's field, and Wagram's ridge!
    Or is thy soul like mountain-tide,
That, swell'd by winter storm and shower,
Rolls down in turbulence of power,
    A torrent fierce and wide;
Reft of these aids, a rill obscure,
Shrinking unnoticed, mean and poor,
    Whose channel shows display'd
The wrecks of its impetuous course,
But not one symptom of the force
    By which these wrecks were made!

## XV.

Spur on thy way!—since now thine ear
Has brook'd thy veterans' wish to hear,
    Who, as thy flight they eyed,
Exclaim'd,—while tears of anguish came,
Wrung forth by pride, and rage, and shame,—
    "O, that he had but died!"
But yet, to sum this hour of ill,
Look, ere thou leavest the fatal hill,
    Back on yon broken ranks—
Upon whose wild confusion gleams
The moon, as on the troubled streams
    When rivers break their banks,
And, to the ruin'd peasant's eye
Objects half seen roll swiftly by,
    Down the dread current hurl'd—
So mingle banner, wain, and gun,
Where the tumultuous flight rolls on
Of warriors, who, when morn begun,
    Defied a banded world.

## XVI.

List — frequent to the hurrying rout,
The stern pursuers' vengeful shout
Tells, that upon their broken rear
Rages the Prussian's bloody spear.
　　So fell a shriek was none,
When Beresina's icy flood
Redden'd and thaw'd with flame and blood,
And, pressing on thy desperate way,
Raised oft and long their wild hurra,
　　The children of the Don.
Thine ear no yell of horror cleft
So ominous, when, all bereft
Of aid, the valiant Polack left —[1]
Ay, left by thee — found soldier's grave
In Leipsic's corpse-encumber'd wave.
Fate, in those various perils past,
Reserved thee still some future cast;
On the dread die thou now hast thrown
Hangs not a single field alone,
Nor one campaign — thy martial fame,
Thy empire, dynasty, and name,
　　Have felt the final stroke;
And now, o'er thy devoted head
The last stern vial's wrath is shed,
　　The last dread seal is broke.[2]

---

[1] [For an account of the death of Poniatowski at Leipsic, see Sir Walter Scott's Life of Bonaparte, vol. vii. p. 588.]

[2] [" I, who with faith unshaken from the first,
　　Even when the tyrant seem'd to touch the skies,
Had look'd to see the high-blown bubble burst,
　　And for a fall conspicuous as his rise,
Even in that faith had look'd not for defeat
So swift, so overwhelming, so complete." — SOUTHEY.]

## XVII.

Since live thou wilt—refuse not now
Before these demagogues to bow,
Late objects of thy scorn and hate,
Who shall thy once imperial fate
Make wordy theme of vain debate.—
Or shall we say, thou stoop'st less low
In seeking refuge from the foe,
Against whose heart, in prosperous life,
Thine hand hath ever held the knife?

 Such homage hath been paid
By Roman and by Grecian voice,
And there were honour in the choice,
 If it were freely made.
Then safely come—in one so low,—
So lost,—we cannot own a foe;
Though dear experience bid us end,
In thee we ne'er can hail a friend.—
Come, howsoe'er—but do not hide
Close in my heart that germ of pride,
Erewhile, by gifted bard espied,
 That "yet imperial hope;"[1]
Think not that for a fresh rebound,
To raise ambition from the ground,
 We yield thee means or scope.

---

[1] [" The Desolator desolate!
 The Victor overthrown!
The Arbiter of others' fate
 A Suppliant for his own!
Is it some yet *imperial hope,*
That with such change can calmly cope?
 Or dread of death alone?
To die a prince—or live a slave—
Thy choice is most ignobly brave!"
    BYRON'S *Ode to Napoleon.*]

In safety come—but ne'er again
Hold type of independent reign;
    No islet calls thee lord,
We leave thee no confederate band,
No symbol of thy lost command,
To be a dagger in the hand
    From which we wrench'd the sword.

## XVIII.

Yet, even in yon sequester'd spot,
May worthier conquest be thy lot
    Than yet thy life has known;
Conquest, unbought by blood or harm,
That needs nor foreign aid nor arm,
    A triumph all thine own.
Such waits thee when thou shalt control
Those passions wild, that stubborn soul,
    That marr'd thy prosperous scene:—
Hear this, from no unmoved heart,
Which sighs, comparing what THOU ART
    With what thou MIGHT'ST HAVE BEEN![1]

## XIX.

Thou, too, whose deeds of fame renew'd
Bankrupt a nation's gratitude,

---

[1] [" 'Tis done—but yesterday a King!
    And arm'd with Kings to strive—
And now thou art a nameless thing;
    So abject—yet alive!
Is this the man of thousand thrones,
Who strew'd our earth with hostile bones,
    And can he thus survive?
Since he, miscalled the Morning Star,
Nor man nor fiend hath fallen so far."
           BYRON'S *Ode to Napoleon.*]

To thine own noble heart must owe
More than the meed she can bestow.
For not a people's just acclaim,
Not the full hail of Europe's fame,
Thy Prince's smiles, thy state's decree,
The Ducal rank, the garter'd knee,
Not these such pure delight afford
As that, when hanging up thy sword,
Well mayst thou think, " This honest steel
Was ever drawn for public weal;
And, such was rightful Heaven's decree,
Ne'er sheathed unless with victory !"

## XX.

Look forth, once more, with soften'd heart.
Ere from the field of fame we part ;[1]
Triumph and sorrow border near,
And joy oft melts into a tear.
Alas! what links of love that morn
Has War's rude hand asunder torn!
For ne'er was field so sternly fought,
And ne'er was conquest dearer bought.
Here piled in common slaughter sleep
Those whom affection long shall weep:
Here rests the sire, that ne'er shall strain
His orphans to his heart again;
The son, whom, on his native shore,
The parent's voice shall bless no more;

---

[1] [" We left the field of battle in such mood
　　As human hearts from thence should bear away;
And musing thus, our purposed route pursued,
　　Which still through scenes of recent bloodshed lay,
Where Prussia late, with strong and stern delight,
Hung on her fated foes to persecute their flight."
　　　　　　　　　　　　　　　SOUTHEY.]

The bridegroom, who has hardly press'd
His blushing consort to his breast;
The husband, whom through many a year
Long love and mutual faith endear.
Thou canst not name one tender tie,
But here dissolved its relics lie!
O! when thou see'st some mourner's veil
Shroud her thin form and visage pale,
Or mark'st the Matron's bursting tears
Stream when the stricken drum she hears
Or see'st how manlier grief, suppress'd,
Is labouring in a father's breast,—
With no enquiry vain pursue
The cause, but think on Waterloo!

## XXI.

Period of honour as of woes,
What bright careers 'twas thine to close!—
Mark'd on thy roll of blood what names
To Britain's memory, and to Fame's,
Laid there their last immortal claims!
Thou saw'st in seas of gore expire
Redoubted Picton's soul of fire—
Saw'st in the mingled carnage lie
All that of Ponsonby could die—
De Lancey change Love's bridal-wreath,
For laurels from the hand of Death—[*]

---

[*] [The Poet's friend, Colonel Sir William De Lancey, married
the beautiful daughter of Sir James Hall, Bart., in April, 1815,
and received his mortal wound on the 18th of June.  See Captain B. Hall's affecting narrative in the first series of his " Fragments of Voyages and Travels," vol. ii. p. 369.]

Saw'st gallant MILLER'S[1] failing eye
Still bent where Albion's banners fly,
And CAMERON,[2] in the shock of steel,
Die like the offspring of Lochiel;
And generous GORDON,[3] 'mid the strife,
Fall while he watch'd his leader's life.—
Ah! though her guardian angel's shield
Fenced Britain's hero through the field,
Fate not the less her power made known,
Through his friends' hearts to pierce his own!

## XXII.

Forgive, brave Dead, the imperfect lay!
Who may your names, your numbers, say?
What high-strung harp, what lofty line,
To each the dear-earn'd praise assign,
From high-born chiefs of martial fame
To the poor soldier's lowlier name?
Lightly ye rose that dawning day,
From your cold couch of swamp and clay,

---

[1] [Colonel Miller, of the Guards—son to Sir Wm. Miller, Lord Glenlee. When mortally wounded in the attack on the Bois de Bossu, he desired to see the colours of the regiment once more ere he died. They were waved over his head, and the expiring officer declared himself satisfied.]

[2] ["Colonel Cameron, of Fassiefern, so often distinguished in Lord Wellington's despatches from Spain, fell in the action at Quatre Bras, (16th June, 1815,) while leading the 92d, or Gordon Highlanders, to charge a body of cavalry, supported by infantry."—*Paul's Letters*, p. 91.]

[3] [Colonel the Honourable Sir Alexander Gordon, brother to the Earl of Aberdeen, who has erected a pillar on the spot where he fell by the side of the Duke of Wellington.]

To fill, before the sun was low,
The bed that morning cannot know.—
Oft may the tear the green sod steep,
And sacred be the heroes' sleep,
   Till time shall cease to run ;
And ne'er beside their noble grave,
May Briton pass and fail to crave
A blessing on the fallen brave
   Who fought with Wellington!

### XXIII.

Farewell, sad Field! whose blighted face
Wears desolation's withering trace;
Long shall my memory retain
Thy shatter'd huts and trampled grain,
With every mark of martial wrong,
That scathe thy towers, fair Hougomont!

---

  [1] [" Beyond these points the fight extended not,
    Small theatre for such a tragedy!
Its breadth scarce more, from eastern Popelot
    To where the groves of Hougomont on high
Rear in the west their venerable head,
And cover with their shade the countless dead.

" But wouldst thou tread this celebrated ground,
    And trace with understanding eyes a scene
Above all other fields of war renown'd,
    From western Hougomont thy way begin;
There was our strength on that side, and there first,
In all its force, the storm of battle burst.—SOUTHEY.

Mr. Southey adds, in a note on these verses: " So important
a battle, perhaps, was never before fought within so small an
extent of ground. I computed the distance between Hougomont
and Popelot at three miles; in a straight line it might probably
not exceed two and a half.

" Our guide was very much displeased at the name which the
battle had obtained in England,—'Why call it the battle of

Yet though thy garden's green arcade
The marksman's fatal post was made,
Though on thy shatter'd beeches fell
The blended rage of shot and shell,
Though from thy blacken'd portals torn,
Their fall thy blighted fruit-trees mourn,
Has not such havoc bought a name
Immortal in the rolls of fame?
Yes—Agincourt may be forgot,
And Cressy be an unknown spot,
    And Blenheim's name be new;
But still in story and in song,
For many an age remember'd long,
Shall live the towers of Hougomont,
    And Field of Waterloo.

Waterloo?' he said,—' Call it Hougomont, call it La Haye Sainte,
call it Popelot,—any thing but Waterloo.' " —*Pilgrimage to
Waterloo.*]

# CONCLUSION.

Stern tide of human Time! that know'st not rest,
But, sweeping from the cradle to the tomb,
Bear'st ever downward on thy dusky breast
Successive generations to their doom;
While thy capacious stream has equal room
For the gay bark where Pleasure's streamers sport,
And for the prison-ship of guilt and gloom,
The fisher skiff, and barge that bears a court,
Still wåfting onward all to one dark silent port;—

Stern tide of Time! through what mysterious change
Of hope and fear have our frail barks been driven!
For ne'er, before, vicissitude so strange
Was to one race of Adam's offspring given.
And sure such varied change of sea and heaven,
Such unexpected bursts of joy and woe,
Such fearful strife as that where we have striven,
Succeeding ages ne'er again shall know,
Until the awful term when Thou shalt cease to flow.

Well hast thou stood, my Country!—the brave fight
Hast well maintain'd through good report and ill;
In thy just cause and in thy native might,
And in Heaven's grace and justice constant still;
Whether the banded prowess, strength, and skill
Of half the world against thee stood array'd,
Or when, with better views and freer will,
Beside thee Europe's noblest drew the blade,
Each emulous in arms the Ocean Queen to aid.

Well art thou now repaid—though slowly rose,
And struggled long with mists thy blaze of fame,
While like the dawn that in the orient glows
On the broad wave its earlier lustre came;
Then eastern Egypt saw the growing flame,
And Maida's myrtles gleam'd beneath its ray,
Where first the soldier, stung with generous shame,
Rivall'd the heroes of the wat'ry way,
And wash'd in foemen's gore unjust reproach away.

Now, Island Empress, wave thy crest on high,
And bid the banner of thy Patron flow,
Gallant Saint George, the flower of Chivalry,
For thou hast faced, like him, a dragon foe,
And rescued innocence from overthrow,
And trampled down, like him, tyrannic might,
And to the gazing world mayst proudly show
The chosen emblem of thy sainted Knight,
Who quell'd devouring pride, and vindicated right.

Yet 'mid the confidence of just renown,
Renown dear-bought, but dearest thus acquired,
Write, Britain, write the moral lesson down:
'Tis not alone the heart with valour fired,
The discipline so dreaded and admired,
In many a field of bloody conquest known;
—Such may by fame be lured, by gold be hired—
'Tis constancy in the good cause alone,
Best justifies the meed thy valiant sons have won.

### END OF THE FIELD OF WATERLOO.

# SONGS AND MISCELLANIES

# SAINT CLOUD.

### [*Paris, 5th September, 1815.*]

---

Soft spread the southern summer night
  Her veil of darksome blue;
Ten thousand stars combined to light
  The terrace of Saint Cloud.

The evening breezes gently sigh'd,
  Like breath of lover true,
Bewailing the deserted pride
  And wreck of sweet Saint Cloud.

The drum's deep roll was heard afar,
  The bugle wildly blew
Good-night to Hulan and Hussar,
  That garrison Saint Cloud.

The startled Naiads from the shade
  With broken urns withdrew,
And silenced was that proud cascade,
  The glory of Saint Cloud.

We sate upon its steps of stone,
  Nor could its silence rue,
When waked, to music of our own,
  The echoes of Saint Cloud.

Slow Seine might hear each lovely note
   Fall light as summer dew,
While through the moonless air they float,
   Prolong'd from fair Saint Cloud.

And sure a melody more sweet
   His waters never knew,
Though music's self was wont to meet
   With Princes at Saint Cloud.

Nor then, with more delighted ear,
   The circle round her drew,
Than ours, when gather'd round to hear
   Our songstress[1] at St. Cloud.

Few happy hours poor mortals pass,—
   Then give those hours their due,
And rank among the foremost class
   Our evenings at Saint Cloud.

---

[1] [These lines were written after an evening spent at Saint Cloud with the late Lady Alvanley and her daughters, one of whom was the songstress alluded to in the text.]

## THE

# DANCE OF DEATH.[1]

### I.

Night and morning were at meeting
    Over Waterloo;
Cocks had sung their earliest greeting;
    Faint and low they crew,
For no paly beam yet shone
On the heights of Mount Saint John;
Tempest-clouds prolong'd the sway
Of timeless darkness over day;
Whirlwind, thunder-clap, and shower,
Mark'd it a predestined hour.
Broad and frequent through the night
Flash'd the sheets of levin-light;
Muskets, glancing lightnings back,
Show'd the dreary bivouack
    Where the soldier lay,
Chill and stiff, and drench'd with rain,
Wishing dawn of morn again,
    Though death should come with day.

### II.

'Tis at such a tide and hour,
Wizard, witch, and fiend, have power,

---

[1] [Originally published in 1815, in the Edinburgh Annual Register, vol. v.]

And ghastly forms through mist and shower
 Gleam on the gifted ken;
And then the affrighted prophet's ear
Drinks whispers strange of fate and fear,
Presaging death and ruin near
 Among the sons of men;—
Apart from Albyn's war-array,
'Twas then grey Allan sleepless lay;
Grey Allan, who, for many a day,
 Had follow'd stout and stern,
Where, through battle's rout and reel,
Storm of shot and hedge of steel,
Led the grandson of Lochiel,
 Valiant Fassiefern.
Through steel and shot he leads no more,
Low laid 'mid friends' and foemen's gore—
But long his native lake's wild shore,
And Sunart rough, and high Ardgower
 And Morven long shall tell,
And proud Bennevis hear with awe,
How, upon bloody Quatre-Bras,
Brave Cameron heard the wild hurra
 Of conquest as he fell.[1]


### III.

'Lone on the outskirts of the host,
The weary sentinel held post,
And heard, through darkness far aloof,
The frequent clang of courser's hoof,
Where held the cloak'd patrol their course,
And spurr'd 'gainst storm the swerving horse;

---

[1] [See note, *ante*, p. 321.]

But there are sounds in Allan's ear,
Patrol nor sentinel may hear,
And sights before his eye aghast
Invisible to them have pass'd,
    When down the destined plain,
'Twixt Britain and the bands of France,
Wild as marsh-borne meteors glance,
Strange phantoms wheel'd a revel dance,
    And doom'd the future slain.—
Such forms were seen, such sounds were heard
When Scotland's James his march prepared
    For Flodden's fatal plain;[1]
Such, when he drew his ruthless sword,
As Choosers of the Slain, adored
    The yet unchristen'd Dane.
An indistinct and phantom band,
They wheel'd their ring-dance hand in hand,
    With gestures wild and dread;
The Seer, who watch'd them ride the storm,
Saw through their faint and shadowy form
    The lightning's flash more red;
And still their ghastly roundelay
Was of the coming battle-fray,
    And of the destined dead.

## IV.

### Song.

Wheel the wild dance
While lightnings glance,

---

[See *ante*, vol. ii., Marmion, canto v., stanzas 24, 25, 26, and
Appendix, Note N, p. 331.]

And thunders rattle loud,
And call the brave
To bloody grave,
   To sleep without a shroud.

Our airy feet,
So light and fleet,
   They do not bend the rye
That sinks its head when whirlwinds rave
And swells again in eddying wave,
   As each wild gust blows by;

But still the corn,
At dawn of morn,
   Our fatal steps that bore,
At eve lies waste,
A trampled paste
   Of blackening mud and gore.

### V.

Wheel the wild dance
While lightnings glance,
   And thunders rattle loud,
And call the brave
To bloody grave,
   To sleep without a shroud.

Wheel the wild dance
Brave sons of France,
   For you our ring makes room
Make space full wide
For martial pride,
   For banner, spear, and plume.
Approach, draw near,
Proud cuirassier!

Room for the men of steel!
Through crest and plate
The broadsword's weight
  Both head and heart shall feel.

## VI.

Wheel the wild dance
While lightnings glance,
  And thunders rattle loud,
And call the brave
To bloody grave,
  To sleep without a shroud.

Sons of the spear!
You feel us near
  In many a ghastly dream;
With fancy's eye
Our forms you spy,
  And hear our fatal scream
With clearer sight
Ere falls the night,
  Just when to weal or woe
Your disembodied souls take flight
On trembling wing—each startled sprite
  Our choir of death shall know.

## VII.

Wheel the wild dance
While lightnings glance,
  And thunders rattle loud,
And call the brave
To bloody grave,
  To sleep without a shroud.

w w

Burst, ye clouds, in tempest showers,
Redder rain shall soon be ours —
    See the east grows wan —
Yield we place to sterner game,
Ere deadlier bolts and direr flame
Shall the welkin's thunders shame;
Elemental rage is tame
    To the wrath of man.

### VIII.

At morn, grey Allan's mates with awe
Heard of the vision'd sights he saw,
    The legend heard him say;
But the Seer's gifted eye was dim,
Deafen'd his ear, and stark his limb,
    Ere closed that bloody day —
He sleeps far from his Highland heath, —
But often of the Dance of Death
    His comrades tell the tale,
On picquet-post, when ebbs the night,
And waning watch-fires glow less bright,
    And dawn is glimmering pale.